Hansford
A Tale of Bacon's Rebellion

by

St. George Tucker

Hansford
A Tale of Bacon's Rebellion
by St. George Tucker

ISBN: 978-93-62203-14-4

Published by

DOUBLE 9 BOOKS

2/13-B, Ansari Road
Daryaganj, New Delhi – 110002
info@double9books.com
www.double9books.com
Tel. 011-40042856

ABOUT THE AUTHOR

St. George Tucker was a Bermudian-born American lawyer, military officer, and professor who taught at the College of William and Mary. He increased the prerequisites for a law degree at the college because he believed lawyers need extensive education. He was a General Court of Virginia judge before joining the Court of Appeals. Tucker supported gradual emancipation of slaves after the American Revolutionary War, as presented to the state assembly in a pamphlet published in 1796. He created an American copy of Blackstone's Commentaries on the Laws of England, which became an essential reference work for many American lawyers and law students in the early nineteenth century. Tucker was born near Port Royal, Bermuda, to English immigrants Anne Butterfield and Colonel Henry Tucker (1713–1787). His father was the great-grandson of George Tucker, who moved to Bermuda from England in 1662. The Tuckers were highly regarded in Port Royal. St. George's older brother, Thomas Tudor Tucker, moved to Virginia in the 1760s after finishing medical school in Scotland and settling in South Carolina before the American Revolutionary War. Another brother was Henry Tucker, who served as President of the Bermuda Council and as acting Governor on occasion. They had a relative named George Tucker, a politician and author.

CONTENTS

PREFACE

It is the design of the author, in the following pages, to illustrate the period of our colonial history, to which the story relates, and to show that this early struggle for freedom was the morning harbinger of that blessed light, which has since shone more and more unto the perfect day.

Most of the characters introduced have their existence in real history—Hansford lived, acted and died in the manner here narrated, and a heart as pure and true as Virginia Temple's mourned his early doom.

In one of those quaint old tracts, which the indefatigable antiquary, Peter Force, has rescued from oblivion, it is stated that Thomas Hansford, although a son of Mars, did sometimes worship at the shrine of Venus. It was his unwillingness to separate forever from the object of his love that led to his arrest, while lurking near her residence in Gloucester. From the meagre materials furnished by history of the celebrated rebellion of Nathaniel Bacon the following story has been woven.

It were an object to be desired, both to author and to reader, that the fate of Thomas Hansford had been different. This could not be but by a direct violation of history. Yet the lesson taught in this simple story, it is hoped, is not without its uses to humanity. Though vice may triumph for a season, and virtue fail to meet its appropriate reward, yet nothing can confer on the first, nor snatch from the last, that substantial happiness which is ever afforded to the mind conscious of rectitude. The self-conviction which stings the vicious mind would make a diadem a crown of thorns. The *mens sibi conscia recti* can make a gallows as triumphant as a throne. Such is the moral which the author designs to convey. If a darker punishment awaits the guilty, or a purer reward is in reserve for the virtuous, we must look for them to that righteous Judge, whose hand wields at once the sceptre of mercy and the sword of justice.

And now having prepared this brief preface, to stand like a portico before his simple edifice, the author would cordially and respectfully make his bow, and invite his guests to enter. If his little volume is read, he will be amply repaid; if approved, he will be richly rewarded.

CHAPTER I

"The rose of England bloomed on Gertrude's cheek;
What though these shades had seen her birth? Her sire
A Briton's independence taught to seek
Far western worlds."

Gertrude of Wyoming.

Among those who had been driven, by the disturbances in England, to seek a more quiet home in the wilds of Virginia, was a gentleman of the name of Temple. An Englishman by birth, he was an unwilling spectator of the revolution which erected the dynasty of Cromwell upon the ruins of the British monarchy. He had never been able to divest his mind of that loyal veneration in which Charles Stuart was held by so many of his subjects, whose better judgments, if consulted, would have prompted them to unite with the revolutionists. But it was a strong principle with that noble party, who have borne in history the distinguished name of Cavaliers, rarely to consult the dictates of reason in questions of ancient prejudice. They preferred rather to err blindly with the long line of their loyal forbears in submission to tyranny, than to subvert the ancient principles of government in the attainment of freedom. They saw no difference between the knife of the surgeon and the sword of the destroyer—between the wholesome medicine, administered to heal, and the deadly poison, given to destroy.

Nor are these strong prejudices without their value in the administration of government, while they are absolutely essential to the guidance of a revolution. They retard and moderate those excesses which they cannot entirely control, and even though unable to avoid the *descensus Averni*, they render that easy descent less fatal and destructive. Nor is there anything in the history of revolutions more beautiful than this steady adherence to ancient principles—this faithful devotion to a fallen prince, when all others have forsaken him and fled. While man is capable of enjoying the blessings of freedom, the memory of Hampden will be cherished and revered; and yet there is something scarcely less attractive in the disinterested loyalty, the generous self-denial, of the devoted Hyde, who left the comforts of home, the pride of country and the allurements of fame, to join in the lonely wanderings of the banished Stuart.

When at last the revolution was accomplished, and Charles and the hopes of the Stuarts seemed to sleep in the same bloody grave, Colonel Temple, unwilling longer to remain under the government of a usurper, left England for Virginia, to enjoy in the quiet retirement of this infant colony, the peace and tranquillity which was denied him at home. From this, the last resting place of the standard of loyalty, he watched the indications of returning peace, and with a proud and grateful heart he hailed the advent of the restoration. For many years an influential member of the House of Burgesses, he at last retired from the busy scenes of political life to his estate in Gloucester, which, with a touching veneration for the past, he called Windsor Hall. Here, happy in the retrospection of a well spent life, and cheered and animated by the affection of a devoted wife and lovely daughter, the old Loyalist looked forward with a tranquil heart to the change which his increasing years warned him could not be far distant.

His wife, a notable dame of the olden time, who was selected, like the wife of the good vicar, for the qualities which wear best, was one of those thrifty, bountiful bodies, who care but little for the government under which they live, so long as their larders are well stored with provisions, and those around them are happy and contented. Possessed of a good mind, and of a kind heart, she devoted herself to the true objects of a woman's life, and reigned supreme at home. Even when her husband had been immersed in the cares and stirring events of the revolution, and she was forced to hear the many causes of complaint urged against the government and stoutly combatted by the Colonel, the good dame had felt far more interest in market money than in ship money—in the neatness of her own chamber, than in the purity of the Star Chamber—and, in short, forgot the great principles of political economy in her love for the more practical science of domestic economy. We have said that at home Mrs. Temple reigned supreme, and so indeed she did. Although the good Colonel held the reins, she showed him the way to go, and though he was the nominal ruler of his little household, she was the power behind the throne, which even the throne submissively acknowledged to be greater than itself.

Yet, for all this, Mrs. Temple was an excellent woman, and devoted to her husband's interests. Perhaps it was but natural that, although with a willing heart, and without a murmur, she had accompanied him to Virginia, she should, with a laudable desire to impress him with her real worth, advert more frequently than was agreeable to the heavy sacrifice which she had made. Nay more, we have but little doubt that the bustle and self-annoyance, the flurry and bluster, which always attended her domestic preparations, were considered as a requisite condiment to give relish to her food. We are at least certain of this, that her frequent strictures on the dress, and criticisms on the manners of her husband, arose from her real pride, and from her desire that to the world he should appear the noble perfection which he was to her. This the good Colonel fully understood, and though sometimes chafed by her incessant taunts, he knew her real worth, and had long since learned to wear his fetters as an ornament.

Since their arrival in Virginia, Heaven had blessed the happy pair with a lovely daughter—a bliss for which they long had hoped and prayed, but hoped and prayed in vain. If hope deferred, however, maketh the heart sick, it loses none of its freshness and delight when it is at last realized, and the fond hearts of her parents were overflowing with love for this their only child. At the time at which our story commences, Virginia Temple (she was called after the fair young colony which gave her birth) had just completed her nineteenth year. Reared for the most part in the retirement of the country, she was probably not possessed of those artificial manners, which disguise rather than adorn the gay butterflies that flutter in the fashionable world, and which passes for refinement; but such conventional proprieties no more resemble the innate refinement of soul which nature alone can impart, than the plastered rouge of an old faded dowager resembles the native rose which blushes on a healthful maiden's cheek. There was in lieu of all this, in the character of Virginia Temple, a freshness of feeling and artless frankness, and withal a refined delicacy of sentiment and expression, which made the fair young girl the pride and the ornament of the little circle in which she moved.

Under the kind tuition of her father, who, in his retired life, delighted to train her mind in wholesome knowledge, she possessed a great advantage over the large majority of her sex, whose education, at that early period, was wofully deficient. Some there were indeed (and in this respect the world has not changed much in the last two centuries), who were tempted to sneer at accomplishments superior to their own, and to hint that a book-worm and a bluestocking would never make a useful wife. But such envious insinuations were overcome by the care of her judicious mother, who spared no pains to rear her as a useful as well as an accomplished woman. With such a fortunate education, Virginia grew up intelligent, useful and beloved; and her good old father used often to say, in his bland, gentle manner, that he knew not whether his little Jeanie was more attractive when, with her favorite authors, she stored her mind with refined and noble sentiments, or when, in her little check apron and plain gingham dress, she assisted her busy mother in the preparation of pickles and preserves.

There was another source of happiness to the fair Virginia, in which she will be more apt to secure the sympathy of our gentler readers. Among the numerous suitors who sought her hand, was one who had early gained her heart, and with none of the cruel crosses, as yet, which the young and inexperienced think add piquancy to the bliss of love; with the full consent of her parents, she had candidly acknowledged her preference, and plighted her troth, with all the sincerity of her young heart, to the noble, the generous, the brave Thomas Hansford.

CHAPTER II

"Heaven forming each on other to depend,
A master, or a servant, or a friend,
Bids each on other for assistance call,
Till one man's weakness grows the strength of all.
Wants, frailties, passions, closer still ally
The common interest, or endear the tie.
To these we owe true friendship, love sincere,
Each homefelt joy that life inherits here."

Essay on Man.

Begirt with love and blessed with contentment, the little family at Windsor Hall led a life of quiet, unobtrusive happiness. In truth, if there be a combination of circumstances peculiarly propitious to happiness, it will be found to cluster around one of those old colonial plantations, which formed each within itself a little independent barony. There first was the proprietor, the feudal lord, proud of his Anglo-Saxon blood, whose ambition was power and personal freedom, and whose highest idea of wealth was in the possession of the soil he cultivated. A proud feeling was it, truly, to claim a portion of God's earth as his own; to stand upon his own land, and looking around, see his broad acres bounded only by the blue horizon walls,[1] and feel in its full force the whole truth of the old law maxim, that he owned not only the surface of the soil, but even to the centre of the earth, and the zenith of the heavens.[2] There can be but little doubt that the feelings suggested by such reflections are in the highest degree favorable to the development of individual freedom, so peculiar to the Anglo-Saxon race, and so stoutly maintained, especially among an agricultural people. This respect for the ownership of land is illustrated by the earliest legislation, which held sacred the title to the soil even from the grasp of the law, and which often restrained the freeholder from alienating his land from the lordly but unborn aristocrat to whom it should descend.

Next in the scale of importance in this little baronial society, were the indented servants, who, either for felony or treason, were sent over to the colony, and bound for a term of years to some one of the planters. In some cases, too, the poverty of the emigrant induced him to submit voluntarily to indentures with the captain of the ship which brought him to the colony, as some compensation for his passage. These servants, we learn, had certain privileges accorded to them, which were not enjoyed by the slave: the service of the former was only temporary, and after the expiration of their term they became free citizens of the colony. The female servants, too, were limited in their duties to such employments as are generally assigned to women, such as cooking, washing and housework; while it was not unusual to see the negro women, as even now, in many portions of the State, managing the plough, hoeing the maize, worming and stripping the tobacco, and harvesting the grain. The colonists had long remonstrated against the system of indented servants, and denounced the policy which thus foisted upon an infant colony the felons and the refuse population of the mother country. But, as was too often the case, their petitions and remonstrances were treated with neglect, or spurned with contempt. Besides being distasteful to them as freemen and Cavaliers, the indented servants had already evinced a restlessness under restraint, which made them dangerous members of the body politic. In 1662, a servile insurrection was secretly organized, which had well nigh proved fatal to the colony. The conspiracy was however betrayed by a certain John Berkenhead, one of the leaders in the movement, who was incited to the revelation by the hope of reward for his treachery; nor was the hope vain. Grateful for their deliverance, the Assembly voted this man his liberty, compensated his master for the loss of his services, and still further rewarded him by a bounty of five thousand pounds of tobacco. Of this reckless and abandoned wretch, we will have much to say hereafter.

Another feature in this patriarchal system of government was the right of property in those inferior races of men, who from their nature are incapable of a high degree of liberty, and find their greatest development, and their truest happiness, in a condition of servitude. Liberty is at last a reward to be attained after a long struggle, and not the inherent right of every man. It is the sword which becomes a weapon of power and defence in the hands of the strong, brave, rational man, but a dangerous plaything when entrusted to the hands of madmen or children. And thus, by the mysterious government of Him, who rules the earth in righteousness, has it been wisely ordained, that they only who are worthy of freedom shall permanently possess it.

The mutual relations established by the institution of domestic slavery were beneficial to both parties concerned. The Anglo-Saxon baron possessed power, which he has ever craved, and concentration and unity of will, which was essential to its maintenance. But that power was tempered, and that will controlled, by the powerful motives of policy, as well as by the dictates of justice and mercy. The African serf, on the other hand, was reduced to slavery, which, from his very nature, he is incapable of despising; and an implicit obedience to the will of his master was essential to the preservation of the relation. But he, too, derived benefits from the institution, which he has never acquired in any other condition; and trusting to the justice, and relying on the power of his master to provide for his wants, he lived a contented and therefore a happy life. Improvident himself by nature, his children were reared without his care, through the helpless period of infancy, while he was soothed and cheered in the hours of sickness, and protected and supported in his declining years. The history of the world does not furnish another example of a laboring class who could rely with confidence on such wages as competency and contentment.

In a new colony, where there was but little attraction as yet, for tradesmen to emigrate, the home of the planter became still more isolated and independent. Every landholder had not only the slaves to cultivate his soil and to attend to his immediate wants, but he had also slaves educated and skilled in various trades. Thus, in this busy hive, the blaze of the forge was seen and the sound of the anvil was heard, in repairing the different tools and utensils of the farm; the shoemaker was found at his last, the spinster at her wheel, and the weaver at the loom. Nor has this system of independent reliance on a plantation for its own supplies been entirely superseded at the present day. There may still be found, in some sections of Virginia, plantations conducted on this principle, where the fleece is sheared, and the wool is carded, spun, woven and made into clothing by domestic labor, and where a few groceries and finer fabrics of clothing are all that are required, by the independent planter, from the busy world beyond his little domain.

Numerous as were the duties and responsibilities that devolved upon the planter, he met them with cheerfulness and discharged them with faithfulness. The dignity of the master was blended with the kind attention of the friend on the one hand, and the obedience of the slave, with the fidelity of a grateful dependent, on the other. And thus was illustrated, in their true beauty, the blessings of that much abused but happy institution, which should ever remain, as it has ever been placed by the commentators of our law, next in position, as it is in interest, to the tender relation of parent and child.

FOOTNOTES:

[1] The immense grants taken up by early patentees, in this country, justifies this language, which might otherwise seem an extravagant hyperbole.

[2] *Cujus est solum, ejus est usque ad cœlum.*

CHAPTER III

"An old worshipful gentleman, who had a great estate,
That kept a brave old house at a bountiful rate, —
With an old lady whose anger one word assuages, —
Like an old courtier of the queen's,
And the queen's old courtier."

Old Ballad.

A pleasant home was that old Windsor Hall, with its broad fields in cultivation around it, and the dense virgin forest screening it from distant view, with the carefully shaven sward on the velvet lawn in front, and the tall forest poplars standing like sentries in front of the house, and the venerable old oak tree at the side, with the rural wooden bench beneath it, where Hansford and Virginia used to sit and dream of future happiness, while the tame birds were singing sweetly to their mates in the green branches above them. And the house, too, with its quaint old frame, its narrow windows, and its substantial furniture, all brought from England and put down here in this new land for the comfort of the loyal old colonist. It had been there for years, that old house, and the moss and lichen had fastened on its shelving roof, and the luxuriant vine had been trained to clamber closely by its sides, exposing its red trumpet flowers to the sun; while the gay humming-bird, with her pretty dress of green and gold, sucked their honey with her long bill, and fluttered her little wings in the mild air so swiftly that you could scarcely see them. Then there was that rude but comfortable old porch, destined to as many uses as the chest of drawers in the tavern of the Deserted Village. Protected by its sheltering roof alike from rain and sunshine, it was often used, in the mild summer weather, as a favorite sitting-room, and sometimes, too, converted into a dining-room. There, too, might be seen, suspended from the nails and wooden pegs driven into the locust pillars, long specimen ears of corn, samples of grain, and different garden seeds tied up in little linen bags; and in the strange medley, Mrs. Temple had hung some long strings of red pepper-pods, sovereign specifics in cases of sore throat, but which seemed, among so many objects of greater interest, to blush with shame at their own inferiority. It was not yet the season when the broad tobacco leaf, brown with the fire of curing, was exhibited, and formed the chief staple of conversation, as well as of trade, with the old crony planters. The wonderful plant was just beginning to suffer from the encroaches of the worm, the only animal, save man, which is life-proof against the deadly nicotine of this cultivated poison.

In this old porch the little family was gathered on a beautiful evening towards the close of June, in the year 1676. The sun, not yet set, was just sinking below the tall forest, and was dancing and flickering gleefully among the trees, as if rejoicing that he had nearly finished his long day's journey. Colonel Temple had just returned from his evening survey of his broad fields of tobacco, and was quietly smoking his pipe, for, like most of his fellow colonists, he was an inveterate consumer of this home production. His good wife was engaged in knitting, an occupation now almost fallen into disuse among ladies, but then a very essential part of the duties of a large plantation. Virginia, with her tambour frame before her, but which she had neglected in the reverie of her own thoughts, was caressing the noble St. Bernard dog which lay at her feet, who returned her caresses by a grateful whine, as he licked the small white hand of his mistress. This dog, a fine specimen of that noble breed, was a present from Hansford, and for that reason, as well as for his intrinsic merits, was highly prized, and became her constant companion in her woodland rambles in search of health and wild flowers. With all the vanity of a conscious favorite, Nestor regarded with well bred contempt the hounds that stalked in couples about the yard, in anxious readiness for the next chase.

As the young girl was thus engaged, there was an air of sadness in her whole mien—such a stranger to her usually bright, happy face, that it did not escape her father's notice.

"Why, Jeanie," he said, in the tender manner which he always used towards her, "you are strangely silent this evening. Has anything gone wrong with my little daughter?"

"No, father," she replied, "at least nothing that I am conscious of. We cannot be always gay or sad at our pleasure, you know."

"Nay, but at least," said the old gentleman, "Nestor has been disobedient, or old Giles is sick, or you have been working yourself into a sentimental sadness over Lady Willoughby's[3] troubles."

"No, dear father; though, in reality, that melancholy story might well move a stouter heart than mine."

"Well, confess then," said her father, "that, like the young French gentleman in Prince Arthur's days, you are sad as night only for wantonness. But what say you, mother, has anything gone wrong in household affairs to cross Virginia?"

"No, Mr. Temple," said the old lady. "Certainly, if Virginia is cast down at the little she has to do, I don't know what ought to become of me. But that's a matter of little consequence. Old people have had their day, and needn't expect much sympathy."

"Indeed, dear mother," said Virginia, "I do not complain of anything that I have to do. I know that you do not entrust as much to me as you ought, or as I wish. I assure you, that if anything has made me sad, it is not you, dear mother," she added, as she tenderly kissed her mother.

"Oh, I know that, my dear; but your father seems to delight in always charging me with whatever goes wrong. Goodness knows, I toil from Monday morning till Saturday night for you all, and this is all the thanks I get. And if I were to work my old fingers to the bone, it would be all the same. Well, it won't last always."

To this assault Colonel Temple knew the best plan was not to reply. He had learned from sad experience the truth of the old adages, that "breath makes fire hotter," and that "the least said is soonest mended." He only signified his consciousness of what had been said by a quiet shrug of the shoulders, and then resumed his conversation with Virginia.

"Well then, my dear, I am at a loss to conjecture the cause of your sadness, and must throw myself upon your indulgence to tell me or not, as you will. I don't think you ever lost anything by confiding in your old father."

"I know I never did," said Virginia, with a gentle sigh, "and it is for the very reason that you always make my foolish little sorrows your own, that I am unwilling to trouble you with them. But really, on the present occasion—I scarcely know what to tell you."

"Then why that big pearl in your eye?" returned her father. "Ah, you little rogue, I have found you out at last. Mother, I have guessed the riddle. Somebody has not been here as often lately as he should. Now confess, you silly girl, that I have guessed your secret."

The big tears that swam in his daughter's blue eyes, and then rolling down, dried themselves upon her cheek, told the truth too plainly to justify denial.

"I really think Virginia has some reason to complain," said her mother. "It is now nearly three weeks since Mr. Hansford was here. A young lawyer's business don't keep him so much employed as to prevent these little courteous attentions."

"We used to be more attentive in our day, didn't we, old lady?" said Colonel Temple, as he kissed his good wife's cheek.

This little demonstration entirely wiped away the remembrance of her displeasure. She returned the salutation with an affectionate smile, as she replied,

"Yes, indeed, Henry; if there was less sentiment, there was more real affection in those days. Love was more in the heart then, and less out of books, than now."

"Oh, but we were not without our little sentiments, too. Virginia, it would have done you good to have seen how gaily your mother danced round the May-pole, with her courtly train, as the fair queen of them all; and how I, all ruffs and velvet, at the head of the boys, and on bended knee, begged her majesty to accept the homage of our loyal hearts. Don't you remember, Bessy, the grand parliament, when we voted you eight subsidies, and four fifteenths to be paid in flowers and candy, for your grand coronation?"

"Oh, yes!" said the old lady; "and then the coronation itself, with the throne made of the old master's desk, all nicely carpeted and decorated with flowers and evergreen; and poor Billy Newton, with his long, solemn face, a paste-board mitre, and his sister's night-gown for a pontifical robe, acting the Archbishop of Canterbury, and placing the crown upon my head!"

"And the game of Barley-break in the evening," said the Colonel, fairly carried away by the recollections of these old scenes, "when you and I, hand in hand, pretended only to catch the rest, and preferred to remain together thus, in what we called the hell, because we felt that it was a heaven to us."[4]

"Oh, fie, for shame!" said the old lady. "Ah, well, they don't have such times now-a-days."

"No, indeed," said her husband; "old Noll came with his nasal twang and puritanical cant, and dethroned May-queens as well as royal kings, and his amusements were only varied by a change from a hypocritical sermon to a psalm-singing conventicle."

Thus the old folks chatted on merrily, telling old stories, which, although Virginia had heard them a hundred times and knew them all by heart, she loved to hear again. She had almost forgotten her own sadness in this occupation of her mind, when her father said—

"But, Bessy, we had almost forgotten, in our recollections of the past, that our little Jeanie needs cheering up. You should remember, my daughter, that if there were any serious cause for Mr. Hansford's absence, he would have written to you. Some trivial circumstance, or some matter of business, has detained him from day to day. He will be here to-morrow, I have no doubt."

"I know I ought not to feel anxious," said Virginia, her lip quivering with emotion; "he has so much to do, not only in his profession, but his poor old mother needs his presence a great deal now; she was far from well when he was last here."

"Well, I respect him for that," said her mother. "It is too often the case with these young lovers, that when they think of getting married, and doing for themselves, the poor old mothers are laid on the shelf."

"And yet," continued Virginia, "I have a kind of presentiment that all may not be right with him. I know it is foolish, but I can't—I can't help it?"

"These presentiments, my child," said her father, who was not without some of the superstition of the time, "although like dreams, often sent by the Almighty for wise purposes, are more often but the phantasies of the imagination. The mind, when unable to account for circumstances by reason, is apt to torment itself with its own fancy—and this is wrong, Jeanie."

"I know all this," replied Virginia, "and yet have no power to prevent it. But," she added, smiling through her tears, "I will endeavor to be more cheerful, and trust for better things."

"That's a good girl; I assure you I would rather hear you laugh once than to see you cry a hundred times," said the old man, repeating a witticism that Virginia had heard ever since her childish trials and tears over broken dolls or tangled hair. The idea was so grotesque and absurd, that the sweet girl laughed until she cried again.

"Besides," added her father, "I heard yesterday that that pestilent fellow, Bacon, was in arms again, and it may be necessary for Berkeley to use some harsh means to punish his insolence. I would not be at all surprised if Hansford were engaged in this laudable enterprise."

"God, in his mercy, forbid," said Virginia, in a faint voice.

"And why, my daughter? Would you shrink from lending the services of him you love to your country, in her hour of need?"

"But the danger, father!"

"There can be but little danger in an insurrection like this. Strong measures will soon suppress it. Nay, the very show of organized and determined resistance will strike terror into the white hearts of these cowardly knaves. But if this were not so, the duty would be only stronger."

"Yes, Virginia," said her mother. "No one knows more than I, how hard it is for a woman to sacrifice her selfish love to her country. But in my day we never hesitated, and I was happy in my tears, when I saw your father going forth to fight for his king and country. There was none of your 'God forbid' then, and you need not expect to be more free from trials than those who have gone before you."

There was no real unkindness meant in this speech of Mrs. Temple, but, as we have before reminded the reader, she took especial delight in magnifying her own joys and her own trials, and in making an invidious comparison of the present day with her earlier life, always to the prejudice of the former. Tenderly devoted to her daughter, and deeply sympathizing in her distress, she yet could not forego the pleasure of reverting to the time when she too had similar misfortunes, which she had borne with such exemplary fortitude. To be sure, this heroism existed only in the dear old lady's imagination, for no one gave way to trials with more violent grief than she. Virginia, though accustomed to her mother's peculiar temper, was yet affected by her language, and her tears flowed afresh.

"Cheer up, my daughter," said her father, "these tears are not only unworthy of you, but they are uncalled for now. This is at last but conjecture of mine, and I have no doubt that Hansford is well and as happy as he can be away from you. But you would have proved a sad heroine in the revolution. I don't think you would imitate successfully the bravery and patriotism of Lady Willoughby, whose memoirs you have been reading. Oh! that was a day for heroism, when mothers devoted their sons, and wives their husbands, to the cause of England and of loyalty, almost without a tear."

"I thank God," said the weeping girl, "that he has not placed me in such trying scenes. With all my admiration for the courage of my ancestors, I have no ambition to suffer their dangers and distress."

"Well, my dear," replied her father, "I trust you may never be called upon to do so. But if such should be your fate, I also trust that you have a strong heart, which would bear you through the trial. Come now, dry your tears, and let me hear you sing that old favorite of mine, written by poor Dick Lovelace. His Lucasta[5] must have been something of the same mind as my Virginia, if she reproved him for deserting her for honour."

"Oh, father, I feel the justice of your rebuke. I know that none but a brave woman deserves the love of a brave man. Will you forgive me?"

"Forgive you, my daughter?—yes, if you have done anything to be forgiven. Your old father, though his head is turned gray, has still a warm place in his heart for all your distresses, my child; and that heart will be cold in death before it ceases to feel for you. But come, I must not lose my song, either."

And Virginia, her sweet voice rendered more touchingly beautiful by her emotion, sang the noble lines, which have almost atoned for all the vanity and foppishness of their unhappy author.

"Tell me not, sweet, I am unkind,
If from the nunnery
Of thy chaste breast and quiet mind,
To war and arms I fly.

"True, a new mistress now I chase,
The first foe in the field,
And with a stronger faith embrace
The sword, the horse, the shield.

"Yet, this inconstancy is such
As you too shall adore;
I had not loved thee, dear, so much,
Loved I not honour more!"

"Yes," repeated the old patriot, as the last notes of the sweet voice died away; "yes, 'I had not loved thee, dear, so much, loved I not honour more!' This is the language of the truly noble lover. Without a heart which rises superior to itself, in its devotion to honour, it is impossible to love truly. Love is not a pretty child, to be crowned with roses, and adorned with trinkets, and wooed by soft music. To the truly brave, it is a god to be worshipped, a reward to be attained, and to be attained only in the path of honour!"

"I think," said Mrs. Temple, looking towards the wood, "that Virginia's song acted as an incantation. If I mistake not, Master Hansford is even now coming to explain his own negligence."

FOOTNOTES:

[3] I have taken these beautiful memoirs, now known to be the production of a modern pen, to be genuine. Their truthfulness to nature certainly will justify me in such a liberty.

[4] The modern reader will need some explanation of this old game, whose terms seem, to the refined ears of the present day, a little profane. Barley-break resembled a game which I have seen played in my own time, called King Cantelope, but with some striking points of difference. In the old game, the play-ground was divided into three parts of equal size, and the middle of these sections was known by the name of

hell. The boy and girl, whose position was in this place, were to attempt, with joined hands, to catch those who should try to pass from one section to the other. As each one was caught, he became a recruit for the couple in the middle, and the last couple who remained uncaught took the places of those in hell, and thus the game commenced again.

[5] The lady to whom the song is addressed. It may be found in Percy's Reliques, or in almost any volume of old English poetry.

CHAPTER IV

"Came there a certain lord, neat, trimly dressed,
Fresh as a bridegroom."
                                        Henry IV.

In truth a young man, well mounted on a powerful bay, was seen approaching from the forest, that lay towards Jamestown. Virginia's cheek flushed with pleasure as she thought how soon all her fears would vanish away in the presence of her lover—and she laughed confusedly, as her father said,

"Aye, come dry your tears, you little rogue—those eyes are not as bright as Hansford would like to see. Tears are very pretty in poetry and fancy, but when associated with swelled eyes and red noses, they lose something of their sentiment."

As the horseman came nearer, however, Virginia found to her great disappointment, that the form was not that of Hansford, and with a deep sigh she went into the house. The stranger, who now drew up to the door, proved to be a young man of about thirty years of age, tall and well-proportioned, his figure displaying at once symmetrical beauty and athletic strength. He was dressed after the fashion of the day, in a handsome velvet doublet, trussed with gay-colored points at the waist to the breeches, which reaching only to the knee, left the finely turned leg well displayed in the closely-fitting white silk stockings. Around his wrists and neck were revealed graceful ruffles of the finest cambric. The heavy boots, which were usually worn by cavaliers, were in this case supplied by shoes fastened with roses of ribands. A handsome sword, with ornamented hilt, and richly chased scabbard, was secured gracefully by his side in its fringed hanger. The felt hat, whose wide brim was looped up and secured by a gold button in front, completed the costume of the young stranger. The abominable fashion of periwigs, which maintained its reign over the realm of fashion for nearly a century, was just beginning to be introduced into the old country, and had not yet been received as orthodox in the colony. The rich chestnut hair of the stranger fell in abundance over his fine shoulders, and was parted carefully in the middle to display to its full advantage his broad intellectual forehead.

But in compliance with custom, his hair was dressed with the fashionable love-locks, plaited and adorned with ribands, and falling foppishly over either ear.

But dress, at last, like "rank, is but the guinea's stamp, the man's the gowd for a' that," and in outward appearance at least, the stranger was of no alloyed metal. There was in his air that easy repose and self-possession which is always perceptible in those whose life has been passed in association with the refined and cultivated. But still there was something about his whole manner, which seemed to betray the fact, that this habitual self-possession, this frank and easy carriage was the result of a studied and constant control over his actions, rather than those of a free and ingenuous heart.

This idea, however, did not strike the simple minded Virginia, as with natural, if not laudable curiosity, she surveyed the handsome young stranger through the window of the hall. The kind greeting of the hospitable old colonel having been given, the stranger dismounted, and the fine bay that he rode was committed to the protecting care of a grinning young African in attendance, who with his feet dangling from the stirrups trotted him off towards the stable.

"I presume," said the stranger, as they walked towards the house, "that from the directions I have received, I have the honor of seeing Colonel Temple. It is to the kindness of Sir William Berkeley that I owe the pleasure I enjoy in forming your acquaintance, sir," and he handed a letter from his excellency, which the reader may take the liberty of reading with us, over Colonel Temple's shoulder.

> "Bight trusty old friend," ran the quaint and formal, yet familiar note. "The bearer of these, Mr. Alfred Bernard, a youth of good and right rare merit, but lately from England, and whom by the especial confidence reposed in him from our noble kinsman Lord Berkeley, we have made our private secretary, hath desired acquaintance with some of the established gentlemen in the colony, the better for his own improvement, to have their good society. And in all good faith, there is none, to whom I can more readily commend him, than Colonel Henry Temple, with the more perfect confidence in his desire to oblige him, who is always as of yore, his right good friend,
>
> "William Berkeley, Kn't.
> *"From our Palace at Jamestown, June 20, A. D. 1676."*

"It required not this high commendation, my dear sir," said old Temple, pressing his guest cordially by the hand, "to bid you welcome to my poor roof. But I now feel that to be a special honour, which would otherwise be but the natural duty of hospitality. Come, right welcome to Windsor Hall."

With these words they entered the house, where Alfred Bernard was presented to the ladies, and paid his devoirs with such knightly grace, that Virginia admired, and Mrs. Temple heartily approved, a manner and bearing, which, she whispered to her daughter, was worthy of the old cavalier days before the revolution. Supper was soon announced—not the awkward purgatorial meal, perilously poised in cups, and eaten with greasy fingers—so dire a foe to comfort and silk dresses—but the substantial supper of the olden time. It is far from our intention to enter into minute details, yet we cannot refrain from adverting to the fact that the good old cavalier grace was said by the Colonel, with as much solemnity as his cheerful face would wear—that grace which gave such umbrage to the Puritans with their sour visages and long prayers, and which consisted of those three expressive words, "God bless us."

"I have always thought," said the Colonel, apologetically, "that this was enough—for where's the use of praying over our meals, until they get so cold and cheerless, that there is less to be thankful for."

"Especially," said Bernard, chiming in at once with the old man's prejudices, "when this brief language contains all that is necessary—for even Omnipotence can but bless us—and we may easily leave the mode to Him."

"Well said, young man, and now come and partake of our homely fare, seasoned with a hearty welcome," said the Colonel, cordially.

Nor loth was Alfred Bernard to do full justice to the ample store before him. A ride of more than thirty miles had whetted an appetite naturally good, and the youth of "right rare merit," did not impress his kind host very strongly with his conversational powers during his hearty meal.

The repast being over, the little party retired to a room, which the old planter was pleased to call his study, but which savored far more of the presence of the sportive Diana, than of the reflecting muses. Over the door, as you entered the room, were fastened the large antlers of some noble deer, who had once bounded freely and gracefully through his native forest. Those broad branches are now, by a sad fatality, doomed to support the well oiled fowling-piece that laid their wearer low. Fishing tackle, shot-pouches, fox brushes, and other similar evidences and trophies of sport, testified to the Colonel's former delight in angling and the chase; but now alas! owing to the growing infirmities of age, though he still cherished his pack, and encouraged the sport, he could only start the youngsters in the neighborhood, and give them God speed! as with horses, hounds, and horns they merrily scampered away in the fresh, early morning. But with his love for these active, manly sports, Colonel Temple was devoted to reading such works as ran with his prejudices, and savored of the most rigid loyalty. His books, indeed, were few, for in that day it was no easy matter to procure books at all, especially for the colonists, who cut off from the great fountain of literature which was then just reviving from the severe drought of puritanism, were but sparingly supplied with the means of information. But a few months later than the time of which we write, Sir William Berkeley boasted that education was at a low ebb in Virginia, and thanked his God that so far there were neither free schools nor printing presses in the colony—the first instilling and the last disseminating rebellious sentiments among the people. Yet under all these disadvantages, Colonel Temple was well versed in the literature of the last two reigns, and with some of the more popular works of the present. Shakspeare was his constant companion, and the spring to which he often resorted to draw supplies of wisdom. But Milton was held in especial abhorrence—for the prose writings of the eloquent old republican condemned unheard the sublime strains of his divine poem.

CHAPTER V

"A man in all the world's new fashion planted,
That hath a mint of phrases in his brain;
One, whom the music of his own vain tongue,
Doth ravish like enchanting harmony;
A man of compliments."

Love's Labor Lost.

"Well, Mr. Bernard," said the old Colonel as they entered the room, "take a seat, and let's have a social chat. We old planters don't get a chance often to hear the news from Jamestown, and I am afraid you will find me an inquisitive companion. But first join me in a pipe. There is no greater stimulant to conversation than the smoke of our Virginia weed."

"You must excuse me," said Bernard, smiling, "I have not yet learned to smoke, although, if I remain in Virginia, I suppose I will have to contract a habit so general here."

"What, not smoke!" said the old man, in surprise. "Why tobacco is at once the calmer of sorrows, the assuager of excitement; the companion of solitude, the life of company; the quickener of fancy, the composer of thought."

"I had expected," returned Bernard, laughing at his host's enthusiasm, "that so rigid a loyalist as yourself, would be a convert to King James's Counterblast. Have you never read that work of the royal pedant?"

"Read it!" cried the Colonel, impetuously. "No! and what's more, with all my loyalty and respect for his memory, I would sooner light my pipe with a page of his Basilicon, than subscribe to the sentiments of his Counterblast."

"Oh, he had his supporters too," replied Bernard, smiling. "You surely cannot have forgotten the song of Cucullus in the Lover's Melancholy;" and the young man repeated, with mock solemnity, the lines,

"They that will learn to drink a health in hell,
Must learn on earth to take tobacco well,
For in hell they drink no wine, nor ale, nor beer,
But fire and smoke and stench, as we do here."

"Well put, my young friend," said Temple, laughing in his turn. "But you should remember that John Ford had to put such a sentiment in the mouth of a Bedlamite. Here, Sandy," he added, kicking a little negro boy, who was nodding in the corner, dreaming, perhaps, of the pleasures of the next 'possum hunt, "Run to the kitchen, Sandy, and bring me a coal of fire."

"And, now, Mr. Bernard, what is the news political and social in the big world of Jamestown?"

"Much to interest you in both respects. It is indeed a part of my duty in this visit, to request that you and the ladies will be present at a grand masque ball to be given on Lady Frances's birth-night."

"A masque in Virginia!" exclaimed the Colonel, "that will be a novelty indeed! But the Governor has not the opportunity or the means at hand to prepare it."

"Oh, yes!" replied Bernard, "we have all determined to do our best. The assembly will be in session, and the good burgesses will aid us, and at any rate if we cannot eclipse old England, we must try to make up in pleasure, what is wanting in brilliancy. I trust Miss Temple will aid us by her presence, which in itself will add both pleasure and brilliancy to the occasion."

Virginia blushed slightly at the compliment, and replied—

"Indeed, Mr. Bernard, the presence which you seem to esteem so highly depends entirely on my father's permission—but I will unite with you in urging that as it is a novelty to me, he will not deny his assent. I should like of all things to go."

"Well, my daughter, as you please—but what says mother to the plan? You know she is not queen consort only, and she must be consulted."

"I am sure, Colonel Temple," said the good lady, "that I do as much to please Virginia as you can. To be sure, a masque in Virginia can afford but little pleasure to me, who have seen them in all their glory in England, but I have no doubt it will be all well enough for the young people, and I am always ready to contribute to their amusement."

"I know that, my dear, and Jeanie can testify to it as well as I. But, Mr. Bernard, what is to be the subject of this masque, and who is the author, or are we to have a rehash of rare Ben Jonson's Golden Age?"

"It is to be a kind of parody of that, or rather a burlesque;" replied Bernard, "and is designed to hail the advent of the Restoration, a theme worthy of the genius of a Shakspeare, though, unfortunately, it is now in far humbler hands."

"A noble subject, truly," said the Colonel, "and from your deprecating air, I have no doubt that we are to be indebted to your pen for its production."

"Partly, sir," returned Bernard, with an assumption of modesty. "It is the joint work of Mr. Hutchinson, the chaplain of his excellency, and myself."

"Oh! Mr. Bernard, are you a poet," cried the old lady in admiration; "this is really an honour. Mr. Temple used to write verses when we were young, and although they were never printed, they were far prettier than a great deal of the lovesick nonsense that they make such a fuss about. I was always begging him to publish, but he never would push himself forward, like others with not half his merit."

"I do not pretend to any merit, my dear madam," said Bernard, "but I trust that with my rigid loyalty, and parson Hutchinson's rigid episcopacy, the roundhead puritans will not meet with more favour than they deserve. Neither of us have been long enough in the colony to have learned from observation the taste of the Virginians, but there is abundant evidence on record that they were the last to desert the cause of loyalty, and to submit to the sway of the puritan Protector."

"Right, my friend, and she ever will be, or else old Henry Temple will seek out some desolate abode untainted with treason wherein to drag out the remainder of his days."

"Your loyalty was never more needed," said Bernard; "for Virginia, I fear, will yet be the scene of a rebellion, which may be but the brief epitome of the revolution."

"Aye, you refer to this Baconian movement. I had heard that the demagogue was again in arms. But surely you cannot apprehend any danger from such a source."

"Well, I trust not; and yet the harmless worm, if left to grow, may acquire fangs. Bacon is eloquent and popular, and has already under his standard some of the very flower of the colony. He must be crushed and crushed at once; and yet I fear the worst from the clemency and delay of Sir William Berkeley."

"Tell me; what is his ground of quarrel?" asked Temple.

"Why, simply that having taken up arms against the Indians without authority, and enraging them by his injustice and cruelty, the governor required him to disband the force he had raised. He peremptorily refused, and demanded a commission from the governor as general-in-chief of the forces of Virginia to prosecute this unholy war."

"Why unholy?" asked the Colonel. "Rebellious as was his conduct in refusing to lay down his arms at the command of the governor, yet I do not see that it should be deemed unholy to chastise the insolence of these savages."

"I will tell you, then," replied Bernard. "His avowed design was to avenge the murder of a poor herdsman by a chief of the Doeg tribe. Instead of visiting his vengeance upon the guilty, he turned his whole force against the Susquehannahs, a friendly tribe of Indians, and chased them like sheep into one of their forts. Five of the Indians relying on the boasted chivalry of the whites, came out of the fort unarmed, to inquire the cause of this unprovoked attack. They were answered by a charge of musketry, and basely murdered in cold blood."

"Monstrous!" cried Temple, with horror. "Such infidelity will incense the whole Indian race against us and involve the country in another general war."

"Exactly so," returned Bernard, "and such is the governor's opinion; but besides this, it is suspected, and with reason too, that this Indian war is merely a pretext on the part of Bacon and a few of his followers, to cover a deeper and more criminal design. The insolent demagogue prates openly about equal rights, freedom, oppression of the mother country, and such dangerous themes, and it is shrewdly thought that, in his wild dreams of liberty, he is taking Cromwell for his model. He has all of the villainy of the old puritan, and a good deal of his genius and ability. But I beg pardon, ladies, all this politics cannot be very palatable to a lady's taste. We will certainly expect you, Mrs. Temple, to be present at the masque; and if Miss Virginia would prefer not to play her part in the exhibition, she may still be there to cheer us with her smiles. I can speak for the taste of all gallant young Virginians, that they will readily pardon her for not concealing so fair a face beneath a mask."

"Ah, I can easily see that you are but lately from England," said Mrs. Temple, delighted with the gallantry of the young man. "Your speech, fair sir, savours far more of the manners of the court than of these untutored forests. Alas! it reminds me of my own young days."

"Well, Mr. Bernard," said the Colonel, interrupting his wife in a reminiscence, which bid fair to exhaust no brief time, "you will find that we have only transplanted old English manners to another soil.

"'Cœlum non animum mutant qui trans mare currunt.'"

"I am glad to see," said Bernard, casting an admiring glance at Virginia, "that this new soil you speak of, Colonel Temple, is so favourably adapted to the growth of the fairest flowers."

"Oh, you must be jesting, Mr. Bernard," said the old lady, "for although I am always begging Virginia to pay more attention to the garden, there are scarcely any flowers there worth speaking of, except a few roses that I planted with my own hands, and a bed of violets."

"You mistake me, my dear madam," returned Bernard, still gazing on Virginia with an affectation of rapture, "the roses to which I refer bloom on fair young cheeks, and the violets shed their sweetness in the depths of those blue eyes."

"Oh, you are at your poetry, are you?" said the old lady.

"Not if poetry extends her sway only over the realm of fiction," said Bernard, laying his hand upon his heart.

"Indeed, Mr. Bernard," said Virginia, not displeased at flattery, which however gross it may appear to modern ears, was common with young cavaliers in former days, and relished by the fair damsels, "I have been taught that flowers flourish far better in the cultivated parterre, than in the wild woods. I doubt not that, like Orlando, you are but playing off upon a stranger the sentiments, which, in reality, you reserve for some faithful Rosalind whom you have left in England."

"You now surprise me, indeed," returned Bernard, "for do you know that among all the ladies that grace English society, there are but few who ever heard of Rosalind or her Orlando, and know as little of the forest of Ardennes as of your own wild forests in Virginia."

"I have heard," said the Colonel, "that old Will Shakspeare and his cotemporaries—peers he has none—have been thrown aside for more modern writers, and I fear that England has gained nothing by the exchange. Who is now your prince of song?"

"There is a newly risen wit and poet, John Dryden by name, who seems to bear the palm undisputed. Waller is old now, and though he still writes, yet he has lost much of his popularity by his former defection from the cause of loyalty."

"Well, for my part, give me old wine, old friends and old poets," said the Colonel. "I confess I like a bard to be consecrated by the united plaudits of two or three generations, before I can give him my ready admiration."

"I should think your acquaintance with Horace would have taught you the fallacy of that taste," said Bernard. "Do you not remember how the old Roman laureate complains of the same prejudice existing in his own day, and argues that on such a principle merit could be accorded to no poet, for all must have their admirers among cotemporaries, else their works would pass into oblivion, before their worth were fairly tested?"

"I cannot be far wrong in the present age at least," said Temple, "from what I learn and from what I have myself seen, the literature of the present reign is disgraced by the most gross and libertine sentiments. As the water of a healthful stream if dammed up, stagnates and becomes the fruitful source of unwholesome malaria, and then, when released, rushes forward, spreading disease and death in its course, so the liberal feelings and manners of old England, restrained by the rigid puritanism of the Protectorate, at last burst forth in a torrent of disgusting and diseased libertinism."

Bernard had not an opportunity of replying to this elaborate simile of the good old Colonel, which, like Fadladeen, he had often used and still reserved for great occasions. Further conversation was here interrupted by a new arrival, which in this case, much to the satisfaction of the fair Virginia, proved to be the genuine Hansford.

CHAPTER VI

"Speak of Mortimer!
Zounds, I will speak of him; and let my soul
Want mercy, if I do not join with him."

Henry IV.

Thomas Hansford, in appearance and demeanour, lost nothing in comparison with the accomplished Bernard. He certainly did not possess in so high a degree the easy assurance which characterized the young courtier, but his self-confidence, blended with a becoming modesty, and his open, ingenuous manners, fully compensated for the difference. There was that in his clear blue eye and pleasant smile which inspired confidence in all whom he approached. Modest and unobtrusive in his expressions of opinion, he was nevertheless firm in their maintenance when announced, and though deferential to superiors in age and position, and respectful to all, he was never servile or obsequious.

The same kind of difference might be traced in the dress of the two young men, as in their manners. With none of the ostentatious display, which we have described as belonging to the costume of Bernard, the attire of Hansford was plain and neat. He was dressed in a grey doublet and breeches, trussed with black silk points. His long hose were of cotton, and his shoes were fastened, not with the gay colored ribbons before described, but with stout leather thongs, such as are still often used in the dress of a country gentleman. His beaver was looped with a plain black button, in front, displaying his fair hair, which was brushed plainly back from his forehead. He, too, wore a sword by his side, but it was fastened, not by handsome fringe and sash, but by a plain belt around his waist. It seemed as though it were worn more for use than ornament. We have been thus particular in describing the dress of these two young men, because, as we have hinted, the contrast indicated the difference in their characters—a difference which will, however, more strikingly appear in the subsequent pages of this narrative.

"Well, my boy," said old Temple, heartily, "I am glad to see you; you have been a stranger among us lately, but are none the less welcome on that account. Yet, faith, lad, there was no necessity for whetting our appetite for your company by such a long absence."

"I have been detained on some business of importance," replied Hansford, with some constraint in his manner. "I am glad, however, my dear sir, that I have not forfeited my welcome by my delay, for no one, I assure you, has had more cause to regret my absence than myself."

"Better late than never, my boy," said the Colonel. "Come, here is a new acquaintance of ours, to whom I wish to introduce you. Mr. Alfred Bernard, Mr. Hansford."

The young men saluted each other respectfully, and Hansford passed on to "metal more attractive." Seated once more by the side of his faithful Virginia, he forgot the presence of all else, and the two lovers were soon deep in conversation, in a low voice.

"I hope your absence was not caused by your mother's increased sickness," said Virginia.

"No, dearest, the old lady's health is far better than it has been for some time. But I have many things to tell you which will surprise, if they do not please you."

"Oh, you have no idea what a fright father gave me this evening," said Virginia. "He told me that you had probably been engaged by the governor to aid in suppressing this rebellion. I fancied that there were already twenty bullets through your body, and made a little fool of myself generally. But if I had known that you were staying away from me so long without any good reason, I would not have been so silly, I assure you."

"Your care for me, dear girl, is very grateful to my feelings, and indeed it makes me very sad to think that I may yet be the cause of so much unhappiness to you."

"Oh, come now," said the laughing girl, "don't be sentimental. You men think very little of ladies, if you suppose that we are incapable of listening to anything but flattery. Now, there's Mr. Bernard has been calling me flowers, and roses, and violets, ever since he came. For my part, I would rather be loved as a woman, than admired as all the flowers that grow in the world."

"Who is this Mr. Bernard?" asked Hansford.

"He is the Governor's private secretary, and a very nice fellow he seems to be, too. He has more poetry at his finger's ends than you or I ever read, and he is very handsome, don't you think so?"

"It is very well that I did not prolong my absence another day," said Hansford, "or else I might have found my place in your heart supplied by this foppish young fribble."[6]

"Nay, now, if you are going to be jealous, I will get angry," said Virginia, trying to pout her pretty lips. "But say what you will about him, he is very smart, and what's more, he writes poetry as well as quotes it."

"And has he told you of all his accomplishments so soon?" said Hansford, smiling; "for I hardly suppose you have seen a volume of his works, unless he brought it here with him. What else can he do? Perhaps he plays the flute, and dances divinely; and may-be, but for 'the vile guns, he might have been a soldier.' He looks a good deal like Hotspur's dandy to my eyes."

"Oh, don't be so ill-natured," said Virginia, "He never would have told about his writing poetry, but father guessed it."

"Your father must have infinite penetration then," said Hansford, "for I really do not think the young gentleman looks much as though he could tear himself from the mirror long enough to use his pen."

"Well, but he has written a masque, to be performed day-after-to-morrow night, at the palace, to celebrate Lady Frances' birth-day. Are you not going to the ball. Of course you'll be invited."

"No, dearest," said Hansford, with a sigh. "Sir William Berkeley might give me a more unwelcome welcome than to a masque."

"What on earth do you mean?" said Virginia, turning pale with alarm. "You have not—"

"Nay, you shall know all to-morrow," replied Hansford.

"Tom," cried Colonel Temple, in his loud, merry voice, "stop cooing there, and tell me where you have been all this time. I'll swear, boy, I thought you had been helping Berkeley to put down that d—d renegade, Bacon."

"I am surprised," said Hansford, with a forced, but uneasy smile, "that you should suppose the Governor had entrusted an affair of such moment to me."

"Zounds, lad," said the Colonel, "I never dreamed that you were at the head of the expedition. Oh, the vanity of youth! No, I suppose my good friends, Colonel Ludwell and Major Beverley, are entrusted with the lead. But I thought a subordinate office—"

"You are mistaken altogether, Colonel," said Hansford. "The business which detained me from Windsor Hall had nothing to do with the suppression of this rebellion, and indeed I have not been in Jamestown for some weeks."

"Well, keep your own counsel then, Tom; but I trust it was at least business connected with your profession. I like to see a young lawyer give his undivided attention to business. But I doubt me, Tom, that you cheat the law out of some of the six hours that Lord Coke has allotted to her."

"I have, indeed, been attending to the preparation of a cause of some importance," said Hansford.

"Well, I'm glad of it, my boy. Who is your client? I hope he gives you a good retainer."

"My fee is chiefly contingent," replied the young lawyer, sorely pressed by the questions of the curious old Colonel.

"Why, you are very laconic," returned Temple, trying to enlist him in conversation. "Come, tell me all about it. I used to be something of a lawyer myself in my youth, didn't I, Bessy?"

"Yes, indeed," said his wife, who was nearly dozing over her eternal knitting; "and if you had stuck to your profession, and not mingled in politics, my dear, we would have been much better off. You know I always told you so."

"I believe you did, Bessy," said the Colonel. "But what's done can't be undone. Take example by me, Tom, d'ye hear, and never meddle in politics, my boy. But I believe I retain some cobwebs of law in my brain yet, and I might help you in your case. Who is your client?"

"The Colony is one of the parties to the cause," replied Hansford; "but the details cannot interest the ladies, you know; I will confer with you some other time on the subject, and will be very happy to have your advice."

All this time, Alfred Bernard had been silently watching the countenance of Hansford, and the latter had been unpleasantly conscious of the fact. As he made the last remark, he saw the keen eyes of Bernard resting upon him with such an expression of suspicion, that he could not avoid wincing. Bernard had no idea of losing the advantage which he thus possessed, and with wily caution he prepared a snare for his victim, more sure of success than an immediate attack would have been.

"I think I have heard something of the case," he said, fixing a penetrating glance on Hansford as he spoke, "and I agree with Mr. Hansford, that its details here would not be very interesting to the ladies. By the way, Colonel, your conjecture, that Mr. Hansford was employed in the suppression of the rebellion, reminds me of a circumstance that I had almost forgotten to mention. You have heard of that fellow Bacon's perjury—"

"Perjury!" exclaimed the Colonel. "No! on the contrary I had been given to understand that, with all his faults, his personal honour was so far unstained, even with suspicion."

"Such was the general impression," returned Bernard, "but it is now proven that he is as capable of the greatest perfidy as of the most daring treason."

"You probably refer, sir, to an affair," said Hansford, "of which I have some knowledge, and on which I may throw some light which will be more favorable to Mr. Bacon."

"Your being able to conjecture so easily the fact to which I allude," said Bernard, "is in itself an evidence that the general impression of his conduct is not so erroneous. I am happy," he added, with a sneer, "that in this free country, a rebel even can meet with so disinterested a defender."

"If you refer, Mr. Bernard," replied Hansford, disregarding the manner of Bernard, "to the alleged infraction of his parole, I can certainly explain it. I know that Colonel Temple does not, and I hope that you do not, wish deliberately to do any man an injustice, even if he be a foe or a rebel."

"That's true, my boy," said the generous old Temple. "Give the devil his due, even he is not as black as he is painted. That's my maxim. How was it, Tom? And begin at the beginning, that's the only way to straighten a tangled skein."

"Then, as I understand the story," said Hansford, in a slow, distinct, voice, "it is this:—After Mr. Bacon returned to Henrico from his expedition against the Indians, he was elected to the House of Burgesses. On attempting to go down the river to Jamestown, to take his seat, he was arrested by Captain Gardiner, on a charge of treason, and brought as a prisoner before Sir William Berkeley. The Governor, expressing himself satisfied with his disclaimer and open recantation of any treasonable design, released him from imprisonment on parole, and, as is reported, promised at the same time to grant him the commission he desired. Mr. Bacon, hearing of the sickness of his wife, returned to Henrico, and while there, secret warrants were issued to arrest him again. Upon a knowledge of this fact he refused to surrender himself under his parole."

"You have made a very clear case of it, if the facts be true," said Bernard, in a taunting tone, "and seem to be well acquainted with the motives and movements of the traitor. I have no doubt there are many among his deluded followers who fail to appreciate the full force of a parole d'honneur."

"Sir!" said Hansford, his face flushing with indignation.

"I only remarked," said Bernard, in reply, "that a traitor to his country knows but little of the laws which govern honourable men. My remark only applied to traitors, and such I conceive the followers and supporters of Nathaniel Bacon to be."

Hansford only replied with a bow.

"And so does Tom," said Temple, "and so do we all, Mr. Bernard. But Hansford knew Bacon before this late movement of his, and he is very loth to hear his old friend charged with anything that he does not deserve. But see, my wife there is nodding over her knitting, and Jeanie's pretty blue eyes, I know, begin to itch. Our motto is, Mr. Bernard, to go to bed with the chickens and rise with the lark. But we have failed in the first to-night, and I reckon we will sleep a little later than lady lark to-morrow. So, to bed, to bed, my lord."

So saying, the hospitable old gentleman called a servant to show the gentlemen to their separate apartments.

"You will be able to sleep in an old planter's cabin, Mr. Bernard," he said, "where you will find all clean and comfortable, although perhaps a little rougher than you are accustomed to. Tom, boy, you know the ways of the house, and I needn't apologize to you. And so pleasant dreams and a good night to you both."

After the Colonel had gone, and before the servant had appeared, Hansford touched Bernard lightly on the shoulder. The latter turned around with some surprise.

"You must be aware, Mr. Bernard," said Hansford, "that your language to-night remained unresented only because of my respect for the company in which we were."

"I did not deem it of sufficient importance," replied Bernard, assuming an indifferent tone, "to inquire whether your motives for silence were respect for the family or regard for yourself."

"You now at least know, sir. Let me ask you whether you made the remark to which I refer with a full knowledge of who I was, and what were my relations towards Mr. Bacon."

"I decline making any explanation of language which, both in manner and expression, was sufficiently intelligible."

"Then, sir," said Hansford, resolutely, "there is but one reparation that you can make," and he laid his hand significantly on his sword.

"I understand you," returned Bernard, "but do not hold myself responsible to a man whose position in society may be more worthy of my contempt than of my resentment."

"The company in which you found me, and the gentleman who introduced us, are sufficient guarantees of my position. If under these circumstances you refuse, you take advantage of a subterfuge alike unworthy of a gentleman or a brave man."

"Even this could scarcely avail you, since the family are not aware of the treason by which you have forfeited any claim to their protection. But I waive any such objection, sir, and accept your challenge."

"Being better acquainted with the place than yourself," said Hansford, "I would suggest, sir, that there is a little grove in rear of the barn-yard, which is a fit spot for our purpose. There will there be no danger of interruption."

"As you please, sir," replied Bernard. "To-morrow morning, then, at sunrise, with swords, and in the grove you speak of."

The servant entered the room at this moment, and the two young men parted for the night, having thus settled in a few moments the preliminaries of a mortal combat, with as much coolness as if it had been an agreement for a fox-hunt.

FOOTNOTES:

[6] A coxcomb, a popinjay.

CHAPTER VII

"'We try this quarrel hilt to hilt.
'Then each at once his falchion drew,
Each on the ground his scabbard threw,
Each looked to sun, and stream, and plain,
As what they ne'er might see again;
Then foot, and point, and eye opposed,
In dubious strife they darkly closed."

Lady of the Lake.

It is a happy thing for human nature that the cares, and vexations, and fears, of this weary life, are at least excluded from the magic world of sleep. Exhausted nature will seek a respite from her trials in forgetfulness, and steeped in the sacred stream of Lethe, like the young Achilles, she becomes invulnerable. It is but seldom that care dares intrude upon this quiet realm, and though it may be truly said that sleep "swift on her downy pinions flies from woe," yet, when at last it does alight on the lid sullied by a tear, it rests as quietly as elsewhere. We have scarcely ever read of an instance where the last night of a convict was not passed in tranquil slumber, as though Sleep, the sweet sister of the dread Terror, soothed more tenderly, in this last hour, the victim of her gloomy brother's dart.

Thomas Hansford, for with him our story remains, slept as calmly on this night as though a long life of happiness and fame stretched out before his eyes. 'Tis true, that ere he went to bed, as he unbelted his trusty sword, he looked at its well-tempered steel with a confident eye, and thought of the morrow. But so fully imbued were the youth of that iron age with the true spirit of chivalry, that life was but little regarded where honour was concerned, and the precarious tenure by which life was held, made it less prized by those who felt that they might be called on any day to surrender it. Hansford, therefore, slept soundly, and the first red streaks of the morning twilight were smiling through his window when he awoke. He rose, and dressing himself hastily, he repaired to the study, where he wrote a few hasty lines to his mother and to Virginia—the first to assure her of his filial love, and to pray her forgiveness for thus sacrificing life for honour; and the second breathing the warm ardour of his heart for her who, during his brief career, had lightened the cares and shared the joys which fortune had strewn in his path. As he folded these two letters and placed them in his pocket, he could not help drawing a deep sigh, to think of these two beings whose fate was so intimately entwined with his own, and whose thread of life would be weakened when his had been severed. Repelling such a thought as unworthy a brave man engaged in an honourable cause, he buckled on his sword and repaired with a firm step to the place of meeting. Alfred Bernard, true to his word, was there.

And now the sun was just rising above the green forest, to the eastward. The hands, as by a striking metonymy those happy laborers were termed, who never knew the cares which environ the head, were just going out to their day's work. Men, women and children, some to plough the corn, and one a merry teamster, who, with his well attended team, was driving to the woods for fuel. And in the barn-yard were the sleek milch cows, smelling fresh with the dewy clover from the meadow, and their hides smoking with the early dew of morning; and the fowls, that strutted and clucked, and cackled, in the yard, all breakfasting on the scanty grains that had fallen from the horse-troughs—all save one inquisitive old rooster, who, flapping his wings and mounting the fence to crow, eyed askant the two young men, as though, a knight himself, he guessed their bloody intent. And the birds, too, those joyous, happy beings, who pass their life in singing, shook the fresh dew from their pretty wings, cleared their throats in the bracing air, and like the pious Persian, pouring forth their hymn of praise to the morning sun, fluttered away to search for their daily food. All was instinct with happiness and beauty. All were seeking to preserve the life which God had given but two, and they stood there, in the bright, dewy morning, to stain the fair robe of nature with blood. It is a sad thought, that of all the beings who rejoice in life, he alone, who bears the image of his Maker, should have wandered from His law.

The men saluted one another coldly as Hansford approached, and Bernard said, with a firm voice, "You see, sir, I have kept my appointment. I believe nothing remains but to proceed."

"You must excuse me for again suggesting," said Hansford, "that we wait a few moments, until these labourers are out of sight. We might be interrupted."

Bernard silently acquiesced, and the combatants stood at a short distance apart, each rapt in his own reflections. What those reflections were may be easily imagined. Both were young men of talent and promise. The one, the favourite of Sir William Berkeley, saw fame and distinction awaiting him in the colony. The other, the beloved of the people, second only to Bacon in their affections, and by that great leader esteemed as a friend and entrusted as a confidant, had scarce less hope in the future. The one a stranger, almost unknown in the colony, with little to care for in the world but self; the other the support of an aged mother, and the pride of a fair and trusting girl—the strong rock, on whose protection the grey lichen of age had rested, and around which the green tendrils of love entwined. Both men of erring hearts, who in a few moments might be summoned to appear at that dread bar, where all the secrets of their hearts are known, and all the actions of their lives are judged. The two combatants were nearly equally matched in the use of the sword. Bernard's superior skill in fence being fully compensated by the superior coolness of his adversary.

Just as the last labourer had disappeared, both swords flashed in the morning sun. The combat was long, and the issue doubtful. Each seemed so conscious of the skill of the other, that both acted chiefly on the defensive. But the protracted length of the fight turned to the advantage of Hansford, who, from his early training and hardy exercise, was more accustomed to endure fatigue. Bernard became weary of a contest of such little interest, and at last, forgetting the science in which he was a complete adept, he made a desperate lunge at the breast of the young colonist. This thrust Hansford parried with such success, that he sent the sword of his adversary flying through the air. In attempting to regain possession of his sword, Bernard's foot slipped, and he fell prostrate to the ground.

"Now yield you," cried the victor, as he stood above the prostrate form of his antagonist, "and take back the foul stain which you have placed upon my name, or, by my troth, you had else better commend yourself to Heaven."

"I cannot choose but yield," said Bernard, rising slowly from the ground, while his face was purple with rage and mortification. "But look ye, sir rebel, if but I had that good sword once more in my hand, I would prove that I can yet maintain my honour and my life against a traitor's arm. I take my life at your hands, but God do so to me, and more also, if the day do not come when you will wish that you had taken it while it was in your power. The life you give me shall be devoted to the one purpose of revenge."

"As you please," said Hansford, eyeing him with an expression of bitter contempt. "Meantime, as you value your life, dedicated to so unworthy an object, let me hear no more of your insolence."

"Nay, by my soul," cried Bernard, "I will not bear your taunts. Draw and defend yourself!" At the same time, with an active spring, he regained possession of his lost sword. But just as they were about to renew the attack, there appeared upon the scene of action a personage so strange in appearance, and so wild in dress, that Bernard dropped his weapon in surprise, and with a vacant stare gazed upon the singular apparition.

The figure was that of a young girl, scarce twenty years of age, whose dark copper complexion, piercing black eyes, and high cheek bones, all proclaimed her to belong to that unhappy race which had so long held undisputed possession of this continent. Her dress was fantastic in the highest degree. Around her head was a plait of peake, made from those shells which were used by the Indians at once as their roanoke, or money, and as their most highly prized ornament of dress. A necklace and bracelets of the same adorned her neck and arms. A short smock, made of dressed deer-skin, which reached only to her knees, and was tightly fitted around the waist with a belt of wampum, but scantily concealed the swelling of her lovely bosom. Her legs, from the knee to the ancle, were bare, and her feet were covered with buckskin sandals, ornamented with beads, such as are yet seen in our western country, as the handiwork of the remnant of this unhappy race. Such a picturesque costume well became the graceful form that wore it. Her long, dark hair, which, amid all these decorations, was her loveliest ornament, fell unbound over her shoulders in rich profusion. As she approached, with light and elastic step, towards the combatants, Bernard, as we have said, dropped his sword in mute astonishment. It is true, that even in his short residence in Virginia, he had seen Indians at Jamestown, but they had come with friendly purpose to ask favors of the English. His impressions were therefore somewhat similar to those of a man who, having admired the glossy coat, and graceful, athletic form of a tiger in a menagerie, first sees that fierce animal bounding towards him from his Indian jungle. The effect upon him, however, was of course but momentary, and he again raised his sword to renew the attack. But his opponent, without any desire of engaging again in the contest, turned to the young girl and said, in a familiar voice, "Well, Mamalis, what brings you to the hall so early this morning?"

"There is danger there," replied the young girl, solemnly, and in purer English than Bernard was prepared to hear. "If you would help me, put up your long knife and follow me."

"What do you mean?" asked Hansford, alarmed by her manner and words.

"Manteo and his braves come to take blood for blood," returned the girl. "There is no time to lose."

"In God's name, Mr. Bernard," said Hansford, quickly, "come along with us. This is no time for private quarrel. Our swords are destined for another use."

"Most willingly," replied Bernard; "our enmity will scarcely cool by delay. And mark me, young man, Alfred Bernard will never rest until he avenges the triumph of your sword this morning, or the foul blot which you have placed upon his name. But let that pass now. Can this creature's statement be relied on?"

"She is as true as Heaven," whispered Hansford. "Come on, for we have indeed but little time to lose; at another time I will afford you ample opportunity to redeem your honour or to avenge yourself. You will not find my blood cooler by delay." And so the three walked on rapidly towards the house, the two young men side by side, after having sworn eternal hostility to one another, but yet willing to forget their private feud in the more important duties before them.

The reader of the history of this interesting period, will remember that there were, at this time, many causes of discontent prevailing among the Indians of Virginia. As has been before remarked, the murder of a herdsman, Robert Hen by name, and other incidents of a similar character, were so terribly avenged by the incensed colonists, not only upon the guilty, but upon friendly tribes, that the discontent of the Indians was wide spread and nearly universal. Nor did it cease until the final suppression of the Indian power by Nathaniel Bacon, at the battle of Bloody Run. This, however, was but the immediate cause of hostilities, for which there had already been, in the opinion of the Indians, sufficient provocation. Many obnoxious laws had been passed by the Assembly, in regard to the savages, that were so galling to their independence, that the seeds of discord and enmity were already widely sown. Among these were the laws prohibiting the trade in guns and ammunition with the Indians; requiring the warriors of the peaceful tribes to wear badges in order that they might be recognized; restricting them in their trade to particular marts; and, above all, providing that the *Werowance*, or chief of a tribe, should hold his position by the appointment of the Governor, and not by the choice of his braves. This last provision, which struck at the very independence of the tribes, was so offensive, that peaceable relations with the Indians could not long be maintained. Add to this the fact, which for its inhumanity is scarcely credible, that the English at Monados, now the island of New York, had, with a view of controlling the monopoly of the trade in furs and skins, inspired the Indians with a bitter hostility toward the Virginians, and it will easily be seen that the magazine of discontent needed but a spark to explode in open hostility.

So much is necessary to be premised in order that the reader may understand the relations which existed, at this period, between the colonists and the Indians around them.

CHAPTER VIII

"And in, the buskined hunters of the deer,
To Albert's home with shout and cymbal throng."

Campbell.

The surprise and horror with which the intelligence of this impending attack was received by the family at Windsor Hall may be better imagined than described. Manteo, the leader of the party, a young Indian of the Pamunkey tribe, was well known to them all. With his sister, the young girl whom we have described, he lived quietly in his little wigwam, a few miles from the hall, and in his intercourse with the family had been friendly and even affectionate. But with all this, he was still ardently devoted to his race, and thirsting for fame; and stung by what he conceived the injustice of the whites, he had leagued himself in an enterprise, which, regardless of favour or friendship, was dictated by revenge.

It was, alas! too late to hope for escape from the hall, or to send to the neighboring plantations for assistance; and, to add to their perplexity, the whole force of the farm, white servants and black, had gone to a distant field, where it was scarcely possible that they could hear of the attack until it was too late to contribute their aid in the defence. But with courage and resolution the gentlemen prepared to make such defence or resistance as was in their power, and, indeed, from the unsettled character of the times, a planter's house was no mean fortification against the attacks of the Indians. Early in the history of the colony, it was found necessary, for the general safety, to enact laws requiring each planter to provide suitable means of defence, in case of any sudden assault by the hostile tribes. Accordingly, the doors to these country mansions were made of the strongest material, and in some cases, and such was the case at Windsor Hall, were lined on the interior by a thick sheet of iron. The windows, too, or such as were low enough to be scaled from the ground, were protected by shutters of similar material. Every planter had several guns, and a sufficient store of ammunition for defence. Thus it will be seen that Windsor Hall, protected by three vigorous men, well armed and stout of heart, was no contemptible fortress against the rude attacks of a few savages, whose number in all probability would not exceed twenty. The greatest apprehension was from fire; but, strange to say, the savages but seldom resorted to this mode of vengeance, except when wrought up to the highest state of excitement.[7]

"At any rate," said the brave old Colonel, "we will remain where we are until threatened with fire, and then at least avenge our lives with the blood of these infamous wretches."

The doors and lower windows had been barricaded, and the three men, armed to the teeth, stood ready in the hall for the impending attack. Virginia and her mother were there, the former pale as ashes, but suppressing her emotions with a violent effort in order to contribute to her mother's comfort. In fact, the old lady, notwithstanding her boast of bravery on the evening before, stood in need of all the consolation that her daughter could impart. She vented her feelings in screams as loud as those of the Indians she feared, and refused to be comforted. Virginia, forgetful of her own equal danger, leant tenderly over her mother, who had thrown herself upon a sofa, and whispered those sweet words of consolation, which religion can alone suggest in the hour of our trial:

"Mother, dear mother," she said, "remember that although earthly strength should fail, we are yet in the hands of One who is mighty."

"Well, and what if we are," cried her mother, whose faith was like that of the old lady, who, when the horses ran away with her carriage, trusted in Providence till the breeching broke. "Well, and what if we are, if in a few minutes our scalps may be taken by these horrible savages?"

"But, dear mother, He has promised—"

"Oh, I don't know whether he has or not—but as sure as fate there they come," and the old lady relapsed into her hysterics.

"Mother, mother, remember your duty as a Christian—remember in whom you have put your trust," said Virginia, earnestly.

"Oh, yes, that's the way. Of course I know nothing of my duty, and I don't pretend to be as good as others. I am nothing but a poor, weak old woman, and must be reminded of my duty by my daughter, although I was a Christian long before she was born. But, for my part, I think it's tempting Providence to bear such a judgment with so much indifference."

"But, Bessy," interposed the Colonel, seeing Virginia was silent under this unusual kind of argument, "your agitation will only make the matter worse. If you give way thus, we cannot be as ready and cool in action as we should. Come now, dear Bessy, calm yourself."

"Oh, yes, it's well to say that, after bringing me all the way into this wild country, to be devoured by these wild Indians. Oh, that I should ever have consented to leave my quiet home in dear old England for this! And all because a protector reigned instead of a king. Protector, forsooth; I would rather have a hundred protectors at this moment than one king."

"Father," said Virginia, in a tremulous voice, "had we not better retire to some other part of the house? We can only incommode you here."

"Right, my girl," said her father. "Take your mother up stairs into your room, and try and compose her."

"Take me, indeed," said his worthy spouse. "Colonel Temple, you speak as if I was a baby, to be carried about as you choose. I assure you, I will not budge a foot from you."

"Stay where you are then," replied Temple, impatiently, "and for God's sake be calm. Ha! now my boys—here they come!" and a wild yell, which seemed to crack the very welkin, announced the appearance of the enemy.

"I think we had all better go to the upper windows," said Hansford, calmly. "There is nothing to be done by being shut up in this dark hall; while there, protected from their arrows, we may do some damage to the enemy. If we remain, our only chance is to make a desperate sally, in which we would be almost certainly destroyed."

"Mr. Hansford," said Virginia, "give me a gun—there is one left—and you shall see that a young girl, in an hour of peril like this, knows how to aid brave men in her own defence."

Hansford bent an admiring glance upon the heroic girl, as he placed the weapon in her hands, while her father said, with rapture, "God bless you, my daughter. If your arm were strong as your heart is brave, you had been a hero. I retract what I said on yesterday," he added in a whisper, with a sad smile, "for you have this day proved yourself worthy to be a brave man's wife."

The suggestion of Hansford was readily agreed upon, and the little party were soon at their posts, shielded by the windows from the attack of the Indians, and yet in a position from which they could annoy the enemy considerably by their own fire. From his shelter there, Bernard, to whom the sight was entirely new, could see rushing towards the hall, a party of about twenty savages, painted in the horrible manner which they adopt to inspire terror in a foe, and attired in that strange wild costume, which is now familiar to every school-boy. Their leader, a tall, athletic young Indian, surpassed them all in the hideousness of his appearance. His closely shaven hair was adorned with a tall eagle's feather, and pendant from his ears were the rattles of the rattlesnake. The only garment which concealed his nakedness was a short smock, or apron, reaching from his waist nearly to his knees, and made of dressed deer skin, adorned with beads and shells. Around his neck and wrists were strings of peake and roanoke. His face was painted in the most horrible manner, with a ground of deep red, formed from the dye of the pocone root, and variegated with streaks of blue, yellow and green. Around his eyes were large circles of green paint. But to make his appearance still more hideous, feathers and hair were stuck all over his body, upon the fresh paint, which made the warrior look far more like some wild beast of the forest than a human being.

Brandishing a tomahawk in one hand, and holding a carbine in the other, Manteo, thus disguised, led on his braves with loud yells towards the mansion of Colonel Temple. How different from the respectful demeanour, and more modest attire, in which he was accustomed to appear before the family of Windsor Hall.

To the great comfort of the inmates, his carbine was the only one in the party, thanks to the wise precaution of the Assembly, in restricting the sale of such deadly weapons to the Indians. His followers, arrayed in like horrible costume with himself, followed on with their tomahawks and bows; their arrows were secured in a quiver slung over the shoulder, which was formed of the skins of foxes and raccoons, rendered more terrible by the head of the animal being left unsevered from the skin. To the loud shrieks and yells of their voices, was added the unearthly sound of their drums and rattles—the whole together forming a discordant medley, which, as brave old John Smith has well and quaintly observed, "would rather affright than delight any man."

All this the besieged inmates of the hall saw with mingled feelings of astonishment and dread, awaiting with intense anxiety the result.

"Now be perfectly quiet," said Hansford, in a low tone, for, by tacit consent, he was looked upon as the leader of the defence. "The house being closed, they may conclude that the family are absent, and so, after their first burst of vengeance, retire. Their bark is always worse than their bite."

Such indeed seemed likely to be the case, for the Indians, arrived at the porch, looked around with some surprise at the barred doors and windows, and began to confer together. Whatever might have been the event of their conference, their actions, however, were materially affected by an incident which, though intended for the best, was well nigh resulting in destruction to the whole family.

FOOTNOTES:

[7] This fact, which I find mentioned by several historians, is explained by Kercheval, in his history of the Valley of Virginia, by the supposition that the Indians for a long time entertained the hope of reconquering the country, and saved property from destruction which might be of use to them in the future. See page 90 of Valley of Va.

CHAPTER IX

"Like gun when aimed at duck or plover,
Kicks back and knocks the shooter over."

There was at Windsor Hall, an old family servant, known alike to the negroes and the "white folks," by the familiar appellation of Uncle Giles. He was one of those old-fashioned negroes, who having borne the heat and burden of the day, are turned out to live in comparative freedom, and supplied with everything that can make their declining years comfortable and happy. Uncle Giles, according to his own account, was sixty-four last Whitsuntide, and was consequently born in Africa. It is a singular fact connected with this race, that whenever consulted about their age, they invariably date the anniversary of their birth at Christmas, Easter or Whitsuntide, the triennial holydays to which they are entitled. Whether this arises from the fact that a life which is devoted to the service of others should commence with a holyday, or whether these three are the only epochs known to the negro, is a question of some interest, but of little importance to our narrative. So it was, that old uncle Giles, in his own expressive phrase was, "after wiking all his born days, done turn out to graze hisself to def." The only business of the old man was to keep himself comfortable in winter by the kitchen fire, and in summer to smoke his old corn-cob pipe on the three legged bench that stood at the kitchen door. Added to this, was the self-assumed duty of "strapping" the young darkies, and lecturing the old ones on the importance of working hard, and obeying "old massa," cheerfully in everything. And so old uncle Giles, with white and black, with old and young, but especially with old uncle Giles himself, was a great character. Among other things that increased his inordinate self-esteem, was the possession of a rusty old blunderbuss, which, long since discarded as useless by his master, had fallen into his hands, and was regarded by him and his sable admirers as a pearl of great price.

Now it so happened, that on the morning to which our story refers, uncle Giles was quietly smoking his pipe, and muttering solemnly to himself in that grumbling tone so peculiar to old negroes. When he learned, however, of the intended attack of the Indians, the old man, who well remembered the earlier skirmishes with the savages, took his old blunderbuss from its resting-place above the door of the kitchen, and prepared himself for action. The old gun, which owing to the growing infirmities of its possessor, had not been called into use for years, was now rusted from disuse and neglect; and a bold spider had even dared to seek, not the bubble reputation, but his more substantial gossamer palace, at the very mouth of the barrel. Notwithstanding all this, the gun had all the time remained loaded, for Giles was too rigid an economist to waste a charge without some good reason. Armed with this formidable weapon, Giles succeeded in climbing up the side of the low cabin kitchen, by the logs which protruded from either end of the wall. Arrived at the top and screening himself behind the rude log and mud chimney, he awaited with a patience and immobility which Wellington might have envied, the arrival of the foe. Here then he was quietly seated when the conference to which we have alluded took place between the Indian warriors.

"Bird flown," said Manteo, the leader of the party. "Nest empty."

Two or three of the braves stooped down and began to examine the soft sandy soil to discover if there were any tracks or signs of the family having left. Fortunately the search seemed satisfactory, for the foot-prints of Bernard's and Hansford's horses, as they were led from the house towards the stable on the previous evening, were still quite visible.

This little circumstance seemed to determine the party, and they had turned away, probably to seek their vengeance elsewhere, or to return at a more propitious moment, when the discharge of a gun was heard, so loud, so crashing, and so alarming, that it seemed like the sudden rattling of thunder in a storm.

Luckily, perhaps for all parties, while the shot fell through the poplar trees like the first big drops of rain in summer, the only damage which was done was in clipping off the feather which was worn by Manteo as a badge of his position. When we say this, however, we mean to refer only to the effect of the *charge*, not of the *discharge* of the gun, for the breech rebounding violently against old Giles shoulder, the poor fellow lost his balance and came tumbling to the ground. The cabin was fortunately not more than ten feet high, and our African hero escaped into the kitchen with a few bruises—a happy compromise for the fate which would have inevitably been his had he remained in his former position. The smoke of his fusil mingling with the smoke from the chimney, averted suspicion, and with the simple-minded creatures who heard the report and witnessed its effects the whole matter remained a mystery.

"Tunder," said one, looking round in vain for the source from which an attack could be made.

"Call dat tunder," growled Manteo, pointing significantly to his moulted plume that lay on the ground.

"Okees[8] mad. Shoot Pawcussacks[9] from osies,"[10] said one of the older and more experienced of the party, endeavouring to give some rational explanation of so inexplicable a mystery.

A violent dispute here arose between the different warriors as to the cause of this sudden anger of the gods; some contending that it was because they were attacking a Netoppew or friend, and others with equal zeal contending that it was to reprove the slowness of their vengeance.

From their position above, all these proceedings could be seen, and these contentions heard by the besieged party. The mixed language in which the men spoke, for they had even thus early appropriated many English words to supply the deficiencies in their own barren tongue, was explained by Mamalis, where it was unintelligible to the whites. This young girl felt a divided interest in the fate of the besieging and besieged parties; for all of her devotion to Virginia Temple could not make her entirely forget the fortunes of her brave brother.

In a few moments, she saw that it was necessary to take some decisive step, for the faction which was of harsher mood, and urged immediate vengeance, was seen to prevail in the conference. The fatal word "fire" was several times heard, and Manteo was already starting towards the kitchen to procure the means of carrying into effect their deadly purpose.

"I see nothing left, but to defend ourselves as we may," said Hansford in a low voice, at the same time raising his musket, and advancing a step towards the window, with a view of throwing it open and commencing the attack.

"Oh, don't shoot," said Mamalis, imploringly, "I will go and save all."

"Do you think, my poor girl, that they will hearken to mercy at your intercession," said Colonel Temple, shaking his head, sorrowfully.

"No!" replied Mamalis, "the heart of a brave knows not mercy. If he gave his ear to the cry of mercy, he would be a squaw and not a brave. But fear not, I can yet save you," she added confidently, "only do not be seen."

The men looked from one to the other to decide.

"Trust her, father," said Virginia, "if you are discovered blood must be shed. She says she can save us all. Trust her, Hansford. Trust her, Mr. Bernard."

"We could lose little by being betrayed at this stage of the game," said Temple, "so go, my good girl, and Heaven will bless you!"

Quick as thought the young Indian left the room, and descended the stairs. Drawing the bolt of the back door so softly, that she scarcely heard it move, herself, she went to the kitchen, where old Giles, a prey to a thousand fears, was seated trembling over the fire, his face of that peculiar ashy hue, which the negro complexion sometimes assumes as an humble apology for pallor. As she touched the old man on the shoulder, he groaned in despair and looked up, showing scarcely anything but the whites of his eyes, while his woolly head, thinned and white with age, resembled ashes sprinkled over a bed of extinguished charcoal. Seeing the face of an Indian, and too terrified to recognize Mamalis, he fell on his knees at her feet, and cried,

"Oh, for de Lord sake, massa, pity de poor old nigger! My lod a messy, massa, I neber shoot anudder gun in all my born days."

"Hush," said Mamalis, "and listen to me. I tell lie, you say it is truth; I say whites in Jamestown; you say so too—went yesterday."

"But bress your soul, missis," said Giles, "sposen dey ax me ef I shot dat cussed gun, me say dat truf too?"

"No, say it was thunder."

At this moment the tall dark form of Manteo entered the room. He started with surprise, as he saw his sister there, and in such company. His dark eye darted a fierce glance at Giles, who quailed beneath its glare. Then turning again to his sister, he said in the Indian tongue, which we freely translate:

"Mamalis with the white man! where is he that I may drown my vengeance in his blood."

"He is gone; he is not within the power of Manteo. Manitou[11] has saved Manteo from the crime of killing his best friend."

"His people have killed my people for the offence of the few, I will kill him for the cruelty of many. For this is the calumet[12] broken. For this is the tree of peace[13] cut down by the tomahawk of war."

"Say not so," replied Mamalis. "Temple is the netoppew[14] of Manteo. He is even now gone to the grand sachem of the long knives, to make Manteo the Werowance[15] of the Pamunkeys."

"Ha! is this true?" asked Manteo, anxiously.

"Ask this old man," returned Mamalis. "They all went to Jamestown yesterday, did they not?" she asked in English of Giles, who replied, in a trembling voice,

"Yes, my massa, dey has all gone to Jimson on yestiddy."

"And I a Werowance!" said the young man proudly, in his own language. "Spirits of Powhatan and Opechancanough, the name of Manteo shall live immortally as yours. His glory shall be the song of our race, and the young men of his tribe shall emulate his deeds. His life shall be brilliant as the sun's bright course, and his spirit shall set in the spirit land, bright with unfading glory."

Then turning away with a lofty step, he proceeded to rejoin his companions.

The stratagem was successful, and Manteo, the bravest, the noblest of the braves, succeeded after some time in persuading them to desist from their destructive designs. In a few moments, to the delight of the little besieged party, the Indians had left the house, and were soon buried in the deep forest.

"Thanks, my brave, generous girl," said Temple, as Mamalis, after the success of her adventure, entered the room. "To your presence of mind we owe our lives."

"But I told a lie," said the girl, looking down; "I said you had gone to make Manteo the Werowance of the Pamunkeys."

"Well, my girl, he shall not want my aid in getting the office. So you, in effect, told the truth."

"No, no; I said you had gone. It was a lie."

"Ah, but, Mamalis," said Virginia, in an encouraging voice, for she had often impressed upon the mind of the poor savage girl the nature of a lie, "when a falsehood is told for the preservation of life, the sin will be freely forgiven which has accomplished so much good."

"Ignatius Loyola could not have stated his favourite principle more clearly, Miss Temple," said Bernard, with a satirical smile. "I see that the Reformation has not made so wide a difference in the two Churches, after all."

"No, Mr. Bernard," said old Temple, somewhat offended at the young man's tone; "the stratagem of the soldier, and the intrigue of the treacherous Jesuit, are very different. The one is the means which brave men may use to accomplish noble ends; the other is the wily machinations of a perfidious man to attain his own base purposes. The one is the skilful fence and foil of the swordsman, the other the subtle and deceitful design of the sneaking snake."

"Still they both do what is plainly a deception, in order to accomplish an end which they each believe to be good. Once break down the barrier to the field of truth, and it is impossible any longer to distinguish between virtue and error."

"Well," said Mrs. Temple, "I am the last to blame the bridge which carries me over, and I'll warrant there is not one here, man or woman, who isn't glad that our lives have been saved by Mamalis's falsehood—for I have not had such a fright in all my days."

FOOTNOTES:

[8] Gods.

[9] Guns.

[10] Heaven.

[11] The good spirit of the Indians.

[12] The pipe of peace.

[13] When a peace was concluded a tree was planted, and the contracting parties declared that the peace should be as long lived as the tree.

[14] The friend or benefactor.

[15] The Werowance, or chief of a tribe, was appointed by the Governor, and this mode of appointment gave great dissatisfaction to the Indians.

CHAPTER X

"Religion, 'tis that doth distinguish us
From their bruit humour,
well we may it know,
That can with understanding argue thus,
Our God is truth, but they cannot do so."
Smith's History.

As may be well imagined, the Indian attack formed the chief topic of conversation at Windsor Hall during the day. Many were the marvellous stories which were called to memory, of Indian warfare and of Indian massacres—of the sad fate of those who had been their victims, the tortures to which their prisoners had been subjected, and the relentless cruelty with which even the tender babe, while smiling in the face of its ruthless murderer, was dashed pitilessly against a tree. Among these narratives, the most painful was that detailing the fate of George Cassen, who, tied to a tree by strong cords, was doomed to see his flesh and joints cut off, one by one, and roasted before his eyes; his head and face flayed with sharp mussel shells, and his belly ripped open; until at last, in the extremity of his agony, he welcomed the very flames which consumed him, and rescued his body from their cruelty.[16]

Uncle Giles, whose premature action had so nearly ruined them all, and yet had probably been the cause of their ultimate safety, was the hero of the day, and loud was the laugh at the incident of the gun and kitchen chimney. The old man's bruises were soon tended and healed, and the grateful creature declared that "Miss Ginny's *lineaments* always did him more good than all the doctors in the world;" and in truth they were good for sore eyes.

It was during the morning's conversation that Bernard learned from his host, and from Virginia, the intimate relations existing between Mamalis and the family at Windsor Hall. Many years before, there had been, about two miles from the hall, an Indian village, inhabited by some of the tribe of the Pamunkeys. Among them was an old chieftain named Nantaquaus,[17] who claimed to be of the same lineage as Powhatan, and who, worn out with war, now resided among his people as their patriarchal counsellor. In the hostilities which had existed before the long peace, which was only ended by the difficulties that gave rise to Bacon's Rebellion, the whole of the inhabitants of the little village had been cut off by the whites, with the exception of this old patriarch and his two orphan grand-children, who were saved through the interposition of Colonel Temple, exerted in their behalf on account of some kindness he had received at their hands. Grateful for the life of his little descendants, for he had long since ceased to care for the prolongation of his own existence, old Nantaquaus continued to live on terms approaching even to intimacy with the Temples. When at length he died, he bequeathed his grand-children to the care of his protector. It was his wish, however, that they should still remain in the old wigwam where he had lived, and where they could best remember him, and, in visions, visit his spirit in the far hunting ground. In compliance with this, his last wish, Manteo and Mamalis continued their residence in that rude old hut, and secured a comfortable subsistence—he by fishing and the chase, and she by the cultivation of their little patch of ground, where maize, melons, pompions, cushaus, and the like, rewarded her patient labour with their abundant growth. Besides these duties, to which the life of the Indian woman was devoted, the young girl in her leisure moments, and in the long winter, made, with pretty skill, mats, baskets and sandals, weaving the former curiously with the long willow twigs which grew along the banks of the neighbouring York river, and forming the latter with dressed deer skin, ornamented with flowers made of beads and shells, or with the various coloured feathers of the birds. Her little manufactures met with a ready sale at the hall, being exchanged for sugar and coffee, and other such comforts as civilization provides; and for the sale of the excess of these simple articles over the home demand, she found a willing agent in the Colonel, who, in his frequent visits to Jamestown, disposed of them to advantage.

Despite these associations, however, Manteo retained much of the original character of his race, and the wild forest life which he led, bringing him into communication with the less civilized members of his tribe, helped to cherish the native-fierceness of his temper. Clinging with tenacity to the superstitions and pursuits of his fathers, his mind was of that sterile soil, in which the seeds of civilization take but little root. His sister, without having herself lost all the peculiar features of her natural character, was still formed in a different mould, and her softer nature had already received some slight impress from Virginia's teachings, which led her by slow but certain degrees towards the truth. His was of that fierce, tiger nature, which Horace has so finely painted in his nervous description of Achilles,

"Impiger, iracundus, inexorabilis, acer!"

While her's can be best understood by her name, Mamalis, which, signifying in her own language a young fawn, at once expressed the grace of her person and the gentleness of her nature.

Such is a brief but sufficient description of the characters and condition of these two young Indians, who play an important part in this narrative. The description, we may well suppose, derived additional interest to Bernard, from its association with the recent exciting scene, and from the interest which his heart began already to entertain for the fair narrator.

But probably the most amusing, if not the most instructive portion of the morning's conversation, was that in which Mrs. Temple bore a conspicuous part. The danger being past, the good woman adverted with much pride to the calmness and fortitude which she had displayed during the latter part of the trying scene. She never suspected that her conduct had been at all open to criticism, for in the excess of her agitation, she had not been aware, either of her manner or her language.

"The fact is, gentlemen," she said, "that while you all displayed great coolness and resolution, it was well that you were not surrounded by timid women to embarrass you with their fears. I was determined that none of you should see my alarm, and I have no doubt you were surprised at my calmness."

"It was very natural for ladies to feel alarm," said Hansford, scarcely able to repress the rising smile, "under circumstances, which inspired even strong men with fear. I only wonder that you bore it so well."

"Ah, it is easy to see you are apologizing for Virginia, and I must confess that once or twice she did almost shake my self-possession a little by her agitation. But poor thing! we should make allowance for her. She is unaccustomed to such scenes. I, who was, you may say, cradled in a revolution, and brought up in civil war, am not so easily frightened."

"No, indeed, Bessy," said old Temple, smiling good humouredly, "so entirely were you free from the prevailing fears, that I believe you were unconscious half the time of what was going on."

"Well, really, Colonel Temple," said the old lady, bristling up at this insinuation, "I think it ill becomes you to be exposing me as a jest before an entire stranger. However, it makes but little difference. It won't last always."

This prediction of his good wife, that "It," which always referred to her husband's conduct immediately before, was doomed like all other earthly things to terminate, was generally a precursor to hysterics. And so she shook her head and patted her foot hysterically, while the Colonel wholly unconscious of any reasonable cause for the offence he had given, rolled up his eyes and shrugged his shoulders in silence.

Leaving the good couple to settle at their leisure those little disputes which never lasted on an average more than five minutes, let us follow

Virginia as she goes down stairs to make some preparation for dinner. As she passed through the hall on her way to the store-room, she saw the graceful form of Mamalis just leaving the house. In the conversation which ensued we must beg the reader to imagine the broken English in which the young Indian expressed herself, while we endeavor to give it a free and more polite translation.

"Mamalis, you are not going home already, are you," said Virginia, in a gentle voice.

"Yes," replied the girl, with a sigh.

"Why do you sigh, Mamalis? Are you unhappy, my poor girl?"

"It is very sad to be alone in my poor wigwam," she replied.

"Then stay with us, Manteo is away, and will probably not be back for some days."

"He would be angry if he came home and found me away."

"Oh, my poor girl," said Virginia, taking her tenderly by the hand, "I wish you could stay with me, and let me teach you as I used to about God and heaven. Oh, think of these things, Mamalis, and they will make you happy even when alone. Wouldn't you like to have a friend always near you when Manteo is away?"

"Oh yes," said the girl earnestly.

"Well, there is just such a Friend who will never desert you; who is ever near to protect you in danger, and to comfort you in distress. Whose eye is never closed in sleep, and whose thoughts are never wandering from his charge."

"That cannot be," said the young Indian, incredulously.

"Yes, it both can be and is so," returned her friend. "One who has promised, that if we trust in him he will never leave us nor forsake us. That friend is the powerful Son of God, and the loving Brother of simple man. One who died to show his love, and who lives to show his power to protect. It is Jesus Christ."

."You told me about him long ago," said Mamalis, shaking her head, "but I never saw him. He never comes to Manteo's wigwam."

"Nay, but He is still your friend," urged Virginia earnestly. "When you left the room this morning on that work of mercy to save us all, I did not see you, and yet I told my father that I knew you would do us good. Were you less my friend because I didn't see you?

"No."

"No," continued Virginia, "you were more my friend, for if you had remained with me, we might all have been lost. And so Jesus has but withdrawn Himself from our eyes that He may intercede with his offended father, as you did with Manteo."

"Does he tell lies for us?" said the girl with artless simplicity, and still remembering her interview with her brother. Virginia felt a thrill of horror pass through her heart as she heard such language, but remembering the ignorance of her poor blinded pupil, she proceeded.

"Oh! Mamalis, do not talk thus. He of whom I speak is not as we are, and cannot commit a sin. But while He cannot commit sin Himself, He can die for the sins of others."

"Well," said the poor girl, seeing that she had unwittingly hurt the feelings of her friend, "I don't understand all that. Your God is so high, mine I can see and understand. But you love your God, I only fear mine."

"And do you not believe that God is good, my poor friend?" said Virginia, with a sigh.

"From Manitou all good proceeds," replied Mamalis, as with beautiful simplicity she thus detailed her simple creed, which she had been taught by her fathers. "From him is life, and joy, and love. The blue sky is his home, and the green earth he has made for his pleasure. The fresh smelling flowers and the pure air are his breath, and the sweet music of the wind through the woods is his voice. The stars that he has sown through heaven, are the pure shells which he has picked up by the rivers which flow through the spirit land; and the sun is his chariot, with which he drives through heaven, while he smiles upon the world. Such is Manitou, whose very life is the good giving; the bliss-bestowing."

"My sweet Mamalis," said Virginia, "you have, indeed, in your ignorance, painted a beautiful picture of the beneficence of God. And can you not—do you not thank this Giver of every good and perfect gift for all his mercies?"

"I cannot thank him for that which he must bestow," said the girl. "We do not thank the flower because its scent is sweet; nor the birds that fill the woods with their songs, because their music is grateful to the ear. Manitou is made to be adored, not to be thanked, for his very essence is good, and his very breath is love."

"But remember, my friend, that the voice of this Great Spirit is heard in the thunder, as well as in the breeze, and his face is revealed in the lightning as well as in the flower. He is the author of evil as well as of good, and should we not pray that He would avert the first, even if He heed not our prayer to bestow the last."

If Virginia was shocked by the sentiments of her pupil before, Mamalis was now as much so. Such an idea as ascribing evil to the great Spirit of the Universe, never entered the mind of the young savage, and now that she first heard it, she looked upon it as little less than open profanity.

"Manitou is not heard in the thunder nor seen in the lightning," she replied. "It is Okee whose fury against us is aroused, and who thus turns blessings into curses, and good into evil. To him we pray that he look not upon us with a frown, nor withhold the mercies that flow from Manitou; that the rains may fall upon our maize, and the sun may ripen it in the full ear; that he send the fat wild deer across my brother's path, and ride on his arrow until it reach its heart; that he direct the grand council in wisdom, and guide the tomahawk in its aim in battle. But I have tarried too long, my brother may await my coming."

"Nay, but you shall not go—at least," said Virginia, "without something for your trouble. You have nearly lost a day, already. And come often and see me, Mamalis, and we will speak of these things again. I will teach you that your Manitou is good, as well as the author of good; and that he is love, as well as the fountain of love in others; that it is to him we should pray and in whom we should trust, and he will lead us safely through all our trials in this life, and take us to a purer spirit land than that of which you dream."

Mamalis shook her head, but promised she would come. Then loading her with such things as she thought she stood in need of, and which the poor girl but seldom met with, except from the same kind hand, Virginia bid her God speed, and they parted; Mamalis to her desolate wigwam, and Virginia to her labours in the household affairs, which had devolved upon her.[18]

FOOTNOTES:

[16] Fact.

[17] This was also the name of the only son of the great Powhatan, as appears by John Smith's letter to the Queen, introducing the Princess Pocahontas.

[18] In the foregoing scene the language of Mamalis has been purposely rendered more pure than as it fell from her lips, because thus it was better suited to the dignity of her theme. As for the creed itself, it is taken from so many sources, that it would be impossible, even if desirable, to quote any authorities. The statements of Smith and Beverley, are, however, chiefly relied upon.

CHAPTER XI

"And will you rend our ancient love asunder,
And join with men in scorning your poor friend."
Midsummer Night's Dream.

While Virginia was thus engaged, she was surprised by hearing a light step behind her, and looking up she saw Hansford pale and agitated, standing in the room.

"What in the world is the matter?" she cried, alarmed at his appearance; "have the Indians—"

"No, dearest, the Indians are far away ere this. But alas! there are other enemies to our peace than they."

"What do you mean?" she said, "speak! why do you thus agitate me by withholding what you would say."

"My dear Virginia," replied her lover, "do you not remember that I told you last night that I had something to communicate, which would surprise and grieve you. I cannot expect you to understand or appreciate fully my motives. But you can at least hear me patiently, and by the memory of our love, by the sacred seal of our plighted troth, I beg you to hear me with indulgence, if not forgiveness."

"There are but few things, Hansford, that you could do," said Virginia, gravely, "that love would not teach me to forgive. Go on. I hear you patiently."

"My story will be brief," said Hansford, "although it may involve sad consequences to me. I need only say, that I have felt the oppressions of the government, under which the colony is groaning; I have witnessed the duplicity and perfidy of Sir William Berkeley, and I have determined with the arm and heart of a man, to maintain the rights of a man."

"What oppressions, what perfidy, what rights, do you mean?" said Virginia, turning pale with apprehension.

"You can scarcely understand those questions dearest. But do you not know that the temporizing policy, the criminal delay of Berkeley, has already made the blood of Englishmen flow by the hand of savages. Even the agony which you this morning suffered, is due to the indirect encouragement given to the Indians by his fatal indulgence."

"And you have proved false to your country," cried Virginia. "Oh! Hansford, for the sake of your honour, for the sake of your love, unsay the word which stains your soul with treason."

"Nay, my own Virginia, understand me. I may be a rebel to my king. I may almost sacrifice my love, but I am true, ever true to my country. The day has passed, Virginia, when that word was so restricted in its meaning as to be confounded with the erring mortal, who should be its minister and not its tyrant. The blood of Charles the First has mingled with the blood of those brave martyrs who perished for liberty, and has thus cemented the true union between a prince and his people. It has given to the world, that useful lesson, that the sovereign is invested with his power, to protect, and not to destroy the rights of his people; that freemen may be restrained by wholesome laws, but that they are freemen still. That lesson, Sir William Berkeley must yet be taught. The patriot who dares to teach him, is at last, the truest lover of his country."

"I scarcely know what you say," said the young girl, weeping, "but tell me, oh, tell me, have you joined your fortunes with a rebel?"

"If thus you choose to term him who loves freedom better than chains, who would rather sacrifice life itself than to drag out a weary existence beneath the galling yoke of oppression, I have. I know you blame me. I know you hate me now," he added, in a sad voice, "but while it was my duty, as a freeman and a patriot, to act thus, it was also my duty, as an honourable man, to tell you all. You remember the last lines of our favourite song,

> "I had not loved thee dear, so much,
> Loved I not honour more."

"Alas! I remember the words but too well," replied Virginia, sadly, "but I had been taught that the honour there spoken of, was loyalty to a king, not treason. Oh, Hansford, forgive me, but how can I, reared as I have been, with such a father, how can I"—she hesitated, unable to complete the fatal sentence.

"I understand you," said Hansford. "But one thing then remains undone. The proscribed rebel must be an outlaw to Virginia Temple's heart. The trial is a sore one, but even this sacrifice can I make to my beloved country. Thus then I give you back your troth. Take it—take it," he cried, and with one hand covering his eyes, he seemed with the other to tear from his heart some treasured jewel that refused to yield its place.

The violence of his manner, even more than the fatal words he had spoken, alarmed Virginia, and with a wild scream, that rang through the old hall, she threw herself fainting upon his neck. The noise reached the ears of the party, who remained above stairs, and Colonel Temple, his wife, and Bernard, threw open the door and stood for a moment silent spectators of the solemn scene. There stood Hansford, his eye lit up with excitement, his face white as ashes, and his strong arm supporting the trembling form of the young girl, while with his other hand he was chafing her white temples, and smoothing back the long golden tresses that had fallen dishevelled over her face.

"My child, my child," shrieked her mother, who was the first to speak, "what on earth is the matter?"

"Yes, Hansford, in the devil's name, what is to pay?" said the old colonel. "Why, Jeanie," he added, taking the fair girl tenderly in his arms, "you are not half the heroine you were when the Indians were here. There now, that's a sweet girl, open your blue eyes and tell old father what is the matter."

"Nothing, dear father," said Virginia, faintly, as she slowly opened her eyes. "I have been very foolish, that's all."

"Nay, Jeanie, it takes more than nothing or folly to steal the bloom away from these rosy cheeks."

"Perhaps the young gentleman can explain more easily," said Bernard, fixing his keen eyes on his rival. "A little struggle, perhaps, between love and loyalty."

"Mr. Bernard, with all his shrewdness, would probably profit by the reflection," said Hansford, coldly, "that as a stranger here, his opinions upon a matter of purely family concern, are both unwelcome and impertinent."

"May be so," replied Bernard with a sneer; "but scarcely more unwelcome than the gross and continued deception practised by yourself towards those who have honoured you with their confidence."

Hansford, stung by the remark, laid his hand upon his sword, but was withheld by Colonel Temple, who cried out with impatience,

"Why, what the devil do you mean? Zounds, it seems to me that my house is bewitched to-day. First those cursed Indians, with their infernal yells, threatening death and destruction to all and sundry; then my daughter here, playing the fool before my face, according to her own confession; and lastly, a couple of forward boys picking a quarrel with one another after a few hours' acquaintance. Damn it, Tom, you were wont to have a plain tongue in your head. Tell me, what is the matter?"

"My kind old friend," said Hansford, with a tremulous voice, "I would fain have reserved for your private ear, an explanation which is now rendered necessary by that insolent minion, whose impertinence had already received the chastisement it deserves, but for an unfortunate interruption."

"Nay, Tom," said the Colonel, "no harsh words. Remember this young man is my guest, and as such, entitled to respect from all under my roof."

"Well then, sir," continued Hansford, "this young lady's agitation was caused by the fact that I have lately pursued a course, which, while I believe it to be just and honourable, I fear will meet with but little favour in your eyes."

"As much in the dark as ever," said the Colonel, perplexed beyond measure, for his esteem for Hansford prevented him from suspecting the true cause of his daughter's disquiet. "Damn it, man, Davus sum non Œdipus. Speak out plainly, and if your conduct has been, as you say, consistent with your honour, trust to an old friend to forgive you. Zounds, boy, I have been young myself, and can make allowance for the waywardness of youth. Been gaming a little too high, hey; well, the rest[19] was not so low in my day, but that I can excuse that, if you didn't ‹pull down the side.'"[20]

"I would fain do the young man a service, for I bear him no ill-will, though he has treated me a little harshly," said Bernard, as he saw Hansford silently endeavouring to frame a reply in the most favourable terms, "I see he is ashamed of his cause, and well he may be; for you must know that he has become a great man of late, and has linked his fate to a certain Nathaniel Bacon."

The old loyalist started as he heard this unexpected announcement, then with a deep sigh, which seemed to come from his very soul, he turned to Hansford and said, "My boy, deny the foul charge; say it is not so."

"It is, indeed, true," replied Hansford, mournfully, "but when—"

"But when the devil!" cried the old man, bursting into a fit of rage; "and you expect me to stand here and listen to your justification. Zounds, sir, I would feel like a traitor myself to hear you speak. And this is the serpent that I have warmed and cherished at my hearth-stone. Out of my house, sir!"

"To think," chimed in Mrs. Temple, for once agreeing fully with her husband, "how near our family, that has always prided itself on its loyalty, was being allied to a traitor. But he shall never marry Virginia, I vow."

"No, by God," said the enraged loyalist; "she should rot in her grave first."

"Miss Temple is already released from her engagement," said Hansford, recovering his calmness in proportion as the other party lost their's. "She is free to choose for herself, sir."

"And that choice shall never light on you, apostate," cried Temple, "unless she would bring my grey hairs in sorrow to the grave."

"And mine, too," said the old lady, beginning to weep.

"I will not trouble you longer with my presence," said Hansford, proudly, "except to thank you for past kindness, which I can never forget. Farewell, Colonel Temple, I respect your prejudices, though they have led you to curse me. Farewell, Mrs. Temple, I will ever think of your generous hospitality with gratitude. Farewell, Virginia, forget that such a being as Thomas Hansford ever darkened your path through life, and think of our past love as a dream. I can bear your forgetfulness, but not your hate. For you, sir," he added, turning to Alfred Bernard, "let me hope that we will meet again, where no interruption will prevent our final separation."

With these words, Hansford, his form proudly erect, but his heart bowed down with sorrow, slowly left the house.

"Are you not a Justice of the Peace?" asked Bernard, with a meaning look.

"And what is that to you, sir?" replied the old man, suspecting the design of the question.

"Only, sir, that as such it is your sworn duty to arrest that traitor. I know it is painful, but still it is your duty."

"And who the devil told you to come and teach me my duty, sir?" said the old man, wrathfully. "Let me tell you, sir, that Tom Hansford, with all his faults, is a d—d sight better than a great many who are free from the stain of rebellion. Rebellion!—oh, my God!—poor, poor Tom."

"Nay, then, sir," said Bernard, meekly, "I beg your pardon. I only felt it my duty to remind you of what you might have forgotten. God forbid that I should wish to endanger the life of a poor young man, whose only fault may be that he was too easily led away by others."

"You are right, by God," said the Colonel, quickly. "He is the victim of designing men, and yet I never said a word to reclaim him. Oh, I have acted basely and not like a friend. I will go now and bring him back, wife; though if he don't repent—zounds!—neither will I; no, not for a million friends."

So saying, the noble-hearted old loyalist, whose impulsive nature was as prompt to redeem as to commit an error, started from the room to reclaim his lost boy. It was too late. Hansford, anticipating the result of the fatal revelation, had ordered his horse even before his first interview with Virginia. The old Colonel only succeeded in catching a glimpse of him from the porch, as at a full gallop he disappeared through the forest.

With a heavy sigh he returned to the study, there to meet with the consolations of his good wife, which were contained in the following words:

"Well, I hope and trust he is gone, and will never darken our doors again. You know, my dear, I always told you that you were wrong about that young man, Hansford. There always seemed to be a lack of frankness and openness in his character, and although I do not like to interpose my objections, yet I never altogether approved of the match. You know I always told you so."

"Told the devil!" cried the old man, goaded to the very verge of despair by this new torture. "I beg your pardon, Bessy, for speaking so hastily, but, damn it, if all the angels in Heaven had told me that Tom Hansford could prove a traitor, I would not have believed it."

And how felt she, that wounded, trusting one, who thus in a short day had seen the hopes and dreams of happiness, which fancy had woven in her young heart, all rudely swept away! 'Twere wrong to lift the veil from that poor stricken heart, now torn with grief too deep for words—too deep, alas! for tears. With her cheek resting on her white hand, she gazed tearlessly, but vacantly, towards the forest where he had so lately vanished as a dream. To those who spoke to her, she answered sadly in monosyllables, and then turned her head away, as if it were still sweet to cherish thus the agony which consumed her. But the bitterest drop in all this cup of woe, was the self-reproach which mingled with her recollection of that sad scene. When he had frankly given back her troth, she, alas! had not stayed his hand, nor by a word had told him how truly, even in his guilt, her heart was his. And now, she thought, when thus driven harshly into the cold world, his only friends among the enemies to truth, his enemies its friends, how one little word of love, or even of pity, might have redeemed him from error, or at least have cheered him in his dark career.

But bear up bravely, sweet one; for heavier, darker sorrows yet must cast their shadows on thy young heart, ere yet its warm pulsations cease to beat, and it be laid at rest.

FOOTNOTES:

[19] Rest was the prescribed limit to the size of the venture.

[20] To pull down the side was a technical term with our ancestors for cheating.

CHAPTER XII

"Wounded in both my honour and my love;
They have pierced me in two tender parts.
Yet, could I take my just revenge,
It would in some degree assuage my smart."
Vanbrugh.

It was at an early hour on the following morning that the queer old chariot of Colonel Temple—one of the few, by the way, which wealth had as yet introduced into the colony—was drawn up before the door. The two horses of the gentlemen were standing ready saddled and bridled, in the care of the hostler. In a few moments, the ladies, all dressed for the journey, and the gentlemen, with their heavy spurs, long, clanging swords, and each with a pair of horseman's pistols, issued from the house into the yard. The old lady, declaring that they were too late, and that, if her advice had been taken, they would have been half way to Jamestown, was the first to get into the carriage, armed with a huge basket of bread, beef's tongue, cold ham and jerked venison, which was to supply the place of dinner on the road. Virginia, pale and sad, but almost happy at any change from scenes where every object brought up some recollection of the banished Hansford, followed her mother; and the large trunk having been strapped securely behind the carriage, and the band-box, containing the old lady's tire for the ball and other light articles of dress, having been secured, the little party were soon in motion.

The hope and joy with which Virginia had looked forward to this trip to Jamestown had been much enhanced by the certainty that Hansford would be there. With the joyousness of her girlish heart, she had pictured to herself the scene of pleasure and festivity which awaited her. The Lady Frances' birth-day, always celebrated at the palace with the voice of music and the graceful dance—with the presence of the noblest cavaliers from all parts of the colony, and the smiles of the fairest damsels who lighted the society of the Old Dominion—was this year to be celebrated with unusual festivities. But, alas! how changed were the feelings of Virginia now!—how blighted were the hopes which had blossomed in her heart!

Their road lay for the most part through a beautiful forest, where the tall poplar, the hickory, the oak and the chestnut were all indigenous, and formed an avenue shaded by their broad branches from the intense rays of the summer sun. Now and then the horses were startled at the sudden appearance of some fairy-footed deer, as it bounded lightly but swiftly through the woods; or at the sudden whirring of the startled pheasant, as she flew from their approach; or the jealous gobble of the stately turkey, as he led his strutting dames into his thicket-harem. The nimble grey squirrel, too, chattered away saucily in his high leafy nest, secure from attack from his very insignificance. Birds innumerable were seen flitting from branch to branch, and tuning their mellow voices as choristers in this forest-temple of Nature. The song of the thrush and the red-bird came sweetly from the willows, whose weeping branches overhung the neighbouring banks of a broad stream; the distant dove joined her mournful melody to their cheerful notes, and the woodpecker, on the blasted trunk of some stricken oak, tapped his rude bass in unison with the happy choir of the forest.

All this Virginia saw and heard, and *felt*—yes, felt it all as a bitter mockery: as if, in these joyous bursts from the big heart of Nature, she were coldly regardless of the sorrows of those, her children, who had sought their happiness apart; as though the avenging Creator had given man naught but the bitter fruit of that fatal tree of knowledge, while he lavished with profusion on all the rest of his creation the choicest fruits that flourished in His paradise.

In vain did Bernard, with his soft and winning voice, point out these beauties to Virginia. In vain, with all the rich stores of his gifted mind, did he seek to alienate her thoughts from the one subject that engrossed them. She scarcely heard what he said, and when at length urged by the impatient nudges of her mother to answer, she showed by her absence of mind how faint had been the impression which he made. A thousand fears for the safety of her lover mingled with her thoughts. Travelling alone in that wild country, with hostile Indians infesting the colony, what, alas! might be his fate! Or even if he should escape these dangers, still, in open arms against his government, proclaimed a rebel by the Governor, a more horrible destiny might await him. And then the overwhelming thought came upon her, that be his fate in other respects what it might—whether he should fall by the cruelty of the savage, the sword of the enemy, or, worst of all, by the vengeance of his indignant country—to her at least he was lost forever.

Avoiding carefully any reference to the subject of her grief, and bending his whole mind to the one object of securing her attention, Alfred Bernard endeavored to beguile her with graphic descriptions of the scenes he had left in England. He spoke—and on such subjects none could speak more charmingly—of the brilliant society of wits, and statesmen, and beauties, which clustered together in the metropolis and the palace of the restored Stuart. Passing lightly over the vices of the court, he dwelt upon its pageantry, its wit, its philosophy, its poetry. The talents of the gay and accomplished, but vicious Rochester, were no more seen dimmed in their lustre by his faithlessness to his wife, or his unprincipled vices in the *beau monde* of London. Anecdote after anecdote, of Waller, of Cowley, of Dryden, flowed readily from his lips. The coffee-houses were described, where wit and poetry, science and art, politics and religion, were discussed by the first intellects of the age, and allured the aspiring youth of England from the vices of dissipation, that they might drink in rich draughts of knowledge from these Pierian springs. The theatre, the masque, the revels, which the genial rays of the Restoration had once more warmed into life, next formed the subjects of his conversation. Then passing from this picture of gay society, he referred to the religious discussions of the day. His eye sparkled and his cheek glowed as he spoke of the triumphs of the established Church over puritanical heresy; and his lip curled, and he laughed satirically, as he described the heroic sufferings of some conscientious Baptist, dragged at the tail of a cart, and whipped from his cell in Newgate to Tyburn hill. Gradually did Virginia's thoughts wander from the one sad topic which had engrossed them, and by imperceptible degrees, even unconsciously to herself, she became deeply interested in his discourse. Her mother, whom the wily Bernard took occasion ever and anon, to propitiate with flattery, was completely carried away, and in the inmost recesses of her heart a hope was hatched that the eloquent young courtier would soon take the place of the rebel Hansford, in the affections of her daughter.

We have referred to a stream, along whose forest-banks their road had wound. That stream was the noble York, whose broad bosom, now broader and more beautiful than ever, lay full in their view, and on which the duck, the widgeon and the gull were quietly floating. Here and there could be seen the small craft of some patient fisherman, as it stood anchored at a little distance from the shore, its white sail shrouding the solitary mast; and at an opening in the woods, about a mile ahead, rose the tall masts of an English vessel, riding safely in the broad harbour of Yorktown—then the commercial rival of Jamestown in the colony.

The road now became too narrow for the gentlemen any longer to ride by the side of the carriage, and at the suggestion of the Colonel, an arrangement was adopted by which he should lead the little party in front, while Bernard should bring up the rear. This precaution was the more necessary, as the abrupt banks of the river, with the dense bushes which grew along them, was a safe lurking place for any Indians who might be skulking about the country.

"A very nice gentleman, upon my word," said Mrs. Temple, when Alfred Bernard was out of hearing. "Virginia, don't you like him?"

"Yes, very much, as far as I have an opportunity of judging."

"His information is so extensive, his views so correct, his conversation so delightful. Don't you think so?"

"Yes, mother," replied Virginia.

"Yes, mother! Why don't you show more spirit?" said her mother. "There you sat moping in the carriage the whole way, looking for all the world as if you didn't understand a word he was saying. That isn't right, my dear; you should look up and show more spirit—d'ye hear!"

"You mistake,mother; I did enjoy the ride very much, and found Mr. Bernard very agreeable."

"Well, but you were so lack-a-daisical and yea, nay, in your manner to him. How do you expect a young man to feel any interest in you, if you never give him any encouragement?"

"Why, mother, I don't suppose Mr. Bernard takes any more interest in me than he would in any casual acquaintance; and, indeed, if he did, I certainly cannot return it. But I will try and cheer up, and be more agreeable for your sake."

"That's right, my dear daughter; remember that your old mother knows what is best for you, and she will never advise you wrong. I think it is very plain that this young gentleman has taken a fancy to you already, and while I would not have you too pert and forward, yet it is well enough to show off, and, in a modest way, do everything to encourage him. You know I always said, my dear, that you were too young when you formed an attachment for that young Hansford, and that you did not know your own heart, and now you see I was right."

Virginia did not see that her mother was right, but she was too well trained to reply; and so, without a word, she yielded herself once more to her own sad reflections, and, true-hearted girl that she was, she soon forgot the fascinations of Alfred Bernard in her memory of Hansford.

They had not proceeded far, when Bernard saw, seated on the trunk of a fallen tree, the dusky form of a young Indian, whom he soon recognized as the leader of the party who the day before had made the attack upon Windsor Hall. The interest which he felt in this young man, whose early history he had heard, combined with a curiosity to converse with one of the strange race to which he belonged, and, as will be seen, a darker motive and a stronger reason than either, induced Bernard to rein up his horse, and permitting his companions to proceed some distance in front, to accost the young Indian. Alfred Bernard, by nature and from education, was perfectly fearless, though he lacked the magnanimity which, united with fearlessness, constitutes bravery. Laying his hand on his heart, which, as he had already learned, was the friendly salutation used with and toward the savages, he rode slowly towards Manteo. The young Indian recognized the gesture which assured him of his friendly intent, and rising from his rude seat, patiently waited for him to speak.

"I would speak to you," said Bernard.

"Speak on."

"Are you entirely alone?"

"Ugh," grunted Manteo, affirmatively.

"Where are those who were with you at Windsor Hall?"

"Gone to Delaware,[21] to Matchicomoco."[22]

"Why did you not go with them?" asked Bernard.

"Manteo love long-knife—Pamunkey hate Manteo—drive him away from his tribe," said the young savage, sorrowfully.

The truth flashed upon Bernard at once. This young savage, who, in a moment of selfish ambition, for his own personal advancement, had withheld the vengeance of his people, was left by those whom he had once led, as no longer worthy of their confidence. In the fate of this untutored son of the forest, the young courtier had found a sterner rebuke to selfishness and ambition than he had ever seen in the court of the monarch of England.

"And so you are alone in the world now?" said Bernard.

"Ugh!"

"With nothing to hope or to live for?"

"One hope left," said Manteo, laying his hand on his tomahawk.

"What is that?"

"Revenge."

"On whom?"

"On long-knives and Pamunkeys."

"If you live for revenge," said Bernard, "we live for nearly the same object. You may trust me—I will be your friend. Do you know me?"

"No!" said Manteo, shaking his head.

"Well, I know you," said Bernard. "Now, what if I help you to the sweet morsel of revenge you speak of?"

"I tank you den."

"Do you know your worst enemy?"

"Manteo!"

"How—why so?"

"I make all my oder enemy."

"Nay, but I know an enemy who is even worse than yourself, because he has made you your own enemy. One who oppresses your race, and is even now making war upon your people. I mean Thomas Hansford."

"Ugh!" said Manteo, with more surprise than he had yet manifested; and for once, leaving his broken English, he cried in his own tongue, "Ahoaleu Virginia." (He loves Virginia Temple.)

"And do you?" said Bernard, guessing at his meaning, and marking with surprise the more than ordinary feeling with which Manteo had uttered these words.

"See dere," replied Manteo, holding up an arrow, which he had already taken from his quiver, as if with the intention of fixing it to his bow-string. "De white crenepo,[23] de maiden, blunt Manteo's arrow when it would fly to her father's heart." At the same time he pointed towards the road along which the carriage had lately passed.

"By the holy Virgin," muttered Bernard, "methinks the whole colony, Indians, negroes, and all, are going stark mad after this girl. And so you hate Hansford, then?" he said aloud.

"No, I can't hate what she loves," replied Manteo, feelingly.

"Why did you aid in attacking her father's house then, yesterday?"

"Long-knives strike only when dey hate; Pamunkey fight from duty. If Manteo drop de tomahawk because he love, he is squaw, not a brave."

"But this Hansford," said Bernard, "is in arms against your people, whom the government would protect."

"Ugh!" grunted the young warrior. "Pamunkey want not long-knives' protect. De grand werowance of long-knives has cut down de peace tree and broke de pipe, and de tomahawk is now dug up. De grand werowance protect red man like eagle protect young hare."

"Nay, but we would be friends with the Indians," urged Bernard. "We would share this great country with them, and Berkeley would be the great father of the Pamunkeys."

The Indian looked with ineffable disdain on his companion, and then turning towards the river, he pointed to a large fish-hawk, who, with a rapid swoop, had caught in his talons a fish that had just bubbled above the water for breath, and borne him far away in the air.

"See dere," said Manteo; "water belong to fish—hawk is fish's friend."

Bernard saw that he had entirely mistaken the character of his companion. The vengeance of the Indians being once aroused, they failed to discriminate between the authors of the injuries which they had received, and those who sought to protect them; and they attributed to the great werowance of the long-knives (for so they styled the Governor of Virginia) all the blame of the attack and slaughter of the unoffending Susquehannahs. But the wily Bernard was not cast down by his ill success, in attempting to arouse the vengeance of Manteo against his rival.

"Your sister is at the hall often, is she not?" he asked, after a brief pause.

"Ugh," said the Indian, relapsing into this affirmative grunt.

"So is Hansford—your sister knows him."

"What of dat?"

"Excuse me, my poor friend," said Bernard, "but I came to warn you that your sister knows him as she should not."

The forest echoed with the wild yell that burst from the lips of Manteo at this cruel fabrication—so loud, so wild, so fearful, that the ducks which had been quietly basking in the sun, and admiring their graceful shadows in the water, were startled, and with an alarmed cry flew far away down the river.

The Indian character, although still barbarous, had been much improved by association with the English. Respect for the female sex, and a scrupulous regard for female purity, which are ever the first results of dawning civilization, had already taken possession of the benighted souls of the Indians of Virginia. More especially was this so with the young Manteo, whose association with the whites, notwithstanding his strong devotion to his own race, had imparted more refinement and purity to his nature than was enjoyed by most of his tribe. Mamalis, the pure, the spotless Mamalis—she, whom from his earliest boyhood he had hoped to bestow on some young brave, who, foremost in the chase, or most successful in the ambuscade, could tell the story of his achievements among the chieftains at the council-fire—it was too much; the stern heart of the young Indian, though "trained from his tree-rocked cradle the fierce extremes of good and ill to bear," burst forth in a gush of agony, as he thus heard the fatal knell of all his pride and all his hope.

Bernard was at first startled by the shriek, but soon regained his composure, and calm and composed regarded his victim. When at length the first violence of grief had subsided, he said, with a soft, mild voice, which fell fresh as dew upon the withered heart of the poor Indian,

"I am sorry for you, my friend, but it is too true. And now, Manteo, what can be your only consolation?"

"Revenge is de wighsacan[24] to cure dis wound," said the poor savage.

"Right. This is the only food for brave and injured men. Well, we understand each other now—don't we?"

"Ugh," grunted Manteo, with a look of satisfaction.

"Very well," returned Bernard, "is your tomahawk sharp?"

"It won't cut deep as dis wound, but I will sharpen it on my broken heart," replied Manteo, with a heavy sigh.

"Right bravely said. And now farewell; I will help you as I can," said Alfred Bernard, as he turned and rode away, while the poor Indian sank down again upon his rude log seat, his head resting on his hands.

"And this the world calls villainy!" mused Bernard, as he rode along. "But it is the weapon with which nature has armed the weak, that he may battle with the strong. For what purpose was the faculty of intrigue bestowed upon man, if it were not to be exercised? and, if exercised at all, why surely it can never be directed to a purer object than the accomplishment of good. Thus, then, what the croaking moralist calls evil, may always be committed if good be the result; and what higher good can be attained in life than happiness, and what purer happiness can there be than revenge? No man shall ever cross my path but once with safety, and this young Virginia rebel has already done so. He has shown his superior skill and courage with the sword, and has made me ask my life at his hands. Let him look to it that he may not have to plead for his own life in vain. This young Indian's thirst will not be quenched but with blood. By the way, a lucky hit was that. His infernal yell is sounding in my ears yet. But Hansford stands in my way besides. This fair young maiden, with her beauty, her intellect, and her land, may make my fortune yet; and who can blame the poor, friendless orphan, if he carve his way to honour and independence even through the blood of a rival. The poor, duped savage whom I just left, said that he was his own worst enemy; I am wiser in being my own best friend. Tell me not of the world—it is mine oyster, which I will open by my wits as well as by my sword. Prate not of morality and philanthropy. Man is a microcosm, a world within himself, and he only is a wise one who uses the world without for the success of the world within. Once supplant this Hansford in the love of his betrothed bride, and I succeed to the broad acres of Windsor Hall. Old Berkeley shall be the scaffolding by which I will rise to power and position, and when he rots down, the building I erect will be but the fairer for the riddance. Who recks the path which he has trod, when home and happiness are in view? What general thinks of the blood he has shed, when the shout of victory rings in his ears? Be true to yourself, Alfred Bernard, though false to all the world beside! At last, good father Bellini, thou hast taught me true wisdom—'Success sanctifies sin.'"

FOOTNOTES:

[21] The name of the village at the confluence of Pamunkey and Mattapony, now called West Point.

[22] Grand Council of the Indians.

[23] A woman.

[24] A root used by the Indians successfully in the cure of all wounds.

CHAPTER XIII

"Is this your joyous city, whose antiquity is of ancient days?"

Isaiah.

"One mouldering tower, o'ergrown with ivy, shows
Where first Virginia's capital arose,
And to the tourist's vision far withdrawn
Stands like a sentry at the gates of dawn.
The church has perished—faint the lines and dim
Of those whose voices raised the choral hymn,
Go read the record on the mossy stone,
'Tis brief and sad—oblivion claims its own!"

Thompson's Virginia.

The traveller, as he is borne on the bosom of the noble James, on the wheezing, grunting steamboat, may still see upon the bank of the river, a lonely ruin, which is all that now remains of the old church at Jamestown. Despite its loneliness and desolation, that old church has its memories, which hallow it in the heart of every Virginian. From its ruined chancel that "singular excellent" Christian and man, good Master Hunt, was once wont, in far gone times, to preach the gospel of peace to those stern old colonists, who in full armour, and ever prepared for Indian interruptions, listened with devout attention. There in the front pew, which stood nearest the chancel, had sat John Smith, whose sturdy nature and strong practical sense were alone sufficient to repel the invasion of heathen savages, and provide for the wants of a famishing colony. Yet, with all the sternness and rigour of his character, his heart was subdued by the power of religion, as he bowed in meek submission to its precepts, and relied with humble confidence upon its promises. The pure light of Heaven was reflected even from that strong iron heart. At that altar had once knelt a dusky but graceful form, the queenly daughter of a noble king; and, her savage nature enlightened by the rays of the Sun of righteousness, she had there received upon her royal brow the sacred sign of her Redeemer's cross. And many a dark eye was bedewed with tears, and many a strong heart was bowed in prayer, as the stout old colonists stood around, and saw the baptismal rite which sealed the profession and the faith of the brave, the beautiful, the generous Pocahontas.

But while this old ruin thus suggests many an association with the olden time, there is nothing left to tell the antiquary of the condition and appearance of Jamestown, the first capital of Virginia. The island, as the narrow neck of land on which the town was built is still erroneously called, may yet be seen; but not a vestige of the simple splendour, with which colonial pride delighted to adorn it, remains to tell the story of its glory or destruction. And yet, to the eye and the heart of the colonist, this little town was a delight: for here were assembled the Governor and his council, who, with mimic pride, emulated the grandeur and the pageant of Whitehall. Here, too, were the burgesses congregated at the call of the Governor, who, with their stately wives and blooming daughters, contributed to the delight of the metropolitan society. Here, too, was the principal mart, where the planters shipped their tobacco for the English market, and received from home those articles of manufacture and those rarer delicacies which the colony was as yet unable to supply. And here, too, they received news from Europe, which served the old planters and prurient young statesmen with topics of conversation until the next arrival; while the young folks gazed with wonder and delight at the ship, its crew and passengers, who had actually been in that great old England of which they had heard their fathers talk so much.

The town, like an old-fashioned sermon, was naturally divided into two parts. The first, which lay along the river, was chiefly devoted to commercial purposes—the principal resort of drunken seamen, and those land harpies who prey upon them for their own subsistence. Here were located those miserable tippling-houses, which the Assembly had so long and so vainly attempted to suppress. Here were the busy forwarding houses, with their dark counting-rooms, their sallow clerks, and their bills of lading. Here the shrewd merchant and the bluff sea-captain talked loudly and learnedly of the laws of trade, the restrictive policy of the navigation laws, and the growing importance of the commercial interests of the colony. And here was the immense warehouse, under the especial control of the government, with its hundreds of hogsheads of tobacco, all waiting patiently their turn for inspection; and the sweating negroes, tearing off the staves of the hogsheads to display the leaf to view, and then noisily hammering them together again, while the impatient inspector himself went the rounds and examined the wide spread plant, and adjudged its quality; proving at the same time his capacity as a connoisseur, by the enormous quid which he rolled pleasantly in his mouth.

But it is the more fashionable part of the town, with which our story has to do; and here, indeed, even at this early day, wealth and taste had done much to adorn the place, and to add to the comfort of the inhabitants. At one end of the long avenue, which was known as Stuart street, in compliment to the royal family, was situated the palace of Sir William Berkeley. Out of his private means and the immense salary of his office, the governor had done much to beautify and adorn his grounds. A lawn, with its well shaven turf, stretched in front of the house for more than a hundred yards, traversed in various directions with white gravelled walks, laid out with much taste, and interspersed with large elms and poplars. In the centre of the lawn was a beautiful summer-house, over which the white jessamine and the honeysuckle, planted by Lady Frances' own hand, clambered in rich profusion. The house, itself, though if it still remained, it would seem rather quaint and old-fashioned, was still very creditable as a work of architecture. A long porch, or gallery, supported by simple Doric pillars, stretched from one end of it to the other, and gave an air of finish and beauty to the building. The house was built of brick, brought all the way from England, for although the colonists had engaged in the manufacture of brick to a certain extent, yet for many years after the time of which we write, they persisted in this extraordinary expense, in supplying the materials for their better class of buildings.

At the other end of Stuart street was the state-house, erected in pursuance of an act, the preamble of which recites the disgrace of having laws enacted and judicial proceedings conducted in an ale-house. This building, like the palace, was surrounded by a green lawn, ornamented with trees and shrubbery, and enclosed by a handsome pale—midway the gate and the portico, on either side of the broad gravel walk, were two handsome houses, one of which was the residence of Sir Henry Chicherley, Vice-President of the Council, and afterwards deputy-governor upon the death of Governor Jeffreys. The other house was the residence of Thomas Ludwell, Secretary to the colony, and brother to Colonel Philip Ludwell, whose sturdy and unflinching loyalty during the rebellion, has preserved his name to our own times.

The state-house, itself, was a large brick building, with two wings, the one occupied by the governor and his council, the other by the general court, composed indeed of the same persons as the council, but acting in a judicial capacity. The centre building was devoted to the House Burgesses exclusively, containing their hall, library, and apartments for different offices. The whole structure was surmounted by a queer looking steeple, resembling most one of those high, peaked hats, which Hogarth has placed on the head of Hudibras and his puritan compeers.

Between the palace and the state-house, as we have said before, ran Stuart street, the thoroughfare of the little metropolis, well built up on either side with stores and the residences of the prominent citizens of the town. There was one peculiarity in the proprietors of these houses, which will sound strangely in the ears of their descendants. Accustomed to the generous hospitality of the present day, the reader may be surprised to learn that most of the citizens of old Jamestown entertained their guests from the country for a reasonable compensation; and so, when the gay cavalier from Stafford or Gloucester had passed a week among the gaieties or business of the metropolis,

> He called for his horse and he asked for his way,
> While the jolly old landlord cried "*Something* to pay."

But when we reflect that Jamestown was the general resort of persons from all sections of the colony, and that the tavern accommodations were but small, we need not be surprised at a state of things so different from the glad and gratuitous welcome of our own day.

Such, briefly and imperfectly described, was old Jamestown, the first capital of Virginia, as it appeared in 1676, to the little party of travellers, whose fortunes we have been following, as they rode into Stuart street, late in the evening of the day on which they left Windsor Hall. The arrival, as is usual in little villages, caused quite a sensation. The little knot of idlers that gathered about the porch of the only regular inn, desisted from whittling the store box, in the demolishing of which they had been busily engaged—and looked up with an impertinent stare at the new comers. Mine host bustled about as the carriage drove up before the door, and his jolly red face grew redder by his vociferous calls for servants. In obedience to his high behest, the servants came—the hostler, an imported cockney, to examine the points of the horses committed to his care, and to measure his provender by their real worth; the pretty Scotch chambermaid to conduct the ladies to their respective rooms, and a brisk and dapper little French barber to attack the colonel vehemently with a clothes-brush, as though he had hostile designs upon the good man's coat.

Bernard, in the meantime, having promised to come for Virginia, and escort her to the famous birth-night ball, rode slowly towards the palace;

now and then casting a haughty glance around him on those worthy gossips, who followed his fine form with their admiring eyes, and whispered among themselves that "Some folks was certainly born to luck; for look ye, Gaffer, there is a young fribble, come from the Lord knows where, and brought into the colony to be put over the heads of many worthier; and for all he holds his head so high, and sneers so mighty handsome with his lip, who knows what the lad may be. The great folk aye make a warm nest for their own bastards, and smooth the outside of the blanket as softly as the in, while honester folks must e'en rough it in frieze and Duffield. But na'theless, I say nothing, neighbor."

CHAPTER XIV

"There was a sound of revelry by night—
And Belgium's capital had gathered then
Her beauty and her chivalry; and bright
The lamps shone o'er fair women and brave men;
A thousand hearts beat happily; and when
Music arose with its voluptuous swell,
Soft eyes looked love to eyes that spoke again,
And all went merry as a marriage bell."
                              Childe Harold.

The ball at Sir William Berkeley's palace was of that character, which, in the fashionable world, is described as brilliant; and was long remembered by those who attended it, as the last scene of revelry that was ever known in Jamestown. The park or lawn which we have described was brilliantly illuminated with lamps and transparencies hung from the trees. The palace itself was a perfect blaze of light. The coaches of the cavaliers rolled in rapid succession around the circular path that led to the palace, and deposited their fair burdens, and then rolled rapidly away to await the breaking up of the ball. Young beaux, fairly glittering with gold embroidery, with their handsome doublets looped with the gayest ribbons, and their hair perfumed and oiled, and plaited at the sides in the most captivating love-knots; their cheeks beplastered with rouge, and their moustache carefully trimmed and brushed, passed gracefully to and fro, through the vast hall, and looked love to soft eyes that spake again. And those young eyes, how brightly did they beam, and how freshly did the young cheeks of their lovely owners blush, even above the rouge with which they were painted, as they met the admiring glance of some favored swain bent lovingly upon them! How graceful, too, the attitude which these fair maidens assumed, with their long trails sweeping and fairly carpeting the floor, or when held up by their tapering fingers, how proudly did they step, as they crossed the room to salute the stately and dignified, but now smiling Lady Frances Berkeley— and she the queenly centre of that vast throng, leaning upon the arm of her noble and venerable husband, with what grace and dignity she bowed her turbaned head in response to their salutations; and with what a majestic air of gratified vanity did she receive the courteous gratulations of the chivalrous cavaliers as they wished her many returns of the happy day, and hoped that the hours of her life would be marked by the lapse of diamond sands, while roses grew under her feet!

Sir William Berkeley, of whose extraordinary character we know far more than of any of the earlier governors of Virginia, was now in the evening of his long and prosperous life. "For more than thirty years he had governed the most flourishing country the sun ever shone upon,"[25] and had won for himself golden opinions from all sorts of people. Happy for him, and happy for his fame, if he had passed away ere he had become "encompassed," as he himself expresses it, "with rebellion, like waters." To all he had endeared himself by his firmness of character and his suavity of manner. In 1659, he was called, by the spontaneous acclaim of the people of Virginia, to assume the high functions of the government, of which he had been deprived during the Protectorate, and, under his lead, Virginia was the first to throw off her allegiance to the Protector, and to declare herself the loyal realm of the banished Charles. Had William Berkeley died before the troublous scenes which now awaited him, and which have cast so dark a shadow upon his character, scarce any man in colonial history had left so pure a name, or been mourned by sincerer tears. Death is at last the seal of fame, and over the grave alone can we form a just estimate of human worth and human virtue.

In person he was all that we delight to imagine in one who is truly great. Age itself had not bent his tall, majestic figure, which rose, like the form of the son of Kish, above all the people. His full black eye was clear and piercing, and yet was often softened by a benevolent expression. And this was the true nature of his heart, formed at once for softness and for rigour. His mouth, though frequently a pleasant smile played around it, expressed the inflexible firmness and decision of his character. No man to friends was more kind and gentle; no man to a foe was more relentless and vindictive. The only indication of approaching age was in the silver colour of his hair, which he did not conceal with the recently introduced periwig, and which, combed back to show to its full advantage his fine broad brow, fell in long silvery clusters over his shoulders.

Around him were gathered the prominent statesmen of the colony, members of the Council and of the House of Burgesses, conversing on various subjects of political interest. Among those who chose this rational mode of entertainment was our old friend, Colonel Henry Temple, who met many an old colleague among the guests, and everywhere received the respect and attention which his sound sense, his sterling worth, and his former services so richly deserved.

The Lady Frances, too, withdrawing her arm from that of her husband, engaged in elegant conversation with the elderly dames who sought her society; now conversing with easy dignity with the accomplished wives of the councillors; now, with high-bred refinement, overlooking the awkward blunders of some of the plainer matrons, whose husbands were in the Assembly; and now smiling good-humouredly at the old-fashioned vanity and assumed dignity of Mrs. Temple. The comparison of the present order of things with that to which she had been accustomed in her earlier days, formed, as usual, the chief theme of this good lady's discourse. But, to the attentive observer, the glance of pride with which from time to time she looked at her daughter, who, with graceful step and glowing cheek, was joining in the busy dance, plainly showed that, in some respects at least, Mrs. Temple had to acknowledge that the bright present had even eclipsed her favourite past.

Yes, to the gay sound of music, amid the bright butterflies of fashion, who flew heartlessly through the mazes of the graceful dance, Virginia Temple moved—with them, but not of them. She had not forgotten Hansford, but she had forgotten self, and, determined to please her mother, she had sought to banish from her heart, for the time, the sorrow which was still there. She had come to the ball with Bernard, and he, seeing well the effort she had made, bent all the powers of his gifted mind to interest her thoughts, and beguile them from the absorbing subject of her grief. She attributed his efforts to a generous nature, and thanked him in her heart for thus devoting himself to her pleasure. She had attempted to return his kindness by an assumed cheerfulness, which gradually became real and natural, for shadows rest not long upon a young heart. They fly from the blooming garden of youth, and settle themselves amid the gloom and ruins of hoary age. And never had Alfred Bernard thought the fair girl more lovely, as, with just enough of pensive melancholy to soften and not to sadden her heart, she moved among the gay and thoughtless throng around her.

The room next to the ball-room was appropriated to such of the guests as chose to engage in cards and dice; for in this, as in many other respects, the colony attempted to imitate the vices of the mother country. It is true the habit of gaming was not so recklessly extravagant as that which disgraced the corrupt court of Charles the Second, and yet the old planters were sufficiently bold in their risks, and many hundreds of pounds of tobacco often hung upon the turn of the dice-box or the pip[26] of a card. Seated around the old fashioned card-table of walnut, were sundry groups of those honest burgesses, who were ready enough in the discharge of their political functions in the state-house, but after the adjournment were fully prepared for all kinds of fun. Some were playing at gleek, and, to the uninitiated, incomprehensible was the jargon in which the players indulged. "Who'll buy the stock?" cries the dealer. "I bid five" — "and I ten" — "and I fifty." Vie, revie, surrevie, capote, double capote, were the terms that rang through the room, as the excited gamesters, with anxious faces, sorted and examined their cards. At another table was primero, or thirty-one, a game very much resembling the more modern game of vingt-et-un; and here, too, loud oaths of "damn the luck," escaped the lips of the betters, as, with twenty-two in their hands, they drew a ten, and burst with a pip too many. Others were moderate in their risks, rattled the dice at tra-trap, and playing for only an angel a game, smoked their pipes sociably together, and talked of the various measures before the Assembly.

Thus the first hours of the evening passed rapidly away, when suddenly the sound of the rebecks[27] ceased in the ball-room, the gaming was arrested in an instant, and at the loud cry of hall-a-hall,[28] the whole company repaired to the long, broad porch, crowding and pushing each other, the unwary cavaliers treading on the long trains of the fair ladies, and receiving a well-merited frown for their carelessness. The object of this general rush was to see the masque, which was to be represented in the porch, illuminated and prepared for the purpose. At one end of the porch a stage was erected, with all the simple machinery which the ingenuity of the youth of Jamestown could devise, to aid in the representation — the whole concealed for the present from the view of the spectators by a green baize curtain.

The object of the masque, imitated from the celebrated court masques of the seventeenth century, which reflected so much honour on rare Ben Jonson, and aided in establishing the early fame of John Milton, was to celebrate under a simple allegory the glories of the Restoration. Alfred Bernard, who had witnessed such a representation in England, first suggested the idea of thus honouring the birth-night of the Lady Frances, and the suggestion was eagerly taken hold of by the loyal young men of the little colonial capital, who rejoiced in any exhibition that might even faintly resemble the revels to which their loyal ancestors, before the revolution, were so ardently devoted.

FOOTNOTES:

[25] This is his own language.

[26] Pip signified the spot on a card.

[27] Fiddles.

[28] The cry of the herald for silence at the beginning of the masque.

CHAPTER XV

"Then help with your call
For a hall, a hall!
Stand up by the wall,
Both good-men and tall,
We are one man's all!"

The Gipsey Metamorphosea.

With the hope that a description of the sports and pastimes of their ancestors may meet with like favour from the reader, we subjoin the following account of this little masque which was prepared for the happy occasion by Alfred Bernard, aided by the grave chaplain, Arthur Hutchinson, and performed by some of the gay gallants and blooming damsels of old Jamestown. We flatly disclaim in the outset any participation in the resentment or contempt which was felt by these loyal Virginians towards the puritan patriots of the revolution.

The curtain rises and discovers the genius of True Liberty, robed in white, with a wreath of myrtle around her brow; holding in her right hand a sceptre entwined with myrtle, as the emblem of peace, and in her left a sprig of evergreen, to represent the fabled Moly[29] of Ulysses. As she advances to slow and solemn music, she kneels at an altar clothed with black velvet, and raising her eyes to heaven, she exclaims:—

"How long, oh Heaven! shall power with impious hand
In cruel bondage bind proud Britain's land,
Or heresy in fair Religion's robe
Usurp her empire and control the globe!—
Hypocrisy in true Religion's name
Has filled the land of Britain long with shame,
And Freedom, captive, languishes in chains,
While with her sceptre, Superstition reigns.
Restore, oh Heaven! the reign of peace and love,
And let thy wisdom to thy people prove
That Freedom too is governed by her rules,—
No toy for children, and no game for fools;—
Freed from restraint the erring star would fly
Darkling, and guideless, through the untravelled sky—

The stubborn soil would still refuse to yield
The whitening harvest of the fertile field;
The wanton winds, when loosened from their caves,
Would drive the bark uncertain through the waves
This magnet lost, the sea, the air, the world,
To wild destruction would be swiftly hurled!
And say, just Heaven, oh say, is feeble man
Alone exempt from thy harmonious plan?
Shall he alone, in dusky darkness grope,
Free from restraint, and free, alas! from hope?
Slave to his passions, his unbridled will,
Slave to himself, and yet a freeman still?
No! teach him in his pride to own that he
Can only in obedience be free—
That even he can only safely move,
When true to loyalty, and true to love."

As she speaks, a bright star appears at the farther end of the stage, and ascending slowly, at length stands over the altar, where she kneels. Extending her arm towards the star, she rises and cries in triumph:—

"I hail the sign, pure as the starry gem,
Which rested o'er the babe of Bethlehem—
My prayer is heard, and Heaven's sublime decree
Will rend our chains, and Britain shall be free!"

Then enters the embodiment of Puritanism, represented in the peculiar dress of the Roundheads—with peaked hat, a quaint black doublet and cloak, rigidly plain, and cut in the straight fashion of the sect; black Flemish breeches, and grey hose; huge square-toed shoes, tied with coarse leather thongs; and around the waist a buff leather belt, in which he wears a sword. He comes in singing, as he walks, one of the Puritan versions, or rather perversions of the Psalms, which have so grossly marred the exquisite beauty of the original, and of which one stanza will suffice the reader:—

"Arise, oh Lord, save me, my God,
For thou my foes hast stroke,
All on the cheek-bone, and the teeth
Of wicked men hast broke."[30]

Then standing at some distance from the altar, he rolls up his eyes, till nothing but the whites can be seen, and is exercised in prayer. With a smile of bitter contempt the genius of True Liberty proceeds:—

"See where he comes, with visage long and grim,
Whining with nasal twang his impious hymn!

See where he stands, nor bows the suppliant knee,
He apes the Publican, but acts the Pharisee—
Snatching the sword of just Jehovah's wrath,
And damning all who leave *his* thorny path.
Now by this wand which Hermes, with a smile,
Gave to Ulysses in the Circean isle,
I will again exert the power divine,
And change to Britons these disgusting swine."

She waves the sprig of Moly over the head of the Puritan three or four times, who, sensible of the force of the charm, cries out:—

"Hah! what is this! strange feelings fill my heart;
Avaunt thee, tempter! I defy thy art—
Up, Israel! hasten to your tents, and smite
These sons of Belial, and th' Amalekite,—
Philistia is upon us with Goliah,
Come, call the roll from twelfth of Nehemiah,[31]
Gird up your loins and buckle on your sword,
Fight with your prayers, your powder, and the word.
How, General 'Faint-not,'[32] has your spirit sunk?
Let not God's soldier yield unto a Monk."[33]

Then, as the charm increases, he continues in a feebler voice:

"Curse on the tempter's art! that heathenish Moly
Has in an instant changed my nature wholly;
The past, with all its triumphs, is a trance,
My legs, once taught to kneel, incline to dance,
My voice, which to some holy psalm belongs,
Is twisting round into these carnal songs.
Alas! I'm lost! New thoughts my bosom swell;
Habakuk, Barebones, Cromwell, fare ye well.
Break up conventicles, I do insist,
Sing the doxology and be dismissed."

As he finishes the last line, the heavy roll of thunder is heard, and suddenly the doors of a dungeon in the background fly open, from which emerges the impersonation of Christmas, followed by the Queen of May. Christmas is represented by a jolly, round-bellied, red-nosed, laughing old fellow, dressed in pure white. His hair is thickly powdered, and his face red with rouge. In his right hand he holds a huge mince-pie, which ever and anon he gnaws with exquisite humour, and in his left is a bowl of generous wassail, from which he drinks long and deeply. His brows are twined with misletoe and ivy, woven together in a fantastic wreath, and to his hair and different parts of his dress are attached long pendants of glass, to represent icicles. As he advances to the right of the stage, there descends from the awning above an immense number of small fragments of white paper, substitutes for snow-flakes, with which that part of the floor is soon completely covered.

The Queen of May takes her position on the left. She is dressed in a robe of pure white, festooned with flowers, with a garland of white roses twined with evergreen upon her brow. In her hand is held the May-pole, adorned with ribbons of white, and blue, and red, alternately wrapped around it, and surmounted with a wreath of various flowers. As she assumes her place, showers of roses descend from above, envelope her in their bloom, and shed a fresh fragrance around the room.

The Genius of Liberty points out the approaching figures to the Puritan, and exclaims:

> "Welcome, ye happy children of the earth,
> Who strew life's weary way with guileless mirth!
> Thus Joy should ever herald in the morn
> On which the Saviour of the world was born,
> And thus with rapture should we ever bring
> Fresh flowers to twine around the brow of Spring.
> Think not, stern mortal, God delights to scan,
> With fiendish joy, the miseries of man;
> Think not the groans that rend your bosom here
> Are music to Jehovah's listening ear.
> Formed by His power, the children of His love,
> Man's happiness delights the Sire above;
> While the light mirth which from his spirit springs
> Ascends like incense to the King of kings."

Christmas, yawning and stretching himself, then roars out in a merry, lusty voice:

> "My spirit rejoices to hear merry voices,
> With a prospect of breaking my fast,
> For with such a lean platter, these days they call latter [34]
> Were very near being my last.

> "In that cursed conventicle, as chill as an icicle,
> I caught a bad cold in my head,
> And some impudent vassal stole all of my wassail,
> And left me small beer in its stead.

"Of all that is royal and all that is loyal
They made a nice mess of mince-meat.
With their guns and gunpowder, and their prayers that are
louder,
But the de'il a mince-pie did I eat.

"No fat sirloin carving, I scarce kept from starving,
And my bones have become almost bare,
As if I were the season of the gunpowder treason,
To be hallowed with fasting and prayer.

"If they fancy pulse diet, like the Jews they may try it,
Though I think it is fit but to die on.
But may the Emanuel long keep this new Daniel
From the den of the brave British Lion.

"In the juice of the barley I'll drink to King Charley,
The bright star of royalty risen,
While merry maids laughing and honest men quaffing
Shall welcome old Christmas from prison."

As he thunders out the last stave of his song, the Queen of May steps
forward, and sings the following welcome to Spring:

"Come with blooming cheek, Aurora,
Leading on the merry morn;
Come with rosy chaplets, Flora,
See, the baby Spring is born.

"Smile and sing each living creature,
Britons, join me in the strain;
Lo! the Spring is come to Nature,
Come to Albion's land again.

"Winter's chains of icy iron
Melt before the smile of Spring;
Cares that Albion's land environ
Fade before our rising king.

"Crown his brow with freshest flowers,
Weave the chaplet fair as May,
While the sands with golden hours
Speed his happy life away.

"Crown his brow with leaves of laurel,
Twined with myrtle's branch of peace—

A hero in fair Britain's quarrel,
A lover when her sorrows cease.

"Blessings on our royal master,
Till in death he lays him down,
Free from care and from disaster,
To assume a heavenly crown."

As she concludes her lay, she places the May-pole in the centre of the stage, and a happy throng of gay young swains and damsels enter and commence the main dance around it. The Puritan watches them at first with a wild gaze, in which horror is mingled with something of admiration. Gradually his stern features relax into a grim smile, and at last, unable longer to restrain his feelings, he bursts forth in a most immoderate and carnal laugh. His feet at first keep time to the gay music; he then begins to shuffle them grotesquely on the floor, and finally, overcome by the wild spirit of contagion, he unites in the dance to the sound of the merry rebecks. While the dance continues, he shakes off the straight-laced puritan dress which he had assumed, and tossing the peaked hat high in the air, appears, amid the deafening shouts of the delighted auditory, in the front of the stage in the rich costume of the English court, and with a royal diadem upon his brow, the mimic impersonation of Charles the Second.

FOOTNOTES:

[29] The intelligent reader, familiar with the Odyssey, need not to be reminded that with this wand of Moly, which Mercury presented to Ulysses, the Grecian hero was enabled to restore his unhappy companions, who, by the magic of the goddess Circe, had been transformed into swine.

[30] A true copy from the records.

[31] "Cromwell," says an old writer, "hath beat up his drums clean through the Old Testament. You may learn the genealogy of our Saviour by the names of his regiment. The muster-master has no other list than the first chapter of St. Matthew." If the Puritan sergeant had lost this roll, Nehemiah XII. would serve him instead.

[32] The actual name of one of the Puritans.

[33] General Monk, the restorer of royalty.

[34] The Puritans believed the period of the revolution to be the latter days spoken of in prophecy.

CHAPTER XVI

"I charge you, oh women! for the love you bear to men, to like as much of this play as please you; and I charge you, oh men! for the love you bear to women, (as I perceive by your simpering, none of you hate them,) that between you and the women the play may please."

As you Like It.

"There is the devil haunts thee, in the likeness of a fat old man; a tun of man is thy companion."

Henry IV.

The good-natured guests at the Governor's awarded all due, and more than due merit to the masque which was prepared for their entertainment. Alfred Bernard became at once the hero of the evening, and many a bright eye glanced towards him, and envied the fair Virginia the exclusive attention which he paid to her. Some young cavaliers there were, whose envy carried them so far, that they sneered at the composition of the young poet; declared the speeches of Liberty to be prosy and tiresome; and that the song of Christmas was coarse, rugged, and devoid of wit; nay, they laughed at the unnatural transformation of the grim-visaged Puritan into the royal Charles, and referred sarcastically to the pretentious pedantry of the young author, in introducing the threadbare story of Ulysses and the Moly into a modern production—and at the inconsistent jumble of ancient mythology and pure Christianity. Bernard heard them not, and if he had, he would have scorned their strictures, instead of resenting them. But he was too much engrossed in conversation with Virginia to heed either the good-natured applause of his friends, or the peevish jealousy of his young rivals. Indeed, the loyalty of the piece amply atoned for all its imperfections, and the old colonists smiled and nodded their heads, delighted at the wholesome tone of sentiment which characterized the whole production.

The character of Christmas was well sustained by Richard Presley,[35] a member of the House of Burgesses, whose jolly good humour, as broad sometimes as his portly stomach, fitted him in an eminent degree for the part. He was indeed one of those merry old wags, who, in an illustrated edition of Milton, might have appeared in L'Allegro, to represent the idea of "Laughter holding both his sides."

Seeing Sir William Berkeley and Colonel Temple engaged in earnest conversation, in one corner of the room, the old burgess bustled, or rather waddled up to them, and remaining quiet just long enough to hear the nature of their conversation chimed in, with,

"Talking about Bacon, Governor? Why he is only imitating old St. Albans, and trying to establish a *novum organum* in Virginia. By God, it seems to me that Sir Nicholas exhausted the whole of his *mediocria firma* policy, and left none of it to his kinsmen. Do you not know what he meant by that motto, Governor?"

"No;" said Sir William, smiling blandly.

"Well, I'll tell you, and add another wrinkle to your face. Mediocria firma, when applied to Bacon, means nothing more nor less than sound middlings. But I tell you what, this young mad-cap, Bacon, will have to adopt the motto of another namesake of his, and ancestor, perhaps, for friars aye regarded their tithes more favourably than their vows of virtue—and were fathers in the church as well by the first as the second birth."

"What ancestor do you allude to now, Dick?" asked the Governor.

"Why, old Friar Bacon, who lamented that time was, time is, and time will be. And to my mind, when time shall cease with our young squealing porker here, we will e'en substitute hemp in its stead."

"Thou art a mad wag, Presley," said the Governor, laughing, "and seem to have sharpened thy wit by strapping it on the Bible containing the whole Bacon genealogy. Come, Temple, let me introduce to your most favourable acquaintance, Major Richard Presley, the Falstaff of Virginia, with as big a paunch, and if not as merry a wit, at least as great a love for sack—aye, Presley?"

"Yes, but indifferent honest, Governor, which I fear my great prototype was not," replied the old wag, as he shook hands with Colonel Temple.

"Well, I believe you can be trusted, Dick," said the Governor, kindly, "and I may yet give you a regiment of foot to quell this modern young Hotspur of Virginia."

"Aye, that would be rare fun," said Presley, with a merry laugh, "but look ye, I must take care to attack him in as favourable circumstances as the true Falstaff did, or 'sblood he might embowell me."

"I would like to own the tobacco that would be raised over your grave then, Dick," said the Governor, laughing, "but never fear but I will supply you with a young Prince Hal, as merry, as wise, and as brave."

"Which is he, then? for I can't tell your true prince by instinct yet."

"There he stands talking to Miss Virginia Temple. You know him, Colonel Temple, and I trust that you have not found that my partiality has overrated his real merit."

"By no means," returned Temple; "I never saw a young man with whom I was more pleased. He is at once so ingenuous and frank, and so intelligent and just in his views and opinions on all subjects—who is he, Sir William? One would judge, from his whole mien and appearance, that noble blood ran in his veins."

"I believe not," replied Berkeley, "or if so, as old Presley would say, he was hatched in the nest where some noble eagle went a birding. I am indebted to my brother, Lord Berkeley, for both my chaplain and my private secretary. Good Parson Hutchinson seems to have been the guardian of Bernard in his youth, but what may be the real relation between them I am unable to say."

"Perhaps, like Major Presley's old Friar Bacon," said Temple, "the good parson may have been guilty of some indiscretion in his youth, for which he would now atone by his kindness to the offspring of his early crime."

"Hardly so," replied the Governor, "or he would probably acknowledge him openly as his son, without all this mystery. I have several times hinted at the subject to Mr. Hutchinson, but it seems to produce so much real sorrow, that I have never pushed my inquiries farther. All that I know is what I tell you, that my brother, in whose parish this Mr. Hutchinson long officiated as rector, recommended him to me—and the young man, who has been thoroughly educated by his patron, or guardian, by the same recommendation, has been made my private secretary."

"He is surely worthy to fill some higher post," said Temple.

"And he will not want my aid in building up his fortunes," returned Berkeley; "but they have only been in the colony about six months as yet— and the young man has entwined himself about my heart like a son. My own bed, alas! is barren, as you know, and it seems that a kind providence had sent this young man here as a substitute for the offspring which has been denied to me. See Temple," he added, in a whisper, "with what admiring eyes he regards your fair daughter. And if an old man may judge of such matters, it is with maiden modesty returned."

"I think that you are at fault," said Temple, with a sigh; "my daughter's affections are entirely disengaged at present."

"Well, time will develope which of us is right. It would be a source of pride and pleasure, Harry, if I could live to see a union between this, my adopted boy, and the daughter of my early friend," said the old Governor, as a tear glistened in his eye; "but come, Presley, the dancing has ceased for a time," he added aloud, "favour the company with a song."

"Oh, damn it, Governor," replied the old burgess, "my songs won't suit a lady's ear. They are intended for the rougher sex."

"Well, never fear," said the Governor, "I will check you if I find you are overleaping the bounds of propriety."

"Very well, here goes then—a loyal ditty that I heard in old England, about five years agone, while I was there on a visit. Proclaim order, and join in the chorus as many as please."

And with a loud, clear, merry voice, the old burgess gave vent to the following, which he sung to the tune of the "Old and Young Courtier;" an air which has survived even to our own times, though adapted to the more modernized words, and somewhat altered measure of the "Old English Gentleman:"—

"Young Charley is a merry prince; he's come unto his own,
And long and merrily may he fill his martyred father's
throne; With merry laughter may he drown old Nolly's
whining groan,And when he dies bequeath his crown to
royal flesh and bone.
Like a merry King of England,
And England's merry King.

"With bumpers full, to royal Charles, come fill the thirsty
glasses, The pride of every loyal heart, the idol of the
masses; Yet in the path of virtue fair, old Joseph far
surpasses,The merry prince, whose sparkling eye delights
in winsome lasses.
Like a merry King of England,
And England's merry King.

"For Joseph from dame Potiphar, as holy men assert,
Leaving his garment in her hand, did naked fly unhurt;
But Charley, like an honest lad, will not a friend desert,
And so he still remains behind, nor leaves his only shirt.

Like a merry King of England,
And England's merry King.

"Then here's to bonny Charley, he is a prince divine,
He hates a Puritan as much as Jews detest a swine;
But, faith, he loves a shade too much his mistresses and
wine, Which makes me fear that he will not supply the
royal line,
With a merry King of England,
And England's merry King."

The singer paused, and loud and rapturous was the applause which he received, until, putting up his hand in a deprecating manner, silence was again restored, and with an elaborate *impromptu*, which it had taken him about two hours that morning to spin from his old brain, he turned to Berkeley, and burst forth again.

"Nor let this mirror of the king by us remain unsung,
To whom the hopes of Englishmen in parlous times have
clung: Let Berkeley's praises still be heard from every loyal
tongue, While Bacon and his hoggish herd be cured, and
then be hung.
Like young rebels of the King,
And the King's young rebels."

Various were the comments drawn forth by the last volunteer stanza of the old loyalist. With lowering looks, some of the guests conversed apart in whispers, for there were a good many in the Assembly, who, though not entirely approving the conduct of Bacon, were favourably disposed to his cause. Sir William Berkeley himself restrained his mirth out of respect for a venerable old man, who stood near him, and towards whom many eyes were turned in pity. This was old Nathaniel Bacon, the uncle of the young insurgent, and himself a member of the council. There were dark rumours afloat, that this old man had advised his nephew to break his parole and fly from Jamestown; but, although suspicion had attached to him, it could never be confirmed. Even those who credited the rumour rather respected the feelings of a near relative, in thus taking the part of his kinsman, than censured his conduct as savouring of rebellion.

FOOTNOTES:

[35] This jovial old colonist is referred to in the T. M. account of the Rebellion.

CHAPTER XVII

"And first she pitched her voice to sing,
Then glanced her dark eye on the king,
And then around the silent ring,
And laughed, and blushed, and oft did say
Her pretty oath, by yea and nay,
She could not, would not, durst not play."

Marmion.

"How did *you* like Major Presley's song?" said Bernard to Virginia, as he leaned gracefully over her chair, and played carelessly with the young girl's fan.

"Frankly, Mr. Bernard," she replied, "not at all. There was only one thing which seemed to me appropriate in the exhibition."

"And what was that?"

"The coarse language and sentiment of the song comported well with the singer."

"Oh, really, Miss Temple," returned Bernard, "you are too harsh in your criticism. It is not fair to reduce the habits and manners of others to your own purer standard of excellence, any more than to censure the scanty dress of your friend Mamalis, which, however picturesque in itself, would scarcely become the person of one of these fair ladies here."

"And yet," said Virginia, blushing crimson at the allusion, "there can be no other standard by which I at least can be governed, than that established by my own taste and judgment. You merely asked me *my* opinion of Major Presley's performance; others, it is true, may differ with me, but their decisions can scarcely affect my own."

"The fact that there is such a wide variance in the taste of individuals," argued Bernard, "should, however, make us cautious of condemning that which may be sustained by the judgment of so many. Did you know, by the way, Miss Virginia, that 'habit' and 'custom' are essentially the same words as 'habit' and 'costume.' This fact—for the history of a nation may almost be read in the history of its language—should convince you that the manners and customs of a people are as changeable as the fashions of their dress."

"I grant you," said Virginia, "that the mere manners of a people may change in many respects; but true taste, when founded on a true appreciation of right, can never change."

"Why, yes it can," replied her companion, who delighted in bringing the young girl out, as he said, and plying her with specious sophisms. "Beauty, certainly, is an absolute and not a relative emotion, and yet what is more changeable than a taste in beauty. The Chinese bard will write a sonnet on the oblique eyes, flat nose and club feet of his saffron Amaryllis, while he would revolt with horror from the fair features of a British lassie. Old Uncle Giles will tell you that the negro of his Congo coast paints his Obi devil white, in order to inspire terror in the hearts of the wayward little Eboes. The wild Indians of Virginia dye their cheeks—"

"Nay, there you will not find so great a difference between us," said Virginia, interrupting him, as she pointed to the plastered rouge on Bernard's cheek. "But really, Mr. Bernard, you can scarcely be serious in an opinion so learnedly argued. You must acknowledge that right and wrong are absolute terms, and that a sense of them is inherent in our nature."

"Well then, seriously, my dear Miss Temple," replied Bernard, "I do not see so much objection to the gay society of England, which is but a reflection from the mirror of the court of Charles the Second."

"When the mirror is stained or imperfect, Mr. Bernard, the image that it reflects must be distorted too. That society which breaks down the barriers that a refined sentiment has erected between the sexes, can never develope in its highest perfection the purity of the human heart."

"Well, I give up the argument," said Bernard, "for where sentiment is alone concerned, there is no more powerful advocate than woman. But, my dear Miss Temple, you who have such a pure and correct taste on this subject, can surely illustrate your own idea by an example. Will you not sing? I know you can—your mother told me so."

"You must excuse me, Mr. Bernard; I would willingly oblige you, but I fear I could not trust my voice among so many strangers."

"You mistake your own powers," urged Bernard. "There is nothing easier, believe me, after the first few notes of the voice, which sound strangely enough I confess, than for any one to recover self-possession entirely. I well remember the first time I attempted to speak before a large audience. When I arose to my feet, my knees trembled, and my lips actually felt heavy as lead. It seemed as though every drop of blood in my system rushed back to my heart. The vast crowd before me was nothing but an immense assemblage of eyes, all bent with the most burning power upon me; and when at length I opened my mouth, and first heard the tones of my own voice, it sounded strange and foreign to my ear. It seemed as though it was somebody else, myself and yet not myself, who was speaking; and my utterance was so choked and discordant, that I would have given worlds if I could draw back the words that escaped me. But after a half dozen sentences, I became perfectly composed and self-possessed, and cared no more for the gaping crowd than for the idle wind which I heed not. So it will be with your singing, but rest assured that the discord of your voice will only exist in your own fancy. Now will you oblige me?"

"Indeed, Mr. Bernard, I cannot say that you have offered much inducement," said Virginia, laughing at the young man's description of his forensic debut. "Nothing but the strongest sense of duty would impel me to pass through such an ordeal as that which you have described. Seriously you must excuse me. I cannot sing."

"Oh yes you can, my dear," said her mother, who was standing near, and heard the latter part of the conversation. "What's the use of being so affected about it! You know you can sing, my dear—and I like to see young people obliging."

"That's right, Mrs. Temple," said Bernard, "help me to urge my petition; I don't think Miss Virginia can be disobedient, even if it were in her power to be disobliging."

"The fact is, Mr. Bernard," said the old lady, "that the young people of the present day require so much persuading, that its hardly worth the trouble to get them to do any thing."

"Well, mother, if you put it on that ground," said Virginia, "I suppose I must waive my objections and oblige you."

So saying, she rose, and taking Bernard's arm, she seated herself at Lady Frances' splendid harp, which was sent from England as a present by her brother-in-law, Lord Berkeley. Drawing off her white gloves, and running her little tapering fingers over the strings, Virginia played a melancholy symphony, which accorded well with the sad words that came more sadly on the ear through the medium of her plaintive voice:—

"Fondly they loved, and her trusting heart
With the hopes of the future bounded,
Till the trumpet of Freedom condemned them to part,
And the knell of their happiness sounded.

"But his is a churl's and a traitor's choice,
Who, deaf to the call of duty,

Would linger, allured by a syren's voice,
On the Circean island of beauty.

"His country called! he had heard the sound,
And kissed the pale cheek of the maiden,
Then staunched with his blood his country's wound,
And ascended in glory to Aidenn.

"The shout of victory lulled him to sleep
The slumber that knows no dreaming,
But a martyr's reward he will proudly reap,
In the grateful tears of Freemen.

"And long shall the maidens remember her love,
And heroes shall dwell on his story;
She died in her constancy like the lone dove,
But he like an eagle in glory.

"Oh let the dark cypress mourn over her grave,
And light rest the green turf upon her;
While over his ashes the laurel shall wave,
For he sleeps in the proud bed of honour."

The reader need not be told that this simple little ballad derived new beauty from the feeling with which Virginia sang it. The remote connection of its story with her own love imparted additional sadness to her sweet voice, and as she dwelt on the last line, her eyes filled with tears and her voice trembled. Bernard marked the effect which had been produced, and a thrill of jealousy shot through his heart at seeing this new evidence of the young girl's constancy.

But while he better understood her feelings than others around her, all admired the plaintive manner in which she had rendered the sentiment of the song, and attributed her emotion to her own refined appreciation and taste. Many were the compliments which were paid to the fair young minstrel by old and young; by simpering beaux and generous maidens. Sir William Berkeley, himself, gallantly kissed her cheek, and said that Lady Frances might well be jealous of so fair a rival; and added, that if he were only young again, Windsor Hall might be called upon to yield its fair inmate to adorn the palace of the Governor of Virginia.

CHAPTER XVIII

"Give me more love or more disdain,
The torrid or the frozen zone;
Bring equal ease unto my pain,
The temperate affords me none;
Either extreme of love or hate,
Is sweeter than a calm estate." —
Thomas Carew.

While Virginia thus received the meed of merited applause at the hands of all who were truly generous, there were some then, as there are many now, in whose narrow and sterile hearts the success of another is ever a sufficient incentive to envy and depreciation. Among these was a young lady, who had hitherto been the especial favourite of Alfred Bernard, and to whom his attentions had been unremittingly paid. This young lady, Miss Matilda Bray, the daughter of one of the councillors, vented her spleen and jealousy in terms to the following purport, in a conversation with the amiable and accomplished Caroline Ballard.

"Did you ever, Caroline, see any thing so forward as that Miss Temple?"

"I am under a different impression," replied her companion. "I was touched by the diffidence and modesty of her demeanor."

"I don't know what you call diffidence and modesty; screeching here at the top of her voice and drowning every body's conversation. Do you think, for instance, that you or I would presume to sing in as large a company as this—with every body gazing at us like a show."

"No, my dear Matilda, I don't think that we would. First, because no one would be mad enough to ask us; and, secondly, because if we did presume, every body would be stopping their ears, instead of admiring us with their eyes."

"Speak for yourself," retorted Matilda. "I still hold to my opinion, that it was impertinent to be stopping other people's enjoyment to listen to her."

"On the contrary, I thought it a most welcome interruption, and I believe that most of the guests, as well as Sir William Berkeley, himself, concurred with me in opinion."

"Well, I never saw any body so spiteful as you've grown lately, Caroline. There's no standing you. I suppose you will say next that this country girl is beautiful too, with her cotton head and blue china eyes."

"I am a country girl myself, Matilda," returned Caroline, "and as for the beauty of Miss Temple, whatever I may think, I believe that our friend, Mr. Bernard, is of that opinion."

"Oh, you needn't think, with your provoking laugh," said Miss Bray, "that I care a fig for Mr. Bernard's attention to her."

"I didn't say so."

"No, but you thought so, and you know you did; and what's more, it's too bad that you should take such a delight in provoking me. I believe it's all jealousy at last."

"Jealousy, my dear Matilda," said her companion, "is a jaundiced jade, that thinks every object is of its own yellow colour. But see, the dance is about to commence again, and here comes my partner. You must excuse me." And with a smile of conscious beauty, Caroline Ballard gave her hand to the handsome young gallant who approached her.

Bernard and Virginia, too, rose from their seats, but, to the surprise of Matilda Bray, they did not take their places in the dance, but walked towards the door. Bernard saw how his old flame was writhing with jealousy, and as he passed her he said, maliciously,

"Good evening, Miss Matilda; I hope you are enjoying the ball."

"Oh, thank you, exceedingly," said Miss Bray, patting her foot hysterically on the floor, and darting from her fine black eyes an angry glance, which gave the lie to her words.

Leaving her to digest her spleen at her leisure, the handsome pair passed out of the ball-room and into the lawn. It was already thronged with merry, laughing young people, who, wearied with dancing, were promenading through the gravelled walks, or sitting on the rural benches, arranged under the spreading trees.

"Oh, this is really refreshing," said the young girl, as she smoothed back her tresses from her brow, to enjoy the delicious river breeze. "Those rooms were very oppressive."

"I scarcely found them so," said Bernard, gallantly; "for when the mind is agreeably occupied we soon learn to forget any inconvenience to which the body may be subjected. But I knew you would enjoy a walk through this fine lawn."

"Oh, indeed I do; and truly, Mr. Bernard," said the ingenuous girl, "I have much to thank you for. Nearly a stranger in Jamestown, you have made my time pass happily away, though I fear you have deprived yourself of the society of others far more agreeable."

"My dear Miss Temple, I will not disguise from you, even to retain your good opinion of my generosity, the fact that my attention has not been so disinterested as you suppose."

"I thank you, sir," said Virginia, "for the compliment; but I am afraid that I have not been so agreeable, in return for your civility, as I should. You were witness to a scene, Mr. Bernard, which would make it useless to deny that I have much reason to be sad; and it makes me more unhappy to think that I may affect others by my gloom."

"I know to what you allude," replied Bernard, "and believe me, fair girl, sweeter to me is this sorrow in your young heart, than all the gaudy glitter of those vain children of fashion whom we have left. But, alas! I myself have much cause to be sad—the future looms darkly before me, and I see but little left in life to make it long desirable."

"Oh, say not so," said Virginia, moved by the air of deep melancholy which Bernard had assumed, but mistaking its cause. "You are young yet, and the future should be bright. You have talents, acquirements, everything to ensure success; and the patronage and counsel of Sir William Berkeley will guide you in the path to honourable distinction. Fear not, my friend, but trust hopefully in the future."

"There is one thing, alas!" said Bernard, in the same melancholy tone, "without which success itself would scarcely be desirable."

"And what is that?" said the young girl, artlessly. "Believe me, you will always find in me, Mr. Bernard, a warm friend, and a willing if not an able counsellor."

"But this is not all," cried Bernard, passionately. "Does not your own heart tell you that there must be something more than friendship to satisfy the longings of a true heart? Oh, Virginia—yes, permit me to call you by a name now doubly dear to me, as the home of my adoption and as the object of my earnest love. Dearest Virginia, sweet though it be to the heart of a lonely orphan, drifting like a sailless vessel in this rugged world, to have such a friend, yet sweeter far would it be to live in the sunlight of your love."

"Mr. Bernard!" exclaimed Virginia, with unfeigned surprise.

"Nay, dearest, do you, can you wonder at this revelation? I had striven, but in vain, to conceal a hope which I knew was too daring. Oh, do not by a word destroy the faint ray which has struggled so bravely in my heart."

"Mr. Bernard," said Virginia, as she withdrew her arm from his, "I can no longer permit this. If your feelings be such as you profess, and as I believe they are—for I know your nature to be honorable—I regret that I can only respect a sentiment which I can never return."

"Oh, say not thus, my own Virginia, just as a new life begins to dawn upon me. At least be not so hasty in a sentence which seals my fate forever."

"I am not too hasty," replied Virginia. "But I would think myself unworthy of the love you have expressed, if I held out hopes which can never be realized. You know my position is a peculiar one. My hand but not my heart is disengaged. Nor could you respect the love of a woman who could so soon forget one with whom she had promised to unite her destiny through life. I have spoken thus freely, Mr. Bernard, because I think it due to your feelings, and because I am assured that what I say is entrusted to an honourable man."

"Indeed, my dear Miss Temple, if such you can only be to me," said her wily lover, "I do respect from my heart your constancy to your first love. That unwavering devotion to another, whom I esteem, because he is loved by you, only makes you more worthy to be won. May I not still hope that time may supply the niche, made vacant in your heart, by another whose whole life shall be devoted to the one object of making you happy?"

"Mr. Bernard, candour compels me to say no, my friend; there are vows which even time, with its destroying hand can never erase, and which are rendered stronger and more sacred by the very circumstances which prevent their accomplishment. Fate, my friend, may interpose her stern decree and forever separate me from the presence of Mr. Hansford, but my heart is still unchangeably his. Ha! what is that?" she added, with a faint scream, as from the little summer-house, which we have before described, there came a deep, prolonged groan.

As she spoke, and as Bernard laid his hand upon his sword to avenge himself upon the intruder, a dark figure issued from the door of the arbor, and stood before them. The young man stood appalled as he recognized by the uncertain light of a neighbouring lamp, the dark, swarthy features of Master Hutchinson, the chaplain of the Governor.

"Put up your sword, young man," said the preacher, gravely; "they who use the sword shall perish by the sword."

"In the devil's name," cried Bernard, forgetful of the presence of Virginia, "how came you here?"

"Not to act the spy at least," said Hutchinson, "such is not my character. Suffice it to say, that I came as you did, to enjoy this fresh air—and sought the quiet of this arbour to be free from the intrusion of others. I have lived too long to care for the frivolities which I have heard, and your secret is safe in my breast—a repository of many a darker confidence than that." With these words the bent form of the melancholy preacher passed out of their sight.

"A singular man," said Bernard, in a troubled voice, "but entirely innocent in his conduct. An abstracted book-worm, he moves through the world like a stranger in it. Will you return now?"

"Thank you," said Virginia, "most willingly—for I confess my nerves are a little unstrung by the fright I received. And now, my friend, pardon me for referring to what has passed, but you will still be my friend, won't you?"

"Oh, certainly," said Bernard, in an abstracted manner. "I wonder," he muttered "what he could have meant by that hideous groan?"

And sadly and silently the rejected lover and his unhappy companion returned to the heartless throng, who still lit up the palace with their hollow smiles.

Alike the joyous dance, the light mirth, and the splendid entertainment passed unheeded by Virginia, as she sat silently abstracted, and returned indifferent answers to the questions which were asked her. And Bernard, the gay and fascinating Bernard, wandered through the crowd, like a troubled spectre, and ever and anon muttered to himself, "I wonder what he could have meant by that hideous groan?"

CHAPTER XIX

"His heart has not half uttered itself yet,
And much remains to do as well as they.
The heart is sometime ere it finds its focus,
And when it does with the whole light of nature
Strained through it to a hair's breadth, it but burns
The things beneath it which it lights to death."

Festus .

And now the ball is over. Mothers wait impatiently for their fair daughters, who are having those many last words so delightful to them, and so provoking to those who await their departure. Carriages again drive to the door, and receive their laughing, bright-eyed burdens, and then roll away through the green lawn, while the lamps throw their broad, dark shadows on the grass. Gay young cavaliers, who have come from a distance to the ball, exchange their slippers for their heavy riding-boots and spurs, and mount their pawing and impatient steeds. Sober-sided old statesmen walk away arm-in-arm, and discuss earnestly the business of the morrow. The gamesters and dicers depart, some with cheerful smiles, chuckling over their gains, and others with empty pockets, complaining how early the party had broken up, and proposing a renewal of the game the next night at the Blue Chamber at the Garter Inn. Old Presley has evidently, to use his own phrase, "got his load," and waddling away to his quarters, he winks his eye mischievously at the lamps, which, under the multiplying power of his optics, have become more in number than the stars. Thus the guests all pass away, and the lights which flit for a few moments from casement to casement in the palace, are one by one extinguished, and all is dark, save where one faint candle gleams through an upper window and betrays the watchfulness of the old chaplain.

And who is he, with his dark, melancholy eyes, which tell so plainly of the chastened heart—he who seeming so gentle and kind to all, reserves his sternness for himself alone—and who, living in love with all God's creatures, seems to hate with bitterness his own nature? It was not then as it is sometimes now, that every man's antecedents were inquired into and known, and that the young coxcomb, who disgraces the name that he bears and the lineage of which he boasts, is awarded a higher station in society than the self-sustaining and worthy son of toil, who builds his reputation on the firmer foundation of substantial worth. Every ship brought new emigrants from England, who had come to share the fate and to develope the destiny of the new colony, and who immediately assumed the position in society to which their own merit entitled them. And thus it was, that when Arthur Hutchinson came to Virginia, no one asked, though many wondered, what had blighted his heart, and cast so dark a shadow on his path. There was one man in the colony, and one alone, who had known him before—and yet Alfred Bernard, with whom he had come to Virginia, seemed to know little more of his history and his character than those to whom he was an entire stranger.

Arthur Hutchinson was in appearance about fifty years of age. His long hair, which had once been black as the raven's wing, but was now thickly sprinkled with grey, fell profusely over his stooping shoulders. There was that, too, in the deep furrows on his broad brow, and in the expression of his pale thin lips which told that time and sorrow had laid their heavy hands upon him. As has been before remarked, by the recommendation of Lord Berkeley, which had great weight with his brother, Hutchinson had been installed as Chaplain to Sir William, and through his influence with the vestry, presented to the church in Jamestown. Although, with his own private resources, the scanty provision of sixteen thousand pounds of tobacco per annum, (rated at about eighty pounds sterling,) was ample for his comfortable support, yet good Master Hutchinson had found it very convenient to accept Sir William Berkeley's invitation to make his home at the palace. Here, surrounded by his books, which he regarded more as cheerful companions, than as grim instructors, he passed his life rather in inoffensive meditation than in active usefulness. The sad and quiet reserve of his manners, which seemed to spring from the memory of some past sorrow, that while it had ceased to give pain, was still having its silent effect upon its victim, made him the object of pity to all around him. The fervid eloquence and earnestness of his sermons carried conviction to the minds of the doubting, arrested the attention of the thoughtless and the wayward, and administered the balm of consolation to the afflicted child of sorrow. The mysterious influence which he exerted over the proud spirit of Alfred Bernard, even by one reproving glance from those big, black, melancholy eyes, struck all who knew them with astonishment. He took but little interest in the political condition of the colony, or in the state of society around him, and while, by this estrangement, and his secluded life, he made but few warm friends, he made no enemies. The good people of the parish were content to let the parson pursue his own quiet life undisturbed, and he lost none of their respect, while he gained much of their regard by his refusal to make the influence of the church the weapon of political warfare.

Hutchinson, who had retired to his room some time before the guests had separated, was quietly reading from one of the old fathers, when his attention was arrested by a low tap at the door, which he at once recognized as Bernard's. At the intimation to come in, the young man entered, and throwing himself into a chair, he rested his face upon his hand, and sighed deeply.

"Alfred," said the preacher, after watching him for a moment in silence, "I am glad you have come. I have somewhat to say to you."

"Well, sir, I will hear you patiently. What would you say?"

"I would warn you against letting a young girl divert you from the pursuit of higher objects than are to be attained by love."

"How, sir?" exclaimed Bernard, with surprise.

"Alfred Bernard, look at me. Read in this pale withered visage, these sunken cheeks, this bent form, and this broken heart, the brief summary of a history which cannot yet be fully known. You have seen and known that I am not as other men—that I walk through the world a stranger here, and that my home is in the dark dungeon of my own bitter thoughts. Would you know what has thus severed the chain which bound me to the world? Would you know what it is that has blighted a heart which might have borne rich fruit, and turned it to ashes? Would you know what is the vulture, too cruel to destroy, which feeds upon this doomed form?"

"In God's name, Mr. Hutchinson, why do you speak thus wildly?" said Bernard, for he had never before heard such language fall from the lips of the reserved and quiet preacher. "I know that you have had your sorrows, for the foot-prints of sorrow are indeed on you, but I have often admired the stoical philosophy with which you have borne the burden of care."

"Stoical philosophy!" exclaimed the preacher, pressing his hand to his heart. "The name that the world has given to the fire which burns here, and whose flame is never seen. Think you the pain is less, because all the heat is concentrated in the heart, not fanned into a flame by the breath of words?"

"Well, call it what you will," said Bernard, "and suffer as you will, but why reserve until to-night a revelation which you have so long refused to make?"

"Simply because to-night I have seen and heard that which induces me to warn you from the course that you are pursuing. Young man, beware how you seek your happiness in a woman's smile."

"You must excuse me, my old friend," said Bernard, smiling, "if I remind you of an old adage which teaches us that a burnt child dreads the fire. If trees were sentient, would you have them to fly from the generous rain of heaven, by which they grow, and live, and bloom, because, forsooth, one had been blasted by the lightning of the storm?"

Hutchinson only replied with a melancholy shake of the head, and the two men gazed at each other in silence. Bernard, with all his sagacity and knowledge of human nature, in vain attempted to read the secret thoughts of his old guardian, whose dark eyes, lit up for a moment with excitement, had now subsided into the pensive melancholy which we have more than once remarked. The affectionate solicitude with which he had ever treated him, prevented Bernard from being offended at his freedom, and yet, with a vexed heart, he vainly strove to solve a mystery which thus seemed to surround Virginia and himself, who, until a few days before, had been entire strangers to each other.

"Alfred Bernard," said the old man at length, with his sweet gentle voice, "do you remember your father? You are very like him."

"How can you ask me such a question, when you yourself have told me so often that I never saw him."

"True, I had forgotten," returned Hutchinson, with a sigh, "but your mother you remember?"

"Oh yes," said the young man, with a tear starting in his eye, "I can never forget her sad, pensive countenance. I have been a wild, bad man, Mr. Hutchinson, but often in my darkest hours, the memory of my mother would come over me, as though her spirit, like a dove, was descending from her place in heaven to watch over her boy. Alas! I feel that if I had followed the precepts which she taught me, I would now be a better and a happier man."

No heart is formed entirely hard; there are moments and memories which melt the most obdurate heart, as the wand of the prophet smote water from the rock. And Alfred Bernard, with all his cold scepticism and selfish nature, was for a moment sincerely repentant.

"I have often thought, Mr. Hutchinson," he continued, "that if it had pleased heaven to give me some near relative on earth, around whom my heart could delight to cling, I would have been a better man. Some kind brother who could aid and sympathize with me in my struggle with the world, or some gentle sister, in whose love I could confide, and to whose sweet society I might repair from the bitter trials of this rugged life; if these had been vouchsafed me, my heart would have expanded into more sympathy with my race than it can ever now feel."

Hutchinson smiled sadly, and replied—

"It has been my object in life, Alfred Bernard, to supply the place of those nearer and dearer objects of affection which have been denied you. I hope in this I have not been unsuccessful."

"I am aware, Mr. Hutchinson," said Bernard, bitterly, "that to you I am indebted for my education and support. I hope I have ever manifested a becoming sense of gratitude, and I only regret that in this alone am I able to repay you."

"And do you think that I wished to remind you of your dependence, Alfred? Oh, no—you owe me nothing. I have discharged towards you a solemn, a sacred duty, which you had a right to claim. I took you, a little homeless orphan, and sought to cultivate your mind and train your heart. In the first you have done more than justice to my tuition and my care. I am proud of the plant that I have reared. But how have you repaid me? You have imbibed sentiments and opinions abhorrent to all just and moral men. You have slighted my advice, and at times have even threatened the adviser."

"If you refer to the difference in our faith," said Bernard, "you must remember that it was from your teachings that I derived the warrant to follow the dictates of my conscience and my reason. If they have led me into error, you must charge it upon these monitors which God has given me. You cannot censure me."

"I confess I am to blame," said the good old man, with a sigh. "But who could have thought, that when, with my hard earnings, I had saved enough to send you to France, in order to give you a more extensive acquaintance with the world you were about to enter—who would have thought that it would result in your imbibing such errors as these! Oh, my son, what freedom of conscience is there in a faith like papacy, which binds your reason to the will of another? And what purity can there be in a religion which you dare not avow?"

"Naaman bowed in the house of Rimmon," returned Bernard, carelessly, "and if the prophet forgave him for thus following the customs of his nation, that he might retain a profitable and dignified position, I surely may be forgiven, under a milder dispensation, for suppressing my real sentiments in order to secure office and preferment."

"Alas!" murmured Hutchinson, bitterly. "Well, it is a sentiment worthy of Edward's son. But go, my poor boy, proud in your reason, which but leads you astray—wresting scripture in order to justify hypocrisy, and profaning religion with vice. You shall not yet want my prayers that you may be redeemed from error."

"Well, good night," said Bernard, as he opened the door. "But do me the justice to say, that though I may be deceitful, I can never be ungrateful, nor can I forget your kindness to a desolate orphan." And so saying, he closed the door, and left the old chaplain to the solitude of his own stricken heart.

CHAPTER XX

"Oh, tiger's heart, wrapt in a woman's hide."
Henry VI.

Brightly shone the sun through the window of the Garter Inn, at which Virginia Temple sat on the morning after the ball at Sir William Berkeley's palace. Freed from the restraints of society, she gave her caged thoughts their freedom, and they flew with delight to Hansford. She reproved herself for the appearance of gaiety which she had assumed, while he was in so much danger; and she inwardly resolved that, not even to please her mother, would she be guilty again of such hypocrisy. She felt that she owed it to Hansford, to herself, and to others, to act thus. To Hansford, because his long and passionate love, and his unstained name, deserved a sacrifice of the world and its joys to him. To herself, because sad as were her reflections on the past, and fearful as were her apprehensions for the future, there was still a melancholy pleasure in dwelling on the memory of her love— far sweeter to her wounded heart than all the giddy gaiety of the world around her. And to others, because, but for her assumed cheerfulness, the feelings of Alfred Bernard, her generous and gifted friend, would have been spared the sore trial to which they had been subjected the night before. She was determined that another noble soul should not make shipwreck of its happiness, by anchoring its hopes on her own broken heart.

Such were her thoughts, as she leaned her head upon her hand and gazed out of the window at the throng of people who were hurrying toward the state-house. For this was to be a great day in legislation. The Indian Bill was to be up in committee, and the discussion would be an able one, in which the most prominent members of the Assembly were to take part. She had seen the Governor's carriage, with its gold and trappings, the Berkeley coat-of-arms, and its six richly caparisoned white horses, roll splendidly by, with an escort of guards, by which Sir William was on public occasions always attended. She had seen the Burgesses, with their reports, their petitions and their bills, some conversing carelessly and merrily as they passed, and others with thoughtful countenance bent upon the ground, cogitating on some favourite scheme for extricating the colony from its dangers. She had seen Alfred Bernard pass on his favourite horse, and he had turned his eyes to the window and gracefully saluted her; but in that brief moment she saw that the scenes through which he had passed the night before were still in his memory, and had made a deep impression on his heart. On the plea of a sick head-ache, she had declined to go with her mother to the "House," and the good old lady had gone alone with her husband, deploring, as she went, the little interest which the young people of the present day took in the politics and prosperity of their country.

While thus silently absorbed in her own thoughts, the attention of Virginia Temple was arrested by the door of her room being opened, and on looking up, she saw before her the tall figure of a strange, wild looking woman, whom she had never seen before. This woman, despite the warmth of the weather, was wrapped in a coarse red shawl, which gave a striking and picturesque effect to her singular appearance. Her features were prominent and regular, and the face might have been considered handsome if it were not for the exceeding coarseness of her swarthy skin. Her jet-black hair, not even confined by a comb, was secured by a black riband behind, and passing over the right shoulder, fell in a heavy mass over her bosom. Her figure was tall and straight as an Indian's, and her bare brawny arms, which escaped from under her shawl, gave indications of great physical strength; while there was that in the expression of her fierce black eye, and her finely formed mouth, which showed that there was no mere woman's heart in that masculine form.

The wild appearance and attire of the woman inspired Virginia with terror at first, but she suppressed the scream which rose to her lips, and in an agitated voice, she asked,

"What would you have with me, madam?"

"What are you frightened at, girl," said the woman in a shrill, coarse voice, "don't you see that I am a woman?"

"Yes, ma'am," said Virginia, trembling, "I am not frightened, ma'am."

"You are frightened—I see you are," returned her strange guest.—"But if you fear, you are not worthy to be the wife of a brave man—come, deny nothing—I can read you like a book—and easier, for it is but little that I know from books, except my Bible."

"Are you a gipsey, ma'am?" said Virginia, softly, for she had heard her father speak of that singular race of vagrants, and the person and language of the stranger corresponded with the idea which she had formed of them.

"A gipsey! no, I am a Virginian—and a brave man's wife, as you would be—but that prejudice and fear keep you still in Egyptian bondage. The time has come for woman to act her part in the world—and for you, Virginia Temple, to act yours."

"But what would you have me to do?" asked Virginia, surprised at the knowledge which the stranger seemed to possess of her history.

"Do!" shrieked the woman, "your duty—that which every human creature, man or woman, is bound before high heaven to do. Aid in the great work which God this day calls upon his Israel to do—to redeem his people from captivity and from the hand of those who smite us."

"My good woman," said Virginia, who now began to understand the character of the strange intruder, "it is not for me, may I add, it is not for our sex to mingle in contests like the present. We can but humbly pray that He who controls the affairs of this world, may direct in virtue and in wisdom, the hearts of both rulers and people."

"And why should we only pray," said the woman sternly, "when did Heaven ever answer prayer, except when our own actions carried the prayer into effect. Have you not learned, have you not known, hath it not been told you from the foundation of the world, that faith without works was dead."

"But there is no part which a woman can consistently take in such a contest as the present, even should she so far forget her true duties as to wish to engage in it."

"Girl, have you read your bible, or are you one of those children of the scarlet woman of Babylon, to whom the word of God is a closed book—to whom the waters from the fountain of truth can only come through the polluted lips of priests—as unclean birds feed their offspring. Do you not know that it was a woman, even Rahab, who saved the spies sent out from Shittem to view the land of promise? Do you not know that Miriam joined with the hosts of Israel in the triumph of their deliverance from the hand of Pharaoh? Do you not know that Deborah, the wife of Lapidoth, judged Israel, and delivered Jacob from the hands of Jabin, king of Canaan, and Sisera the captain of his host—and did not Jael, the wife of Heber the Kenite, rescue Israel from the hands of Sisera? Surely she fastened the nail in a sure place, and the wife of Sisera, tarried long ere his chariot should come—and shall we in these latter days of Israel be less bold than they? Tell me not of prayers, Virginia Temple, cowards alone pray blindly for assistance. It is the will of God that the brave should be often under Heaven, the answerers of their own prayers."

"And pray tell me," said Virginia, struck with the wild, biblical eloquence of the Puritan woman, "why you have thus come to me among so many of the damsels of Virginia, to urge me to engage in this enterprise."

"Because I was sent. Because one of the captains of our host has sought the hand of Virginia Temple. Ah, blush, maiden, for the blush of shame well becomes one who has deserted her lover, because he has laid aside every weight, and pressed forward to the prize of his high calling. Yet a little while, and the brave men of Virginia will be here to show the malignant Berkeley, that the servant is not greater than his lord—that they who reared up this temple of his authority, can rase it to the ground and bury him in its ruins. I come from Thomas Hansford, to ask that you will under my guidance meet him where I shall appoint to-night."

"This is most strange conduct on his part," said Virginia, flushing with indignation, "nor will I believe him guilty of it. Why did he entrust a message like this to you instead of writing?"

"A warrior writes with his sword and in blood," replied the woman. "Think you that they who wander in the wilderness, are provided with pen or ink to write soft words of love to silly maidens? But he foresaw that you would refuse, and he gave me a token—I fear a couplet from a carnal song."

"What is it?" cried Virginia, anxiously.

"'I had not loved thee, dear, so much,
Loved I not honour more,'"

said the woman, in a low voice. "Thus the words run in my memory."

"And it is indeed a true token," said Virginia, "but once for all, I cannot consent to this singular request."

"Decide not in haste, lest you repent at leisure," returned the woman, "I will come to-night at ten o'clock to receive your final answer. And regret not, Virginia Temple, that your fate is thus linked with a brave man. The babe unborn will yet bless the rising in this country—and children shall rise up and call us blest.[36] And, oh! as you would prove worthy of him who loves you, abide not thou like Reuben among the sheep-folds to hear the bleating of the flocks, and you will yet live to rejoice that you have turned a willing ear to the words and the counsel of Sarah Drummond."

There was a pause of some moments, during which Virginia was wrapt in her own reflections concerning the singular message of Hansford, rendered even more singular by the character and appearance of the messenger. Suddenly she was startled from her reverie by the blast of a trumpet, and the distant trampling of horses' hoofs. Sarah Drummond also started at the sound, but not from the same cause, for she heard in that sound the blast of defiance—the trumpet of freedom, as its champions advanced to the charge.

"They come, they come," she said, in her wild, shrill voice; "my Lord, my Lord, the chariots of Israel and the horsemen thereof—I go, like Miriam of old, to prophecy in their cause, and to swell their triumph. Farewell. Remember, at ten o'clock to-night I return for your final answer."

With these words she burst from the room, and Virginia soon seen her tall form, with hasty strides, moving toward the place from which the sound proceeded.

FOOTNOTES:

[36] This was her very language during the rebellion.

CHAPTER XXI

"Men, high minded men,
With powers as far above dull brutes endued,
In forest, brake or den,
As beasts excel cold rocks and brambles rude;
Men, who their duties know,
But know their rights, and knowing dare maintain,
These constitute a state."

Sir William Jones.

And nearer, and nearer, came the sound, and the cloud of dust which already rose in the street, announced their near approach. And then, Virginia saw emerging from that cloud a proud figure, mounted on a splendid grey charger, which pranced and champed his bit, as though proud of the noble burden which he bore. And well he might be proud, for that young gallant rider was Nathaniel Bacon, a man who has left his name upon his country's history, despite the efforts to defame him, as the very embodiment of the spirit of freedom. And he looked every inch a hero, as with kingly mien and gallant bearing he rode through that crowded street, the great centre of attraction to all.

Beside him and around him were those, his friends and his companions, who had sworn to share his success, or to perish in the attempt.

There was the burley Richard Lawrence, not yet bent under the weight of his growing years. There was Carver, the bold, intrepid and faithful Carver, whose fidelity yet lives historically in his rough, home-brewed answer to the Governor, that "if he served the devil he would be true to his trust." There too was the young and graceful form of one whose name has been honoured by history, and cherished by his descendants—whose rising glory has indeed been eclipsed by others of his name more successful, but not more worthy of success—nor can that long, pure cavalier lineage boast a nobler ancestor than the high-souled, chivalrous, and devoted Giles Bland. There too were Ingram, and Walklate, and Wilford, and Farloe, and Cheesman, and a host of others, whom time would fail us to mention, and yet, each one of whom, a pioneer in freedom's cause, deserves to be freshly remembered. And there too, and the heart of Virginia Temple beat loud and quick as she beheld him, was the gallant Hansford, whom she loved so well; and as she gazed upon his noble figure, now foremost in rebellion, the old love came back gushing into her heart, and she half forgave his grievous sin, and loved him as before.

These all passed on, and the well-regulated band of four hundred foot-soldiers, all armed and disciplined for action, followed on, ready and anxious to obey their noble leader, even unto death. Among these were many, who, through their lives had been known as loyalists, who upheld the councils of the colony in their long resistance to the usurpation of the Protector, and who hailed the restoration of their king as a personal triumph to each and all. There too were those who had admired Cromwell, and sustained his government, and some few grey-headed veterans who even remembered to have fought under the banner of John Hampden— Cavaliers and Roundheads, Episcopalians and Dissenters; old men, who had heretofore passed through life regardless of the forms of government under which they lived; and young men, whose ardent hearts burned high with the spirit of liberty—all these discordant elements had been united in the alembic of freedom, and hand-in-hand, and heart-in-heart, were preparing for the struggle. And Virginia Temple thought, as she gazed from the window upon their manly forms, that after all, rebellion was not confined to the ignoble and the base.

On, on, still on, and now they have reached the gate which is the grand entrance to the state-house square. The crowd of eager citizens throng after them, and with the fickle sympathy of the mob unite in loud shouts of "Long live Bacon, the Champion of Freedom." And now they are drawn up in bristling column before the hall of the assembly, while the windows are crowded thick with the pale, anxious faces of the astounded burgesses. But see! the leaders dismount, and their horses are given in charge to certain of the soldiers. Conspicuous among them all is Nathaniel Bacon, from his proud and imperial bearing as he walks with impatient steps up and down the line, and reads their resolution in the faces of the men.

"What will he do!" is whispered from the white and agitated lips of the trembling burgesses.

"This comes of the faithless conduct of Berkeley," says one.

"Yes; I always said that Bacon should have his commission," says another.

"It is downright murder to deny him the right to save the colony from the savages," says a third.

"And we must suffer for the offences of a despotic old dotard," said the first speaker.

"Say you so, masters," cried out old Presley, wedging his huge form between two of his brethren at the window—and all his loyalty of the preceding night having oozed out at his fingers' ends, like Bob Acres' courage, at the first approach of danger—"say you so; then, by God, it is my advice to let him put out the fire of his own raising."

But see there! Bacon and his staff are conferring together. It will soon be known what is his determination. It is already read in his fierce and angry countenance as he draws his sword half way from its scabbard, and frowns upon the milder councils of Hansford and Bland. Presently a servant of one of the members comes in with pale, affrighted looks, and whispers to his master. He has overheard the words of Bacon, which attended that ominous gesture.

"I will bear a little while. But when you see my sword drawn from my scabbard, thus, let that be the signal for attack. Then strike for freedom, for truth, and for justice."

The burgesses look in wild alarm at each other. What is to be done? It were vain to resist. They are unarmed. The rebels more than quadruple Governor, Council, and Assembly. Let those suffer who have incurred the wrath of freemen. Let the lightning fall upon him who has called it down. For ourselves, let us make peace.

In a moment a white handkerchief suspended on the usher's rod streams from the window, an emblem of peace, an advocate for mercy, and with one accordant shout, which rings through the halls of the state-house, the burgesses declare that he shall have his commission.

Bacon sees the emblem. He hears the shout. His dark eye flashes with delight as he hails this bloodless victory over the most formidable department of the government. The executive dare not hold out against the will of the Assembly. But the victory is not yet consummated.

Suddenly from the lips of the excited soldiery comes a wild cry, and following the direction of their eyes, he sees Sir William Berkeley standing at the open window of the Council Chamber. Yes, there stands the proud old man, with form erect and noble—his face somewhat paler, and his eagle eye somewhat brighter than usual. But these are the only signs he gives of emotion, as he looks down upon that hostile crowd, with a smile of bitter scorn encircling his lip. He quails not, he blenches not, before that angry foe. His pulse beats calmly and regularly, for it is under the control of the brave great heart, which knows no fear. And there he stands, all calm and silent, like a firm-set rock that defies in its iron strength the fury of the storm that beats against it.

Yet Berkeley is in danger. He is the object, the sole object, of the bitter hate of that incensed and indignant soldiery. He has pledged and he has broken his word to them, and when did broken faith ever fail to arouse the indignation of Virginians? He has denied them the right to protect, by organized force, their homes and their firesides from the midnight attacks of ruthless savages. He has advised the passage of laws restricting their commerce, and reducing the value of their staples. He has urged the erection of forts throughout the colony, armed with a regular soldiery, supported in their idleness by the industry of Virginians, and whose sole object is to check the kindling flame of liberty among the people. He has sanctioned and encouraged the exercise of power by Parliament to tax an unrepresented colony. He has advised and upheld His Majesty in depriving the original patentees of immense tracts of land, and lavishing them as princely donations upon fawning favourites. He has refused to represent to the king the many grievances of the colony, and to urge their redress, and, although thus showing himself to be a tyrant over a free people, he has dared to urge, through his servile commissioners, his appointment as Governor for life.

Such were some of the many causes of discontent among the colonists which had so inflamed them against Sir William Berkeley. And now, there he stood before them, calm in spite of their menaces, unrelenting in spite of their remonstrances. Without a word of command, and with one accord a hundred fusils were pointed at the breast of the brave old Governor. It was a moment of intense excitement—of terrible suspense. But even then his courage and his self-reliance forsook him not. Tearing open his vest, and presenting himself at the window more fully to their attack, he cried out in a firm voice:

"Aye, shoot! 'Fore God, a fair mark. Infatuated men, bury your wrongs here in my heart. I dare you to do your worst!"

"Down with your guns!" shouted Bacon, angrily. But it needed not the order of their leader to cause them to drop their weapons in an instant. The calm smile which still played around the countenance of the old Governor, the unblenching glance of that eagle eye, and the unawed manner in which he dared them to revenge, all had their effect in allaying the resentment of the soldiers. And with this came the memory of the olden time, when he was so beloved by his people, because so just and gentle. Something of this old feeling now returned, and as they lowered their weapons a tear glistened in many a hardy soldier's eye.

With the quick perception of true genius, Nathaniel Bacon saw the effect produced. Well aware of the volatile materials with which he had to work, he dreaded a revolution in the feelings of the men. Anxious to smother the smouldering ashes of loyalty before they were fanned into a flame, he cried with a loud voice,

"Not a hair of your head shall be touched. No, nor of any man's. I come for justice, not for vengeance. I come to plead for the mercy which ill-judged and cruel delay has long denied this people. I come to plead for the living—my argument may be heard from the dead. The voices of murdered Englishmen call to you from the ground. We demand a right, guaranteed by the sacred and inviolable law of self-preservation! A right! guaranteed by the plighted but violated word of an English knight and a Virginia Governor. A right! which I now hold by the powerful, albeit unwritten, sanction of these, the sovereigns of Virginia."

The last artful allusion of Bacon entirely restored the confidence of his soldiers, and with loud cries they shouted in chorus, "And we will have it!—we will have it!"

Berkeley listened patiently to this brief address, and then turned from the window where he was standing, and took his seat at the council-table. Here, too, he was surrounded by many who, either alarmed at the menaces of the rebels, and convinced of the futility of resisting their demands, or, what is more probable, who had a secret sympathy in the causes of the rebellion, exerted all their influence in mollifying the wrath and obstinacy of the old Governor. But it was all in vain. To every argument or persuasion which was urged, his only reply was,

"To have forced from me by rebels the trust confided in me by my king! To yield to force what I denied to petition! No, Gentlemen; 'fore God, if the authority of my master's government must be overcome in Virginia, let me perish with it. I wish no higher destiny than to be a martyr, like my royal master, Charles the First, to the cause of truth and justice. Let them rob me of my life when they rob me of my trust."

While thus the councillors were vainly endeavoring to persuade the old man to yield to the current which had so set against him, he was surprised by a slight touch on his shoulder, and on looking up he saw Alfred Bernard standing before him. The young man bent over, and in a low whisper uttered these significant words:

"The commission, extorted by force, is null and void when the duress is removed."

Struck by a view so apposite to his condition, and so entirely tallying with his own wishes, the impetuous old Governor fairly leaped from his chair and grasped the hand of his young adviser.

"Right, by God!" he said; "right, my son. Gentlemen, this young man's counsel is worth all of your's. Out of the mouth of babes and sucklings—however, Alfred, you would not relish a compliment paid at the expense of your manhood."

"What does the young man propose?" drawled the phlegmatic old Cole, who was one of the council board.

"That I should yield to the current when I must, and resist it when I can," cried Berkeley, exultingly. "Loyalty must only bow to the storm, as the tree bows before the tempest. The most efficient resistance is apparent concession."

The councillors were astounded. Sprung from that chivalric Anglo-Saxon race, who respected honour more than life, and felt a stain like a wound, they could scarcely believe their senses when they thus heard the Governor of Virginia recommending deceit and simulation to secure his safety. To them, rebellion was chiefly detestable because it was an infraction of the oath of loyalty. It could scarcely be more base than the premeditated perjury which Sir William contemplated. Many an angry eye and dark scowl was bent on Alfred Bernard, who met them with an easy and defiant air. The silence that ensued expressed more clearly than words the disapprobation of the council. At length old Ballard, one of the most loyal and esteemed members of the council, hazarded an expression of his views.

"Sir William Berkeley, let me advise you as your counsellor, and warn you as your friend, to avoid the course prescribed by that young man. What effect can your bad faith with these misguided persons have, but to exasperate them?—and when once aroused, and once deceived, be assured that all attempts at reconciliation will be vain. I speak plainly, but I do so because not only your own safety, but the peace and prosperity of the colony are involved in your decision. Were not the broken pledges of that unhappy Stuart, to whom you have referred, the causes of that fearful revolution which alienated the affections of his subjects and at length cost him his life? Charles Stuart has not died in vain, if, by his death and his sufferings, he has taught his successors in power that candour, moderation and truth are due from a prince to his people. But, alas! what oceans of blood must be shed ere man will learn those useful lessons, which alone can ensure his happiness and secure his authority."

"Zounds, Ballard," said the incensed old ruler, "you have mistaken your calling. I have not heard so fine a sermon this many a day, and, 'fore

God, if you will only renounce politics, and don gown and cassock, I will have you installed forthwith in my dismal Hutchinson's living. But," he added, more seriously, as the smile of bitter derision faded from his lips, "I well e'en tell you that you have expressed yourself a matter too freely, and have forgotten what you owe to position and authority."

"I have forgotten neither, sir," said Ballard, firmly but calmly. "I owe respect to position, even though I may not have it for the man who holds that position; and when authority is abused, I owe it alike to myself and to the people to check it so far as I may."

The flush of passion mounted to the brow of Berkeley, as he listened to these words; but with a violent effort he checked the angry retort which rose to his lips, and turning to the rest of the council, he said:

"Well, gentlemen, I will submit the proposition to you. Shall the commission of General of the forces of Virginia be granted to Nathaniel Bacon?"

"Nay, Governor," interposed another of the council, "we would know whether you intend—"

"It is of my actions that you must advise. Leave my motives to me. What do you advise? Shall the commission be granted?"

"Aye," was responded in turn by each of the councillors at the board, and at the same moment the heavy tramp of approaching footsteps was heard, and Bacon, attended by Lawrence, Bland and Hansford, entered the chamber.

The council remained seated and covered, and preserved the most imperturbable silence. It was a scene not unlike that of that ancient senate, who, unable to resist the attack of barbarians, evinced their pride and bravery by their contemptuous silence. The sun was shining brightly through the western windows of the chamber, and his glaring rays, softened and coloured by the rich red curtains of damask, threw a deeper flush upon the cheeks of the haughty old councillors. With their eyes fixed upon the intruders, they patiently awaited the result of the interview. On the other hand, the attitude and behaviour of the rebels was not less calm and dignified. They had evidently counselled well before they had determined to intrude thus upon the deliberations of the council. It was with no angry or impatient outburst of passion, with no air of triumph, that they came. They knew their rights, and had come to claim and maintain them.

There were two men there, and they the youngest of that mixed assembly, who viewed each other with looks of darker hatred than the rest. The wound inflicted in Hansford's heart at Windsor Hall had not yet been healed—and with that tendency to injustice so habitual to lovers, with the proclivity of all men to seek out some one whom they may charge as the author of their own misfortune, he viewed Bernard with feelings of distrust and enmity. He felt, too, or rather he feared, that the heart left vacant by his own exclusion from it, might be filled with this young rival. Bernard, on the other hand, had even stronger reason of dislike, and if such motives could operate even upon the noble mind of Hansford, with how much greater force would they impress the selfish character of the young jesuit. The recollection of that last scene with Virginia in the park, of her unwavering devotion to her rebel lover, and her disregard of his own feelings came upon him now with renewed force, as he saw that rebel rival stand before him. Even if filial regard for her father's wishes and a sense of duty to herself would forever prevent her alliance with Hansford, Alfred Bernard felt that so long as his rival lived there was an insuperable obstacle to his acquisition of her estate, an object which he prized even more than her love. Thus these two young men darted angry glances at each other, and forgot in their own personal aggrievements, the higher principles for which they were engaged of loyalty on the one hand, and liberty on the other.

Bacon was the first to break silence.

"Methinks," he said, "that your honours are not inclined to fall into the error of deciding in haste and repenting at leisure."

"Mr. Bacon," said Berkeley, "you must be aware that the appearance of this armed force tends to prejudice your claims. It would be indecorous in me to be over-awed by menaces, or to yield to compulsion. But the necessities of the time demand that there should be an organized force, to resist the encroachments of the Indians. It is, therefore, not from fear of your threats, but from conviction of this necessity that I have determined to grant you the commission which you ask, with full power to raise, equip, and provision an army, and with instructions, that you forthwith proceed to march against the savages."

Bacon could scarcely suppress a smile at this boastful appearance of authority and disavowal of compulsion, on the part of the proud old Governor. It was with a thrill of rapture that he thus at last possessed the great object of his wishes. Already idolized by the people, he only needed a legal recognition of his authority to accomplish the great ends that he had in view. As the commission was made out in due form, engrossed and sealed, and handed to him, he clutched it eagerly, as though it were a sceptre of royal power. Little suspecting the design of the wily Governor, he felt all his confidence in him restored at once, and from his generous heart he forgave him all the past.

"This commission, though military," he said, proudly, "is the seal of restored tranquillity to the colony. Think not it will be perverted to improper uses. Royalty is to Virginians what the sun is to the pious Persian. Virginia was the last to desert the setting sun of royalty, and still lingered piously and tearfully to look upon its declining rays. She was the first to hail the glorious restoration of its light, and as she worshipped its rising beams, she will never seek to quench or overcloud its meridian lustre. I go, gentlemen, to restore peace to the fireside and confidence to the hearts of this people. The sword of my country shall never be turned against herself."

The heightened colour of his cheek, and the bright flashing of his eye, bespoke the pride and delight of his heart. With a profound bow he turned from the room, and with his aids, he descended to rejoin his anxious and expectant followers. In a few moments the loud shout of the soldiery was heard testifying their satisfaction at the result. The names of Berkeley and of Bacon were upon their lips—and as the proud old Governor gazed from the window at that happy crowd, and saw with the admiring eye of a brave man, the tall and martial form of Nathaniel Bacon at their head, he scarcely regretted in that moment that his loyal name had been linked with the name of a traitor.

CHAPTER XXII

"Me glory summons to the martial scene,
The field of combat is the sphere of men;
Where heroes war the foremost place I claim,
The first in danger, as the first in fame."

Pope's Iliad.

We return to Virginia Temple, who, although not an eye-witness of the scene which we have just described, was far from being disinterested in its result. The words of the singular woman, with whom she had conversed, had made some impression upon her mind. Although disgusted with the facility with which Dame Drummond had distorted and perverted Scripture to justify her own wild absurdities, Virginia still felt that there was much cause for self-reproach in her conduct to her lover. She felt every assurance that though he might err, he would err from judgment alone; and how little did she know of the questions at issue between the aroused people and the government. Indeed, when she saw the character of those with whom Hansford was associated—men not impelled by the blind excitement of a mob, but evidently actuated by higher principles of right and justice, her heart misgave her that, perhaps, she had permitted prejudice to carry her too far in her opposition to their cause. The struggle in her mind was indeed an unequal one. It was love pleading against ignorant prejudice, and that at the forum of a woman's heart. Can it be wondered at that Virginia Temple, left to herself, without an adviser, yielded to the powerful plea, and freely and fully forgave her rebel lover? And when she thought, too, that, however guilty to his country, he had, at least, been ever faithful to her, she added to her forgiveness of him the bitterest self-reproach. On one thing she was resolved, that notwithstanding the apparent indelicacy of such a course, she would grant him the interview which he requested, and if she could not win him from his error, at least part from him, though forever, as a friend. She felt that it was due to her former love, and to his unwavering devotion, to grant this last request.

Once determined on her course, the hours rolled heavily away until the time fixed for her appointment with Hansford. Despite her attempt to prove cheerful and unconcerned, her lynx-eyed mother detected her sadness, but was easily persuaded that it was due to a slight head-ache, with which she was really suffering, and which she pleaded as an excuse. The old lady was more easily deceived, because it tallied with her own idea, that Jamestown was very unhealthy, and that she, herself, could never breathe its unwholesome air without the most disastrous consequences to her health.

At length, Colonel Temple, having left the crowd of busy politicians, who were discussing the events of the day in the hall, returned with his good wife to their own room. Virginia, with a beating heart, resumed her watch at the window, where she was to await the coming of Sarah Drummond. It was a warm, still night. Scarcely a breath of air was stirring the leaves of the long line of elms that adorned the street. She sat watching the silent stars, and wondering if those bright worlds contained scenes of sorrow and despair like this; or were they but the pure mansions which the Comforter was preparing in his heavenly kingdom for those disconsolate children of earth who longed for that peace which he had promised when he told his trusting disciples "Let not your heart be troubled, neither let it be afraid." How apt are the sorrowing souls of earth to look thus into the blue depths of heaven, and in their selfishness to think that Nature, with her host of created beings, was made for them. She chose from among those shining worlds, one bright and trembling star, which stood apart, and there transported on the wings of Fancy or Faith, she lived in love and peace with Hansford. Sweet was that star-home to the trusting girl, as she watched it in its slow and silent course through heaven. Free from the cares which vex the spirit in this dark sin-world, that happy star was filled with love, and the blissful pair who knew it as their home, felt no change, save in the "grateful vicissitude of pleasure and repose." Such was the picture which the young girl, with the pencil of hope, and the colours of fancy painted for her soul's eye. But as she gazed, the star faded from her sight, and a dark and heavy cloud lowered from the place where it had stood.

At the same moment, as if the vision in which she had been rapt was something more than a dream, the door of her chamber opened, and Sarah Drummond entered. The heart of Virginia Temple nearly failed her, as she thought of the coincidence in time of the disappearance of the star and the summons to her interview with Hansford. Her companion marked her manner, and in a more gentle voice than she had yet assumed, she said,

"Why art thou cast down, maiden? Let not your heart sink in the performance of a duty. Have you decided?"

"Must I meet him alone?" asked Virginia. "Oh, how could he make a request so hard to be complied with!"

"Alone!" said Sarah, with a sneer. "Yes, silly girl, reared in the school that would teach that woman's virtue is too frail even to be tempted. Yes, alone! She who cannot trust her honour to a lover, knows but little of the true power of love."

"I will follow you," replied Virginia, firmly, and throwing a shawl loosely around her, she rose from her seat and prepared to go.

"Come on, then," said Sarah, quickly, "there is no time to be lost. In an hour, at most, the triumphant defenders of right will be upon their march."

The insurgents, wearied with their long march the night and day before, and finding no accommodation for their numbers in the inn, or elsewhere, had determined to seek a few hours repose in the green lawn surrounding the state-house, previous to their night march upon the Indians. It was here that Hansford had appointed to meet and bid farewell to his betrothed Virginia. Half leading, half dragging the trembling girl, who had already well nigh repented her resolution, Sarah Drummond walked rapidly down the street, in the direction of the state-house. Arrived at the gate, their further progress was arrested by a rough, uncouth sentinel, who in a coarse voice demanded who they were.

"I am Sarah Drummond," said the woman, promptly, "and this young maiden would speak with Major Hansford."

"Why, 'stains, dame, what has become of all your religion, that you should turn ribibe on our hands, and be bringing young hoydens this time o' night to the officers. For shame, Dame Drummond."

"Berkenhead," cried the woman, fiercely, "we all know you for a traitor and a blasphemer, who serve but for the loaves and fishes, and not for the pure word. You gained your liberty, you know, by betraying your fellows in the insurrection of '62, and are a base pensioner upon the bounty of the Assembly for your cowardice and treason. But God often maketh the carnal-minded of this world to fulfil his will, and so we must e'en bear with you yet a little while. Come, let us pass."

"Nay, dame," said the old soldier, "I care but little for your abuse; but duty is duty, and so an' ye give me not the shibboleth, as old Noll's canters would say, you may e'en tramp back. You see, I've got some of your slang, and will fight the devil with his own fire: 'And there fell of the children of Ephraim, at the passage of the Jordan—'"

"Hush, blasphemer!" said Sarah, impatiently. "But if you must have the pass before you can admit us, take it." And she leaned forward and whispered in his ear the words, "Be faithful to the cause."

"Right as a trivet," said Berkenhead, "and so pass on. A fig for the consequences, so that my skirts are clear."

Relieved from this embarrassment, Sarah Drummond and her trembling companion passed through the gate, and proceeded up the long gravelled walk which led to the state-house. They had not gone far before Virginia Temple descried a dark form approaching them, and even before she could recognize the features, her heart told her it was Hansford. In another moment she was in his arms.

"My own Virginia, my loved one," he cried, regardless of the presence of Mrs. Drummond, "I scarcely dared hope that you would have kept your promise to say farewell. Come, dearest, lean on my arm, I have much to tell you. You, my kind dame, remain here for a few moments—we will not detain you long."

Quietly yielding to his request, Virginia took her lover's arm, and they walked silently along the path, leaving the good dame Drummond to digest alone her crude notions about the prospects of Israel.

"Is it not singular," said Hansford at length, "that before you came, I thought the brief hour we must spend together was far too short to say half that I wish, and now I can say nothing. The quiet feeling of love, of pure and tranquil love, banishes every other thought from my heart."

"I fear—I fear," murmured Virginia, "that I have done very wrong in consenting to this interview."

"And why, Virginia," said her lover, "even the malefactor is permitted the poor privilege of bidding farewell forever to those around him—and am I worse than he?"

"No, Hansford, no," replied Virginia, "but to come thus with a perfect stranger, at night, and without my father's permission, to an interview with one who has met with his disapprobation—"

"True love," replied Hansford, sadly, "overleaps all such feeble barriers as these—where the happiness of the loved one is concerned."

"And, therefore, I came," returned the young girl, "but you forget, Hansford, that the relation which once existed between us has, by our mutual consent, been dissolved—what then was proper cannot now be permitted."

"If such be the case," replied Hansford, in an offended tone, "Miss Temple must be aware that I am the last person to urge her to continue in a course which her judgment disapproves. May I conduct you to your companion?"

Virginia did not at first reply. The coldness of manner which she had assumed was far from being consonant with her real feelings, and the ingenuous girl could no longer continue the part which she attempted to represent. After a brief pause, the natural affection of her nature triumphed, and with the most artless frankness she said,

"Oh, no, Hansford, my tongue can no longer speak other language than that which my heart dictates. Forgive me for what I have said. We cannot part thus."

"Thanks, my dearest girl," he cried, "for this assurance. The future is already too dark, for the light of hope to be entirely withdrawn. These troublous times will soon be over, and then—"

"Nay, Hansford," said Virginia, interrupting him, "I fear you cannot even then hope for that happiness which you profess to anticipate in our union. These things I have thought of deeply and sorrowfully. Whatever may be the issue of this unnatural contest, to us the result must be the same. My father's prejudices—and without his consent, I would never yield my hand to any one—are so strong against your cause, that come what may, they can never be removed."

"He must himself, ere long, see the justice of our cause," said Hansford, confidently. "It is impossible that truth can long be hid from one, who, like your noble father, must ever be desirous of its success."

"And do you think," returned Virginia, "that having failed to arrive at your conclusions in his moments of calm reflection, he will be apt to change his opinions under the more formidable reasoning of the bayonet? Believe me, Hansford, that scenes like those which we have this day witnessed, can never reconcile the opposing parties in this unhappy strife."

"It is true, too true," said Hansford, sorrowfully; "and is there then no hope?"

"Yes, there is a hope," said Virginia, earnestly. "Let not the foolish pride of consistency prevent you from acknowledging an error when committed. Boldly and manfully renounce the career into which impulse has driven you. Return to your allegiance—to your ancient faith; and believe me, that Virginia Temple will rejoice more in your repentance than if all the honours of martial glory, or of civic renown, were showered upon you. She would rather be the trusting wife of the humble and repentant servant of his king, than the queen of a sceptered usurper, who clambered to the throne through the blood of the martyrs of faith and loyalty."

"Oh, Virginia!" said Hansford, struggling hard between duty and love.

"I know it is hard to conquer the fearful pride of your heart," said Virginia; "but, Hansford, 'tis a noble courage that is victorious in such a contest. Let me hear your decision. There is a civil war in your heart," she added, more playfully, "and that rebel pride must succumb to the strong arm of your own self-government."

"In God's name, tempt me no further!" cried Hansford. "We may well believe that man lost his high estate of happiness by the allurements of woman, since even now the cause of truth is endangered by listening to her persuasions."

"I had hoped," replied the young girl, aroused by this sudden change of manner on the part of her lover, "that the love which you have so long professed was something more than mere profession. But be it so. The first sacrifice which you have ever been called upon to make has estranged your heart forever, and you toss aside the love which you pretended so fondly to cherish, as a toy no longer worthy of your regard."

"This is unkind, Virginia," returned Hansford, in an injured tone. "I have not deserved this at your hands. Sorely you have tempted me; but, thank God, not even the sweet hope which you extend can allure me from my duty. If my country demand the sacrifice of my heart, then let the victim be bound upon her altar. The sweet memories of the past, the love which still dwells in that heart, the crushed hopes of the future, will all unite to form the sad garland to adorn it for the sacrifice."

The tone of deep melancholy with which Hansford uttered these words showed how painful had been the struggle through which he had passed. It had its effect, too, upon the heart of Virginia. She felt how cruel had been her language just before—how unjust had been her charge of inconstancy. She saw at once the fierce contest in Hansford's breast, in which duty had triumphed over love. Ingenuous as she ever was, she acknowledged her fault, and wept, and was forgiven.

"And now," said Hansford, more calmly, "my own Virginia—for I may still call you so—in thus severing forever the chain which has bound us, I do not renounce my love, nor the deep interest which I feel in your future destiny. I love you too dearly to wish that you should still love me; find elsewhere some one more worthy than I to fill your heart. Forget that you ever loved me; if you can, forget that you ever knew me. And yet, as a friend, let me warn you, with all the sincerity of my heart, to beware of Alfred Bernard."

"Of whom?" asked Virginia, in surprise.

"Of that serpent, who, with gilded crest and subtle guile, would intrude into the garden of your heart," continued Hansford, solemnly.

"Why, Hansford," said Virginia, "you scarcely know the young man of whom you speak. Like you, my friend, my affections are buried in the past. I can never love again. But yet I would not have you wrong with unjust suspicions one who has never done you wrong. On the contrary, even in my brief intercourse with him, his conduct towards you has been courteous and generous."

"How hard is it for innocence to suspect guile," said Hansford. "My sweet girl, these very professions of generosity towards me, have but sealed my estimate of his character. For me he entertains the deadliest hate. Against me he has sworn the deadliest vengeance. I tell you, Virginia, that if ever kindly nature implanted an instinct in the human heart to warn it of approaching danger, she did so when first I looked upon that man. My subsequent knowledge of him but strengthened this intuition. Mild, insinuating, and artful, he is more to be feared than an open foe. I dread a villain when I see him smile."

"Hush! we are overheard," said Virginia, trembling, and looking around, Hansford saw Arthur Hutchinson, the preacher, emerging from the shadow of an adjacent elm tree.

"Young gentleman," said Hutchinson, in his soft melodious voice, "I have heard unwillingly what perhaps I should not. He who would speak in the darkness of the night as you have spoken of an absent man, does not care to have many auditors."

"And he who would screen himself in that darkness, to hear what he should not," retorted Hansford, haughtily, "is not the man to resent what he has heard, I fear. But what I say, I am ready to maintain with my sword— and if you be a friend of the individual of whom I have spoken, and choose to espouse his quarrel, let me conduct this young lady to a place of safety, and I will return to grant such satisfaction as you or your principal may desire."

"This young maiden will tell you," said Hutchinson, "that I am not one of those who acknowledge that bloody arbiter between man and man, to which you refer."

"Oh, no!" cried Virginia, in an agitated voice; "this is the good parson Hutchinson, of whom you have heard."

"And you, maiden," said Hutchinson, "are not in the path of duty. Think you it is either modest or becoming, to leave your parents and your home, and seek a clandestine interview with this stranger. Return to your home. You have erred, grossly erred in this."

"Nay," cried Hansford, in a threatening voice, "if you say ought in reproach of this young lady, by heavens, your parson's coat will scarce protect you from the just punishment of your insolence;" then suddenly checking himself, he added, "Forgive me, sir, this hasty folly. I believe you mean well, although your language is something of the most offensive. And say to your friend Mr. Bernard, all that you have heard, and tell him for Major Hansford, that there is an account to be settled between us, which I have not forgotten."

"Hansford!" cried the preacher, with emotion, "Hansford, did you say? Look ye, sir, I am a minister of peace, and cannot on my conscience bear your hostile message. But I warn you, if your name indeed be Hansford, that you are in danger from the young man of whom you speak. His blood is hot, his arm is skilful, and towards you his purpose is not good."

"I thank you for your timely warning, good sir," returned Hansford, haughtily; "but you speak of danger to one who regards it not." Then turning to Virginia, he said in a low voice, "'Tis at least a blessing, that the despair which denies to the heart the luxury of love, at least makes it insensible to fear."

"And are you such an one," said Hutchinson, overhearing him; "and is it on thee that the iniquities of the father will be visited. Forbid it, gracious heaven, and forgive as thou would'st have me forgive the sins of the past."

"Mr. Hutchinson," said Hansford, annoyed by the preacher's solemn manner and mysterious words, "I know nothing, and care little for all this mystery. Your brain must be a little disordered—for I assure you, that as I was born in the colony, and you are but a recent settler here, it is impossible that there can be any such mysterious tie between us as that at which you so darkly hint."

"The day may come," replied Hutchinson, in the same solemn manner, "when you will know all to your cost—and when you may find that care and sorrow can indeed shake reason on her throne."

"Well, be it so, but as you value your safety, urge me no further with these menaces. But pardon me, how came you in this enclosure? Know you not that you are within the boundaries of the General's camp, against his strict orders?"

"Aye," replied the preacher, "I knew that the rebels were encamped hereabout, but I did not, and do not, see by what right they can impede a peaceful citizen in his movements."

"Reverend sir," said Hansford, "you have the reputation of having a sound head on your shoulders, and should have a prudent tongue in your head. I would advise you, therefore, to refrain from the too frequent use of that word 'rebel,' which just fell from you. But it is time we should part. I will conduct you to the gate lest you find some difficulty in passing the sentry, and you will oblige me, kind sir, by seeing this young lady to her home." Then turning to Virginia, he whispered his brief adieu, and imprinting a long, warm kiss upon her lips, he led the way in silence to the gate. Here they parted. She to return to her quiet chamber to mourn over hopes thus fled forever, and he to forget self and sorrow in the stirring events of martial life.

CHAPTER XXIII

"In the service of mankind to be
A guardian god below; still to employ
The mind's brave ardour in heroic aims,
Such as may raise us o'er the grovelling herd
And make us shine forever—that is life."

Thomson.

In a short time the bustle and stir in the camp of the insurgents announced that their little army was about to commence its march. Nathaniel Bacon rode slowly along Stuart street, at the head of the soldiery, and leaving Jamestown to the east, extended his march towards the falls of James river. Here, he had received intelligence that the hostile tribes had gathered to a head, and he determined without delay to march upon them unawares, and with one decisive blow to put an end to the war. Flushed with triumph, he thought, the soldiery would more willingly and efficiently turn their arms against the government, and aid in carrying out his darling project of effecting some organic changes in the charter of the colony; if, indeed, it was not already his purpose to dissolve the political connection of Virginia with the mother country.

The little party rode on in silence for several miles, for each was buried in his own reflections. Bacon, with his own peculiar views of ambition and glory, felt but little sympathy with those who united in the rebellion for the specific object of a march against the savages. Hansford was meditating on the heavy sacrifice which he had made for his country's service, and striving to see, in the dim future, some gleam of hope which might cheer him in his gloom. Lawrence and Drummond, the two most influential leaders in the movement, had been left behind in Jamestown, their place of residence, to watch the movements of Berkeley, in whose fair promises none of the insurgents seemed to place implicit confidence. The rest of the little party had already exhausted in discussion the busy events of the day, and remained silent from want of material for conversation.

At length, however, Bacon, whose knowledge of human nature had penetrated the depths of Hansford's heart, and who felt deeply for his favourite, gave him the signal to advance somewhat in front of their comrades, and the following conversation took place:

"And so, my friend," said Bacon, in the mild, winning voice, which he knew so well how to assume; "and so, my friend, you have renounced your dearest hopes in life for this glorious enterprise."

Hansford only answered with a sigh.

"Take it not thus hardly," continued Bacon. "Think of your loss as a sacrifice to liberty. Look to the future for your happiness, to a redeemed and liberated country for your home — to glory as your bride."

"Alas!" said Hansford, "glory could never repay the loss of happiness. Believe me, General, that personal fame is not what I covet. Far better would it be for me to have been born and reared in obscurity, and to pass my brief life with those I love, than for the glittering bauble, glory, to give up all that is dear to the heart."

"And do you repent the course you have taken," asked Bacon, with some surprise.

"Repent! no; God forbid that I should repent of any sacrifice which I have made to the cause of my country. But it is duty that prompts me, not glory. For as to this selfsame will-o'-the-wisp, which seems to allure so many from happiness, I trust it not. I am much of the little Prince Arthur's mind —

'By my Christendom,
So I were out of prison and kept sheep,
I should be as merry as the day is long.'

Duty is the prison which at last keeps man from enjoying his own happier inclination."

"There you are wrong, Hansford," said Bacon, "duty is the poor drudge, which, patient in its harness, pursues the will of another. Glory is the wild, unconfined eagle, that impatient of restraint would soar to a heaven of its own."

"And is it such an object as this that actuates you in our present enterprise?" asked Hansford.

"Both," replied the enthusiastic leader. "Man, in his actions, is controlled by many forces — and duty is chiefly prized when it waits as the humble handmaiden on glory. But in this enterprise other feelings enter in to direct my course. Revenge against these relentless wolves of the forest for the murder of a friend — revenge against that proud old tyrant, Berkeley, who, clothed in a little brief authority, would trample me under his feet, — love of my country, which impels me to aid in her reformation, and to secure her liberty—and, nay, don't frown,—desire for that fame which is to the mere discharge of plain duty what the spirit is to the body—which directs and sustains it here, but survives its dissolution. Are not these sufficient motives of action?"

"Pardon me, General," said Hansford, "but I see only one motive here which is worthy of you. Self-preservation, not revenge, could alone justify an assault upon these misguided savages—and your love of country is sufficient inducement to urge you to her protection and defence. But these motives are chiefly personal to yourself. How can you expect them to affect the minds of your followers?"

"Look ye, Major Hansford," said Bacon, "I speak to you as I do not to most men—because I know you have a mind and a heart superior to them—I would dare not attempt to influence you as I do others; but do you see those poor trusting fellows that are following in our wake? These men help men like you and me to rise, as feathers help the eagle to soar above the clouds. But the proud bird may moult a feather from his pinion without descending from his lofty pride of place."

"And this then is what you call liberty?" said Hansford, a little offended at the overbearing manner of the young demagogue.

"Certainly," returned Bacon, calmly, "the only liberty for which the mass of mankind are fitted. The instincts of nature point them to the man most worthy to control their destinies. Their brute force aids in elevating him to power—and then he returns upon their heads the blessings with which they have entrusted him. Do you remember the happy compliment of my old namesake of St. Albans to Queen Elizabeth? Royalty is the heaven which, like the blessed sun, exhales the moisture from the earth, and then distilling it in gentle rains, it falleth on the heads of those from whom she has received it."

"I remember the compliment, which beautiful though it may be in imagery, I always thought was but the empty flattery of a vain old royal spinster by an accomplished courtier. I never suspected that St. Albans, far less his relative, Nathaniel Bacon, believed it to be true. And so, with all your high flown doctrines of popular rights and popular liberty, you are an advocate for royalty at last."

"Nay, you mistake me, I will not say wilfully," replied Bacon, in an offended tone, "I merely used the sentiment as an illustration of what I had been saying. The people must have rulers, and my idea of liberty only extends to their selection of them. After that, stability in government requires that the power of the people should cease, and that of the ruler begin. You may purify the stream through which the power flows, by constantly resorting to the fountain head; but if you keep the power pent up in the fountain, like water, it will stagnate and become impure, or else overflow its banks and devastate that soil which it was intended to fertilize."

"Our ideas of liberty, I confess," said Hansford, "differ very widely. God grant that our antagonistic views may not prejudice the holy cause in which we are now engaged."

"Well, let us drop the subject then," said Bacon, carelessly, "as there is so little prospect of our agreeing in sentiment. What I said was merely meant to while away this tedious journey, and make you forget your own private griefs. But tell me, what do you think of the result of this enterprise?"

"I think it attended with great danger," replied Hansford.

"I had not thought," returned Bacon, with something between a smile and a sneer, "that Thomas Hansford would have considered the question of peril involved in a contest like this."

"I am at a loss to understand your meaning," said Hansford, indignantly. "If you think I regard danger for myself, I tell you that it is a feeling as far a stranger to my bosom as to your own, and this I am ready to maintain. If you meant no offence, I will merely say that it is the part of every general to 'sit down and consider the cost' before engaging in any enterprise."

"Why will you be so quick to take offence?" said Bacon. "Do I not know that fear is a stranger to your breast?—else why confide in you as I have done? But I spoke not of the danger attending our enterprise. To me danger is not a matter of indifference, it is an object of desire. They who would bathe in a Stygian wave, to render them invulnerable, are not worthy of the name of heroes. It is only the unmailed warrior, whose form, like the white plume of Navarre, is seen where danger is the thickest, that is truly brave and truly great."

"You are a singular being, Bacon," said Hansford, with admiration, "and were born to be a hero. But tell me, what is it that you expect or hope for poor Virginia, when all your objects may be attained? She is still but a poor, helpless colony, sapped of her resources by a relentless sovereign, and expected to submit quietly to the oppressions of those who would enslave her."

"By heavens, no!" cried Bacon, impetuously. "It shall never be. Her voice has been already heard by haughty England, and it shall again be heard in thunder tones. She who yielded not to the call of an imperious dictator—she who proposed terms to Cromwell—will not long bear the insulting oppression of the imbecile Stuarts. The day is coming, and now is, when on this Western continent shall arise a nation, before whose potent sway even Britain shall be forced to bow. Virginia shall be the Rome and England shall be the Troy, and history will record the annals of that haughty and imperious kingdom chiefly because she was the mother of this western Rome. Yes," he continued, borne along impetuously by his own gushing thoughts, "there shall come a time when Freedom will look westward for her home, and when the oppressed of every nation shall watch with anxious eye that star of Freedom in its onward course, and follow its bright guidance till it stands over the place where Virginia—this young child of Liberty—is; and oh! Hansford, will it then be nothing that we were among those who watched the infant breathings of that political Saviour—who gave it the lessons of wisdom and of virtue, and first taught it to speak and proclaim its mission to the world? Will it then be nothing for future generations to point to our names, and, in the language of pride and gratitude, to cry, there go the authors of our freedom?"

So spake the young enthusiast, thus dimly foreshadowing the glory that was to be—the freedom which, just one hundred years from that eventful period, burst upon the world. He was not permitted, like Simeon of old, to see the salvation for which he longed, and for which he wrought. And yet he helped to plant the germ, which expanded into the wide-spreading tree, and his name should not be forgotten by those who rejoice in its fruit, or rest secure beneath its shade.

Thus whiling away the hours of the night in such engrossing subjects, Hansford had nearly forgotten his sorrows in the visions of the future. How beneficent the Providence which thus enables the mind to receive from without entirely new impressions, which soften down, though they cannot erase, the wounds that a harsh destiny has inflicted.

But it is time that the thread of our narrative was broken, in order to follow the fortunes of an humble, yet worthy character of our story.

CHAPTER XXIV

"I am sorry for thee; thou art come to answer
A stony adversary, an inhuman wretch,
Uncapable of pity, void and empty
From any claim of mercy."
Merchant of Venice.

It was on a bright and beautiful morning—for mysterious nature often smiles on the darkest deeds of her children—that a group of Indians were assembled around the council-fire in one of the extensive forest ranges of Virginia. Their faces painted in the most grotesque and hideous manner, the fierceness of their looks, and the savageness of their dress, would alone have inspired awe in the breast of a spectator. But on the present occasion, the fatal business in which they were engaged imparted even more than usual wildness to their appearance and vehemence to their manner. Bound to a neighbouring tree so tightly as to produce the most acute pain to the poor creature, was an aged negro, who seemed to be the object of the vehement eloquence of his savage captors. Although confinement, torture, and despair had effected a fearful change, by tracing the lines of great suffering on his countenance, yet it would not have been difficult even then to recognize in the poor trembling wretch our old negro friend at Windsor Hall.

After discovering the deception that had been practised on them by Mamalis, and punishing the selfish ambition of Manteo, by expelling him from their tribe, the Indian warriors returned to Windsor Hall, and finding the family had escaped, seized upon old Giles as the victim on whom to wreak their vengeance. With the savage cruelty of their race, his tormentors had doomed him, not to sudden death, which would have been welcome to the miserable wretch, but to a slow and lingering torture.

It would be too painful to dwell long upon the nature of the tortures thus inflicted upon their victims. With all their coarseness and rudeness of manner and life, the Indians had arrived at a refinement and skill in cruelty which the persecutors of the reformers in Europe might envy, but to which they had never attained. Among these, tearing the nails from the hands and feet, knocking out the teeth with a club, lacerating the flesh with rough, dull muscle and oyster-shells, inserting sharp splinters into the wounded flesh, and then firing them until the unhappy being is gradually roasted to death—these were among the tortures more frequently inflicted. From the threats and preparations of his captors, old Giles had reason to apprehend that the worst of these tortures he would soon be called upon to endure.

There is, thank God, a period, when the burdens of this life become so grievous, that the prayer of the fabled faggot-binder may rise sincerely on the lips, and when death would indeed be a welcome friend—when it is even soothing to reflect that,

"We bear our heavy burdens but a journey,
Till death unloads us."

Such was the period at which the wretched negro had now arrived. He listened, therefore, with patient composure to the fierce, threatening language of the warriors, which his former association with Manteo enabled him, when aided by their wild gesticulation, to comprehend. But it was far from the intention of the Indians to release him yet from his terrible existence. One of the braves approaching the poor helpless wretch with a small cord of catgut, such as was used by them for bow-strings, prepared to bind it tightly around his thumb, while the others gathering around in a circle waved their war-clubs high in air to inflict the painful bastinado. When old Giles saw the Indian approach, and fully comprehended his design, his heart sank within him at this new instrument of torture, and in despairing accents he groaned—

"Kill me, kill me, but for de Lord's sake, massa, don't put dat horrid thing on de poor old nigga."

Regardless of his cries, the powerful Indian adjusted the cord, and with might and main drew it so tightly around the thumb that it entered the flesh even to the bone, while the poor negro shrieked in agony. Then, to drown the cry, the other savages commencing a wild, rude chant, let their war-clubs descend upon their victim with such force that he fainted. Just at this moment the quick ears of the Indians caught the almost inaudible sound of approaching horsemen, and as they paused to satisfy themselves of the truth of their suspicions, Bacon and his little band of faithful followers appeared full in sight. Leaving their victim in a moment, the savages prepared to defend themselves from the assault of their intruders, and with the quickness of thought, concealing themselves behind the trees and undergrowth of the forest, they sent a shower of arrows into the unwary ranks of their adversaries.

"By Jove, that had like to have been my death-stroke," cried Bacon, as an arrow directed full against his breast, glanced from a gilt button of his coat and fell harmless to the ground. But others of the party were not so fortunate as their leader. Several of the men, pierced by the poisoned arrows of the enemy, fell dead.

Notwithstanding the success of this first charge of the Indians, Bacon and his party sustained the shock with coolness and intrepidity. Their gallant leader, himself careless of life or safety, led the charge, and on his powerful horse he was, like the royal hero to whom he had compared himself, ever seen in the thickest of the carnage. Well did he prove himself that day worthy of the confidence of his faithful followers.

Nor loth were the Indians to return their charge. Although their party only amounted to about fifty, and Bacon's men numbered several hundred, yet was the idea of retreat abhorrent to their martial feelings. Screening themselves with comparative safety behind the large forest trees, or lying under the protection of the thick undergrowth, they kept up a constant attack with their arrows, and succeeded in effecting considerable loss to the whites, who, incommoded by their horses, or unaccustomed to this system of bush fighting, failed to produce a corresponding effect upon their savage foe.

There was something in the religion of these simple sons of the forest which imparted intrepid boldness to their characters, unattainable by ordinary discipline. The material conception which they entertained of the spirit-world, where valour and heroism were the passports of admission, created a disregard for life such as no civilized man could well entertain. In that new land, to which death was but the threshold, their pursuits were the same in character, though greater in degree, as those in which they here engaged. There they would be welcomed by the brave warriors of a former day, and engage still in fierce contests with hostile tribes. There they would enjoy the delights of the chase through spirit forests, deeper and more gigantic than those through which they wandered in life. Theirs was the Valhalla to which the brave alone were admitted, and among whose martial habitants would continue the same emulation in battle, the same stoicism in suffering, as in their forest-world. Such was the character of their simple religion, which created in their breasts that heroism and fortitude, in danger or in pain, that has with one accord been attributed to them.

But despite their valour and resolution, the contest, with such disparity of numbers, must needs be brief. Bacon pursued each advantage which he gained with relentless vigour, ever and anon cheering his followers, and crying out, as he rushed onward to the charge, "Don't let one of the bloody dogs escape. Remember, my gallant boys, the peace of your firesides and the lives and safety of your wives and children. Remember the brave men who have already fallen before the hand of the savage foe."

Faithful to his injunction, the overwhelming power of the whites soon strewed the ground with the bodies of the brave savages. The few who remained, dispirited and despairing, fled through the forest from the irresistible charge of the enemy.

Meantime the unfortunate Giles had recovered from the swoon into which he had fallen, and began to look wildly about him, as though in a dream. To the fact that the contending parties had been closely engaged, and that from this cause not a gun had been fired, the old negro probably owed his life. With the superstition of his race, the poor creature attributed this fortunate succour to a miraculous interposition of Providence in his behalf; and when he saw the last of his oppressors flying before the determined onslaught of the white men, he fervently cried,

"Thank the Lord, for he done sent his angels to stop de lion's mouf, and to save de poor old nigger from dere hands."

"Hallo, comrades," said Berkenhead, when he espied the poor old negro bound to the tree, "who have we here? This must be old Ochee[37] himself, whom the Lord has delivered into our hands. Hark ye," he added, proceeding to unbind him, "where do you come from? — or are you in reality the evil one, whom these infidel red-skins worship?"

"Oh, no, Massa, I a'ant no evil sperrit. A sperrit hab not flesh and bones as you see me hab."

"Nay," returned the coarse-hearted soldier, "that reasoning won't serve your purpose, for there is precious little flesh and blood about you, old man. The most you can lay claim to is skin and bones."

Hansford, who had been standing a little distance off, was attracted by this conversation, and turning in the direction of the old negro, was much surprised to recognize, under such horrible circumstances, the quondam steward, butler and factotum of Windsor Hall. Nor was Giles' surprise less in meeting with Miss Virginia's "buck" in so secluded a spot. It was with difficulty that Hansford could prevent him from throwing his arms around his neck; but giving the old man a hearty shake of the hand, he asked him the story of his captivity, which Giles, with much importance, proceeded to relate. But he had scarcely begun his narrative, when the attention of the insurgents was attracted by the approach of two horsemen, who advanced towards them at a rapid rate, as though they had some important intelligence to communicate.

FOOTNOTES:

[37] The evil spirit, sometimes called Opitchi Manitou, and worshipped by the Indians.

CHAPTER XXV

"Who builds his hope in air of your fair looks,
Lives like a drunken sailor on a mast."
Richard III.

The new comers were Lawrence and Drummond, who, as will be recollected by the reader, were left in Jamestown to watch the proceedings of the Governor, and to convey to Bacon any needful intelligence concerning them. Although he had, in the first impulse of triumph after receiving his commission, confided fully in the promises of the vacillating Berkeley, yet, on reflection, Bacon did not rely very implicitly upon them. The Governor had once before broken his word in the affair of the parole, promising to grant the commission which he craved, upon condition of his confession of his former disloyal conduct and his promise to amend. Bacon was not the man to be twice deceived, and it did not therefore much surprise him to see the two patriots so soon after his departure from Jamestown, nor to hear the strange tidings which they had come to detail.

"Why, how is this, General?" said Lawrence. "You have had bloody work already, it seems; and not without some loss to your own party."

"Yes, there they lie," returned Bacon. "God rest their brave souls! But being dead, they yet speak—speak to us to avenge their death on the bloody savages who have slaughtered them, and to proclaim the insane policy of Berkeley in delaying our march against the foe. But what make you from Jamestown?"

"Bad news or good, General, as you choose to take it," replied Lawrence. "Berkeley has dissolved the Assembly in a rage, because they supported you in your demand of yesterday, and has himself, with his crouching minions, retired to Gloucester."

"To Gloucester!" cried Bacon. "That is indeed news. But what can the old dotard mean by such a movement?"

"He has already made known his reasons," returned Lawrence. "He has cancelled your commission, and proclaimed you, and all engaged with you, as rebels and traitors."

"Why, this is infamous!" said Bacon. "Is the old knave such an enemy to truth that it cannot live upon his lips for one short day? And who, pray, is rash enough to uphold him in his despotism, or base enough to screen him in his infamy?"

"It was whispered as we left," said Drummond, "that a certain Colonel Henry Temple had avouched the loyalty of Gloucester, and prevailed upon the Governor to make his house his castle, during what he is pleased to term this unhappy rebellion."

"And by my soul," said Bacon, fiercely, "I will teach this certain Colonel Henry Temple the hazard that he runs in thus abetting tyranny and villainy. If he would not have his house beat down over his ears, he were wise to withdraw his aid and support; else, if his house be a castle at all, it is like to be a castle in Spain."

Hansford, who was an eager listener, as we may suppose, to the foregoing conversation, was alarmed at this determination of his impulsive leader. He knew too well the obstinate loyalty of Temple to doubt that he would resist at every hazard, rather than deliver his noble guest into the hands of his enemies. He felt assured, too, that if the report were true, Virginia had accompanied her father to Gloucester, and his very soul revolted at the idea of her being subjected to the disagreeable results which would flow from an attack upon Windsor Hall. The only chance of avoiding the difficulty, was to offer his own mediation, and in the event, which he foresaw, of Colonel Temple refusing to come to terms, he trusted that there was at least magnanimity enough left in the old Governor to induce him to seek some other refuge, rather than to subject his hospitable and loyal host to the consequences of his kindness. There was indeed some danger attending such a mission in the present inflamed state of Berkeley's mind. But this, Hansford held at naught. Hastily revolving in his mind these thoughts, he ventured to suggest to Bacon, that an attack upon Colonel Temple's house would result in the worst consequences to the cause of the patriots; that it would effect no good, as the Governor might again promise, and again recant—and, that it would be difficult to induce his followers to embark in an enterprise so foreign to the avowed object of the expedition, and against a man whose character was well known, and beloved by the people of the Colony.

Bacon calmly heard him through, as though struck with the truth of the views he presented, and then added with a sarcastic smile, which stung Hansford to the quick, "and moreover, the sight of soldiers and of fire-arms might alarm the ladies."

"And, if such a motive as that did influence my opinion," said Hansford, "I hope it was neither unworthy a soldier or a man."

"Unworthy alike of both," replied Bacon, "of a soldier, because the will and command of his superior officer should be his only law—and of a man, because, in a cause affecting his rights and liberties, any sacrifice of feeling should be willingly and cheerfully made."

"That sacrifice I now make," said Hansford, vainly endeavouring to repress his indignation, "in not retorting more harshly to your imputation. The time may yet come when no such sacrifice shall be required, and when none, I assure you, shall be made."

"And, when it comes, young man," returned Bacon, haughtily, "be assured that I will not be backward in affording you an opportunity of defending yourself—meantime you are under my command—and will please remember that you are so. But, gentlemen," he continued, turning to the others, "what say you to our conduct in these circumstances. Shall we proceed to Powhatan, against the enemy of a country to which we are traitors, or shall we march on this mendacious old Knight, and once again wipe off the stigma which he has placed upon our names?"

"I think," said Lawrence, after a pause of some moments, "that there is a good deal of truth in the views presented by Major Hansford. But, could not some middle course be adopted. I don't exactly see how it can be effected, but, if the Governor were met by remonstrance of his injustice, and informed of our determination to resist it as such, it seems to me that he would be forced to recant this last proclamation, and all would be well again."

"And who think you would carry the remonstrance," said Bacon. "It would be about as wise to thrust your head in a lion's mouth, as to trust yourself in the hands of the old fanatic. I know not whom we could get to bear such a mission," he added, smiling, "unless our friend Ingram there, who having been accustomed to ropes in his youth, if report speaks true, need have no fear of them in age."[38]

"In faith, General," replied the quondam rope-dancer, "I am only expert in managing the cable when it supports my feet. But I have never been able to perform the feat of dancing on nothing and holding on by my neck."

"General Bacon," said Hansford, stepping forward, "I am willing to execute your mission to the Governor."

"My dear boy," said Bacon, grasping him warmly by the hand, "forgive me for speaking so roughly to you just now, I am almost ready to cut my tongue out of my head for having said anything to wound your feelings. But damn that old treacherous fox, he inflamed me so, that I must have let out some of my bad humour or choked in retaining it."

Hansford returned his grasp warmly, perhaps the more ready to forgive and forget, as he saw a prospect of attaining his object in protecting the family of his friend from harm.

"But you shall not go," continued Bacon. "It were madness to venture within the clutch of the infuriated old madman."

"Whatever were the danger," said Hansford, "this was my proposition, and on me devolves the peril, if peril there be in its execution. But there is really none. Colonel Temple, although a bigot in his loyalty, is the last person to violate the rites of hospitality or to despise a flag of truce. And Sir William Berkeley dare not disregard either whilst under his roof."

"Well, so let it be then," said Bacon, "but I fear that you place too much reliance on the good faith of your old friend Temple. Believe me, that these Tories hold a doctrine in their political creed, very much akin to the Papal doctrine of intolerance. 'Faith towards heretics, is infidelity to religion.' But you must at least take some force with you."

"I believe not," returned our hero, "the presence of an armed force would be an insuperable barrier to a reconciliation. I will only take my subaltern, Berkenhead, yonder, and that poor old negro, in whose liberation I sincerely rejoice. The first will be a companion, and in case of danger some protection; and the last, if you choose," he added smiling, "will be a make-peace between the political papist and the rebel heretic."

"Well, God bless you, Hansford," said Bacon, with much warmth, "and above all, forget my haste and unkindness just now. We must learn to forgive like old Romans, if we would be valiant like them, and so

'When I am over-earnest with you, Hansford,
You'll think old Berkeley chides, and leave me so.'"

"With all my heart, my noble General," returned Hansford, laughing, "and now for my mission—what shall I say on behalf of treason to his royal highness?"

"Tell him," said Bacon, gravely, "that Nathaniel Bacon, by the grace of God, and the special trust and confidence of Sir William Berkeley, general-in-chief of the armies of Virginia, desires to know for what act of his, since such trust was reposed in him, he and his followers have been proclaimed as traitors to their king. Ask him for what reason it is that while pursuing the common enemies of the country—while attacking in their lairs the wolves and lions of the forest, I, myself, am mercilessly assaulted like a savage wild beast, by those whom it is my object to defend. Tell him that I require him to retract the proclamation he has issued without loss of time, and in the event of his refusal, I am ready to assert and defend the rights of freemen by the last arbiter between man and man. Lastly, say to him, that I will await his answer until two days from this time, and should it still prove unfavourable to my demands, then woe betide him."

Charged with the purport of his mission, Hansford shook Bacon cordially by the hand, and proceeded to prepare for his journey. As he was going to inform his comrade, old Lawrence gently tapped him on the shoulder, and whispered, "Look ye, Tom, I like not the appearance of that fellow Berkenhead."

"He is faithful, I believe," said Hansford, in the same tone; "a little rough and free spoken, perhaps, but I do not doubt his fidelity."

"I would I were of the same mind," returned his companion; "but if ever the devil set his mark upon a man's face that he might know him on the resurrection morning, he did so on that crop-eared Puritan. Tell me, aint he the same fellow that got his freedom and two hundred pounds for revealing the insurrection of sixty-two?"

"The same, I believe," said Hansford, carelessly; "but what of that?"

"Why simply this," said the honest old cavalier, "that faith is like a walking-cane. Break it once and you may glue it so that the fracture can scarcely be seen by the naked eye; but it will break in the same place if there be a strain upon it."

"I hope you are mistaken," said Hansford; "but I thank you for your warning, and will not disregard it. I will be on my guard."

"Here, Lawrence," cried Bacon, "what private message are you sending to the Governor, that you must needs be delaying our ambassador? We have a sad duty to perform. These brave men, who have fallen in our cause, must not be suffered to lie a prey to vultures. Let them be buried as becomes brave soldiers, who have died right bravely with their harness on. I would there were some one here who could perform the rites of burial—but their requiem shall be sung with our song of triumph. Peace to their souls! Comrades, prepare their grave, and pay due honour to their memory by discharging a volley of musketry over them. I wot they well loved the sound while living—nor will they sleep less sweetly for it now."

By such language, and such real or affected interest in the fate of those who followed his career, Nathaniel Bacon won the affection of his soldiery. Never was there a leader, even in the larger theatres of action, more sincerely beloved and worshipped—and to this may be attributed in a great degree the wonderful power which he possessed over the minds of his followers—moulding their opinions in strict conformity with his own; breathing into them something of the ardent heroism which inspired his own soul, and making them thus the willing and subservient instruments of his own ambitious designs.

With sad countenances the soldiers proceeded to obey the order of their general. Scooping with their swords and bayonets a shallow grave in the soft virgin soil of the forest, they committed the bodies of their comrades to the ground, earth to earth, ashes to ashes, dust to dust—and as they screened their ashes forever from the light of day, the "aisles of the dim woods" echoed back the loud roar of the unheard, unheeded honour which they paid to the memory of the dead.

FOOTNOTES:

[38] He was in truth a rope-dancer in his early life.

CHAPTER XXVI

"But the poor dog, in life the dearest friend,
The first to welcome, foremost to defend,
Whose honest heart is still his master's own;
Who labours, fights, lives, breathes for him alone,
Unhonoured falls, unnoticed all his worth,
Denied in heaven the soul he had on earth."

Byron.

When the last sad rites of burial had been performed over the grave of those who had fallen, Hansford, accompanied by Berkenhead and old Giles, proceeded to the discharge of the trust which had been reposed in him. It was indeed a mission fraught with the most important consequences to the cause of the insurgents, to the family at Windsor Hall, and to himself personally. It required both a cool head and a brave heart to succeed in its execution. Hansford well knew that the first burst of rage from the old Governor, on hearing the bold proposition of the rebels, would be dangerous, if not fatal to himself; and with all the native boldness of his character, it would be unnatural if he failed to feel the greatest anxiety for the result. But even if *he* escaped the vengeance of Berkeley, he feared the impulsive nature of Bacon, in the event of the refusal of Sir William to comply with his demands, would drive him into excesses ruinous to his cause, and dangerous alike to the innocent and the guilty. If Temple's obstinacy and chivalry persisted in giving refuge to the Governor, what, he thought, might be the consequences to her, whose interest and whose safety he held so deeply at heart! Thus the statesman, the lover, and the individual, each had a peculiar interest in the result, and Hansford felt like a wise man the heavy responsibility he had incurred, although he resolved to encounter and discharge it like a bold one.

It was thus, with a heavy heart that he proceeded on his way, and buried in these reflections he maintained a moody silence, little regarding the presence of his two companions. Old Giles, too, had his own food for reflection, and vouchsafed only monosyllables in reply to the questions and observations of the loquacious Berkenhead. But the soldier was not to be repulsed by the indifference of the one, or the laconic answers of the other of his companions. Finding it impossible to engage in conversation, he contented himself with soliloquy, and in a low, muttering voice, as if to himself, but intended as well for the ears of his commander, he began an elaborate comparison of the army of Cromwell, in which he had served, and the army of the Virginia insurgents.

"To be sure, they both fought for liberty, but after that there is monstrous little likeness between 'em. Old Noll was always acting himself, and laying it all to Providence when he was done; while General Bacon, cavorting round, first after the Indians and then after the Governor, seems hardly to know what he is about, and yet, I believe, trusts in Providence at last more than Noll, with all his religion; and, faith, it seems to me it took more religion to do him than most any man I ever see. First psalm singing, and then fighting, and then psalm singing agen, and then more fighting—for all the world like a brick house with mortar stuck between. But I trow that it was the fighting that made the house stand, after all. And yet I believe, for all the saints used to nickname me a sinner, and call me one of the spawn of the beast, because I would get tired of the Word sometimes—and, by the same token, old brother Purge-the-temple Whithead had a whole dictionary of words, much less the one—yet, for all come and gone, I believe I would rather hear a long psalm, than to be doomed to solitary confinement to my own thoughts, as I am here."

"And so you have served in old Noll's army, as you call it," said Hansford, smiling in spite of himself, and willing to indulge the old Oliverian with some little notice.

"Oh, yes, Major," replied Berkenhead, delighted to have gained an auditor at last; "and a rare service it was too. A little too much of what they called the church militant, and the like, for me; but for all that the fellows fought like devils, if they did live like saints—and, what was rare to me, they did not deal the less lightly with their swords for the fervour of their prayers, nor pray the less fervently for their enemies after they had raked them with their fire, or hacked them to pieces with their swords. 'Faith, an if there had been many more battles like Dunbar and Worcester, they had as well have blotted that text from their Bible, for precious few enemies did they have to pray for after that."

"You did not agree with these zealots in religion, then," said Hansford. "Prythee, friend, of what sect of Christians are you a member?"

"Well, Major, to speak the truth and shame the devil, as they say, my religion has pretty much gone with my sword. As a soldier must change his coat whenever he changes his service, so I have thought he should make his faith—the robe of his righteousness, as they call it—adapt itself to that of his employer."

"The cloak of his hypocrisy, you mean," said Hansford, indignantly. "I like not this scoffing profanity, and must hear no more of it. He who is not true to his God is of a bad material for a patriot. But tell me," he added, seeing that the man seemed sufficiently rebuked, "how came you to this colony?"

"Simply because I could not stay in England," replied Berkenhead. "Mine has been a hard lot, Major; for I never got what I wanted in this life. If I was predestined for anything, as old Purge-the-temple used to say we all were, it seems to me it was to be always on the losing side. When I fought for freedom in England, I gained bondage in Virginia for my pains; and when I refused to seek my freedom, and betrayed my comrades in the insurrection of sixty-two, lo, and behold! I was released from bondage for my reward. What I will gain or lose by this present movement, I don't know; but I have been an unlucky adventurer thus far."

"I have heard of your behaviour in sixty-two," said Hansford, "but whether such conduct be laudable or censurable, depends very much upon the motive that prompted you to it. You came to this country then as an indented servant?"

"Yes, sold, your honour, for the thirty pieces of silver, like Joseph was sold into Egypt by his brethren."

"I suspect that the resemblance between yourself and that eminent patriarch ceased with the sale."

"It is not for me to say, your honour. But in the present unsettled state of affairs, who knows who may be made second only to Pharaoh over all Egypt? I wot well who will be our Pharaoh, if we gain our point; and I have done the state some service, and may yet do her more."

"By treachery to your comrades, I suppose," said Hansford, disgusted with the conceit and self-complacency of the man.

"Now, look ye here, Major, if I was disposed to be touchy, I might take exception at that remark. But I have seen too much of life to fly off at the first word. The axe that flies from the helve at the first stroke, may be sharp as a grindstone can make it, but it will never cut a tree down for all that."

"And if you were to fly off, as you call it, at the first or the last word," said Hansford, haughtily, "you would only get a sound beating for your pains. How dare you speak thus to your superior, you insolent knave!"

"No insolence, Major," said Berkenhead, sulkily; "but for the matter of speaking against your honour, I have seen my betters silenced in their turn, by their superiors."

"Silence, slave!" cried Hansford, his face flushing with indignation at this allusion to his interview with Bacon, which he had hoped, till now, had been unheard by the soldiers. "But come," he added, reflecting on the imprudence of losing his only friend and ally in this perilous adventure, "you are a saucy knave, but I suppose I must e'en bear with you for the present. We cannot be far from Windsor Hall, I should think."

"About two miles, as I take it, Major," said Berkenhead, in a more respectful manner. "I used to live in Gloucester, not far from the hall, and many is the time I have followed my master through these old woods in a deer chase. Yes, there is Manteo's clearing, just two miles from the hall."

Scarcely were the words out of the speaker's mouth, when, to the surprise of the little party, a large dog of the St. Bernard's breed leaped from a thicket near them, and bounded towards Hansford.

"Brest ef it a'ant old Nestor," said Giles, whose tongue had at length been loosened by the sight of the family favourite, and he stooped down as he spoke to pat the dog upon the head. But Nestor's object was clearly not to be caressed. Frisking about in a most extraordinary manner, now wagging his tail, now holding it between his legs, now bounding a few steps in front of Hansford's horse, and anon crouching by his side and whining most piteously, he at length completed his eccentric movements by standing erect upon his hind legs and placing his fore feet against the breast of his old master. Struck with this singular conduct, Hansford, reining in his horse, cried out, "The poor dog must be mad. Down, Nestor, down I tell you!"

Well was it for our hero that the faithful animal refused to obey, for just at that moment an arrow was heard whizzing through the air, and the noble dog fell transfixed through the neck with the poisoned missile, which else had pierced Hansford's heart.[39] The alarm caused by so sudden and unexpected an attack had not passed off, before another arrow was buried deep in our hero's shoulder. But quick as were the movements of the attacking party, the trained eye of Berkenhead caught a glimpse of the tall form of an Indian as it vanished behind a large oak tree, about twenty yards from where they stood. The soldier levelled his carbine, and as Manteo (for the reader has probably already conjectured that it was he) again emerged from his hiding place to renew the attack, he discharged his piece with deadly aim and effect. With a wild yell of horror, the young warrior sprang high in the air, and fell lifeless to the ground.

Berkenhead was about to rush forward towards his victim, when Hansford, who still retained his seat on the horse, though faint from pain and loss of blood, cried out, "Caution, caution, for God's sake, there are more of the bloody villains about." But after a few moments' pause, the apprehension of a further attack passed away, and the soldier and Giles repaired to the spot. And there in the cold embrace of death, lay the brave young Indian, his painted visage reddened yet more by the life-blood which still flowed from his wound. His right hand still grasped the bow-string, as in his last effort to discharge the fatal arrow. A haughty smile curled his lip even in the moment in which the soul had fled, as if in that last struggle his brave young heart despised the pang of death itself.

Gazing at him for a moment, yet long enough for old Giles to recognize the features of Manteo in the bloody corpse, they returned to Hansford, whose condition indeed required their immediate assistance. Drawing out the arrow, and staunching the blood as well as they could with his scarf, Berkenhead bandaged it tightly, and although still in great pain, the wounded man was enabled slowly to continue his journey. A ride of about half an hour brought the little party to the door of Windsor Hall.

FOOTNOTES:

[39] An incident somewhat similar to this is on record as having actually occurred.

CHAPTER XXVII

"I'll tell thee truth—
Too oft a stranger to the royal ear,
But far more wholesome than the honeyed lies
That fawning flatterers offer."
Any Port in a Storm.

Brief as was the time which had elapsed, the old hall presented a different appearance to Hansford, from that which it maintained when he last left it under such disheartening circumstances. The notable mistress of the mansion had spared no pains to prepare for the reception of her honoured guest; and, although she took occasion to complain to her good husband of his inconsiderate conduct, in foisting all these strangers upon her at once, yet she inwardly rejoiced at the opportunity it presented for a display of her admirable housewifery. Indeed, the ease-loving old Colonel almost repented of his hospitality, amid the bustle and hurry, the scolding of servants, and the general bad humour which were all necessary incidents to the good dame's preparation. Having finally "brought things to something like rights," as she expressed it, her next care was to provide for the entertainment of her distinguished guest, which to the mind of the benevolent old lady, consisted not in sparkling conversation, or sage counsels, (then, alas! much needed by the Governor,) but in spreading a table loaded with a superabundance of delicacies to tempt his palate, and cause him to forget his troubles. It was a favourite saying of hers, caught up most probably in her early life, during the civil war in England, that if the stomach was well garrisoned with food, the heart would never capitulate to sorrow.

But the truth of this apothegm was not sustained in the present instance. Her hospitable efforts, even when united with the genial good humour and kindness of her husband were utterly unavailing to dispel the gloom which hung over the inmates of Windsor Hall. Sir William Berkeley was himself dejected and sad, and communicated his own dejection to all around him. Indeed, since his arrival at the Hall, he had found good reason to repent his haste in denouncing the popular and gifted young insurgent. The pledge made by Colonel Temple of the loyalty of the people of Gloucester, had not been redeemed—at least so far as an active support of the Governor was concerned. Berkeley's reception by them was cold and unpromising. The enthusiasm which he had hoped to inspire no where prevailed, and the old man felt himself deserted by those whose zealous co-operation he had been led to anticipate. It was true that they asserted in the strongest terms their professions of loyal devotion, and their willingness to quell the first symptoms of rebellion, but they failed to see anything in the conduct of Bacon to justify the harsh measures of Berkeley towards him and his followers. "Lip-service—lip-service," said the old Governor, sorrowfully, as their decision was communicated to him, "they draw near to me with their mouth, and honour me with their lips, but their heart is far from me." But, notwithstanding his disappointment, nothing could shake the proud spirit of Berkeley in his inflexible resolution, to resist any encroachments on his prerogative; and, so providing his few followers with arms from the adjacent fort on York River, he prepared to maintain his power and his dignity by the sword.

Such was the state of things on the evening that Thomas Hansford and his companions arrived at Windsor Hall. The intelligence of their arrival created much excitement, and the inmates of the mansion differed greatly in their opinions as to the intention of the young rebel. Poor Mrs. Temple, in whose mind fear always predominated over every other feeling, felt assured that Hansford had come, attended by another "ruffian," forcibly to abduct Virginia from her home—and a violent fit of hysterics was the result of her suspicions. Virginia herself, vacillating between hope and fear, trusted, in the simplicity of her young, girlish heart, that her lover had repented of his grievous error, and had come to claim her love, and to sue to the Governor for pardon. Sir William Berkeley saw in the mission of Hansford, a faint hope that the rebels, alarmed by his late proclamation, had determined to return to their allegiance, and that Hansford was the bearer of a proposition to this effect, imploring at the same time the clemency and pardon of the government, against which they had so grievously offended.

"And they shall receive mercy, too, at my hands, "said the old knight, as a tear glistened in his eye. "They have learned to fear the power of the government, and to respect its justice, and they shall now learn to love its merciful clemency. God forbid, that I should chasten my repenting people, except as children, for their good."

"Not so fast, my honoured Governor," said Philip Ludwell, who, with the other attendants of Berkeley, had gathered around him in the porch; "you may be mistaken in your opinion. I believe—I know—that your wish is father to the thought in this matter. But look at the resolution and determined bearing of that young man. Is his the face or the bearing of a suppliant?"

Ludwell was right. The noble countenance of Hansford, always expressive, though sufficiently respectful to the presence which he was about to enter, indicated any thing rather than tame submission. His face was very pale, and his lip quivered for a moment as he approached the anxious crowd of loyalists, who remained standing in the porch, but it was at once firmly compressed by the strength of resolution. As he advanced, he raised his hat and profoundly saluted the Governor, and then drawing himself up to his full height, he stood silently awaiting some one to speak. Colonel Temple halted a moment between his natural kindness for his friend and his respect for the presence of Sir William Berkeley. The first feeling prompted him to rush up to Hansford, and greeting him as of old, to give him a cordial welcome to the hall—but the latter feeling prevailed. Without advancing, then, he said in a tone, in which assumed displeasure strove in vain to overcome his native benevolence—

"To what cause am I to attribute this unexpected visit of Mr. Hansford?"

"My business is with Sir William Berkeley," replied Hansford, respectfully, "and I presume I am not mistaken in supposing that I am now in his presence."

"And what would you have from me young man," said Berkeley, coldly; "your late career has estranged you and some of your friends so entirely from their Governor, that I feel much honoured by this evidence of your returning affection."

"Both I and my friends, as far as I may speak for them," returned Hansford, in the same calm tone, "have ever been ready and anxious to show our devotion to our country and its rulers, and our present career to which your excellency has been pleased to allude, is in confirmation of the fact. That we have unwittingly fallen under your displeasure, sir, I am painfully aware. To ascertain the cause of that displeasure is my reason for this intrusion."

"The cause, young man," said Berkeley, "is to be found in your own conduct, for which, may I hope, you have come for pardon?"

"I regret to say that you are mistaken in your conjecture," replied Hansford. "As it is impossible that our conduct could have invoked your displeasure, so it is equally impossible that we should sue for pardon for an offence which we have never committed."

"And, prithee, what then is your worshipful pleasure, fair sir," said Berkeley, ironically; "perhaps, in the abundance of your mercy, you have come to grant pardon, if you do not desire it. Nay!" he exclaimed, seeing Hansford shake his head; "then, peradventure, you would ask me to abdicate my government in favour of young Cromwell. I beg pardon— young Bacon, I should say—the similarity of their views is so striking, that as my memory is but a poor one, I sometimes confound their names. Well! any thing in reason. Nay, again!—well then, I am at a loss to conjecture, and you must yourself explain the object of your visit."

"I would fain convey my instructions to Sir William Berkeley's private ear," said Hansford, unmoved by the irony of the old knight.

"Oh pardon me, fair sir," said Berkeley; "yet, in this I *must* crave your pardon, indeed. A sovereign would never wittingly trust himself alone with a rebel, and neither will I, though only an obscure colonial Governor. There are none but loyal ears here, and I trust Mr. Hansford has no tidings which can offend them."

"I am sure," said Hansford, in reply, "that Sir William Berkeley does not for a moment suspect that I desired to see him in private from any sinister or treasonable motive."

"I know, sir," said Berkeley, angrily, "that you have proved yourself a traitor, and, therefore, I have the best reason for suspecting you of treasonable designs. But I have no time—no disposition to dally with you thus. Tell me, what new treason, that my old ears are yet strangers to, I am yet doomed to hear?"

"My instructions are soon told," said Hansford, repressing his indignation. "General Nathaniel Bacon, by virtue of your own commission, Commander-in-chief of the forces of Virginia, desires to know, and has directed me to inquire, for what cause you have issued a proclamation declaring both him and his followers traitors to their country and king?"

Berkeley stood the shock much better than Hansford expected. His face flushed for a moment, but only for a moment, as he replied,—

"This is certainly an unusual demand of a rebel; but sir, as I have nothing to fear from an exposure of my reasons, I will reply, that Nathaniel Bacon is now in arms against the government of Virginia."

"Not unless the government of Virginia be allied with the Indians, against whom he is marching," said Hansford, calmly.

"Aye, but it is well known," returned Berkeley, "that he has covert views of his own to attain, under pretext of this expedition against the Indians."

"Why, then," replied Hansford, "if they are covert from his own followers, proclaim them traitors with himself; or, if covert from the government, how can you ascertain that they are treasonable? But, above all, if you suspected such traitorous designs, why, by your commission, elevate him to a position in which he may be able to execute them with success?"

"'Fore God, gentlemen, this is the most barefaced insolence that I have ever heard. For yourself, young man, out of your own mouth will I judge you, and convict you of treason; and for your preceptor—whose lessons, I doubt not, you repeat by rote—you may tell him that his commission is null and void, because obtained by force and arms."

"I had not expected to hear Sir William Berkeley make such an acknowledgment," returned Hansford, undauntedly. "You yourself declared that the commission was not given from fear of threats; and even if this were not so, the argument would scarce avail—for on what compulsion was it that your signature appears in a letter to his majesty, warmly approving the conduct of General Bacon, and commending him for his zeal, talents and patriotism?"[40]

"Now, by my knighthood," said Berkeley, stung by this last unanswerable argument, "I will not be bearded thus by an insolent, braggart boy. Seize him!" he cried, turning to Bernard and Ludwell, who stood nearest him. "He is my prisoner, and as an example to his vile confederates, he shall hang in half an hour, until his traitorous tongue has stopped its vile wagging."

Hansford made no attempt to escape, but, as the two men approached to disarm and bind him, he fixed his fine blue eyes full upon Colonel Temple, and said, mildly,

"Shall this be so? Though Sir William Berkeley should fail to respect my position, as the bearer of a peaceable message from General Bacon, I trust that the rites of hospitality may not be violated, even in my humble person."

Colonel Temple was much embarrassed. Notwithstanding the recent conduct of Hansford had alienated him to a great degree, he still entertained a strong affection for his boy—nor could he willingly see him suffer a wrong when he had thus so confidingly trusted to his generosity. But, apart from his special interest in Hansford, the old Virginian had a religious regard for the sacred character of a guest, which he could never forget. And yet, his blind reverence for authority—the bigoted loyalty which has always made the English people so cautious in resistance to oppression, and which retarded indeed our own colonial revolution—made him unwilling to oppose his character of host to the authority of the Governor. He looked first at Sir William Berkeley, and his resolution was made; he turned to Hansford, and as he saw his noble boy standing resolutely there, without a friend to aid him, it wavered. The poor old gentleman was sadly perplexed, but, after a brief struggle, his true, generous heart conquered, and he said, turning to Sir William:

"My honoured sir, I trust you will not let this matter proceed any further here. My house, my life, my all, is at the service of the king and of his representative; but I question how far we are warranted in proceeding to extremities with this youth, seeing that although he is rather froward and pert in his manners, he may yet mean well after all."

"Experience should have taught me," replied Berkeley, coldly, for his evil genius was now thoroughly aroused, "not to place too much confidence in the loyalty of the people of Gloucester. If Colonel Temple's resolution to aid the crumbling power of the government has wavered at the sight of a malapert and rebellious boy, I had better relieve him of my presence, which must needs have become irksome to him."

"Nay, Sir William," returned Temple, reddening at the imputation, "you shall not take my language thus. Let the youth speak for himself; if he breathes a word of treason, his blood be on his own head—my hand nor voice shall be raised to save him. But I am unable to construe any thing which he has yet said as treasonable." Then turning to Hansford, he added, "speak, Mr. Hansford, plainly and frankly. What was your object in thus coming? Were you sent by General Bacon, or did you come voluntarily?"

"Both," replied Hansford, with a full appreciation of the old man's unfortunate position. "It was my proposition that some officer of the army should wait upon the Governor, and ascertain the truth of his rumoured proclamation. I volunteered to discharge the duty in person."

"And in the event of your finding it to be true," said Berkeley, haughtily, "what course did you then intend to pursue?"

This was a dangerous question; for Hansford knew that to express the design of the insurgents in such an event, would be little less than a confession of treason. But he had a bold heart, and without hesitation, but still maintaining his respectful manner, he replied,—

"I might evade an answer to your question, by saying, that it would then be time enough to consider and determine our course. But I scorn to do so, even when my safety is endangered. I answer candidly then, that in such an event the worst consequences to the country and to yourself would ensue. It was to prevent these consequences, and as far as I could to intercede in restoring peace and quiet to our distracted colony, that I came to implore you to withdraw this proclamation. Otherwise, sir, the sword of the avenger is behind you, and within two days from this time you will be compelled once more to yield to a current that you cannot resist. Comply with my request, and peace and harmony will once more prevail; refuse, and let who will triumph, the unhappy colony will be involved in all the horrors of civil war."

There was nothing boastful in the manner of Hansford, as he uttered these words. On the contrary, his whole bearing, while it showed inflexible determination, attested his sincerity in the wish that the Governor, for the good of the country, would yield to the suggestion. Nor did Sir William Berkeley, in spite of his indignation, fail to see the force and wisdom of the views presented; but he had too much pride to acknowledge it to an inferior.

"Now, by my troth," he cried, "if this be not treason, I am at a loss to define the term. I should think this would satisfy even your scepticism, Colonel Temple; for it seems we must consult you in regard to our course while under your roof. You would scarcely consent, I trust, to a self-convicted traitor going at large."

"Of course you act in the premises, according to your own judgment," replied Temple, coldly, for he was justly offended at the overbearing manner of the incensed old Governor, "but since you have appealed to me for my opinion, I will e'en make bold to say, that as this young man came in the character of an intercessor, you might well be satisfied with his parole. I will myself be surety for his truth."

"Parole, forsooth, and do you not think I have had enough of paroles from these rebel scoundrels—zounds, their faith is like an egg-shell, it is made to be broken."

"With my sincere thanks to my noble friend," said Hansford, "for his obliging offer, I would not accept it if I could. Unconscious of having done any thing to warrant this detention, I am not willing to acknowledge its justice, by submitting to a qualified imprisonment."

"It is well," said Berkeley, haughtily; "we will see whether your pride is proof against an ignominious death. Disarm him and hold him in close custody until my farther pleasure shall be known."

As he said this, Hansford was disarmed, and led away under a strong guard to the apartment which Colonel Temple reluctantly designated as the place of his confinement.

Meantime Berkenhead had remained at the gate, guarded by two of the soldiers of the Governor; while old Giles, with a light heart, had found his way back to his old stand by the kitchen door, and was detailing to his astonished cronies the unlucky ventures, and the providential deliverance, which he had experienced. But we must forbear entering into a detailed account of the old man's sermon, merely contenting ourselves with announcing, that such was the effect produced, that at the next baptizing day, old Elder Snivel was refreshed by a perfect pentecost of converts, who attributed their "new birf" to the wrestling of "brudder Giles."

We return to Berkenhead, who, at the command of Col. Ludwell, was escorted, under the guard before mentioned, into the presence of Sir William Berkeley. The dogged and insolent demeanour of the man was even more displeasing to the Governor than the quiet and resolute manner of Hansford, and in a loud, threatening voice, he cried,

"Here comes another hemp-pulling knave. 'Fore God, the colony will have to give up the cultivation of tobacco, and engage in raising hemp, for we are like to have some demand for it. Hark ye, sir knave—do you know the nature of the message which you have aided in bearing from the traitor Bacon to myself?"

"Not I, your honour—no more than my carbine knows whether it is loaded or not. It's little the General takes an old soldier like me into his counsels; but I only know it is my duty to obey, if I were sent to the devil with a message," and the villain looked archly at the Governor.

"Your language is something of the most insolent," said Sir William. "But tell me instantly, did you have no conversation with Major Hansford on your way hither, and if so, what was it?"

"Little else than abuse, your honour," returned Berkenhead, "and a threat that I would be beat over the head if I didn't hold my tongue; and as I didn't care to converse at such a disadvantage, I was e'en content to keep my own counsel for the rest of the way."

"Do you, or do you not, consider Bacon and his followers to be engaged in rebellion against the government?"

"Rebellion, your honour!" cried the renegade. "Why, was it not your honour's self that sent us after these salvages? An' I thought there was any other design afloat, I would soon show them who was the rebel. It is not the first time that I have done the State some service by betraying treason."

"Look ye," said the Governor, eyeing the fellow keenly, "if I mistake not, you are an old acquaintance. Is your name Berkenhead?"

"The same, at your honour's service."

"And didn't you betray the servile plot of 1662, and get your liberty and a reward for it?"

"Yes, your honour, but I wouldn't have you think that it was for the reward I did it?"

"Oh, never mind your motives. If you are Judas, you are welcome to your thirty pieces of silver," said the Governor, with a sneer of contempt. "But to make the analogy complete, you should be hanged for your service."

"No, faith," said the shrewd villain, quickly. "Judas hanged himself, and it would be long ere ever I sought the apostle's elder tree.[41] And besides, his was the price of innocent blood, and mine was not. Look at my hand, your honour, and you will see what kind of blood I shed."

Berkeley looked at the fellow's hand, and saw it stained with the crimson life-blood of the young Indian. With a thrill of horror, he cried, "What blood is that, you infernal villain?"

"Only fresh from the veins of one of these painted red-skins," returned Berkenhead. "And red enough he was when I left him; but, forsooth, he reckons that the paint cost him full dear. He left his mark on Major Hansford, though, before he left."

"Where did this happen?" said Berkeley, astonished.

"Oh, not far from here. The red devil was a friend at the hall here, too, or as much so as their bloody hearts will let any of them be. Colonel Temple, there, knows him, and I have seen him when I lived in Gloucester. A fine looking fellow, too; and if his skin and his heart had been both white, there would have been few better and braver dare-devils than young Manteo."

As he pronounced the name, a wild shriek rent the air, and the distracted Mamalis rushed into the porch. Her long hair was all dishevelled and flying loosely over her shoulders, her eye was that of a maniac in his fury, and tossing her bare arms aloft, she shrieked, in a wild, harsh voice,

"And who are you, that dare to spill the blood of kings? Look to it that your own flows not less freely in your veins."

Berkenhead turned pale with fright, and shrinking from the enraged girl, muttered, "the devil!"—while Temple, in a low voice, whispered to the Governor the necessary explanation, "She is his sister."

"Yes, his sister!" cried the girl, wildly, for she had overheard the words. "His only sister!—and my blood now flows in no veins but my own. But the stream runs more fiercely as the channel is more narrow. Look to it—look to it!" And, with another wild shriek, the maddened girl rushed again into the house. It required all the tender care of Virginia Temple to pacify the poor creature. She reasoned, she prayed, she endeavoured to console her; but her reasons, her prayers, her sweet words of consolation, were all lost upon the heart of the Indian maiden, who nourished but one fearful, fatal idea—revenge!

FOOTNOTES:

[40] This was indeed true, and renders the conduct of Berkeley entirely inexplicable.

[41] The name given to the tree on which Judas hanged himself.

CHAPTER XXVIII

"His flight was madness."
        Macbeth.

Yes, Virginia! She who had so much reason for consolation herself, forgot her own sorrows for the time, in administering the oil of consolation to the poor, wounded, broken-hearted savage girl. She had been sitting at the window of the little parlour, where she could witness the whole scene, and hear the whole interview between the Governor and Hansford; and oh! how her heart had sunk within her as she heard the harsh sentence of the stern old knight, which condemned her noble, friendless lover to imprisonment, perhaps to death; and yet, a maiden modesty restrained her from yielding to the impulse of the moment, to throw herself at the feet of Berkeley, confess her love, and implore his pardon. Alas! ill-fated maiden, it would have been in vain—as she too truly, too fatally discovered afterwards.

The extraordinary appearance and conduct of Mamalis broke up for the present any further conference with Berkenhead, who—his mendacity having established his innocence in the minds of the loyalists—walked off with a swaggering gait, rather elated than otherwise with the result of his interview. Alfred Bernard followed him until they turned an angle of the house, and stood beneath the shade of one of the broad oaks, which spread its protecting branches over the yard.

Meantime the Governor, with such of his council as had attended him to Windsor Hall, retired to the study of the old Colonel, which had been fitted up both for the chamber of his most distinguished guest and for the deliberations of the council. The subject which now engaged their attention was one of more importance than any that had ever come before them since the commencement of the dissensions in Virginia. The mission of Hansford, while it had failed of producing the effect which he so ardently desired, had, notwithstanding, made a strong impression upon the mind of the Governor. He saw too plainly that it would be vain to resist the attack of Bacon, at the head of five hundred men, among whom were to be ranked the very chivalry of Virginia; while his own force consisted merely of his faithful adherents in the council, and about fifty mercenary troops, whose sympathies with the insurgents were strongly suspected.

"I see," said the old man, gloomily, as he took his seat at the council-board, "that I must seek some other refuge. I am hunted like a wild beast from place to place, through a country that was once my own, and by those who were once the loving subjects of my king."

"Remain here!" said the impulsive old Temple. "The people of Gloucester will yet rally around your standard, when they see open treason is contemplated; and should they still refuse, zounds, we may yet offer resistance with my servants and slaves."

"My dear friend," said Berkeley, sorrowfully, "if all Virginians were like yourself, there would have been no rebellion—there would have been no difficulty in suppressing one, if attempted. But alas! the loyalty of the people of Gloucester has already been weighed in the balance and found wanting. No, I have acted hastily, foolishly, blindly. I have warmed this serpent into life by my forbearance and indulgence, and must at last be the victim of its venom and my folly. Oh! that I had refused the commission, which armed this traitor with legal power. I have put a sword into the hands of an enemy, and may be the first to fall by it."

"It is useless to repine over the past," said Philip Ludwell, kindly; "but the power of these rebels cannot last long. The people who are loyal at heart will fall from their support, and military aid will be received from England ere long. Then the warmed reptile may be crushed."

"To my mind," said Ballard, "it were better to repair the evil that has been done by retracing our steps, rather than to proceed further. When a man is over his depth, he had better return to the shore than to attempt to cross the unfathomable stream."

"Refrain from enigmas, if you please," said Berkeley, coldly, "and tell me to what you refer."

"Simply," replied Ballard, firmly, "that all this evil has resulted from your following the jesuitical counsel of a boy, rather than the prudent caution of your advisers. My honoured sir, forgive me if I say it is now your duty to acquiesce in the request of Major Hansford, and withdraw your proclamation."

"And succumb to traitors!" cried Berkeley. "Never while God gives me breath to reiterate it. He who would treat with a traitor, is himself but little better than a traitor."

The flush which mounted to the brow of Ballard attested his indignation at this grave charge; but before he had time to utter the retort which rose to his lips, Berkeley added,

"Forgive me, Ballard, for my haste. But the bare idea of making terms with these audacious rebels roused my very blood. No, no! I can die in defence of my trust, but I cannot, will not yield it."

"But it is not yielding," said Ballard.

"Nay—no more of that," interrupted Berkeley; "let us devise some other means. I have it," he added, after a pause. "Accomac is still true to my interest, and divided from the mainland by the bay, is difficult of access. There will I pitch my tent, and sound my defiance—and when aid shall come from England, these proud and insolent traitors shall feel the power of my vengeance the more for this insult to my weakness."

This scheme met with the approbation of all present, with the exception of old Ballard, who shook his head, and muttered, that he hoped it might all be for the best. And so it was determined that early the next morning the loyal refugees should embark on board a vessel then lying off Tindal's Point, and sail for Accomac.

"And we will celebrate our departure by hanging up that young rogue, Hansford, in half an hour," said Berkeley.

"By what law, may it please your excellency?" asked Ballard, surprised at this threat.

"By martial law."

"And for what offence?"

"Why zounds, Ballard, you have turned advocate-general for all the rebels in the country," said Berkeley, petulantly.

"No, Sir William, I am advocating the cause of justice and of my king."

"Well, sir, what would you advise? To set the rogue at liberty, I suppose, and by our leniency to encourage treason."

"By no means," said Ballard. "But either to commit him to custody until he may be fairly tried by a jury of his peers, or to take him with you to Accomac, where, by further developments of this insurrection, you may better judge of the nature of his offence."

"And a hospitable reception would await me in Accomac, forsooth, if I appeared there with a prisoner of war, whom I did not have the firmness to punish as his crime deserves. No, by heaven! I will not be encumbered with prisoners. His life is forfeit to the law, and as he would prove an apostle of liberty, let him be a martyr to his cause."

"Let me add my earnest intercession to that of Colonel Ballard," said Temple, "in behalf of this unhappy man. I surely have some claim upon your benevolence, and I ask his life as a personal boon to me."

"Oh, assuredly, since you rely upon your hospitable protection to us, you should have your fee," said Berkeley, with a sneer. "But not in so precious a coin as a rebel's life. If you have suffered by the protection afforded to the deputy of your king, you shall not lack remuneration. But the coin shall be the head of Carolus II.;[42] this rebel's head I claim as my own."

"Now, by heaven!" returned Temple, thoroughly aroused, "it requires all my loyalty to stomach so foul an insult. My royal master's exchequer could illy remunerate me for the gross language heaped upon me by his deputy. But let this pass. You are my guest, sir; and that I cannot separate the Governor from the man, I am prevented from resenting an insult, which else I could but little brook."

"As you please, mine host," replied Berkeley. "But, in truth, I have wronged you, Temple. But think, my friend, of the pang the shepherd must feel, when he finds that he has let a wolf into his fold, which he is unable to resist. Oh, think of this, and bear with me!"

Temple knew the old Governor too well to doubt the sincerity of this retraxit, and with a cordial grasp of the hand, he assured Berkeley of his forgiveness. "And yet," he added, warmly, "I cannot forget the cause I advocate, for this first rebuff. Believe me, Sir William, you will gain nothing, but lose much, by proceeding harshly against this unhappy young man. In the absence of any evidence of his guilt, you will arouse the indignation of the colonists to such a height, that it will be difficult to pacify them."

"Pardon me, Sir William Berkeley," said Bernard, who had joined the party, "but would it not be well to examine this knave, Berkenhead, touching the movements and intentions of the insurgents, and particularly concerning any expressions which may have fallen from this young gentleman? If it shall appear that he is guiltless of the crime imputed to him, then you may safely yield to the solicitations of these gentlemen, and liberate him. But if it shall appear that he is guilty, they, in their turn, cannot object to his meeting the penalty which his treason richly deserves."

"Now, by heaven, the young man speaks truthfully and wisely," said Temple, assured, by the former interview with Berkenhead, that he knew of nothing which could convict the prisoner. "Nor do I see, Sir William, what better course you can adopt than to follow his counsel."

"Truly," said Berkeley, "the young man has proven himself the very Elihu of counsellors. 'Great men are not always wise, neither do the aged understand judgment. But there is a spirit in man, and the inspiration of the Almighty giveth them understanding.' Yet I fear, Colonel Temple, you will scarcely, after my impetuosity just now, deem me a Job for patience, though Alfred may be an Elihu for understanding. Your counsel is good, young man. Let the knave be brought hither to testify, and look ye that the prisoner be introduced to confront him. My friends, Ballard and Temple, are such sticklers for law, that we must not deviate from Magna Charta or the Petition of Right. But stay, we will postpone this matter till the morrow. I had almost forgotten it was the Sabbath. Loyal churchmen should venerate the day, even when treason is abroad in the land. Meantime, let the villain Berkenhead be kept in close custody, lest he should escape."

FOOTNOTES:

[42] The coin during the reign of Charles II.

CHAPTER XXIX

"I tell thee what, my friend,
He is a very serpent in my way."
King John.

The reader will naturally desire to know what induced the milder counsel recommended by Alfred Bernard to the Governor. If we have been successful in impressing upon the mind of the reader a just estimate of the character of the young jesuit, he will readily conjecture that it was from no kindly feeling for his rival, and no inherent love of justice that he suggested such a policy; and if he be of a different opinion, he need only go back with us to the interview between Bernard and Berkenhead, to which allusion was made in the chapter immediately preceding the last.

We have said that Alfred Bernard followed the renegade rebel until they stood together beneath a large oak tree which stood at the corner of the house. Here they stopped as if by mutual, though tacit consent, and Berkenhead turning sharply around upon his companion, said in an offended tone—"What is your further will with me sir?"

"You seem not to like your comrade Major Hansford?"

"Oh well enough," replied Berkenhead; "there are many better and many worse than him. But I don't see how the likes and the dislikes of a poor soldier can have any concernment with you."

"I assure you," said Bernard, "it is from no impertinent curiosity, but a real desire to befriend you, that I ask the question. The Governor strongly suspects your integrity, and that you are concealing from him more than it suits you to divulge. Now, I would do you a service and advise you how you may reinstate yourself in his favour."

"Well, that seems kind on the outside," said the soldier, "seeing as you seems to be one of the blooded gentry, and I am nothing but a plain Dunstable.[43] But rough iron is as soft as polished steel."

"I believe you," said Bernard. "Now you have not much reason to waste your love on this Major Hansford. He threatened to beat you, as you say, and a freeborn Englishman does not bear an insult like that with impunity."

"No, your honour," replied the man, "and I've known the day when a Plymouth cloak[44] would protect me from insult as well as a frieze coat from cold. But I am too old for that now, and so I had better swallow an insult dry, than butter it with my own marrow."

"And are there not other modes of revenge than by a blow? Where are your wits, man? What makes the man stronger than the horse that carries him? I tell you, a keen wit is to physical force what your carbine is to the tomahawk of these red-skins. It fires at a distance."

The old soldier looked up with a gleam of intelligence, and Bernard continued—

"Bethink you, did you hear nothing from Hansford by which you might infer that his ultimate design was to overturn the government?"

"Why I can't exactly say that I did," returned the fellow. "To be sure they all prate about liberty and the like, but I reckon that is an Englishman's privilege, providing he takes it out in talking. But there may be fire in the bed-straw for all my ignorance."[45]

"Well, I am sorry for you," said Bernard, "for if you could only remember any thing to convict this young rebel, I would warrant you a free pardon and a sound neck."

"Well, now, as I come to think of it," said the unscrupulous renegade, "there might be some few things he let drop, not much in themselves, but taken together, as might weave a right strong tow; and zounds, I don't think a man can be far wrong to untwist the rope about his own neck by tying it to another. For concerning of life, your honour, while I have no great care to risk it in battle, I don't crave to choke it out with one of these hemp cravats. And so being as I have already done the state some service, I feel it my duty to save her if I can."

"Now, thanks to that catch-word of the rogue," muttered Bernard, "I am like to have easy work to-night. Hark ye, Mr. Berkenhead," he added, aloud, "I think it is likely that the Governor may wish to ask you a question or two touching this matter of which we have been speaking. In the meantime here is something which may help you to get along with these soldiers," and he placed a sovereign in the fellow's hand.

"Thank your honour," said Berkenhead, humbly, "and seeing its not in the way of bribe, I suppose I may take it."

"Oh, no bribe," replied Bernard, smiling, "but mark me, tell a good story. The stronger your evidence the safer is your head."

Bernard returned, as we have seen, to the Governor, for the further development of his diabolical designs, and in a short time Berkenhead, under a guard of soldiers, was conducted to his quarters for the night, in a store-house which stood in the yard some distance from the house.

As the house to which the renegade insurgent was consigned was deemed sufficiently secure, and the soldiers wearied with a long march, were again to proceed on their journey on the morrow, it was not considered necessary to place a guard before the door of this temporary cell—the precaution, however, being taken to appoint a sentry at each side of the mansion-house, and at the door of the apartment in which the unhappy Hansford was confined.

FOOTNOTES:

[43] An old English expression for a rough, honest fellow.

[44] A bludgeon.

[45] There may be danger in the design.

CHAPTER XXX

"Ha! sure he sleeps—all's dark within save what
A lamp, that feebly lifts a sickly flame,
By fits reveals. His face seems turned to favour
The attempt. I'll steal and do it unperceived."
Mourning Bride.

All were wrapt in silence and in slumber, save the weary sentinels, who paced drowsily up and down before the door of the house, humming in a low tone the popular Lillibullero, or silently communing with their brother sentry in the sky. The family, providing for the fatigues of the following day, had early retired to rest, and even Virginia, worn down by excitement and agitation, having been assured by her father of the certain safety of Hansford, had yielded to the restoring influences of sleep. How little did the artless girl, or her unsuspicious father, suppose that beneath their roof they had been cherishing a demon, who, by his wily machinations, was weaving a web around his innocent victim, cruel and inextricable.

We have said that all save the watchful sentinels were sleeping; but one there was from whose eyes and from whose heart revenge had driven sleep. Mamalis—the poor, hapless Mamalis—whose sorrows had been forgotten in the general excitement which had prevailed—Mamalis knew but one thought, and that was no dream. Her brother, the pride and refuge of her maiden heart, lay stiff and murdered by the way-side—his death unwept, his dirge unsung, his brilliant hopes of fame cut off ere they had fully budded. And his murderer was near her! Could she hesitate? Had she not been taught, in her simple faith, that the blood of the victim requires the blood of his destroyer? The voice of her brother's blood called to her from the ground. Nor did it call in vain. It is true, he had been harsh, nay sometimes even cruel to her, but when was woman's heart, when moved to softness, ever mindful of the wrongs she had endured? Ask yourself, when standing by the lifeless corse of one whom you have dearly loved, if then you can remember aught but kindness, and love, and happiness, in your association with the loved one. One gentle word, one sweet smile, one generous action, though almost faded from the memory before, obscures forever all the recollection of wrongs inflicted and injuries endured.

She was in the room occupied by Virginia Temple. Oh, what a contrast between the two! Yes, there they were—Revenge and Innocence! The one lay pure and beautiful in sleep; her round, white arm thrown back upon the pillow, to form a more snowy resting place for her lovely cheek. From beneath her cap some tresses had escaped, which, happy in release, were sporting in the soft air that wooed them through the open window. Her face, at other times too spiritually pale, was now slightly flushed by the sultry warmth of the night. A smile of peaceful happiness played around her lips, as she dreamed, perhaps, of some wild flower ramble which in happier days she had had with Hansford. Her snowy bosom, which in her restlessness she had nearly bared, was white and swelling as a wave which plays in the calm moonlight. Such was the beautiful being who lay sleeping calmly in the arms of Innocence, while the dark, but not less striking, form of the Indian girl bent over, to discover if she slept. She was dressed as we have before described, with the short deer-skin smock, extending to her knees, and fitted closely round the waist with a belt of wampum. Her long black hair was bound by a simple riband, and fell thickly over her shoulders in dark profusion. In her left hand she held a lamp, and it was fearful to mark, by its faint, glimmering light, the intense earnestness of her countenance. There were some traces of tears upon her cheek, but these were nearly dried. Her bright black eyes were lighted by a strange, unnatural fire, which they never knew before. It seemed as though you might see them in the dark. In her right hand she held a small dagger, which *he* had given her as a pledge of a brother's love. Fit instrument to avenge a brother's death!

She seemed to be listening and watching to hear or see the slightest movement from the slumbering maiden. But all was still!

"I slept not thus," she murmured, "the night I heard him vow his vengeance against your father. Before the birds had sung their morning song I came to warn you. Now all I loved, my country, my friends, my brother, have gone forever, and none shares the tears of the Indian maiden."

She turned away with a sigh from the bedside of Virginia, and carefully replaced the dagger in her belt. She then took a key which was lying on the table and clutched it with an air of triumph. That key she had stolen from the pocket of Alfred Bernard while he slept—for what will not revenge, and woman's revenge, dare to do. Then taking up a water pitcher, and extinguishing the light, she softly left the room.

As she endeavoured to pass the outer door she was accosted by the hoarse voice of the sentinel—"Who comes there?" he cried.

"A friend," she answered, timidly.

"You cannot pass, friend, without a permit from the Governor. Them's his orders."

"I go to bring some water for the sick maiden," she said earnestly, showing him the pitcher. "She is far from well. Let her not suffer for a draught of water."

"Well," said the pliant soldier, yielding; "you are a good pleader, pretty one. That dark face of yours looks devilish well by moonlight. What say you; if I let you pass, will you come and sit with me when you get back? It's damned lonesome out here by myself."

"I will do any thing you wish when I return," said the girl.

"Easily won, by Wenus," said the gallant soldier, as he permitted Mamalis to pass on her supposed errand.

Freed from this obstruction, she glided rapidly through the yard, and soon stood before the door of the small house which she had learned was appropriated as the prison of Berkenhead. Turning the key softly in the lock, she pulled the latch-string and gently opened the door. A flood of moonlight streamed upon the floor, encumbered with a variety of plantation utensils. By the aid of this light Mamalis soon recognized the form and features of the fated Berkenhead, who was sleeping in one corner of the room. She knelt over him and feasted her eyes with the anticipation of her deep revenge. Fearing to be defeated in her design, for with her it was the foiled attempt and "not the act which might confound," she bared his bosom and sought his heart. The motion startled the sleeping soldier. "The devil," he said, half opening his eyes; "its damned light." Just as he pronounced the last word the fatal dagger of Mamalis found its way into his heart. "It is all dark now," she said, bitterly, and rising from her victim, she glided through the door and left him with his God.

With the native shrewdness of her race, Mamalis did not forget that she had still to play a part, and so without returning directly to the house, she repaired to the well and filled her pitcher. She even offered the sentinel a drink as she repassed him on her return, and promising once more to come back, when she had carried the water to the "sick maiden," she stole quietly into the room occupied by Bernard, replaced the key in his pocket as before, and hastened up stairs again.

And there seated once more by the bedside of the sleeping Virginia, the young Indian girl sang, in a low voice, at once her song of triumph and her brother's dirge, in that rich oriental improvisation for which the Indians were so remarkable. We will not pretend to give in the original words of this beautiful requiem, but furnish the reader, in default of a better, with the following free translation, which may give some faint idea of its beauty:—

"They have plucked the flower from the garden of my heart, and have torn the soil where it tenderly grew. He was bright and beautiful as the bounding deer, and the shaft from his bow was as true as his unchanging soul! Rest with the Great Spirit, soul of my brother!

"The Great Spirit looked down in pity on my brother; Manitou has snatched him from the hands of the dreadful Okee. On the shores of the spirit-land, with the warriors of his tribe he sings the song of his glory, and chases the spirit deer over the immaterial plains! Rest with the Great Spirit, soul of my brother!

"But I, his sister, am left lonely and desolate; the hearth-stone of Mamalis is deserted. Yet has my hand sought revenge for his murder, and my bosom exults over the destruction of his destroyer! Rest with the Great Spirit, soul of my brother!

"Rest with the Great Spirit, soul of Manteo, till Mamalis shall come to enjoy thy embraces. Then welcome to thy spirit home the sister of thy youth, and reward with thy love the avenger of thy death! Rest with the Great Spirit, soul of my brother!"

As her melancholy requiem died away, Mamalis rose silently from the seat, and bent once more over the form of the sleeping Virginia. As she felt the warm breath of the pure young girl upon her cheek, and watched the regular beating of her heart, and then contrasted the purity of the sleeping maiden with her own wild, guilty nature, she started back in horror. For the first time she felt remorse at the commission of her crime, and with a heavy sigh she hurriedly left the room, as though it were corrupted by her presence.

CHAPTER XXXI

"And smile, and smile, and smile, and be a villain."
King John.

Great was the horror of the loyalists, on the following morning, at the discovery of the horrible crime which had been perpetrated; but still greater was the mystery as to who was the guilty party. There was no mode of getting admittance to the house in which Berkenhead was confined, except through the door, the key of which was in the possession of Alfred Bernard. Even if the position and standing of this young man had not repelled the idea that he was cognizant of the crime, his own unfeigned surprise at the discovery, and the absence of any motive for its commission, acquitted him in the minds of all. And yet, if this hypothesis was avoided, it was impossible to form any rational theory on the subject. There were but two persons connected with the establishment who could be presumed to have any plausible motive for murdering Berkenhead. Hansford might indeed be suspected of a desire to suppress evidence which would be dangerous to his own safety, but then Hansford was himself in close confinement. Mamalis, too, had manifested a spirit, the evening before, towards the unhappy man, which might very naturally subject her to suspicion; but, besides that, she played her part of surprise to perfection—it could not be conceived how she had gotten possession of the key of the room. The sentinel might indeed have thrown much light upon the subject, but he kept his own counsel for fear of the consequences of disobedience to orders; and he boldly asserted that no one had left the house during the night. This evidence, taken in connection with the fact that the young girl was found sleeping, as usual, in the little room adjoining Virginia's chamber, entirely exculpated her from any participation in the crime. Nothing then was left for it, but to suppose that the unhappy man, in a fit of desperation, had himself put a period to his existence. A little investigation might have easily satisfied them that such an hypothesis was as groundless as the rest; for it was afterwards ascertained by Colonel Temple, after a strict search, that no weapon was found on or near the body, nor in the apartment where it lay. But Sir William Berkeley, anxious to proceed upon his way to Accomac, and caring but little, perhaps, for the fate of a rebel, whose life was probably shortened but a few hours, gave the affair a very hurried and summary examination. Bernard, with his quick sagacity, discovered, or at least shrewdly suspected, the truth, and Mamalis felt, as he fixed his dark eyes upon her, that he had read the mystery of her heart. But, for his own reasons, the villain for the present maintained the strictest silence on the subject.

But this catastrophe, so fatal to Berkenhead, was fortunate for young Hansford. The Governor, more true to his word to loyalists than he had hitherto been to the insurgents, released our hero from imprisonment, in the absence of any testimony against him. And, to the infinite chagrin of Alfred Bernard, his rival, once more at liberty, was again, in the language of the treacherous Plantagenet, "a very serpent in his way." He had too surely discovered, that so long as Hansford lived, the heart of Virginia Temple, or what he valued far more, her hand, could never be given to another; and yet he felt, that if he were out of the way, and that heart, though widowed, free to choose again, the emotions of mistaken gratitude would prompt her to listen with favour to his suit. With all his faults, too, and with his mercenary motives, Bernard was not without a feeling, resembling love, for Virginia. We are told that there are fruits and flowers which, though poisonous in their native soil, when transplanted and cherished under more genial circumstances, become at once fair to the eye and wholesome to the taste. It is thus with love. In the wild, sterile heart of Alfred Bernard it had taken root, and poisoned all his nature; but yet it was the same emotion which shed a genial influence over the manly heart of Hansford. If it had been otherwise, there were some as fair, and many far more wealthy, in his adopted colony, than Virginia Temple. But she was at once adapted to his interests, his passions, and his intellect. She could aid his vaulting ambition by sharing with him her wealth; she could control, by the strength of her character, and the sweetness of her disposition, his own wild nature; and she could be the instructive and congenial companion of his intellect. And all this rich treasure might be his but for the existence, the rivalry of the hated Hansford. Still his ardent nature led him to hope. With all his heart he would engage in quelling the rebellion, which he foresaw was about to burst upon the colony; and then revenge, the sweetest morsel to the jealous mind, was his. Meantime, he must look the innocent flower, but be the serpent under it; and curbing his own feelings, must, under pretence of friendship and interest for a rival, continue to plot his ruin. Alfred Bernard was equal to the task.

It was with these feelings that he sought Virginia Temple on the eve of his departure from Windsor Hall. The young girl was seated, with her lover, on a rude, rustic bench, beneath the large oak where Bernard had, the evening before, had an interview with the unfortunate Berkenhead. As he approached, she rose, and with her usual winning frankness of manner, she extended her hand.

"Come, Mr. Bernard," she said, "I have determined that you and Major Hansford shall be friends."

"Most willingly, on my part," said the smooth-tongued Bernard. "And I think I have given the best evidence of my disposition to be so, by aiding feebly in restoring to Miss Temple an old friend, when she must now so soon part with her more recent acquaintance."

"I am happy to think," said Hansford, whose candour prevented him from suppressing entirely the coldness of his manner, "that I am indebted to Mr. Bernard for any interest he may have taken in my behalf. I hope, sir, you will now add to the obligation under which I at present rest to you, by apprising me in what manner you have so greatly obliged me."

"Why, you must be aware," replied Bernard, "that your present freedom from restraint is due to my interposition with Sir William Berkeley."

"Oh yes, indeed," interposed Virginia, "for I heard my father say that it was Mr. Bernard's wise suggestion, adopted by the Governor, which secured your release."

"Hardly so," returned Hansford, "even if such were his disposition. But, if I am rightly informed, your assistance only extended to a very natural request, that I should not be judged guilty so long as there was no evidence to convict me. If I am indebted to Mr. Bernard for impressing upon the mind of the Governor a principle of law as old, I believe, as Magna Charta, I must e'en render him the thanks which are justly his due, and which he seems so anxious to demand."

"Mr. Hansford," said Virginia, "why will you persist in being so obstinate? Is it such a hard thing, after all, for one brave man to owe his life to another, or for an innocent man to receive justice at the hands of a generous one? And at least, I should think, she added, with the least possible pout, "that, when I ask as a favour that you should be friends, you should not refuse me."

"Indeed, Miss Virginia," said Alfred Bernard, without evincing the slightest mark of displeasure; "you urge this reconciliation too far. If Major Hansford have some secret cause of enmity or distrust towards me, of which I am ignorant, I beg that you will not force him to express a sentiment which his heart does not entertain. And as for his gratitude, which he seems to think that I demand, I assure you, that for any service which I may have done him, I am sufficiently compensated by my own consciousness of rectitude of purpose, and nobly rewarded by securing your approving smile."

"Nobly, generously said, Mr. Bernard," replied Virginia, "and now I have indeed mistaken Mr. Hansford's character if he fail to make atonement for his backwardness, by a full, free, and cordial reconciliation."

"I must needs give you my left hand, then," said Hansford, extending his hand with as much cordiality as he could assume; "my right arm is disabled as you perceive, by a wound inflicted by one of the enemies of my country, against whom it would seem it is treason to battle."

"Nay, if you go into that hateful subject again," said Virginia, "I fear there is not much cordiality in your heart yet."

"Oh! you are mistaken, Miss Temple," said Bernard, gaily; "you must remember the old adage, that the left is nearest to the heart. Believe me, Major Hansford and myself will be good friends yet, and when we hereafter shall speak of our former estrangement, it will only be to remember by whose gentle influence we were reconciled. But permit me to hope, Major, that your wound is not serious."

"A mere trifle, I believe, sir," returned Hansford, "but I am afraid I will suffer some inconvenience from it for some time, as it is the sword arm; and in these troublous times it may fail me, when it should be prepared to defend."

"An that were the only use to which you would apply it," said Virginia, half laughing, and half in earnest, "I would sincerely hope that it might never heal."

"Oh fear not but that it will soon heal," said Bernard. "The most dangerous wounds are inflicted here," laying his hand upon his heart; "a wound dealt not by a savage, but by an angel; not from the arrow of the ambushed Indian, but from the quiver of the mischievous little blind boy—and the more fatal, because we insanely delight to inflame the wound instead of seeking to cure it."

"Well really, Mr. Bernard," said Virginia, rallying the gay young euphuist, "the flowers of gallantry which you have brought from Windsor Court, thanks to your fostering care, flourish quite as sweetly in this wilderness of Windsor Hall. Take pity on an illiterate colonial girl, and tell me whether this is the language of Waller, Cowley or Dryden?"

"It is the language of the heart, Miss Temple, on the present occasion at least," said Bernard, gravely; "for I am admonished that it is time I should say farewell. Without flowers or poetry, Miss Virginia, I bid you adieu. May you be happy, and derive from your association with others that high enjoyment which you are so capable of bestowing. Farewell, Major Hansford, we may meet again, I trust, when it will not be necessary to invoke the interposition of a fair mediator to effect a reconciliation."

Hansford well understood the innuendo contained in the last words of Bernard, but taking the well-timed hint, refrained from expressing it more clearly, and gave his hand to his rival with every appearance of cordiality. And Virginia, misconstruing the words of the young jesuit, frankly extended her own hand, which he pressed respectfully to his lips, and then turned silently away.

"Well, I am delighted," said Virginia to her lover, when they were thus left alone, "that you are at last friends with Bernard. You see now that I was right and you were wrong in our estimates of his character."

"Indeed I do not, my dear Virginia; on the contrary, this brief interview has but confirmed my previously formed opinion."

"Oh! that is impossible, Hansford; you are too suspicious, indeed you are. I never saw more refinement and delicacy blended with more real candour. Indeed, Hansford, he is a noble fellow."

"I am sorry to differ with you, dearest; but to my mind his refinement is naught but Jesuitical craft; his delicacy the result of an educational schooling of the lip, to conceal the real feelings of his heart; and his candour but the gilt washing which appears like gold, but after all, only hides the baser metal beneath it."

"Well, in my life I never heard such perversion! Really, Hansford, you will make me think you are jealous."

"Jealous, Virginia, jealous!" said Hansford, in a sorrowful tone. "Alas! if I were even capable of such a feeling, what right have I to entertain it? Your heart is free, and torn from the soil which once cherished it, may be transplanted elsewhere, while the poor earth where once it grew can only hope now and then to feel the fragrance which it sheds on all around. No, not jealous, Virginia, whatever else I may be!"

"You speak too bitterly, Hansford; have I not assured you that though a harsh fate may sever us; though parental authority may deny you my hand, yet my heart is unalterably yours. But tell me, why it is that you can see nothing good in this young man, and persist in perverting every sentiment, every look, every expression to his injury?"

Before Hansford could reply, the shrill voice of Mrs. Temple was heard, crying out; "Virginia Temple, Virginia Temple, why where can the child have got to!"—and at the same moment the old lady came bustling round the house, and discovered the unlawful interview of the lovers.

Rising hastily from her seat, Virginia advanced to her mother, who, without giving her time to speak, even had she been so inclined, sang out at the top of her voice—"Come along, my daughter. Here are the guests in your father's house kept waiting in the porch to tell you good-bye, and you, forsooth, must be talking, the Lord knows what, to that young scape-gallows yonder, who hasn't modesty enough to know when and where he's wanted."

"Dear mother, don't speak so loud," whispered the poor girl.

"Don't talk so loud, forsooth—and why? They that put themselves where they are not wanted and not asked, must expect to hear ill of themselves."

"There comes my pretty Jeanie," said her old father, as he saw her approach. "And so you found her at last, mother. Come here, dearest, we have been waiting for you."

The sweet tones of that gentle voice, which however harsh at times to others, were ever modulated to the sweetest music when he spoke to her, fell upon the ears of the poor confused and mortified girl, in such comforting accents, that the full heart could no longer restrain its gushing feelings, and she burst into tears. With swollen eyes and with a heavy heart she bade adieu to the several guests, and as Sir William Berkeley, in the mistaken kindness of his heart, kissed her cheek, and whispered that Bernard would soon return and all would be happy again, she sobbed as if her gentle heart would break.

"I always tell the Colonel that he ruins the child," said Mrs. Temple to the Governor, with one of her blandest smiles, on seeing this renewed exhibition of sensibility. "It was not so in our day, Lady Frances; we had other things to think about than crying and weeping. Tears were not so shallow then."

Lady Frances Berkeley nodded a stately acquiescence to this tribute to the stoicism of the past, and made some sage, original and relevant reflection, that shallow streams ever were the most noisy—and then kissing the weeping girl, repeated the grateful assurance that Bernard would not be long absent, and that she herself would be present at the happy bridal, to taste the bride's cake and quaff the knitting cup,[46] with other like consolations well calculated to restore tranquillity and happiness to the bosom of the disconsolate Virginia.

And so the unfortunate Berkeley commenced that fatal flight, which contributed so largely to divert the arms of the insurgents from the

Indians to the government, and to change what else might have been a mere unauthorized attack upon the common enemies of the country into a protracted and bloody civil war.

Hansford did not long remain at Windsor Hall, after the departure of the loyalists. He would indeed have been wanting in astuteness if he had not inferred from the direct language of Mrs. Temple that he was an unwelcome visitant at the mansion. But more important, if not more cogent reasons urged his immediate departure. He saw at a glance the fatal error committed by Berkeley in his flight to Accomac, and the immense advantage it would be to the insurgents. He wished, therefore, without loss of time to communicate the welcome intelligence to Bacon and his followers, who, he knew, were anxiously awaiting the result of his mission.

Ordering his horse, he bade a cordial adieu to the good old colonel, who, as he shook his hand, said, with a tear in his eye, "Oh, my boy, my boy! if your head were as near right as I believe your heart is, how I would love to welcome you to my bosom as my son."

"I hope, my kind, my noble friend," said Hansford, "that the day may yet come when you will see that I am not wholly wrong. God knows I would almost rather err with you than to be right with any other man." Then bidding a kind farewell to Mrs. Temple and Virginia, to which the old lady responded with due civility, but without cordiality, he vaulted into the saddle and rode off—and as long as the house was still in view, he could see the white 'kerchief of Virginia from the open window, waving a last fond adieu to her unhappy lover.

FOOTNOTES:

[46] A cup drunk at the marriage ceremony in honour of the bride.

CHAPTER XXXII

"The abstract and brief chronicle of the time."
Hamlet.

It is not our purpose to trouble the reader with a detailed account of all the proceedings of the famous Rebellion, which forms the basis of our story. We, therefore, pass rapidly over the stirring incidents which immediately succeeded the flight of Sir William Berkeley. Interesting as these incidents may be to the antiquary or historian, they have but little to do with the dramatis personæ of this faithful narrative, in whose fate we trust our readers are somewhat interested. Accomac is divided from the mainland of Virginia by the broad Chesapeake Bay. Although contained in the same grant which prescribed the limits to the colony, and although now considered a part of this ancient commonwealth, there is good reason to believe that formerly it was considered in a different light. In one of the earliest colonial state papers which has been preserved, the petition of Morryson, Ludwell & Smith, for a reformed charter for the colony, the petitioners are styled the "agents for the governor, council and burgesses of the country of Virginia *and territory of Accomac;*" and although this form of phraseology appears in but few of the records, yet it would appear that the omission was the result of mere convenience in style, just as Victoria is more frequently styled the Queen of England, than called by her more formal title of Queen of the United Kingdoms of Great Britain and Ireland, by the Grace of God, Defender of the Faith. It was, therefore, not without reason, that Nathaniel Bacon, glad at least of a pretext for advancing his designs, should have considered the flight of Sir William Berkeley to Accomac as a virtual abdication of his authority, more especially as it had been ordained but two years before by the council at Whitehall, that the governor should be actually a resident of Virginia, unless when summoned by the King to England or elsewhere. At least it was a sufficient pretext for the young insurgent, who, in the furtherance of his designs did not seem to be over-scrupulous in regard to the powers with which he was clothed. But twelve years afterwards a similar pretext afforded by the abdication of James the Second, relieved the British government of one of the most serious difficulties which has arisen in her constitutional history.

Without proceeding on his expedition against the Indians, Bacon had no sooner heard of the abdication of the governor than he retired to the Middle Plantation, the site of the present venerable city of Williamsburg. Here, summoning a convention of the most prominent citizens from all parts of the colony, he declared the government vacated by the voluntary abdication of Berkeley, and in his own name, and the name of four members of the council, proceeded to issue writs for a meeting of the Assembly. It is but just to the memory of this great man to say, that this Assembly, convened by his will, and acting, as may well be conceived, almost exclusively under his dictation, has left upon our statute books laws "the most wholesome and good," for the benefit of the colony, and the most conducive to the advancement of rational liberty. The rights of property remained inviolate— the reforms were moderate and judicious, and the government of the colony proceeded as quietly and calmly after the accomplishment of the revolution, as though Sir William Berkeley were still seated in his palace as the executive magistrate of Virginia. A useful lesson did this young colonial rebel teach to modern reformers who would defame his name—the lesson that reform does not necessarily imply total change, and that there is nothing with which it is more dangerous to tamper than long established usage. The worst of all quacks are those who would administer their sovereign nostrums to the constitution of their country.

The reader of history need not be reminded that the expedition of Bland and Carver, designed to surprise Sir William Berkeley in his new retreat, was completely frustrated by the treachery of Larimore, and its unfortunate projectors met, at the hands of the stern old Governor, a traitor's doom. Thus the drooping hopes of the loyalists were again revived, and taking advantage of this happy change in the condition of affairs, Berkeley with his little band of faithful adherents returned by sea to Jamestown, and fortified the place to the best of their ability against the attacks of the rebels.

Nor were the insurgents unwilling to furnish them an opportunity for a contest. The battle of Bloody Run is memorable in the annals of the colony as having forever annihilated the Indian power in Eastern Virginia. Like the characters in Bunyan's sublime vision, this unhappy race, so long a thorn in the side of the colonists, had passed away, and "they saw their faces no more." But his very triumph over the savage enemies of his country, well nigh proved the ruin of the young insurgent. Many of his followers, who had joined him with a bona fide design of extirpating the Indian power, now laid down their arms, and retired quietly to their several homes. Bacon was thus left with only about two hundred adherents, to prosecute the civil war which the harsh and dissembling policy of Berkeley had invoked; while the Governor was surrounded by more than three times that number, with the entire navy of Virginia at his command, and, moreover, secure behind the fortifications of Jamestown. Yet did not the brave young hero shrink from the contest. Though reduced in numbers, those that remained were in themselves a host. They were all men of more expanded views, and more exalted conceptions of liberty, than many of the medley crew who had before attended him. They fought in a holier cause than when arrayed against the despised force of their savage foes, and, moreover, they fought in self-defence. For, too proud and generous to desert their leader in his hour of peril, each of his adherents lay under the proscriptive ban of the revengeful Governor, as a rebel and a traitor. No sooner, therefore, did Bacon hear of the return of Berkeley to Jamestown, than, with hasty marches, he proceeded to invest the place. It is here, then, that we resume the thread of our broken narrative.

CHAPTER XXXIII

"When Liberty rallies
Once more in thy regions, remember me then."

Byron.

It was on a calm, clear morning in the latter part of the month of September, that the little army of Nathaniel Bacon, wearied and worn with protracted marches, and with hard fought battles, might be seen winding through the woodland district to the north of Jamestown. The two cavaliers, who led the way a little distance ahead of the main body of the insurgents, were Bacon and his favourite comrade, Hansford—engaged, as before, in an animated, but now a more earnest conversation. The brow of the young hero was more overcast with care and reflection than when we last saw him. The game, which he had fondly hoped was over, had yet to be played, and the stake that remained was far more serious than any which had yet been risked. During the brief interval that his undisputed power existed, the colony had flourished and improved, and the bright dream which he had of her approaching delivery from bondage, seemed about to be realized. And now it was sad and disheartening to think that the battle must again be fought, and with such odds against him, that the chances of success were far more remote than ever. But Bacon was not the man to reveal his feelings, and he imparted to others the cheerfulness which he failed to feel himself. From time to time he would ride along the broken ranks, revive their drooping spirits, inspire them with new courage, and impart fresh ardor into their breasts for the glorious cause in which they were engaged. Then rejoining Hansford, he would express to him the fears and apprehensions which he had so studiously concealed from the rest.

It was on one of these occasions, after deploring the infatuated devotion of so many of the colonists to the cause of blind loyalty, and the desertion of so many on whom he had relied to co-operate in his enterprize, that he said, bitterly:

"I fear sometimes, my friend, that we have been too premature in our struggle for liberty. Virginia is not yet ready to be free. Her people still hug the chains which enslave them."

"Alas!" said Hansford, "it is too true that we cannot endue the infant in swaddling bands with the pride and strength of a giant. The child who learns to walk must meet with many a fall, and the nation that aspires to freedom will often be checked by disaster and threatened with ruin."

"And this it is," said Bacon, sorrowfully, "that makes me sick at heart. Each struggle to be free sinks the chain of the captive deeper into his flesh. And should we fail now, my friend, we but tighten the fetters that bind us."

"Think not thus gloomily on the subject," replied Hansford. "Believe me, that you have already done much to develope the germ of freedom in Virginia. It may be that it may not expand and grow in our brief lives; and even though our memory may pass away, and the nation we have served may fail to call us blessed, yet they will rejoice in the fruition of that freedom for which we may perish. Should the soldier repine because he is allotted to lead a forlorn hope? No! there is a pride and a glory to know, that his death is the bridge over which others will pass to victory."

"God bless your noble soul, Hansford," said Bacon, with the intensest admiration. "It is men like you and not like me who are worthy to live in future generations. Men who, regardless of the risk or sacrifice of self, press onward in the discharge of duty. Love of glory may elevate the soul in the hour of triumph, but love of duty, and firmness resolutely to discharge it, can alone sustain us in the hour of peril and trial."

This was at last the difference between the two men. Intense desire for personal fame, united with a subordinate love of country impelled Bacon in his course. Inflexible resolution to discharge a sacred duty, an entire abnegation of self in its performance, and the strongest convictions of right constituted the incentives to Hansford. It was this that in the hour of their need sustained the heart of Hansford, while the more selfish but noble heart of his leader almost sank within him; and yet the effects upon the actions of the two were much the same. The former, unswayed by circumstances however adverse, pressed steadily and firmly on; while the latter, with the calmness of desperation, knowing that safety, and (what was dearer) glory, lay in the path of success, braced himself for the struggle with more than his usual resolution.

"But, alas!" continued Bacon, in the same melancholy tone, "if we should fail, how hard to be forgotten. Your name and memory to perish among men forever—your very grave to be neglected and uncared for; and this living, breathing frame, instinct with life, and love, and glory, to pass away and mingle with the dust of the veriest worm which crawls upon the earth. Oh, God! to be forgotten, to leave no impress on the world but what the next flowing tide may efface forever. Think of it, realize it, Hansford—to be forgotten!"

"It would, indeed, be a melancholy thought," said Hansford, with a deep sympathy for his friend—"if this were all. But when we remember that we stand but on the threshold of existence, and have a higher, a holier destiny to attain beyond, we need care but little for what is passing here. I have sometimes thought, my friend, that as in manhood we sometimes smile at the absurd frivolities which caught our childish fancy, so when elevated to a higher sphere we would sit and wonder at the interest which we took in the trifling pleasures, the empty honours, and the glittering toys of this present life."

"And do you mean to say that honour and glory are nothing here?"

"Only so far as they reflect the honour and glory which are beyond."

"Pshaw, man!" cried Bacon, "you do not, you cannot think so. You ask me the reason of this desire for fame and remembrance when we are dust. I tell you it is an instinct implanted in us by the Almighty to impel us to glorious deeds."

"Aye," said Hansford, quietly, "and when that desire, by our own indulgence, becomes excessive, just as the baser appetites of the glutton or the debauchee, it becomes corrupt and tends to our destruction."

"You are a curious fellow, Hansford," said Bacon, laughing, "and should have been one of old Noll's generals—for I believe you can preach as well as you can fight, and believe me that is no slight commendation. But you must excuse me if I cannot agree with you in all of your sentiments. I am sorry to say that old Butler's 'pulpit drum ecclesiastic' seldom beat me to a church parade while I was in England, and here in Virginia they send us the worst preachers, as they send us the worst of every thing. But a truce to the subject. Tell me are you a believer in presentiments?"

"Surely such things are possible, but I believe them to be rare," replied his companion. "Future events certainly make an impression upon the animal creation, and I know not why man should be exempt entirely from a similar law. The migratory birds will seek a more southern clime, even before a change of weather is indicated by the wind, and the appearance of the albatross, or the bubbling of the porpoise, if we may believe the sailors' account, portend a storm."

"These phenomena," suggested Bacon, "may easily be explained by some atmospheric influence, insensible to our nature, but easily felt by them."

"I might answer," replied Hansford, "that if insensible to us, we are not warranted in presuming their existence. But who can tell in the subtle mechanism of the mind how sensitive it may be to the impressions of coming yet unseen events. At least, all nations have believed in the existence of such an influence, and the Deity himself has deigned to use it through his prophets, in the revelation of his purposes to man."

"Well, true or not," said Bacon, in a low voice, "I have felt the effect of such a presentiment in my own mind, and although I have tried to resist its influence I have been unable to do so. There is something which whispers to me, Hansford, that I will not see the consummation of my hopes in this colony—and that dying I shall leave behind me an inglorious name. For what at last is an unsuccessful patriot but a rebel. And oh, as I have listened to the monitions of this demon, it seemed as though the veil of futurity were raised, and I could read my fate in after years. Some future chronicler will record this era of Virginia's history, and this struggle for freedom on the part of her patriot children will be styled rebellion; our actions misrepresented; our designs misinterpreted; and I the leader and in part the author of the movement will be handed down with Wat Tyler and Jack Cade to infamy, obloquy and reproach."

"Think not thus gloomily," said Hansford, "the feelings you describe are often suggested to an excited imagination by the circumstances with which it is surrounded; just as dreams are the run mad chroniclers of our daily thoughts and hopes and apprehensions. You should not yield to them, General, they unman you or at least unfit you for the duties which lie before you."

"You are right," returned Bacon; "and I banish them from me forever. I have half a mind to acknowledge myself your convert, Hansford; eschew the gaily bedizzened Glory, and engage your demure little Quaker, Duty, as my handmaiden in her place."

"I will feel but too proud of such a convert to my creed," said Hansford laughing. "And now what of your plans on Jamestown?"

"Why to tell you the truth," said Bacon gravely; "I am somewhat at fault in regard to my actions there. I could take the town in a day, and repulse those raw recruits of the old Governor with ease, if they would only sally out. But I suspect the old tyrant will play a safe game with me—and securely ensconced behind his walls, will cut my brave boys to pieces with his cannon before I can make a successful breach."

"You could throw up breastworks for your protection," suggested Hansford.

"Aye, but I fear it would be building a stable after the horse was stolen. With our small force we could not resist their guns while we were

constructing our fortifications. But I will try it by night, and we may succeed. The d——d old traitor—if he would only meet me in open field, I could make my way 'through twenty times his stop.'"

"Well, we must encounter some risk," replied Hansford. "I have great hopes from the character of his recruits, too. Though they number much more than ourselves, yet they serve without love, and in the present exhausted exchequer of the colony, are fed more by promises than money."

"They are certainly not likely to be fed by *angels*," said Bacon, "as some of the old prophets are said to have been. But, Hansford, an idea has just struck me, which is quite a new manœuvre in warfare, and from which your ideas of chivalry will revolt."

"What is it?" asked Hansford eagerly.

"Why if it succeeds," returned Bacon, "I will warrant that Jamestown is in our hands in twenty-four hours, without the loss of more blood than would fill a quart canteen."

"Bravo, then, General, if you add such an important principle to the stock of military tactics, I'll warrant that whispering demon lied, and that you will retain both Glory and Duty in your service."

"I am afraid you will change your note, Thomas, when I develope my plan. It is simply this—to detail a party of men to scour the country around Jamestown, and collect the good dames and daughters of our loyal councillors. If we take them with us, I'll promise to provide a secure defence against the enemies' fire. The besieged will dare not fire a gun so long as there is danger of striking their wives and children, and we, in the meantime, secure behind this temporary breastwork, will prepare a less objectionable defence. What think you of the plan, Hansford?"

"Good God!" cried Hansford, "You are not in earnest General Bacon?"

"And why not?" said Bacon, in reply. "If such a course be not adopted, at least half of the brave fellows behind us will be slaughtered like sheep. While no harm can result to the ladies themselves, beyond the inconvenience of a few hours' exposure to the night air, which they should willingly endure to preserve life."

Hansford was silent. He knew how useless it was to oppose Bacon when he had once resolved. His chivalrous nature revolted at the idea of exposing refined and delicate females to such a trial. And yet he could not deny that the project if successfully carried out would be the means of saving much bloodshed, and of ensuring a speedy and easy victory to the insurgents.

"Why, what are you thinking of, man," said Bacon gaily. "I thought my project would wound your delicate sensibilities. But to my mind there is more real chivalry and more true humanity in sparing brave blood to brave hearts, than in sacrificing it to a sickly regard for a woman's feelings."

"The time has been when brave blood would have leaped gushing from brave hearts," said Hansford proudly, "to protect woman from the slightest shadow of insult."

"Most true, my brave Chevalier Bayard," said Bacon, in a tone of unaffected good humor, "and shall again—and mine, believe me, will not be more sluggish in such a cause than your own. But here no insult is intended and none will be given. These fair prisoners shall be treated with the respect due to their sex and station. My hand and sword for that. But the time has been when woman too was willing to sacrifice her shrinking delicacy in defence of her country. Wot ye how Rome was once saved by the noble intercession of the wife and mother of Caius Marcus—or how the English forces were beaten from the walls of Orleans by the heroic Joan, or how—"

"You need not multiply examples," said Hansford interrupting him, "to show how women of a noble nature have unsexed themselves to save their country. Your illustrations do not apply, for they did voluntarily what the ladies of Virginia must do upon compulsion. But, sir, I have no more to say. If you persist in this resolution, unchivalrous as I believe it to be, yet I will try to see my duty in ameliorating the condition of these unhappy females as far as possible."

"And in me you shall have been a most cordial coadjutor," returned Bacon. "But, my dear fellow, your chivalry is too shallow. Excuse me, if I say that it is all mere sentiment without a substratum of reason. Now look you— you would willingly kill in battle the husbands of these ladies, and thus inflict a life-long wound upon them, and yet you refuse to pursue a course by which lives may be saved, because it subjects them to a mere temporary inconvenience. But look again. Have you no sympathy left for the wives, no chivalry for the daughters of our own brave followers, whose hearts will be saved full many a pang by a stratagem, which will ensure the safety of their protectors. Believe me, my dear Hansford, if chivalry be nought but a mawkish sentiment, which would throw away the real substance of good, to retain the mere shadow reflected in its mirror, like the poor dog in the fable—the sooner its reign is over the better for humanity."

"But, General Bacon," said Hansford, by no means convinced by the sophistry of his plausible leader, "if the future chronicler of whom you

spoke, should indeed write the history of this enterprise, he will record no fact which will reflect less honour upon your name, than that you found a means for your defence in the persons of defenceless women."

"So let it be, my gallant chevalier," replied Bacon, gaily, determined not to be put out of humour by Hansford's grave remonstrance. "But you have taught me not to look into future records for my name, or for the vindication of my course—and your demure damsel Duty has whispered that I am in the path of right. Look ye, Hansford, don't be angry with your friend; for I assure you on the honour of a gentleman, that the dames themselves will bear testimony to the chivalry of Nathaniel Bacon. And besides, my dear fellow, we will not impress any but the sterner old dames into our service. You know the older they are the better they will serve for material for an *impregnable* fortress."

So saying, Bacon ordered a halt, and communicating to his soldiers his singular design, he detailed Captain Wilford and a party of a dozen men, selected on account of their high character, to capture and bring into his camp the wives of certain of the royalists, who, though residing in the country, had rallied to the support of Sir William Berkeley, on his return to Jamestown. In addition to these who were thus found in their several homes, the detailed corps had intercepted the carriage of our old friend, Colonel Temple; for the old loyalist had no sooner heard of the return of Sir William Berkeley, than he hastened to join him at the metropolis, leaving his wife and daughter to follow him on the succeeding day. What was the consternation and mortification of Thomas Hansford as he saw the fair Virginia Temple conducted, weeping, into the rude camp of the insurgents, followed by her high-tempered old mother, who to use the chaste and classic simile of Tony Lumpkin, "fidgeted and spit about like a Catherine wheel."

CHAPTER XXXIV

"It is the cry of women, good, my lord."
Macbeth.

Agreeably with the promise of Bacon, the captured ladies were treated with a respect and deference which allayed in a great degree their many apprehensions. Still they could not refrain from expressions of the strongest indignation at an act so unusual, so violent, and so entirely at war with the established notions of chivalry at the time. As the reader will readily conjecture, our good friend, Mrs. Temple, was by no means the most patient under the wrongs she had endured, and resisting the kind attentions of those around her, she was vehement in her denunciations of her captors, and in her apprehensions of a thousand imaginary dangers.

"Oh my God!" she cried, "I know that they intend to murder us. To think of leaving a quiet home, and being exposed to such treatment as this. Oh, my precious husband, if he only knew what a situation his poor Betsey was in at this moment; but never mind, as sure as I am a living woman, he shall know it, and then we will see."

"My dear Mrs. Temple," said Mrs. Ballard, another of the captives, "do not give way to your feelings thus. It is useless, and will only serve to irritate these men."

"Men! they are not men!" returned the excited old lady, refusing to be comforted. "Men never would have treated ladies so. They are base, cruel, inhuman wretches, and, as I said before, if I live, to get to Jamestown, Colonel Temple shall know of it too—so he shall."

"But reflect, my dear friend, that our present condition is not affected by this very natural resolution which you have made, to inform your husband of your wrongs. But whatever may be the object of these persons, I feel assured that they intend no personal injury to us."

"No personal injury, forsooth; and have we not sustained it already. Look at my head-tire, all done up nicely just before I left the hall, and now scarcely fit to be seen. And is it nothing to be hauled all over the country with a party of ruffians, that I would be ashamed to be caught in company with; and who knows what they intend?"

"I admit with you, my dear madam," said Mrs. Ballard, "that such conduct is unmanly and inexcusable, and I care not who hears me say so. But still," she added in a low voice, "we have the authority of scripture to make friends even of the mammon of unrighteousness."

"Friends! I would die first. I who have been moving in the first circles, the wife of Colonel Temple, who, if he had chosen, might have been the greatest in the land, to make friends with a party of mean, sneaking, cowardly ruffians. Never—and I'll speak my mind freely too—they shall see that I have a woman's tongue in my head and know how to resent these injuries. Oh, for shame! and to wear swords too, which used to be the badge of gentlemen and cavaliers, who would rather have died than wrong a poor, weak, defenceless woman—much less to rob and murder her."

"Well, let us hope for the best, my friend," said Mrs. Ballard; "God knows I feel as you do, that we have been grossly wronged; but let us remember that we are in the hands of a just and merciful Providence, who will do with us according to his holy will."

"I only know that we are in the hands of a parcel of impious and merciless wretches," cried the old lady, who, as we have seen on a former occasion, derived but little comfort from the consolations of religion in the hour of trial. "I hope I have as much religion as my fellows, who pretend to so much more—but I should like to know what effect that would have on a band of lawless cut-throats?"

"He has given us his holy promise," said Virginia, in a solemn, yet hopeful voice of resignation, "that though we walk through the valley and the shadow of death, he will be with us—his rod and his staff will comfort us—yea, he prepareth a table for us in the presence of our enemies, our cup runneth over."

"Well, I reckon I know that as well as you, miss; but it seems there is but little chance of having a table prepared for us here," retorted her mother, whose fears and indignation had whetted rather than allayed her appetite. "But I think it is very unseemly in a young girl to be so calm under such circumstances. I know that when I was your age, the bare idea of submitting to such an exposure as this would have shocked me out of my senses."

Virginia could not help thinking, that considering the lapse of time since her mother was a young girl, there had been marvellously little change wrought in her keen sensibility to exposure; for she was already evidently "shocked out of her senses." But she refrained from expressing such a dangerous opinion, and replied, in a sad tone—

"And can you think, my dearest mother, that I do not feel in all its force our present awful condition! But, alas! what can we do. As Mrs. Ballard truly says, our best course is to endeavour to move the coarse sympathies of these rebels, and even if they should not relent, they will at least render our condition less fearful by their forbearance and respect. Oh, my mother! my only friend in this dark hour of peril and misfortune, think not so harshly of your daughter as to suppose that she feels less acutely the horrors of her situation, because she fails to express her fears." And so saying, the poor girl drew yet closer to her mother, and wept upon her bosom.

"I meant not to speak unkindly, dear Jeanie," said the good-hearted old lady, "but you know, my child, that when my fears get the better of me, I am not myself. It does seem to me, that I was born under some unlucky star. Ever since I was born the world has been turning upside down; and God knows, I don't know what I have done that it should be so. But first, that awful revolution in England, and then, when we came here to pass our old days in peace and quiet, this infamous rebellion. And yet I must say, I never knew any thing like this. There was at least some show of religion among the old Roundheads, and though they were firm and demure enough, and hated all kinds of amusement, and cruel enough too with all their psalm singing, to cut off their poor king's head, yet they always treated women with respect and decency. But, indeed, even the rebels of the present day are not what they used to be."

Virginia could scarcely forbear smiling, amid her tears, at this new application of her mother's favourite theory. The conversation was here interrupted by the approach of a young officer, who, bowing respectfully to the bevy of captive ladies, said politely, that he was sorry to intrude upon their presence, but that, as it was time to pursue their journey, he had come to ask if the ladies would partake of some refreshment before their ride.

"If they could share the rough fare of a soldier, it would bestow a great favour and honour upon him to attend to their wishes; and indeed, as it would be several hours before they could reach Jamestown, they would stand in need of some refreshment, ere they arrived at more comfortable quarters."

"As your unhappy prisoners, sir," said Mrs. Ballard, with great dignity, "we can scarcely object to a soldier's fare. Prisoners have no choice but to take the food which the humanity of their jailers sets before them. Your apology is therefore needless, if not insulting to our misfortunes."

"Well, madam," returned Wilford, in the same respectful tone, "I did not mean to offend you, and regret that I have done so through mistaken kindness. May I add that, in common with the rest of the army, I deplore the necessity which has compelled us to resort to such harsh means towards yourselves, in order to ensure success and safety."

"I deeply sympathize with you in your profound regret," said Mrs. Ballard, ironically. "But pray tell me, sir, if you learned this very novel and chivalric mode of warfare from the savages with whom you have been contending, or is it the result of General Bacon's remarkable military genius?"

"It is the result of the stern necessity under which we rest, of coping with a force far superior to our own. And I trust that while your ladyships can suffer but little inconvenience from our course, you will not regret your own cares, if thereby you might prevent an effusion of blood."

"Oh, that is it," replied Mrs. Ballard, in the same tone of withering irony. "I confess that I was dull enough to believe that the self-constituted, self-styled champions of freedom had courage enough to battle for the right, and not to screen themselves from danger, as a child will seek protection behind its mother's apron, from the attack of an enraged cow."

"Madam, I will not engage in an encounter of wits with you. I will do you but justice when I say that few would come off victors in such a contest. But I have a message from one of our officers to this young lady, I believe, which I was instructed to reserve for her private ear."

"There is no need for a confidential communication," said Virginia Temple, "as I have no secret which I desire to conceal from my mother and these companions in misfortune. If, therefore, you have aught to say to me, you may say it here, or else leave it unexpressed."

"As you please, my fair young lady," returned Wilford. "My message concerns you alone, but if you do not care to conceal it from your companions, I will deliver it in their presence. Major Thomas Hansford desires me to say, that if you would allow him the honour of an interview of a few moments, he would gladly take the opportunity of explaining to you the painful circumstances by which you are surrounded, in a manner which he trusts may meet with your approbation."

"Say to Major Thomas Hansford," replied Virginia, proudly, "that, as I am his captive, I cannot prevent his intrusion into my presence. I cannot refuse to hear what he may have to speak. But tell him, moreover, that no explanation can justify this last base act, and that no reparation can erase it from my memory. Tell him that she who once honoured him, and loved him, as all that was noble, and generous, and chivalric, now looks back upon the past as on a troubled dream; and that, in future, if she should hear his name, she will remember him but as one who, cast in a noble mould, might have been worthy of the highest admiration, but, defaced by an indelible stain, is cast aside as worthy alike of her indignation and contempt."

As the young girl uttered the last fatal words, she sank back into her grassy seat by her mother's side, as though exhausted by the effort she had made. She had torn with violent resolution from her breast the image which had so long been enshrined there—not only as a picture to be loved, but as an idol to be worshipped—and though duty had nerved and sustained her in the effort, nothing could assuage the anguish it inflicted. She did not love him then, but she had loved him; and her heart, like the gloomy chamber where death has been, seemed more desolate for the absence of that which, though hideous to gaze upon, was now gone forever.

Young Wilford was deeply impressed with the scene, and could not altogether conceal the emotion which it excited. In a hurried and agitated voice he promised to deliver her message to Hansford, and bowing again politely to the ladies, he slowly withdrew.

In a few moments one of the soldiers came with the expected refreshment, which certainly justified the description which Wilford had given. It was both coarse and plain. Jerked venison, which had evidently been the property of a stag with a dozen branches to his horns, and some dry and moulding biscuit, completed the homely repast. Virginia, and most of her companions, declined partaking of the unsavoury viands, but Mrs. Temple, though bitterly lamenting her hard fate, in dooming her to such hard fare, worked vigorously away at the tough venison with her two remaining molars—asserting the while, very positively, that no such venison as that existed in her young days, though, to confess the truth, if we may judge from the evident age of the deceased animal, it certainly did.

CHAPTER XXXV

"Yet, though dull hate as duty should be taught,
I know that thou wilt love me; though my name
Should be shut from thee, as a spell still fraught
With desolation,—and a broken claim;
Though the grave closed between us, 'twere the same."
Childe Harold.

The daylight had entirely disappeared, and the broad disc of the full September moon was just appearing above the eastern horizon, when Bacon and his followers resumed their march. Each of the captive ladies was placed upon a horse, behind one of the officers, whose heavy riding cloak was firmly girt to the horse's back, to provide a more comfortable seat. Thus advancing, at a constant, but slow pace, to accommodate the wearied soldiers, they pursued their onward course toward Jamestown. It was Bacon's object to arrive before the town as early as possible in the night, so as to secure the completion of their intrenchments and breastworks before the morning, when he intended to commence the siege. And now, as they are lighted on their way by the soft rays of the autumnal moon, let us hear the conversation which was passing between one of the cavaliers and his fair companion, as they rode slowly along at some distance from the rest.

We may well suppose that Thomas Hansford, forced thus reluctantly to engage in a policy from which his very soul revolted, would not commit the charge of Virginia's person to another. She, at least, should learn, that though so brutally impressed into the service of the rebel army, there was an arm there to shield her from danger and protect her from rudeness or abuse. She, at least, should learn that there was one heart there, however despised and spurned by others, which beat in its every throb for her safety and happiness.

Riding, as we have said, a little slower than the rest, so as to be a little out of hearing, he said, in a low voice, tremulous with half suppressed emotion, "Miss Temple cannot be ignorant of who her companion is?"

"Your voice assures me," replied Virginia, "that my conjecture is right, and that I am in the presence of one who was once an honoured friend.

But had your voice and form changed as entirely as your heart, I could never have recognized in the rebel who scruples not to insult a defenceless woman, the once gallant and chivalrous Hansford."

"And do you, can you believe that my heart has indeed so thoroughly changed?"

"I would fain believe so, else I am forced to the conclusion that I have, all my life, been deceived in a character which I deemed worthy of my love, while it was only the more black because it was hypocritical."

"Virginia," said Hansford, with desperation, "you shall not talk thus; you shall not think thus of me."

"As my captor and jailer," returned the brave hearted young maiden, "Mr. Hansford may, probably, by force, control the expression of my opinions—but thank God! not even you can control my thoughts. The mind, at least, is free, though the body be enslaved."

"Nay, do not mistake my meaning, dear Virginia," said her lover. "But alas! I am the victim of misconstruction. Could you, for a moment, believe that I was capable of an act which you have justly described as unmanly and unchivalrous?"

"What other opinion can I have?" said Virginia. "I find you acting with those who are guilty of an act as cowardly as it is cruel. I find you tacitly acquiescing in their measures, and aiding in guarding and conducting their unhappy captives—and I received from you a message in which you pretend to say that you can justify that which is at once inexcusable before heaven, and in the court of man's honour. Forgive me, if I am unable to separate the innocent from the guilty, and if I fail to see that your conduct is more noble in this attempt to shift the consequences of your crime upon your confederates."

"Now, by Heaven, you wrong me!" returned Hansford. "My message to you was mistaken by Captain Wilford. I never said I could justify your capture; I charged him to tell you I could justify myself. And as for my being found with those who have committed this unmanly act, as well might you be deemed a participator in their actions now, because of your presence here. I remonstrated, I protested against such a course—and when at last adopted I denounced it as unworthy of men, and far more unworthy of soldiers and freemen."

"And yet, when overwhelmed by the voices of others, you quietly acquiesce, and remain in companionship with those whose conduct you had denounced."

"What else could I do?" urged Hansford. "My feeble arm could not resist the action of two hundred-men; and it only remained for me to continue here, that I might secure the safety and kind treatment of those who were the victims of this rude violence. Alas! how little did I think that so soon you would be one of those unhappy victims, and that my heart would deplore, for its own sake, a course from which my judgment and better nature already revolted."

The scales fell from Virginia's eyes. She now saw clearly the bitter trial through which her lover had been called to pass, and recognized once more the generous, self-denying nature of Hansford. The stain upon his pure fame, to use her own figure, was but the effect of the false and deceptive lens through which she had looked, and now that she saw clearly, it was restored to its original purity and beauty.

"And is this true, indeed?" she said, in a happy voice. "Believe me, Hansford, the relief which I feel at this moment more than compensates for all that I have endured. The renewed assurance of your honour atones for all. Can you forgive me for harbouring for a moment a suspicion that you were aught but the soul of honour?"

"Forgive you, dearest?" returned Hansford. "Most freely—most fully! But scarcely can I forgive those who have so wronged you. Cast in a common lot with them, and struggling for a common cause, I cannot now withdraw from their association; and indeed, Virginia, I will be candid, and tell you freely that I would not if I could."

"Alas!" said Virginia, "and what can be the result of your efforts. Sooner or later aid must come from England, and crush a rebellion whose success has only been ephemeral. And what else can be expected or desired, since we have already seen how lost to honour are those by whom it is attempted. Would you wish, if you could, to subject your country to the sway of men, who, impelled only by their own reckless passions, disregard alike the honour due from man and the respect due to woman?"

"You mistake the character of these brave men, Virginia. I believe sincerely that General Bacon was prompted to this policy by a real desire to prevent the unnecessary loss of life; and though this humanity cannot entirely screen his conduct from reprehension, yet it may cast a veil over it. Bold and reckless though he be, his powerful mind is swayed by many noble feelings; and although he may commit errors, they nearly lose their grossness in his ardent love of freedom, and his exalted contempt of danger."

"His love of freedom, I presume, is illustrated by his forcible capture of unprotected females," returned Virginia; "and his contempt of danger, by his desire to interpose his captives between himself and the guns of his enemies."

"I have told you," said Hansford, "that this conduct is incapable of being justified, and in this I grant that Bacon has grievously erred."

"Then why continue to unite your fortunes to a man whose errors are so gross and disgraceful, and whose culpable actions endanger your own reputation with your best friends?"

"Because," said Hansford, proudly, "we are engaged in a cause, in the full accomplishment of which the faults and errors of its champion will be forgotten, and ransomed humanity will learn to bless his name, scarcely less bright for the imperfections on its disc."

"Your reasoning reminds me," said Virginia, "of the heretical sect of Cainites, of whom my father once told me, who exalted even Judas to a hero, because by his treason redemption was effected for the world."

"Well, my dear girl," replied Hansford, "you maintain your position most successfully. But since you quote from the history of the Church, I will illustrate my position after the manner of a sage old oracle of the law. Sir Edward Coke once alluded to the fable, that there was not a bird that flitted through the air, but contributed by its donations to complete the eagle's nest. And so liberty, whose fittest emblem is the eagle, has its home provided and furnished by many who are unworthy to enjoy the home which they have aided in preparing. Admit even, if you please, that General Bacon is one of these unclean birds, we cannot refuse the contribution which he brings in aid of the glorious cause which we maintain."

"Aye, but he is like, with his vaulting ambition, to be the eagle himself," returned Virginia; "and to say truth, although I have great confidence in your protection, I feel like a lone dove in his talons, and would wish for a safer home than in his eyrie."

"You need fear no danger, be assured, dearest Virginia," said Hansford, "either for yourself or your mother. It is a part of his plan to send one of the ladies under our charge into the city, to apprise the garrison of our strange manœuvre; and I have already his word, that your mother and yourself will be the bearers of this message. In a few moments, therefore, your dangers will be past, and you will once more be in the arms of your noble old father."

"Oh thanks, thanks, my generous protector," cried the girl, transported at this new prospect of her freedom. "I can never forget your kindness, nor cease to regret that I could ever have had a doubt of your honour and integrity."

"Oh forget that," returned Hansford, "or remember it only that you may acknowledge that it is often better to bear with the circumstances which we cannot control, than by hasty opposition to lose the little influence we may possess with those in power. But see the moonlight reflected from the steeple of yonder church. We are within sight of Jamestown, and you will be soon at liberty. And oh! Virginia," he said sorrowfully, "if it should be decreed in the book of fate, that when we part to-night we part forever, and if the name of Hansford be defamed and vilified, you at least, I know, will rescue his honour from reproach—and one tear from my faithful Virginia, shed upon a patriot's grave, will atone for all the infamy which indignant vengeance may heap upon my name."

So saying, he spurred his horse rapidly onward, until he overtook Bacon, who, with the precious burden under his care, as usual, led the way. And a precious burden it might well be called, for by the light of the moon the reader could have no difficulty in recognizing in the companion of the young general of the insurgents, our old acquaintance, Mrs. Temple. In the earlier part of their journey she had by no means contributed to the special comfort of her escort—now, complaining bitterly of the roughness of the road, she would grasp him around the waist with both arms, until he was in imminent peril of falling from his horse, and then when pacified by a smoother path and an easier gait, she would burst forth in a torrent of invective against the cowardly rebels who would misuse a poor old woman so. Bacon, however, while alike regardless of her complaints of the road, the horse, or himself, did all in his power to mollify the old lady, by humouring her prejudices as well as he could; and when he at last informed her of the plan by which she and her daughter would so soon regain their liberty, her temper relaxed, and she became highly communicative. She was, indeed, deep in a description of some early scenes of her life, and was telling how she had once seen the bonnie young Charley with her own eyes, when he was hiding from the pursuit of the Roundheads, and how he commended her loyalty, and above all her looks; and promised when he came to his own to bestow a peerage on her husband for his faithful adherence to the cause of his king. The narrative had already lasted an hour or more when Hansford and Virginia rode up and arrested the conversation, much to the relief of Bacon, who was gravely debating in his own mind whether it was more agreeable to hear the good dame's long-winded stories about past loyalty, or to submit to her vehement imprecations on present rebellion.

The young general saluted Virginia courteously as she approached, expressing the hope that she had not suffered from her exposure to the night air, and then turned to Hansford, and engaged in conversation with him on matters of interest connected with the approaching contest.

But as his remarks will be more fully understood, and his views developed in the next chapter, we forbear to record them here. Suffice it to say, that among other things it was determined, that immediately upon their arrival before Jamestown, Mrs. Temple and Virginia, under the escort of Hansford, should be conducted to the gate of the town, and convey to the Governor and his adherents the intelligence of the capture of the wives of the loyalists. We will only so far anticipate the regular course of our narrative as to say, that this duty was performed without being attended with any incident worthy of special remark; and that Hansford, bidding a sad farewell to Virginia and her mother, committed them to the care of the sentinel at the gate, and returned slowly and sorrowfully to the insurgent camp.

CHAPTER XXXVI

"How yet resolves the Governor of the town?
This is the latest parle
we will admit.If I begin the battery once again,
I will not leave the half achieved Harfleur,
Till in her ashes she lie buried."
King Henry V.

And now was heard on the clear night air the shrill blast of a solitary trumpet breathing defiance, and announcing to the besieged loyalists, the presence of the insurgents before the walls of Jamestown. Exhausted by their long march, and depressed by the still gloomy prospect before them, the thinned ranks of the rebel army required all the encouraging eloquence of their general, to urge them forward in their perilous duty. Nor did they need it long. Drawing his wearied, but faithful followers around him, the young and ardent enthusiast addressed them in language like the following:

"Soldiers,"

"Animated by a desire to free your country from the incursions of a savage foe, you have crowned your arms with victory and your lives with honor. You have annihilated the Indian power in Virginia, and in the waters of the brook which was the witness of your victory, you have washed away the stains of its cruelty. The purple blood which dyed that fatal stream, has even now passed away; Yet your deeds shall survive in the name which you have given it. And future generations, when they look upon its calm and unstained bosom, will remember with grateful hearts, those brave men who have given security to their homes, and will bless your patriot names when they repeat the story of Bloody Run.

"For this you have been proclaimed traitors to your country and rebels to your king. Traitors to a country within whose borders the Indian war whoop has been hushed by your exertions! Rebels to your king for preserving Virginia, the brightest jewel in his crown, from inevitable ruin! But though you have accomplished much, much yet remains undone. Then nerve your stout hearts and gird on your armour once more for the contest. Though your enemies are not to be despised, they are not to be feared. *They* fight as mercenaries uninspired by the cause which they have espoused. *You* battle for freedom, for honor and for life. Your freedom is threatened by the oppressions of a relentless tyrant and a subservient Assembly. Your honor is assailed, for you are publicly branded as traitors. Your lives are proscribed by those who have basely charged your patriotism as treason, and your defence of your country as rebellion. Be not dismayed with the numbers of your foes. Think only that it is yours to lessen them. Remember that Peace can never come to you, though you woo it never so sweetly. You must go to it, even though your way thither lay through a sea of blood. You will find me ever where danger is thickest. I will share your peril now and your reward hereafter."

Inspired with new ardour, by the words and still more by the example of their leader, the soldiers proceeded to the task of constructing a breastwork for their defence. Bacon himself at imminent risk to his person, drew with his own hands the line for the entrenchment, while the soldiers prepared for themselves a secure defence from attack by a breastwork composed of felled trees, earth, and brushwood. It was a noble sight, I ween, to see these hardy patriots of the olden time, nearly sinking under fatigue, yet working cheerfully and ardently in the cause of freedom—to hear their axes ringing merrily through the still night air, and the tall forest trees falling with a heavy crash, as they were preparing their rude fortifications; and to look up on the cold, silent moon, as she watched them from her high path in heaven, and you might almost think, smiled with cold disdain, to think that all their hopes would be blasted, and their ardour checked by defeat, while she in her pride of fulness would traverse that same high arch twelve hundred times before the day-star of freedom dawned upon the land.

Meantime the besieged loyalists having heard with surprise and consternation, the story of Mrs. Temple and Virginia, were completely confounded. Fearing to fire a single gun, lest the ball intended for their adversaries might pierce the heart of some innocent woman, they were forced to await with impatience the completion of the works of the insurgents. The latter had not the same reason for forbearance, and made several successful sorties upon the palisades, which surrounded the town, effecting several breaches, and killing some men, but without loss to any their own party. Furious at the successful stratagems of the rebels and fearing an accession to their number from the surrounding country, Sir William Berkeley at length determined to make a sally from the town, and test the strength and courage of his adversaries in an open field. Bacon, meanwhile, having effected his object in securing a sufficient fortification, with much courtesy dismissed the captive ladies, who went, rejoicing at their liberation, to tell the story of their wrongs to their loyal husbands.

The garrison of Jamestown consisting of about twenty cavalier loyalists, and eight hundred raw, undisciplined recruits, picked up by Berkeley during his stay in Accomac, were led on firmly towards the entrenchments of the rebels, by Beverley and Ludwell, who stood high in the confidence of the Governor, and in the esteem of the colony, as brave and chivalrous men. Among the subordinate officers in the garrison was Alfred Bernard, rejoicing in the commission of captain, but recently conferred, and burning to distinguish himself in a contest against the rebels. From their posts behind the entrenchment, the insurgents calmly watched the approach of their foes. Undismayed by their numbers, nearly four times as great as their own, they awaited patiently the signal of their general to begin the attack. Bacon, on his part, with all the ardour of his nature, possessed in an equal degree the coolness and prudence of a great general, and was determined not to risk a fire, until the enemy was sufficiently near to ensure heavy execution. When at length the front line of the assailants advanced within sixty yards of the entrenchment, he gave the word, which was obeyed with tremendous effect, and then without leaving their posts, they prepared to renew their fire. But it was not necessary. Despite the exhortations and prayers of their gallant officers, the royal army, dismayed at the first fire of the enemy, broke ranks and retreated, leaving their drum and their dead upon the field. In vain did Ludwell exhort them, in the name of the king, to return to the assault; in vain did the brave Beverley implore them as Virginians and Englishmen not to desert their colors; in vain did Alfred Bernard conjure them to retrieve the character of soldiers and of men, and to avenge the cause of wronged and insulted women upon the cowardly oppressors. Regardless alike of king, country or the laws of gallantry, the soldiers ran like frightened sheep, from their pursuers, nor stopped in their flight until once more safely ensconced behind their batteries, and under the protection of the cannon from the ships. The brave cavaliers looked aghast at this cowardly defection, and stood for a moment irresolute, with the guns of the insurgents bearing directly upon them. Bacon could easily have fired upon them with certain effect, but with the magnanimity of a brave man, he was struck with admiration for their dauntless courage, and with pity for their helplessness. Nor was he by any means anxious to pursue them, for he feared lest a victory so easily won, might be a stratagem of the enemy, and that by venturing to pursue, he might fall into an ambuscade. Contenting himself, therefore, with the advantage he had already gained, he remained behind his entrenchment, determined to wait patiently for the morrow, before he commenced another attack upon the town.

CHAPTER XXXVII

"Let's leave this town; for they are hairbrained slaves,
And hunger will enforce them to be more eager.
Of old I know them; rather with their teeth
The walls they'll tear down, than forsake the siege."

King Henry VI.

It was very late, but there were few in Jamestown on that last night of its existence that cared to sleep. Those who were not kept awake by the cares of state or military duties, were yet suffering from an intense apprehension, which denied them repose. There was "hurrying to and fro," along Stuart street, and "whispering with white lips," among the thronging citizens. Ever siding with the stronger party, and inclined to attribute to the besieged Governor the whole catalogue of evils under which the colony was groaning, many of the lower classes of the citizens expressed their sympathy with Nathaniel Bacon, and only awaited a secret opportunity to desert to his ranks. A conspiracy was ripening among the soldiery to open the gates to the insurgents, and surrender at once the town and the Governor into their hands—but over-awed by the resolute boldness of their leader, and wanting in the strength of will to act for themselves, they found it difficult to carry their plan into execution.

Sir William Berkeley, with a few of his steady adherents and faithful friends, was anxiously awaiting, in the large hall of the palace, the tidings of the recent sally upon the besiegers. Notwithstanding the superior numbers of his men, he had but little confidence either in their loyalty or courage, while he was fully conscious of the desperate bravery of the insurgents. While hope whispered that the little band of rebels must yield to the overwhelming force of the garrison, fear interposed, to warn him of the danger of defection and cowardice in his ranks. As thus he sat anxiously endeavouring to guess the probable result of his sally, heavy footsteps were heard ascending the stairs. The heart of the old Governor beat thick with apprehension, and the damp drops wrung from him by anxiety and care, stood in cold beads upon his brow.

"What news?" he cried, in a hoarse, agitated voice, as Colonel Ludwell, Robert Beverley, and Alfred Bernard entered the room. "But I read it in your countenances! All is lost!"

"Yes, Governor Berkeley," said Philip Ludwell, "all is lost! we have not even the melancholy consolation of Francis, 'that our honour is preserved.' The cowardly hinds who followed us, fled from the first charge of the rebels, like frightened hares. All attempts to rally them were in vain, and many of them we understand have joined with the rebels."

As the fatal tidings fell upon his ear, Berkeley pressed his hand to his forehead, and sobbed aloud. The heart of the brave old loyalist could bear no more—and all the haughty dignity of his nature gave way in a flood of bitter tears. But the effect was only transient, and nerving himself, he controlled his feelings once more by the energy of his iron will.

"How many still remain with us?" he asked, anxiously, of Ludwell.

"Alas! sir, if the rumour which we heard as we came hither be true— none, absolutely none. There was an immense crowd gathered around the tavern, listening to the news of our defeat from one of the soldiers, and as we passed a loud and insulting cry went up of "Long live Bacon! and down with tyranny!" The soldiers declared that they would not stain their hands with the blood of their fellow-subjects; the citizens as vehemently declared that the town itself should not long harbour those who had trampled on their rights. Treason stalks abroad boldly and openly, and I fear that the loyalty of Virginia is confined to this room."

"Now, Heaven help me," said Berkeley, sadly, "for the world has well nigh deserted me. And yet, if I fall, I shall fall at my post, and the trust bestowed upon me by my king shall be yielded only with my life."

"It were madness to think of remaining longer here," said Beverley; "the rebels, with the most consummate courage, evince the most profound prudence and judgment. Before the dawn they will bring their cannon to bear upon our ships and force them to withdraw from the harbour, and then all means of escape being cut off, we will be forced to surrender on such terms as the enemy may dictate."

"We will yield to no terms," replied Berkeley. "For myself, death is far preferable to dishonour. Rather than surrender the trust which I have in charge, let us remain here, until, like the brave senators of Rome, we are hacked to pieces at our posts by the swords of these barbarians."

"But what can you expect to gain by such a desperate course," said old Ballard, who, though not without a sufficient degree of courage, would prefer rather to admire the heroism of the Roman patriots in history, than to vie with them in their desperate resolution.

"I expect to retain my honour," cried the brave old Governor. "A brave man may suffer death—he can never submit to dishonour."

"My honoured Governor," said Major Beverley, whose well-known courage and high-toned chivalry gave great effect to his counsel; "believe me, that we all admire your steady loyalty and your noble heroism. But reflect, that you gain nothing by desperation, and it is the part of true courage not to hazard a desperate risk without any hope of success. God knows that I would willingly yield up my own life to preserve unsullied the honour of my country, and the dignity of my king; but I doubt how far we serve his real interests by a deliberate sacrifice of all who are loyal to his cause."

"And what then would you advise?" said the Governor, in an irritated manner. "To make a base surrender of our persons and our cause, and to grant to these insolent rebels every concession which their insolence may choose to demand? No! gentlemen, sooner would William Berkeley remain alone at his post, until his ashes mingled with the ashes of this palace, than yield one inch to rebels in arms."

"It is not necessary," returned Beverley. "You may escape without loss of life or compromise of honour, and reserve until a future day your vengeance on these disloyal barbarians."

Berkeley was silent.

"Look," continued Beverley, leading the old loyalist to the window which overlooked the river; "by the light of dawn you can see the white sails of the Adam and Eve, as she rests at anchor in yonder harbor. There is still time to escape before the rebels can suspect our design. Once upon the deck of that little vessel, with her sails unfurled to this rising breeze, you may defy the threats of the besiegers. Then once more to your faithful Accomac, and when the forces from England shall arrive, trained bands of loyal and brave Britons, your vengeance shall then be commensurate with the indignities you have suffered."

Still Berkeley hesitated, but his friends could see by the quiver of his lip, that the struggle was still going on, and that he was thinking with grim satisfaction of that promised vengeance.

"Let me urge you," continued Beverley, encouraged by the effect which he was evidently producing; "let me urge you to a prompt decision. Will you remain longer in Jamestown, this nest of traitors, and expose your faithful adherents to certain death? Is loyalty so common in Virginia, that you will suffer these brave supporters of your cause to be sacrificed? Will you leave their wives and daughters, whom they can no longer defend, to the insults and outrages of a band of lawless adventurers, who have shown that they disregard the rights of men, and the more sacred deference due to a woman? We have done all that became us, as loyal citizens, to do. We have sustained the standard of the king until it were madness, not courage, further to oppose the designs of the rebels. Beset by a superior force, and with treason among our own citizens, and defection among our own soldiers—with but twenty stout hearts still true and faithful to their trust—our alternative is between surrender and death on the one hand, and flight and future vengeance on the other. Can you longer hesitate between the two? But see, the sky grows brighter toward the east, and the morning comes to increase the perils of the night. I beseech you, by my loyalty and my devotion to your interest, decide quickly and wisely."

"I will go," replied Berkeley, after a brief pause, in a voice choking with emotion. "But God is my witness, that if I only were concerned, rebellion should learn that there was a loyalist who held his sacred trust so near his heart, that it could only be yielded with his life-blood. But why should I thus boast? Do with me as you please—I will go."

No sooner was Berkeley's final decision known, than the whole palace was in a state of preparation. Hurriedly putting up such necessaries as would be needed in their temporary exile, the loyalists were soon ready for their sudden departure. Lady Frances, stately as ever, remained perhaps rather longer before her mirror, in the arrangement of her tire, than was consistent with their hasty flight. Virginia Temple scarcely devoted a moment for her own preparations, so constantly was her assistance required by her mother, who bustled about from trunk to trunk, in a perfect agony of haste—found she had locked up her mantle, which was in the very bottom of an immense trunk, and finally, when she had put her spectacles and keys in her pocket, declared that they were lost, and required Virginia to search in every hole and corner of the room for them. But with all these delays—ever incident to ladies, and old ones especially, when starting on a journey—the little party were at length announced to be ready for their "moonlight flitting." Sadly and silently they left the palace to darkness and solitude, and proceeded towards the river. At the bottom of the garden, which ran down to the banks of the river, were two large boats, belonging to the Governor, and which were often used in pleasure excursions. In these the fugitives embarked, and under the muscular efforts of the strong oarsmen, the richly freighted boats scudded rapidly through the water towards the good ship "Adam and Eve," which lay at a considerable distance from the shore, to avoid the guns of the insurgents.

Alfred Bernard had the good fortune to have the fair Virginia under his immediate charge; but the hearts of both were too full to improve the opportunity with much conversation. The young intriguer, who cared but little in his selfish heart for either loyalists or rebels, still felt that he had placed his venture on a wrong card, and was about to lose. The hopes of preferment which he had cherished were about to be dissipated by the ill fortune of his patron, and the rival of his love, crowned with success, he feared, might yet bear away the prize which he had so ardently coveted. Virginia Temple had more generous cause for depression than he. Hers was the hard lot to occupy a position of neutrality in interest between the contending parties. Whichever faction in the State succeeded, she must be a mourner; for, in either case, she was called upon to sacrifice an idol which she long had cherished, and which she must now yield for ever. They sat together near the stern of the boat, and watched the moonlight diamonds which sparkled for a moment on the white spray that dropped from the dripping oar, and then passed away.

"It is thus," said Bernard, with a heavy sigh. "It is thus with this present transient life. We dance for a moment upon the white waves of fortune, rejoicing in light and hope and joy—but the great, unfeeling world rolls on, regardless of our little life, while we fade even while we sparkle, and our places are supplied by others, who in their turn, dance and shine, and smile, and pass away, and are forgotten!"

"It is even so," said Virginia, sadly—then turning her blue eyes upward, she added, sweetly, "but see, Mr. Bernard, the moon which shines so still and beautiful in heaven, partakes not of the changes of these reflected fragments of her brightness. So we, when reunited to the heaven from which our spirits came, will shine again unchangeable and happy."

"Yes, my sweet one," replied her lover passionately, "and were it my destiny to be ever thus with you, and to hear the sweet eloquence of your pure lips, I would not need a place in heaven to be happy."

"Mr. Bernard," said Virginia, "is this a time or place to speak thus? The circumstances by which we are surrounded should check every selfish thought for the time, in our care for the more important interests at stake."

"My fair, young loyalist," said Bernard, "and is it because of the interest excited in your bosom by the fading cause of loyalty, that you check so quickly the slightest word of admiration from one whom you have called your friend? Nay, fair maiden, be truthful even though you should be cruel."

"To be candid, then, Mr. Bernard," returned Virginia, "I thought we had long ago consented not to mention that subject again. I hope you will be faithful to your promise."

"My dearest Virginia, that compact was made when your heart had been given to another whom you thought worthy to reign there. Surely, you cannot, after the events of to-night oppose such an obstacle to my suit. Your gentle heart, my girl, is too pure and holy a shrine to afford refuge to a rebel, and a profaner of woman's sacred rights."

"Mr. Bernard," said Virginia, "another word on this subject, and I seek refuge myself from your insults. You, who are the avowed champion of woman's rights, should know that she owns no right so sacred as to control the affections of her own heart. I have before told you in terms too plain to be misunderstood, that I can never love you. Force me not to repeat what you profess may give you pain, and above all force me not by your unwelcome and ungenerous assaults upon an absent rival to substitute for the real interest which I feel in your happiness, a feeling more strong and decided, but less friendly."

"You mean that you would hate me," said Bernard, cut to the heart at her language, at once so firm and decided, yet so guarded and courteous. "Very well," he added, with an hauteur but illy assumed. "I trust I have more independence and self-respect than to intrude my attentions or conversation where they are unwelcome. But see, our journey is at an end, and though Miss Temple might have made it more pleasant, I am glad that we are freed from the embarrassment that we both must feel in a more extended interview."

And now the loud voice of Captain Gardiner is heard demanding their names and wishes, which are soon told. The hoarse cable grates harshly along the ribs of the vessel, and the boats are drawn up close to her broadside, and the loyal fugitives ascending the rude and tremulous rope-ladder, stand safe and sound upon the deck of the Adam and Eve.

Scarcely had Berkeley and his adherents departed on their flight from Jamestown, when some of the disaffected citizens of the town, seeing the lights in the palace so suddenly extinguished, shrewdly suspected their design. Without staying to ascertain the truth of their suspicions, they hastened with the intelligence to General Bacon, and threw open the gates to the insurgents. Highly elated with the easy victory they had gained over the loyalists, the triumphant patriots forgetting their fatigue and hunger, marched into the city, amid the loud acclamations of the fickle populace. But to the surprise of all there was still a gloom resting upon Bacon and his officers. That cautious and far-seeing man saw at a glance, that although he had gained an immense advantage over the royalists, in the capture of the metropolis, it was impossible to retain it in possession long. As soon as his army was dispersed, or engaged in another quarter of the colony, it would be easy for Berkeley, with the navy under his command, to return to the place, and erect once more the fallen standard of loyalty.

While then, the soldiery were exulting rapturously over their triumph, Bacon, surrounded by his officers, was gravely considering the best policy to pursue.

"My little army is too small," he said, "to leave a garrison here, and so long as they remain thus organized peace will be banished from the colony; and yet I cannot leave the town to become again the harbour of these treacherous loyalists."

"I can suggest no policy that is fit to pursue, in such an emergency," said Hansford, "except to retain possession of the town, at least until the Governor is fairly in Accomac again."

"That, at best," said Bacon, "will only be a dilatory proceeding, for sooner or later, whenever the army is disbanded, the stubborn old governor will return and force us to continue the war. And besides I doubt whether we could maintain the place with Brent besieging us in front, and the whole naval force of Virginia, under the command of such expert seamen as Gardiner and Larimore, attacking us from the river. No, no, the only way to untie the Gordian knot is to cut it, and the only way to extricate ourselves from this difficulty is to burn the town."

This policy, extreme as it was, in the necessities of their condition was received with a murmur of assent. Lawrence and Drummond, devoted patriots, and two of the wealthiest and most enterprising citizens of the town, evinced their willingness to sacrifice their private means to secure the public good, by firing their own houses. Emulating an example so noble and disinterested, other citizens followed in their wake. The soldiers, ever ready for excitement, joined in the fatal work. A stiff breeze springing up, favored their design, and soon the devoted town was enveloped in the greedy flames.

From the deck of the Adam and Eve, the loyalists witnessed the stern, uncompromising resolution of the rebels. The sun was just rising, and his broad, red disc was met in his morning glory with flames as bright and as intense as his own. The Palace, the State House, the large Garter Tavern, the long line of stores, and the Warehouse, all in succession were consumed. The old Church, the proud old Church, where their fathers had worshipped, was the last to meet its fate. The fire seemed unwilling to attack its sacred walls, but it was to fall with the rest; and as the broad sails of the gay vessel were spread to the morning breeze, which swelled them, that devoted old Church was seen in its raiment of fire, like some old martyr, hugging the flames which consumed it, and pointing with its tapering steeple to an avenging Heaven.

CHAPTER XXXVIII

"We take no note of time but by its loss."
Young.

It is permitted to the story teller, like the angels of ancient metaphysicians, to pass from point to point, and from event to event, without traversing the intermediate space or time. A romance thus becomes a moving panorama, where the prominent objects of interest pass in review before the eyes of the spectator, and not an atlas or chart, where the toiling student, with rigid scrutiny must seek the latitude and longitude of every object which meets his view.

Availing ourselves of this privilege, we will pass rapidly over the events which occurred subsequently to the burning of Jamestown, and again resume the narrative where it more directly affects the fortunes of Hansford and Virginia. We will then suppose that it is about the first of January, 1677, three months after the circumstances detailed in the last chapter. Nathaniel Bacon, the arch rebel, as the loyal historians and legislators of his day delighted to call him, has passed away from the scenes of earth. The damp trenches of Jamestown, more fatal than the arms of his adversaries, have stilled the restless beating of that bold heart, which in other circumstances might have insured success to the cause of freedom. An industrious compiler of the laws of Virginia, and an ingenious commentator on her Colonial History, has suggested from the phraseology of one of the Acts of the Assembly, that Bacon met his fate by the dagger of the assassin, employed by the revengeful Berkeley. But the account of his death is too authentic to admit of such a supposition, and the character of Sir William Berkeley, already clouded with relentless cruelty, is happily freed from the foul imputation, that to the prejudices and sternness of the avenging loyalist he added the atrocity of a malignant fiend. We have the most authentic testimony, that Nathaniel Bacon died of a dysentery, contracted by his exposure in the trenches of Jamestown, at the house of a Dr. Pate, in the county of Gloucester; and that the faithful Lawrence, to screen his insensate clay from the rude vengeance of the Governor, gave the young hero a grave in some unknown forest, where after life's fitful fever he sleeps well.

The cause of freedom, having lost its head, fell a prey to discord and defection. In the selection of a leader to succeed the gallant Bacon, dissensions prevailed among the insurgents, and disgusted at last with the trials to which they were exposed, and wearied with the continuance of a civil war, the great mass of the people retired quietly to their homes. Ingram and Walklate, who attempted to revive the smouldering ashes of the rebellion, were the embodiments of frivolity and stupidity, and were unable to retain that influence over the stern and high-toned patriots which was essential to united action. Deprived of their support, as may be easily conjectured, there was no longer any difficulty in suppressing the ill-fated rebellion; and Walklate, foreseeing the consequences of further resistance, resolved to make a separate peace for himself and a few personal friends, and to leave his more gallant comrades to their fate. The terms of treaty proposed by Berkeley were dispatched by Captain Gardiner to the selfish leader, who, with the broken remnant of the insurgents, was stationed at West Point. He acceded to the terms with avidity, and thus put a final end to a rebellion, which, even at that early day, was so near securing the blessings of rational freedom to Virginia.

Meantime, the long expected aid from England had arrived, and Berkeley, with an organized and reliable force at his command, prepared, with grim satisfaction, to execute his terrible vengeance upon the proscribed and fugitive insurgents. Major Beverley, at the head of a considerable force, was dispatched in pursuit of such of the unhappy men as might linger secreted in the woods and marshes near the river—and smaller parties were detailed for the same object in other parts of the colony. Many of the fugitives were captured and brought before the relentless Governor. There, mocked and insulted in their distress, the devoted patriots were condemned by a court martial, and with cruel haste hurried to execution. The fate of the gallant Lawrence, to whom incidental allusion has been frequently made in the foregoing pages, was long uncertain—but at last those interested in his fate were forced to the melancholy conclusion, that well nigh reduced to starvation in his marshy fastness, with Roman firmness, the brave patriot fell by his own hand, rather than submit to the ruthless cruelty of the vindictive Governor.

Thomas Hansford was among those who were proscribed fugitives from the vengeance of the loyalists. He had in vain endeavoured to rally the dispirited insurgents, and to hazard once more the event of a battle with the royal party. He indignantly refused to accept the terms, so readily embraced by Walklate, and determined to share the fate of those brave comrades, in whose former triumph he had participated. And now, a lonely wanderer, he eluded the vigilant pursuit of his enemies, awaiting with anxiety, the respite which royal interposition would grant, to the unabating vengeance of the governor. He was not without strong hope that the clemency which reflected honour on Charles the Second, towards the enemies of his father, would be extended to the promoters of the ill-fated rebellion in Virginia. In default of this, he trusted to make his escape into Maryland, after the eagerness of pursuit was over, and there secretly to embark for England — where, under an assumed name, he might live out the remnant of his days in peace and security, if not in happiness. It was with a heavy heart that he looked forward to even this remote chance of escape and safety — for it involved the necessity of leaving, for ever, his widowed mother, who leaned upon his strong arm for support; and his beloved Virginia, in whose smiles of favour, he could alone be happy. Still, it was the only honourable chance that offered, and while as a brave man he had nerved himself for any fate, as a good man, he could not reject the means of safety which were extended to him.

While these important changes were taking place in the political world, the family at Windsor Hall were differently affected by the result. Colonel Temple, in the pride of his gratified loyalty, could not disguise his satisfaction even from his unhappy daughter, and rubbed his hands gleefully as the glad tidings came that the rebellion had been quelled. The old lady shared his happiness with all her heart, but mingled with her joy some of the harmless vanity of her nature. She attributed the happy result in a good degree to the counsel and wisdom of her husband, and recurred with great delight to her own bountiful hospitality to the fugitive loyalists. Nay, in the excess of her self-gratulation, she even hinted an opinion, that if Colonel Temple had remained in England, the cause of loyalty would have been much advanced, and that General Monk would not have borne away the palm of having achieved the glorious restoration.

But these loyal sentiments of gratulation met with no response in the heart of Virginia Temple. The exciting scenes through which she had lately passed had left their traces on her young heart. No more the laughing, thoughtless, happy girl whom we have known, shedding light and gaiety on all around her, she had gained, in the increased strength and development of her character, much to compensate for the loss. The furnace which evaporates the lighter particles of the ore, leaves the precious metal in their stead. Thus is it with the trying furnace of affliction in the formation of the human character, and such was its effect upon Virginia. She no longer thought or felt as a girl. She felt that she was a woman, called upon to act a woman's part; and relying on her strengthened nature, but more upon the hand whose protection she had early learned to seek, she was prepared to act that part. The fate of Hansford was unknown to her. She had neither seen nor heard from him since that awful night, when she parted from him at the gate of Jamestown. Convinced of his high sense of honour, and his heroic daring, she knew that he was the last to desert a falling cause, and she trembled for his life, should he fall into the hands of the enraged and relentless Berkeley. But even if her fears in this respect were groundless, the future was still dark to her. The bright dream which she had cherished, that he to whom, in the trusting truth of her young heart, she had plighted her troth, would share with her the joys and hopes of life, was now, alas! dissipated forever. A proscribed rebel, an outcast from home, her father's loyal prejudices were such that she could never hope to unite her destiny with Hansford. And yet, dreary as the future had become, she bore up nobly in the struggle, and, with patient submission, resigned her fate to the will of Heaven.

Her chief employment now was to train the mind of the young Mamalis to truth, and in this sacred duty she derived new consolation in her affliction. The young Indian girl had made Windsor Hall her home since the death of her brother. The generous nature of Colonel Temple could not refuse to the poor orphan, left alone on earth without a protector, a refuge and a home beneath his roof. Nor were the patient and prayerful instructions of Virginia without their reward. The light which had long been struggling to obtain an entrance to her heart, now burst forth in the full effulgence of the truth, and the trusting Mamalis had felt, in all its beauty and reality, the assurance of the promise, "Come unto me all ye that labour and are heavy laden, and I will give you rest." Her manners, which, with all of her association with Virginia, had something of the wildness of the savage, were now softened and subdued. Her picturesque but wild costume, which reminded her of her former life, was discarded for the more modest dress which the refinement of civilization had prescribed. Her fine, expressive countenance, which had often been darkened by reflecting the wild passions of her unsubdued heart, was now radiant with peaceful joy; and as you gazed upon the softened expression, the tranquil and composed bearing of the young girl, you might well "take knowledge of her that she had been with Jesus."

CHAPTER XXXIX

"Farewell and blessings on thy way,
Where'r thou goest, beloved stranger,
Better to sit and watch that ray,
And think thee safe though far away,
Than have thee near me and in danger."
Lalla Roohk.

Moonlight at Windsor Hall! The waning, January moon shone coldly and brightly, as it rose above the dense forest which surrounded the once more peaceful home of Colonel Temple. The tall poplars which shaded the quiet yard were silvered with its light, and looked like medieval knights all clad in burnished and glistening mail. The crisp hoarfrost that whitened the frozen ground sparkled in the mellow beams, like twinkling stars, descended to earth, and drinking in with rapture the clear light of their native heaven. Not a sound was heard save the dreary, wintry blast, as it sighed its mournful requiem over the dead year, "gone from the earth for ever."

Virginia Temple had not yet retired to rest, although it was growing late. She was sitting alone, in her little chamber, and watching the glowing embers on the hearth, as they sparkled for a moment, and shed a ruddy light around, and then were extinguished, throwing the whole room into dark shadow. Sad emblem, these fleeting sparks, of the hopes that had once been bright before her, assuming fancied shapes of future joy and peace and love, and then dying to leave her sad heart the darker for their former presence. In the solitude of her own thoughts she was taking a calm review of her past life—her early childhood—when she played in innocent mirth beneath the shade of the oaks and poplars that still stood unchanged in the yard—her first acquaintance with Hansford, which opened a new world to her young heart, replete with joys and treasures unknown before—all the thrilling events of the last few months—her last meeting with her lover, and his prayer that she at least would not censure him, when he was gone—her present despondency and gloom—all these thoughts came in slow and solemn procession across her mind, like dreary ghosts of the buried past.

Suddenly she was startled from her reverie by the sound of a low, sweet, familiar voice, beneath her window, and, as she listened, the melancholy spirit of the singer sought and found relief in the following tender strains:

"Once more I seek thy quiet home,
My tale of love to tell,
Once more from danger's field I come,
To breathe a last farewell!
Though hopes are flown,
Though friends are gone;
Yet wheresoe'r I flee,
I still retain,
And hug the chain
Which binds my soul to thee.

"My heart, like some lone chamber left,
Must, mouldering, fall at last;
Of hope, of love, of thee bereft,
It lives but in the past.
With jealous care,
I cherish there
The web, however small,
That memory weaves,
And mercy leaves,
Upon that ruined wall.

"Though Tyranny, with bloody laws,
May dig my early grave,
Yet death, when met in Freedom's cause,
Is sweetest to the brave;
Wedded to her,
Without a fear,
I'll mount her funeral pile,
Welcome the death
Which seals my faith,
And meet it with a smile.

"While, like the tides, that softly swell
To kiss their mother moon,
Thy gentle soul will soar to dwell
In visions with mine own;
As skies distil
The dews that fill
The blushing rose at even,

So blest above,
I'll mourn thy love
And weep for thee in heaven."

It needed not the well-known voice of Hansford to assure the weeping girl that he was near her. The burden of that sad song, which found an echo in her own heart, told her too plainly that it could be only he. It was no time for delicate scruples of propriety. She only knew that he was near her and in danger. Rising from her chair, and throwing around her a shawl to protect her from the chill night air, she hastened to the door. In another moment they were in each other's arms.

"Oh, my own Virginia," said Hansford, "this is too, too kind. I had only thought to come and breathe a last farewell, and then steal from your presence for ever. I felt that it was a privilege to be near you, to watch, unseen, the flickering light reflected from your presence. This itself had been reward sufficient for the peril I encounter. How sweet then to hear once more the accents of your voice, and to feel once more the warm beating of your faithful heart."

"And could you think," said Virginia, as she wept upon his shoulder, "that knowing you to be in danger, I could fail to see you. Oh, Hansford! you little know the truth of woman's love if you can for a moment doubt that your misfortune and your peril have made you doubly dear."

"Yet how brief must be my stay. The avenger is behind me, and I must soon resume my lonely wandering."

"And will you again leave me?" asked Virginia, in a reproachful tone.

"Leave you, dearest, oh, how sweet would be my fate, after all my cares and sufferings, if I could but die here. But this must not be. Though I trust I know how to meet death as a brave man, yet it is my duty, as a good man, to leave no honourable means untried to save my life."

"But your danger cannot be so great, dearest," said Virginia, tenderly. "Surely my father—"

"Would feel it his duty," said Hansford, interrupting her, "to deliver me up to justice; and feeling it to be such, he would have the moral firmness to discharge it. Poor old gentleman! like many of his party, his prejudice perverts his true and generous heart. My poor country must suffer long before she can overcome the opposition of bigoted loyalty. Forgive me for speaking thus of your noble father, Virginia—but prejudices like these are the thorns which spring up in his heart and choke the true word of freedom, and render it unfruitful. Is it not so, dearest?"

"You mistake his generous nature," said Virginia, earnestly. "You mistake his love for me. You mistake his sound judgment. You mistake his high sense of honour. Think you that he sees no difference between the man who, impelled by principle, asserts what he believes to be a right, and him, who for his own selfish ends and personal advancement, would sacrifice his country. Yes, my dear friend, you mistake my father. He will gladly interpose with the Governor and restore you to happiness, to freedom, and to—"

She paused, unable to proceed for the sobs that choked her utterance, and then gave vent to a flood of passionate grief.

"You would add, 'and to thee,'" said Hansford, finishing the sentence. "God knows, my girl, that such a hope would make me dare more peril than I have yet encountered. But, alas! if it were even as you say, what weight would his remonstrance have with that imperious old tyrant, Berkeley? It would be but the thistle-down against the cannon ball in the scales of his justice."

"He dare not refuse my father's demands," said Virginia. "One who has been so devoted to his cause, who has sacrificed so much for his king, and who has afforded shelter and protection to the Governor himself in the hour of his peril and need, is surely entitled to this poor favour at his hands. He dare not refuse to grant it."

"Alas! Virginia, you little know the character of Sir William Berkeley, when you say he dares not. But the very qualities which you claim, and justly claim, for your father, would prevent him from exerting that influence with the Governor which your hopes whisper would be so successful—'His noble nature' would prompt him at any sacrifice to yield personal feeling to a sense of public duty. 'His love for you' would prompt him to rescue you from the *rebel* who dared aspire to your hand. 'His sound judgment' would dictate the maxim, that it were well for one man to die for the people; and his 'high sense of honour' would prevent him from interposing between a condemned *traitor* and his deserved doom. Be assured, Virginia, that thus would your father reason; and with his views of loyalty and justice, I could not blame him for the conclusion to which he came."

"Then in God's name," cried Virginia, in an agony of desperation, for she saw the force of Hansford's views, "how can you shun this threatening danger? Whither can you fly?"

"My only hope," said Hansford, gloomily, "is to leave the Colony and seek refuge in Maryland, though I fear that this is hopeless. If I fail in this, then I must lurk in some hiding place until instructions from England may arrive, and check the vindictive Berkeley in his ruthless cruelty."

"And is there a hope of that!" said Virginia, quickly.

"There is a faint hope, and that slender thread is all that hangs between me and a traitor's doom. But I rely with some confidence upon the mild and humane policy pursued by Charles toward the enemies of his father. At any rate, it is all that is left me, and you know the proverb," he added, with a sad smile, "'A drowning man catches at straws.' Any chance, however slight, appears larger when seen through the gloom of approaching despair, just as any object seems greater when seen through a mist."

"It is not, it shall not be slight," said the hopeful girl, "we will lay hold upon it with firm and trusting hearts, and it will cheer us in our weary way, and then—"

But here the conversation was interrupted by the sound of approaching footsteps, and the light, graceful form of Mamalis stood before them. The quick ear of the Indian girl had caught the first low notes of Hansford's serenade, even while she slept, and listening attentively to the sound, she had heard Virginia leave the room and go down stairs. Alarmed at her prolonged absence, Mamalis could no longer hesitate on the propriety of ascertaining its cause, and hastily dressing herself, she ran down to the open door and joined the lovers as we have stated.

"We are discovered," said Hansford, in a surprised but steady voice. "Farewell, Virginia." And he was about to rush from the place, when Virginia interposed.

"Fear nothing from her," she said. "Her trained ear caught the sounds of our voices more quickly than could the duller senses of the European. You are in no danger; and her opportune presence suggests a plan for your escape."

"What is that?" asked Hansford, anxiously.

"First tell me," said Virginia, "how long it will probably be before the milder policy of Charles will arrest the Governor in his vengeance."

"It is impossible to guess with accuracy—if, indeed, it ever should come. But the king has heard for some time of the suppression of the enterprise, and it can scarcely be more than two weeks before we hear from him. But to what does your question tend?"

"Simply this," returned Virginia. "The wigwam of Mamalis is only about two miles from the hall, and in so secluded a spot that it is entirely unknown to any of the Governor's party. There we can supply your present wants, and give you timely warning of any approaching danger. The old wigwam is a good deal dilapidated, but then it will at least afford you shelter from the weather."

"And from that ruder storm which threatens me," said Hansford, gloomily. "You are right. I know the place well, and trust it may be a safe retreat, at least for the present. But, alas! how sad is my fate,—to be skulking from justice like a detected thief or murderer, afraid to show my face to my fellow in the open day, and starting like a frightened deer at every approaching sound. Oh, it is too horrible!"

"Think not of it thus," said Virginia, in an encouraging voice. "Remember it only as the dull twilight that divides the night from the morning. This painful suspense will soon be over; and then, safe and happy, we will smile at the dangers we have passed."

"No, Virginia," said Hansford, in the same gloomy voice, "you are too hopeful. There is a whispering voice within that tells me that this plan will not succeed, and that we cannot avoid the dangers which threaten me. No," he cried, throwing off the gloom which hung over him, while his fine blue eye flashed with pride. "No! The decree has gone forth! Every truth must succeed with blood. If the blood of the martyrs be the seed of the Church, it may also enrich the soil where liberty must grow; and far rather would I that my blood should be shed in such a cause, than that it should creep sluggishly in my veins through a long and useless life, until it clotted and stagnated in an ignoble grave."

"Oh, there spoke that fearful pride again," said Virginia, with a deep sigh; "the pride that pursues its mad career, unheeding prudence, unguided by judgment, until it is at last checked by its own destruction. And would you not sacrifice the glory that you speak of, for me?"

"You have long since furnished me the answer to that plea, my girl," he replied, pressing her tenderly to his heart. "Do you remember, Lucasta,

'I had not loved thee, dear, so much,
Loved I not honour more.'

Believe me, my Virginia, it is an honourable and not a glorious name I seek. Without the latter, life still would be happy and blessed when adorned by your smiles. Without the former, your smile and your love would add bitterness to the cup that dishonour would bid me quaff. And now, Virginia, farewell. The night air has chilled you, dearest—then go, and remember me in your dreams. One fond kiss, to keep virgined upon my lips till we meet again. Farewell, Mamalis—be faithful to your kind mistress." And then imprinting one long, last kiss upon the fair cheek of the trusting Virginia, he turned from the door, and was soon lost from their sight in the dense forest.

Once more in her own little room, Virginia, with a grateful heart, fell upon her knees, and poured forth her thanks to Him, who had thus far prospered her endeavours to minister to the cares and sorrows of her lover. With a calmer heart she sought repose, and wept herself to sleep with almost happy tears. Hansford, in the mean time, pursued his quiet way through the forest, his pathway sufficiently illumined by the pale moonlight, which came trembling through the moaning trees. The thoughts of the young rebel were fitfully gloomy or pleasant, as despondency and hope alternated in his breast. In that lonely walk he had an opportunity to reflect calmly and fully upon his past life. The present was indeed clouded with danger, and the future with uncertainty and gloom. Yet, in this self-examination, he saw nothing to justify reproach or to awaken regret. He scanned his motives, and he felt that they were pure. He reviewed his acts, and he saw in them but the struggles of a brave, free man in the maintenance of the right. The enterprise in which he had engaged had indeed failed, but its want of success did not affect the holiness of the design. Even in its failure, he proudly hoped that the seeds of truth had been sown in the popular mind, which might hereafter germinate and be developed into freedom. As these thoughts passed through his mind, a dim dream of the future glories of his country flashed across him. The bright heaven of the future seemed to open before him, as before the eyes of the dying Stephen—but soon it closed again, and all was dark.

The wigwam which he entered, after a walk of about half an hour, was desolate enough, but its very loneliness made it a better safeguard against the vigilance of his pursuers. He closed the aperture which served for the door, with the large mat used for the purpose; then carefully priming his pistols, which he kept constantly by him in case of surprise, and wrapping his rough horseman's coat around him, he flung himself upon a mat in the centre of the wigwam, and sank into a profound slumber.

CHAPTER XL

"He should be hereabouts. The doubling hare,
When flying from the swift pursuit of hounds,
Baying loud triumph, leaves her wonted path,
And seeks security within her nest."

The Captive.

On the evening which followed the events narrated in the last chapter, a party of half a dozen horsemen might be seen riding leisurely along the road which led to Windsor Hall. From their dress and bearing they might at once be recognized as military men, and indeed it was a detachment of the force sent by Sir William Berkeley in search of such of the rebels as might be lurking in different sections of the country. At their head was Alfred Bernard, his tall and graceful form well set off by the handsome military dress of the period. Dignified by a captaincy of dragoons, the young intriguer at last thought himself on the high road to success, and his whole course was marked by a zealous determination to deserve by his actions the confidence reposed in him. For this his temper and his cold, selfish nature eminently fitted him. The vindictive Governor had no fear but that his vengeance would be complete, so long as Alfred Bernard acted as his agent.

As the party approached the house, Colonel Temple, whose attention was arrested by such an unusual appearance in the then peaceful state of the country, came out to meet them, and with his usual bland courtesy invited them in, at the same time shaking Bernard warmly by the hand. The rough English soldiers, obeying the instructions of their host, conducted their horses to the stable, while the young captain followed his hospitable entertainer into the hall. Around the blazing fire, which crackled and roared in the broad hearth, the little family were gathered to hear the news.

"Prythee, Captain Bernard, for I must not forget your new title," said the colonel, "what is the cause of this demonstration? No further trouble with the rebels?"

"No, no," replied Bernard, "except to smoke the cowardly fellows out of their holes. In the words of your old bard, we have only scotched the snake, not killed it—and we are now seeking to bring the knaves to justice."

"And do you find them difficult to catch?" said the Colonel. "Is the scotched snake an 'anguis in herba?'"

"Aye, but they cannot escape us. These worshippers of liberty, who would fain be martyrs to her cause, shall not elude the vigilance of justice. I need not add, that you are not the object of our search, Colonel."

"Scarcely, my lad," returned Temple, with a smile, "for my mythology has taught me, that these kindred deities are so nearly allied that the true votaries of liberty will ever be pilgrims to the shrine of justice."

"And the pseudo votaries of freedom," continued Bernard, "who would divide the sister goddesses, should be offered up as a sacrifice to appease the neglected deity."

"Well, maybe so," returned Temple; "but neither religion nor government should demand human sacrifices to a great extent. A few of the prominent leaders might well be cut off to strike terror into the hearts of the rest. Thus the demands of justice would be satisfied, consistently with clemency which mercy would dictate."

"My dear sir, a hecatomb would not satisfy Berkeley. I am but his minister, and could not, if I would, arrest his arm. Even now I come by his express directions to ascertain whether any of the rebels may be secreted near your residence. While he does not for a moment suspect your loyalty, yet one of the villains, and he among the foremost in the rebellion, has been traced in this direction."

"Sir," cried Temple, colouring with honest indignation; "dare you suspect that I could harbour a rebel beneath my roof! But remember, that I would as lief do that, abhorrent though it be to my principles, as to harbour a spy."

"My dear sir," said Bernard, softly, "you mistake me most strangely, if you suppose that I could lodge such a suspicion for a moment in my heart; nor have I come as a spy upon your privacy, but to seek your counsel. Sir William Berkeley is so well convinced of your stern and unflinching faith, that he enjoins me to apply to you early for advice as to how I should proceed in my duty."

"Well, my dear boy," said Temple, relapsing into good humour, for he was not proof against the tempting bait of flattery, "you must pardon the haste of an old man, who cannot bear any imputation upon his devotion to the cause of his royal master. While I cannot aid you in your search, my house is freely open to yourself and your party for such time as you may think proper to use it."

"You have my thanks, my dear sir," said Bernard, "and indeed you are entitled to the gratitude of the whole government. Sir William Berkeley bade me say that he could never forget your kindness to him and his little band of fugitives; and Lady Frances often says that she scarcely regrets the cares and anxiety attending her flight, since they afforded her an opportunity of enjoying the society of Mrs. Temple in her own home, where she so especially shines."

"Indeed, we thank them both most cordially," said Mrs. Temple. "It was a real pleasure to us to have them, I am sure; and though we hardly had time to make them as comfortable as they might have been, yet a poor feast, seasoned with a warm welcome, is fit for a king."

"I trust," said Bernard, "that Miss Virginia unites with you in the interest which you profess in the cause of loyalty. May I hope, that should it ever be our fortune again to be thrown like stranded wrecks upon your hospitality, her welcome will not be wanting to our happiness."

"It will always give me pleasure," said Virginia, "to welcome the guests of my parents, and to add, as far as I can, to their comfort, whoever they may be—more particularly when those guests are among my own special friends."

"Of which number I am proud to consider myself, though unworthy of such an honour," said Bernard. "But excuse me for a few moments, ladies, I have somewhat to say to my sergeant before dinner. I will return anon—as soon as possible; but you know, Colonel, duty should ever be first served, and afterwards pleasure may be indulged. Duty is the prim old wife, who must be duly attended to, and then Pleasure, the fair young damsel, may claim her share of our devotion. Aye, Colonel?"

"Nay, if you enter the marriage state with such ideas of its duties as that," returned the Colonel, smiling, "I rather think you will have a troublesome career before you. But your maxim is true, though clothed in an allegory a little too licentious. So, away with you, my boy, and return as soon as you can, for I have much to ask you."

Released from the restraints imposed by the presence of the Colonel and the ladies, Bernard rubbed his hands and chuckled inwardly as he went in search of his sergeant.

"I am pretty sure we are on the right scent, Holliday," he said, addressing a tall, strapping old soldier of about six feet in height. "This prejudiced old steed seemed disposed to kick before he was spurred—and, indeed, if he knew nothing himself, there is a pretty little hind here, who I'll warrant is not so ignorant of the hiding-place of her young hart."

"But I tell you what, Cap'n, it's devilish hard to worm a secret out of these women kind. They'll tell any body else's secret, fast enough, but d—n me if it don't seem as how they only do that to give more room to keep their own."

"Well, we must try at any rate. It is not for you to oppose with your impertinent objections what I may choose order. I hope you are soldier enough to have learned that it is only your duty to obey."

"Oh! yes, Cap'n. I've learned that lesson long ago—and what's more, I learned it on horseback, but, faith, it was one of those wooden steeds that made me do all the travelling. Why, Lord bless me, to obey! It's one of my ten commandments. I've got it written in stripes that's legible on my shoulders now. 'Obey your officers in all things that your days may be long and your back unskinned.'"

"Well, stop your intolerable nonsense," said Bernard, "and hear what I would say. We stay here to-night. There is an Indian girl who lives here, a kind of upper servant. You must manage to see her and talk with her. But mind, nothing of our object, or your tongue shall be blistered for it. Tell her that I wish to see her, beneath the old oak tree to night, at ten o'clock. If she refuses, tell her to 'remember Berkenhead.' These words will act as a charm upon her. Remember—Hush, here comes the Colonel."

It will be remembered by the reader that the magic of these two words, which were to have such an influence upon the young Mamalis, was due to the shrewd suspicion of Alfred Bernard, insinuated at the time, that she was the assassin of the ill-fated Berkenhead. By holding this simple rod, *in terrorem*, over the poor girl, Bernard now saw that he might wield immense power over her, and if the secret of Hansford's hiding-place had been confided to her, he might easily extort it either by arousing her vengeance once more, or in default of that by a menace of exposure and punishment for the murder. But first he determined to see Virginia, and make his peace with her; and under the plausible guise of sympathy in her distress and pity for Hansford, to excite in her an interest in his behalf, even while he was plotting the ruin of her lover.

With his usual pliancy of manner, and control over his feelings, he engaged in conversation with Colonel Temple, humouring the well-known prejudices of the old gentleman, and by a little dexterous flattery winning over the unsuspicious old lady to his favor. Even Virginia, though her heart misgave her from the first that the arrival of Bernard boded no good to her lover, was deceived by his plausible manners and attracted by his brilliant conversation. So the tempter, with the graceful crest, and beautiful colours of the subtle serpent beguiled Eve far more effectually, than if in his own shape he had attempted to convince her by the most specious sophisms.

CHAPTER XLI

"Was ever woman in this humour wooed?"
Richard III.

Dinner being over, the gentlemen remained according to the good old custom, to converse over their wine, while Virginia retired to the quiet little parlour, and with some favourite old author tried to beguile her thoughts from the bitter fears which she felt for the safety of Hansford. But it was all in vain. Her eyes often wandered from her book, and fixed upon the blazing, hickory fire, she was lost in a painful reverie. As she weighed in her mind the many chances in favour of, and against his escape, she turned in her trouble to Him, who alone could rescue her, and with the tears streaming down her pale cheeks, she murmured in bitter accents, "Oh, Lord! in Thee have I trusted, let me never be confounded." Even while she spoke, she was surprised to hear immediately behind her, the well-known voice of Alfred Bernard, for so entirely lost had she been in meditation that she had not heard his step as he entered the room.

"Miss Temple, and in tears!" he said, with well assumed surprise. "What can have moved you thus, Virginia?"

"Alas! Mr. Bernard, you who have known my history and my troubles for the last few bitter months, cannot be ignorant that I have much cause for sadness. But," she added, with a faint attempt to smile, "had I known of your presence, I would not have sought to entertain you with my sorrows."

"The troubles that you speak of are passed, Miss Temple," said Bernard, affecting to misunderstand her, "and as the Colony begins to smile again in the beams of returning peace, you, fair Virginia, should also smile in sympathy with your namesake."

"Mr. Bernard, you must jest. You at least should have known, ere this, that my individual sorrows are not so dependent upon the political condition of the Colony. You at least should have known, sir, that the very peace you boast of may be the knell of hopes more dear to a woman's heart than even the glory and welfare of her country."

"Miss Temple," returned Bernard, with a grave voice, "since you are determined to treat seriously what I have said, I will change my tone. Though you choose to doubt my sincerity, I must express the deep sympathy which I feel in your sorrows, even though I know that these sorrows are induced by your apprehensions for the fate of a rival."

"And that sympathy, sir, is illustrated by your present actions," said Virginia, bitterly. "You would be at the same time the Judean robber and the good Samaritan, and while inflicting a deadly wound upon your victim, and stripping him of cherished hopes, you would administer the oil and wine of your mocking sympathy."

"I might choose to misunderstand your unkind allusions, Miss Temple," replied Bernard, "but there is no need of concealment between us. You have rightly judged the object of my mission, but in this I act as the officer of government, not as the ungenerous rival of Major Hansford."

"So does the public executioner," replied Virginia, "but I am not aware that in its civil and military departments as well as in the navy, our government impresses men into her service against their will."

"You seem determined to misunderstand me, Virginia," said Alfred, with some warmth; "but you shall learn that I am not capable of the want of generosity which you attribute to me. Know then, that it was from a desire to serve you personally through your friend, that I urged the governor to let me come in pursuit of Major Hansford. Suppose, instead, he should fall in the hands of Beverley. Cruel and relentless as that officer has already shown himself to be, his prisoner would suffer every indignity and persecution, even before he was delivered to the tender mercies of Sir William Berkeley — while in me, as his captor, you may rest assured that for your sake, he would meet with kindness and indulgence, and even my warm mediation with the governor in his behalf."

"Oh, then," cried Virginia, trusting words so softly and plausibly spoken, "if you are indeed impelled by a motive so generous and disinterested, it is still in your power to save him. Your influence with the Governor is known, and one word from your lips might control the fate of a brave man, and restore happiness and peace to a broken-hearted girl. Oh! would not this amply compensate even for the neglect of duty? Would it not be far nobler to secure the happiness of two grateful hearts, than to shed the blood of a brave and generous man, and to wade through that red stream to success and fame? Believe me, Mr. Bernard, when you come to die, the recollection of such an act will be sweeter to your soul than all the honour and glory which an admiring posterity could heap above your cold, insensate ashes. If I am any thing to you; if my happiness would be an object of interest to your heart; and if my love, my life-long love, would be worthy of your acceptance, they are yours. Forgive the boldness, the freedom with which

I have spoken. It may be unbecoming in a young girl, but let it be another proof of the depth, the sincerity of my feelings, when I can forget a maiden's delicacy in the earnestness of my plea."

It was impossible not to be moved with the earnest and touching manner of the weeping girl, as with clasped hands and streaming eyes, she almost knelt to Bernard in the fervent earnestness of her feelings. Machiavellian as he was, and accustomed to disguise his heart, the young man was for a moment almost dissuaded from his design. Taking Virginia gently by the hand, he begged her to be calm. But the feeling of generosity which for a moment gleamed on his heart, like a brief sunbeam on a stormy day, gave way to the wonted selfishness with which that heart was clouded.

"And can you still cling with such tenacity to a man who has proven himself so unworthy of you," he said; "to one who has long since sacrificed you to his own fanatical purposes. Even should he escape the fate which awaits him, he can never be yours. Your own independence of feeling, your father's prejudices, every thing conspires to prevent a union so unnatural. Hansford may live, but he can never live to be your husband."

"Who empowered you to prohibit thus boldly the bans between us, and to dissolve our plighted troth?" said Virginia, with indignation.

"You again mistake me," replied Bernard. "God forbid that I should thus intrude upon what surely concerns me not. I only expressed, my dear friend, what you know full well, that whatever be the fate of Major Hansford, you can never marry him. Why, then, this strange interest in his fate?"

"And can you think thus of woman's love? Can you suppose that her heart is so selfish that, because her own cherished hopes are blasted, she can so soon forget and coldly desert one who has first awakened those sweet hopes, and who is now in peril? Believe me, Mr. Bernard, dear as I hold that object to my soul, sad and weary as life would be without one who had made it so happy, I would freely, aye, almost cheerfully yield his love, and be banished for ever from his presence, if I could but save his life."

"You are a noble girl," said Alfred, with admiration; "and teach me a lesson that too few have learned, that love is never selfish. But, yet, I cannot relinquish the sweet reward which you have promised for my efforts in behalf of Hansford. Then tell me once more, dear girl, if I arrest the hand of justice which now threatens his life; if he be once more restored to liberty and security, would you reward his deliverer with your love?"

"Oh, yes!" cried the trusting girl, mistaking his meaning; "and more, I would pledge his lasting gratitude and affection to his generous preserver."

"Nay," said Bernard, rather coldly, "that would not add much inducement to me. But you, Virginia," he added, passionately, "would you be mine—would the bright dream of my life be indeed realized, and might I enshrine you in my faithful heart, as a sacred idol, to whom in hourly adoration I might bow?"

"How mean you, sir," exclaimed Virginia, with surprise. "I fear you have misunderstood my words. My love, my gratitude, my friendship, I promised, but not my heart."

"Then, indeed, am I strangely at fault," said Bernard, with a sneering laugh. "The love you would bestow, would be such as you would feel towards the humblest boor, who had done you a service; and your gratitude but the natural return which any human being would make to the dog who saves his life. Nay, mistress mine, not so platonic, if you please. Think you that, for so cold a feeling as friendship and gratitude, I would rescue this skulking hound from the lash of his master, which he so richly deserves, or from the juster doom of the craven cur, the rope and gallows. No, Virginia Temple, there is no longer any need of mincing matters between us. It is a simple question of bargain and sale. You have said that you would renounce the love of Hansford to save his life. Very well, one step more and all is accomplished. The boon I ask, as the reward of my services, is your heart, or at least your hand. Yield but this, and I will arrest the malice of that doting old knight, who, with his fantastic tricks, has made the angels laugh instead of weep. Deny me, and by my troth, Thomas Hansford meets a traitor's doom."

So complete was the revulsion of feeling from the almost certainty of success, to the despair and indignation induced by so base a proposition, that it was some moments before Virginia Temple could speak. Bernard mistaking the cause of her silence, deemed that she was hesitating as to her course, and pursuing his supposed advantage, he added, tenderly,— "Cheer, up Virginia; cheer up, my bride. I read in those silent tears your answer. I know the struggle is hard, and I love you the more that it is so. It is an earnest of your future constancy. In a short time the trial will be over, and we will learn to forget our sorrows in our love. He who is so unworthy of you will have sought in some distant land solace for your loss, which will be easily attained by his pliant nature. A traitor to his country, will not long mourn the loss of his bride."

"'Tis thou who art the traitor, dissembling hypocrite," cried Virginia, vehemently. "Think you that my silence arose from a moment's consideration of your base proposition? I was stunned at beholding such a monster in the human form. But I defy you yet. The governor shall learn how the fawning favourite of his palace, tears the hand that feeds him—and those who can protect me from your power, shall chastise your insolence. Instead of the love and gratitude I promised, there, take my lasting hate and scorn."

And the young girl proudly rising erect as she spoke, her eyes flashing, but tearless, her bosom heaving with indignation, her nostrils dilated, and her hand extended in bitter contempt towards the astonished Bernard, shouted, "Father, father!" until the hall rung with the sound.

Happily for Alfred Bernard, Colonel Temple and his wife had left the house for a few moments, on a visit to old Giles' cabin, the old man having been laid up with a violent attack of the rheumatics. The wily intriguer was for once caught in his own springe. He had overacted his part, and had grossly mistaken the character of the brave young girl, whom he had so basely insulted. He felt that if he lost a moment, the house would be alarmed, and his miserable hypocrisy exposed. Rushing to Virginia, he whispered, in an agitated voice, which he failed to control with his usual self-command,

"For God's sake, be silent. I acknowledge I have done wrong; but I will explain. Remember Hansford's life is in your hands. Come, now, dear Virginia, sit you down, I will save him."

The proud expression of scorn died away from the curled lips of the girl, and interest in her lover's fate again took entire possession of her heart. She paused and listened. The wily Jesuit had again conquered, and He who rules the universe with such mysterious justice, had permitted evil once more to triumph over innocence.

"Yes," repeated Bernard, regaining his composure with his success; "I will save him. I mistook your character, Miss Temple. I had thought you the simple-hearted girl, who for the sake of her lover's life would sell her heart to his preserver. I now recognize in you the high-spirited woman, who, conscious of right, would meet her own despair in its defence. Alas! in thus losing you for ever, I have just found you possessed of qualities which make you doubly worthy to be won. But I resign you to him whom you have chosen, and in my admiration for the woman, I have almost lost my hatred for the man. For your sake, Miss Temple, Major Hansford shall not want my warm interposition with the Governor in his behalf. Let my reward be your esteem or your contempt, it is still my duty thus to atone for the wound which I have unfortunately inflicted on your feelings. You will excuse and respect my wish to end this painful interview."

And so he left the room, and Virginia once more alone, gave vent to her emotions so long suppressed, in a flood of bitter tears.

"Well, Holliday," said Bernard, as he met that worthy in the hall, "I hope you have been more fortunate with the red heifer than I with the white hind—what says Mamalis?"

"The fact is, Cap'n, that same heifer is about as troublesome a three year old as I ever had the breaking on. She seemed bent on hooking me."

"Did you not make use of the talisman I told you of?" asked Bernard.

"Well, I don't know what you call a tell-us-man," said Holliday, "but I told her that you said she must remember Backinhead, and I'll warrant it was tell-us-woman soon enough. Bless me, if she didn't most turn white, for all her red skin, and she got the trimbles so that I began to think she was going to have the high-strikes—and so says she at last; says she, in kind of choking voice like, 'Well, tell him I will meet him under the oak tree, as he wishes.'"

"Very well," said Bernard, "we will succeed yet, and then your hundred pounds are made—my share is yours already if you be but faithful to me—I am convinced he has been here," he continued, musing, and half unconscious of Holliday's presence. "The hopeful interest that Virginia feels, her knowledge of the fact that he still lives and is at large, and the apprehensions which mingle with her hopes, all convince me that I'm on the right track. Well, I'll spoil a pretty love affair yet, before it approaches its consummation. Fine girl, too, and a pity to victimize her. Bless me, how majestic she looked; with what a queen-like scorn she treated me, the cold, insensate intriguer, as they call me. I begin to love her almost as much as I love her land—but, beware, Alfred Bernard, love might betray you. My game is a bold and desperate one, but the stake for which I play repays the risk. By God, I'll have her yet; she shall learn to bow her proud head, and to love me too—and then the fair fields of Windsor Hall will not be less fertile for the price which I pay for them in a rival's blood—and such a rival. He scorned and defied me when the overtures of peace were extended to him; let him look to it, that in rejecting the olive, he has not planted the cypress in its stead. Thus revenge is united with policy in the attainment of my object, and—What are you staring at, you gaping idiot?" he cried, seeing the big, pewter coloured eyes of Holliday fixed upon him in mute astonishment.

"Why, Cap'n, damme if I don't believe you are talking in your sleep with your eyes open."

"And what did you hear me say, knave?"

"Oh, nothing that will ever go the farther for my hearing it. It's all one to me whether you're working for your country or yourself in this matter, so long as my pretty pounds are none the less heavy and safe."

"I'm working for both, you fool," returned Bernard. "Did you ever know a general or a patriot who did not seek to serve himself as well as his country?"

"Well, no," retorted the soldier, "for what the world calls honour, and what the rough soldier calls money, is at last only different kinds of coin of the same metal."

"Well, hush your impudence," said Bernard, "and mind, not a word of what you have heard, or you shall feel my power as well as others. In the meantime, here is a golden key to lock your lips," and he handed the fellow a sovereign, which he greedily accepted.

"Thank you, Cap'n," said Holliday, touching his hat and pocketing the money; "you need not be afraid of me, for I've seen tricks in my time worth two of that. And for the matter of taking this yellow boy, which might look to some like hush-money, the only difference between the patriot and me is, that he gets paid for opening his mouth, and I for keeping mine shut."

"You are a saucy knave," said Bernard, reassured by the fellow's manner; "and I'll warrant you never served under old Noll's Puritan standard. But away with you, and remember to be in place at ten o'clock to-night, and come to me at this signal," and he gave a shrill whistle, which Holliday promised to understand and obey.

And so they separated, Bernard to while away the tedious hours, by conversing with the old Colonel, and by endeavouring to reinstate himself in the good opinion of Virginia, while Holliday repaired to the kitchen, where, in company with his comrades and the white servants of the hall, he emptied about a half gallon of brown October ale.

CHAPTER XLII

"He sat her on a milk-white steed,
And himself upon a grey;
He never turned his face again,
But he bore her quite away."
                    The Knight of the Burning Pestle.

"Oh, woe is me for Gerrard! I have brought
Confusion on the noblest gentleman
That ever truly loved."
                    The Triumph of Love.

The night, though only starry, was scarce less lovely for the absence of the moon. So bright indeed was the milky way, the white girdle, with which the night adorns her azure robe, that you might almost imagine the moon had not disappeared, but only melted and diffused itself in the milder radiance of that fair circlet.

As was always the custom in the country, the family had retired at an early hour, and Bernard quietly left the house to fulfil his engagement with Mamalis. They stood, he and the Indian girl, beneath the shade of the old oak, so often mentioned in the preceding pages. With his handsome Spanish cloak of dark velvet plush, thrown gracefully over his shoulders, his hat looped up and fastened in front with a gold button, after the manner of the times, Alfred Bernard stood with folded arms, irresolute as to how he should commence a conversation so important, and requiring such delicate address. Mamalis stood before him, with that air of nameless but matchless grace so peculiar to those, who unconstrained by the arts and affectations of society, assume the attitude of ease and beauty which nature can alone suggest. She watched him with a look of eagerness, anxious on her part for the silence to be broken, that she might learn the meaning and the object of this strange interview.

Alfred Bernard was too skillful an intriguer to broach abruptly the subject which, most absorbed his thoughts, and which had made him seek this interview, and when at last he spoke, Mamalis was at a loss to guess what there was in the commonplaces which he used, that could be of interest to him. But the wily hypocrite led her on step by step, until gradually and almost unconsciously to herself he had fully developed his wishes.

"You live here altogether, now, do you not?" he asked, kindly.

"Yes."

"Are they kind to you?"

"Oh yes, they are kind to all."

"And you are happy?"

"Yes, as happy as those can be who are left alone on earth."

"What! are there none of your family now living?"

"No, no!" she replied, bitterly; "the blood of Powhatan now runs in this narrow channel," and she held out her graceful arms, as she spoke, with an expressive gesture.

"Alas! I pity you," said Bernard, sighing. "We are alike in this—for my blood is reduced to as narrow a channel as your own. But your family was very numerous?"

"Yes, numerous as those stars—and bright and beautiful as they."

"Judging from the only Pleiad that remains," thought Bernard, "you may well say so—and can you," he added, aloud, "forgive those who have thus injured you?"

"Forgive, oh yes, or how shall I be forgiven! Look at those stars! They shine the glory of the night. They vanish before the sun of the morning. So faded my people before the arms of the white man—and yet I can freely forgive them all!"

"What, even those who have quenched those stars!" said Bernard, with a sinister meaning in his tone.

"You mistake," replied Mamalis, touchingly. "They are not quenched. The stars we see to-night, though unseen on the morrow, are still in heaven."

"Nay, Mamalis," said Bernard, "the creed of your fathers taught not thus. I thought the Indian maxim was that blood alone could wipe out the stain of blood."

"I love the Christian lesson better," said Mamalis, softly. "And you, Mr. Bernard, should not try to shake my new born faith. 'Love your enemies— bless them that curse you—pray for them that despitefully use you and persecute you—that you may be the children of your Father which is in heaven.' The orphan girl on earth would love to be the child of her father in heaven."

The sweet simplicity with which the poor girl thus referred to the precepts and promises of her new religion, derived more touching beauty from the broken English with which she expressed them. An attempt to describe her manner and accent would be futile, and would detract from the simple dignity and sweetness with which she uttered the words. We leave the reader from his own imagination to fill up the picture which we can only draw in outline. Bernard saw and felt the power of religion in the heart of this poor savage, and he hesitated what course he should pursue. He knew that her strongest feeling in life had been her affection for her brother. That had been the chord which earliest vibrated in her heart, and which as her heart expanded only increased in tension that added greater sweetness to its tone. It was on this broken string, so rudely snapped asunder, that he resolved to play—hoping thus to strike some harsh and discordant notes in her gentle heart.

"You had a brother, Mamalis," he said, abruptly; "the voice of your brother's blood calls to you from the ground."

"My brother!" shrieked the girl, startled by the suddenness of the allusion.

"Aye, your murdered brother," said Bernard, marking with pleasure the effect he had produced, "and it is in your power to avenge his death. Dare you do it?"

"Oh, my brother, my poor lost brother," she sobbed, the stoical indifference of the savage, pressed out by the crushed heart of the sister, "if by this hand thy death could be avenged."

"By your hand he can be avenged," said Bernard, seeing her pause. "It has not yet been done. That stupid knave, in a moment of vanity, claimed for himself the praise of having murdered a chieftain, but the brave Manteo fell by more noble hands than his."

"In God's name, who do you mean?" asked Mamalis.

"I can only tell you that it is now in your power to surrender his murderer to justice, and to his deserved fate."

Mamalis was silent. She guessed that it was Hansford to whom Bernard had thus vaguely alluded. The struggle seemed to be a desperate one. There in the clear starlight, with none to help, save Him, in whom she had learned to trust, she wrestled with the tempter. But that dark scene of her life, which still threw its shadow on her redeemed heart, again rose up before her memory. The lesson was a blessed one. How often thus does the recollection of a former sin guard the soul from error in the future. Surely, in this, too, God has made the wrath of man to praise him. With the aid thus given from on high, the trusting soul of Mamalis triumphed over temptation.

"I know not why you tempt me thus, Mr. Bernard," she said, more calmly, "nor why you have brought me here to-night. But this I know, that I have learned that vengeance belongs to God. It were a crime for mortal man, frail at best, to usurp the right of God. My brother is already fearfully avenged."

Twice beaten in his attempt to besiege the strong heart of the poor Indian, by stratagem, the wily Bernard determined to pursue a more determined course, and to take the resisting citadel by a coup d'etat. He argued, and argued rightly, that a sudden charge would surprise her into betraying a knowledge of Hansford's movements. No sooner, therefore, had the last words fallen from her lips, than he seized her roughly by the arm, and exclaimed,

"So you, then, with all your religious cant, are the murderess of Thomas Hansford!"

"The murderess! Of Hansford! Is he then dead," cried the girl, bewildered by the sudden charge, "How did they find him?"

"Find him!" cried Bernard, triumphantly, "It is easy finding what we hide ourselves. We have proven that you alone are aware of his hiding place, and you alone, therefore, are responsible for his safety. It was for this confession that I brought you here to-night."

"So help me Heaven," said the trembling girl, terrified by the web thus woven around her, "If he be dead, I am innocent of his death."

"The assassin of Berkenhead may well be the murderess of Hansford," said Bernard. "It is easier to deny than to prove. Come, my mistress, tell me when you saw him."

"Oh, but this morning, safe and well," said Mamalis. "Indeed, my hand is guiltless of his blood."

"Prove it, then, if you can," returned Bernard. "You must know our English law presumes him guilty, who is last with the murdered person, unless he can prove his innocence. Show me Hansford alive, and you are safe. If I do not see him by sunrise, you go with me to answer for his death, and to learn that your accursed race is not the only people who demand blood for blood."

Overawed by his threats, and his stern manner, so different from the mild and respectful tone in which he had hitherto addressed her, Mamalis sank upon the ground in an agony of alarm. Bernard disregarded her meek and silent appeal for mercy, and sternly menaced her when she attempted to scream for assistance.

"Hush your savage shrieking, you bitch, or you'll wake the house; and then, by God, I'll choke you before your time. I tell you, if the man is alive, you need fear no danger; and if he be dead, you have only saved the sheriff a piece of dirty work, or may be have given him another victim."

"For God's sake, do me no harm," cried Mamalis, imploringly. "I am innocent—indeed I am. Think you that I would hurt a hair of the head of that man whom Virginia Temple loves?"

This last remark was by no means calculated to make her peace with Bernard; but his only reply was by the shrill whistle which had been agreed upon as a signal between Holliday and himself. True to his promise, and obedient to the command of his superior, the soldier made his appearance on the scene of action with a promptitude that could only be explained by the fact that he had concealed himself behind a corner of the house, and had heard every word of the conversation. Too much excited to be suspicious, Bernard did not remark on his punctuality, but said, in a low voice:

"Go wake Thompson, saddle the horses, and let's be off. We have work before us. Go!" And Holliday, with habitual obedience, retired to execute the order.

"And now," said Bernard, in an encouraging tone, to Mamalis, "you must go with me. But you have nothing to fear, if Hansford be alive. If, however, my suspicions be true, and he has been murdered by your hand, I will still be your friend, if you be but faithful."

The horses were quickly brought, and Bernard, half leading, half carrying the poor, weeping, trembling maiden, mounted his own powerful charger, and placed her behind him. The order of march was soon given, and the heavy sound of the horses' feet was heard upon the hard, crisp, frozen ground. Mamalis, seeing her fate inevitable, whatever it might be, awaited it patiently and without a murmur. Never suspecting the true motive of Bernard, and fully believing that he was *bona fide* engaged in searching for the perpetrators of some foul deed, she readily consented, for her own defence, to conduct the party to the hiding place of the hapless Hansford. Surprised and shocked beyond measure at the intelligence of his fate, she almost forgot her own situation in her concern for him, and was happy in aiding to bring to justice those who, as she feared, had murdered him. She was surprised, indeed, that she had heard nothing of the circumstance from

Virginia, as she would surely have done, had Bernard mentioned it to the family. But in her ignorance of the rules of civilized life, she attributed this to the forms of procedure, to the necessity for secrecy — to anything rather than the true cause. Nor could she help hoping that there might be still some mistake, and that Hansford would be found alive and well, thus establishing her own innocence, and ending the pursuit.

Arrived nearly at the wigwam, she mentioned the fact to Bernard, who in a low voice commanded a halt, and dismounting with his men, he directed Mamalis to guide them the remaining distance on foot. Leaving Thompson in charge of the horses, until he might be called to their assistance, Bernard and Holliday silently followed the unsuspecting Indian girl along the narrow path. A short distance ahead, they could discern the faint smoke, as it curled through the opening at the top of the wigwam and floated towards the sky. This indication rendered it probable that the object of their search was still watching, and thus warned them to greater caution in their approach. Bernard's heart beat thick and loud, and his cheek blanched with excitement, as he thus drew near the lurking place of his enemy. He shook Holliday by the arm with impatient anger, as the heavy-footed soldier jarred the silence by the crackling of fallen leaves and branches. And now they are almost there, and Mamalis, whose excitement was also intense, still in advance, saw through a crevice in the door the kneeling form of the noble insurgent, as he bowed himself by that lonely fire, and committed his weary soul to God.

"He is here! he lives!" she shouted. "I knew that he was safe!" and the startled forest rang with the echoes of her voice.

"The murder is out," cried Bernard, as followed by Holliday, he rushed forward to the door, which had been thrown open by their guide; but ere he gained his entrance, the sharp report of a pistol was heard, and the beautiful, the trusting Mamalis fell prostrate on the floor, a bleeding martyr to her constancy and faith. Hansford, roused by the sudden sound of her voice, had seized the pistol which, sleeping and waking, was by his side, and hearing the voice of Bernard, he had fired. Had the ball taken effect upon either of the men, he might yet have been saved, for in an encounter with a single man he would have proved a formidable adversary. But inscrutable are His ways, whose thoughts are not as our thoughts, and all that the puzzled soul can do, is humbly to rely on the hope that

"God is his own interpreter,
And he will make it plain."

And she, the last of her dispersed and ruined lineage, is gone. In the lone forest, where the wintry blast swept unobstructed, the giant trees moaned sadly and fitfully over their bleeding child; and the bright stars, that saw the heavy deed, wept from their place in heaven, and bathed her lovely form in night's pure dews. She did not long remain unburied in that forest, for when Virginia heard the story of her faith and loyalty from the rude lips of Holliday, the pure form of the Indian girl, still fresh and free from the polluting touch of the destroyer, was borne to her own home, and followed with due rites and fervent grief to the quiet tomb. In after days, when her sad heart loved to dwell upon these early scenes, Virginia placed above the sacred ashes of her friend a simple marble tablet, long since itself a ruin; and there, engraven with the record of her faith, her loyalty and her love, was the sweet assurance, that in her almost latest words, the trusting Indian girl had indeed become one of "the children of her Father which is in Heaven."

CHAPTER XLIII

"Let some of the guard be ready there.
For me?
Must I go like a traitor thither?"
Henry VIII.

The reader need not be told that Hansford, surprised and unarmed, for his remaining pistol was not at hand, and his sword had been laid aside for the night, was no match for the two powerful men who now rushed upon him. To pinion his arms closely behind him, was the work of a moment, and further resistance was impossible. Seeing that all hope of successful defence was gone, Hansford maintained in his bearing the resolute fortitude and firmness which can support a brave man in misfortune, when active courage is no longer of avail.

"I suppose, I need not ask Mr. Bernard," he said, "by what authority he acts—and yet I would be glad to learn for what offence I am arrested."

"The memory of your former acts should teach you," returned Bernard, coarsely, "that your offence is reckoned among the best commentators of the law as high treason."

"A grievous crime, truly," replied Hansford, "but one of which I am happily innocent, unless, indeed, a skirmish with the hostile Indians should be reckoned as such, or Sir William Berkeley should be presumptuous enough to claim to be a king; in which latter case, he himself would be the traitor."

"He is at least the deputy of the king," said Bernard, haughtily, "and in his person the majesty of the king has been assailed."

"Unfortunately, for your reasoning," replied Hansford, "the term for which Berkeley was appointed governor has expired some years since."

"That miserable subterfuge will scarcely avail, since you tacitly acknowledged his authority by acting under his commission. But I have no time to be discussing with you on the nature of your offence, of which, at least, I am not the judge. I will only add, that conscious innocence is not found skulking in dark forests, and obscure hiding places. Call Thompson, with the horses, Holliday. It is time we were off."

"One word, before we leave," said Hansford, sadly. "My pistol ball took effect, I know; who is its victim?"

"A poor Indian girl, who conducted us to your fastness," said Bernard. "I had forgotten her myself, till now. Look, Holliday, does she still live?"

"Dead as a herring, your honour," said the man, as he bent over the body, with deep feeling, for, though accustomed to the flow of blood, he had taken a lively interest in the poor girl, from what he had seen and overheard. "And by God, Cap'n, begging your honour's pardon, a brave girl she was, too, although she was an Injin."

"Poor Mamalis," said Hansford, tenderly, "you have met with an early and a sad fate. I little thought that she would betray me."

"Nay, wrong not the dead," interposed Bernard, "I assure you, she knew nothing of the object of our coming. But all's fair in war, Major, and a little intrigue was necessary to track you to this obscure hold."

"Well, farewell, poor luckless maiden! And so I've killed my friend," said Hansford, sorrowfully. "Alas! Mr. Bernard, my arm has been felt in battle, and has sent death to many a foe. But, God forgive me! this is the first blood I have ever spilt, except in battle, and this, too, flows from a woman."

"Think not of it thus," said Bernard, whose hard nature could not but be touched by this display of unselfish grief on the part of his prisoner. "It was but an accident, and should not rest heavily on your soul. Stay, Holliday, I would not have the poor girl rot here, either. Suppose you take the body to Windsor Hall, where it will be treated with due respect. Thompson and myself can, meantime, attend the prisoner."

"Look ye, Cap'n," said Holliday, with the superstition peculiar to vulgar minds; "'taint that I'm afeard exactly neither, but its a mighty dissolute feeling being alone in a dark night with a corp. I'd rather kill fifty men, than to stay by myself five minutes, with the smallest of the fifty after he was killed."

"Well, then, you foolish fellow, go to the hall to-night and inform them of her death, and excuse me to Colonel Temple for my abrupt departure, and meet me with the rest of the men at Tindal's Point as soon as possible. I will bide there for you. But first help me to take the poor girl's body into the wigwam. I suppose she will rest quietly enough here till morning. Major Hansford," he added, courteously, "our horses are ready I perceive. You can take Holliday's there. He can provide himself with another at the hall. Shall we ride, sir?"

With a sad heart the captive-bound Hansford mounted with difficulty the horse prepared for him, which was led by Thompson, while Bernard rode by his side, and with more of courtesy than could be expected from him, endeavoured to beguile the way with conversation with his prisoner.

Meanwhile Holliday, whistling for company, and ever and anon looking behind him warily, to see whether the disembodied Mamalis was following him, bent his steps towards the hall, to communicate to the unsuspecting Virginia the heavy tidings of her lover's capture. The rough soldier, although his nature had been blunted by long service and familiarity with scenes of distress, was not without some feelings, and showed even in his rude, uncultivated manners, the sympathy and tenderness which was wanting in the more polished but harder heart of Alfred Bernard.

CHAPTER XLIV

"Go to Lord Angelo,
And let him learn to know, when maidens sue,
Men give like gods; but when they weep and kneel,
All their petitions are as freely theirs,
As they themselves would owe them."

Measure for Measure.

It were impossible to describe the silent agony of Virginia Temple, when she learned from Holliday, on the following morning, the capture of Hansford. She felt that it was the wreck of all her hopes, and that the last thread which still hung between her and despair was snapped. But even in that dark hour, her strength of mind, and her firmness of purpose forsook her not. There was still a duty for her to perform in endeavouring to procure his pardon, and she entertained, with the trusting confidence of her young heart, the strong hope that Berkeley would grant her request. On this sacred errand she determined to go at once. Although she did not dream of the full extent of Bernard's hypocrisy, yet all his efforts had been unavailing to restore full confidence in his sincerity. She dared not trust a matter of such importance to another, especially when she had reason to suspect that that other was far from being friendly in his feelings towards her lover. Once determined on her course, she lost no time in informing her parents of her resolution; and so, when they were all seated around the breakfast-table, she said quietly, but firmly—

"I am going to Accomac to-day, father."

"To where!" cried her mother; "why surely, child, you must be out of your senses."

"No, dearest mother, my calmness is not an indication of insanity. If I should neglect this sacred duty, you might then indeed tremble for my reason."

"What in the world are you thinking of, Jeanie!" said her father, in his turn surprised at this sudden resolution; "what duties can call you to Accomac?"

"I go to save life," replied Virginia. "Can you wonder, my father, that when I see all that I hold dearest in life just trembling on the verge of destruction, I should desire to do all in my power to save it."

"You are right, my child," replied her father, tenderly; "if it were possible for you to accomplish any good. But what can you do to rescue Hansford from the hand of justice?"

"Of justice!" said Virginia, "and can you unite with those, my dear father, who profane the name of justice by applying it to the relentless cruelty with which blind vengeance pursues its victims?"

"Ah, Jeanie!" said her father, smiling, as he pressed her hand tenderly; "you should remember, in language of the quaint old satirist, Butler,

'No thief e'er felt the halter draw,
With good opinion of the law;'

and although I would not apply the bitter couplet to my little Jeanie in its full force, yet she must own that her interest in its present application, prevents her from being a very competent judge of its propriety and justice."

"But surely, dear father, you cannot think that these violent measures against the unhappy parties to the late rebellion, are either just or politic?"

"I grant, my child, that to my own mind, a far more humane policy might be pursued consistent with the ends of justice. To inspire terror in a subject is not the surest means to secure his allegiance or his love for government. I am sure, if you were afraid of your old father, and always in dread of his wrath and authority, you would not love him as you do, Jeanie—and government is at last nothing but a larger family."

"Well, then," returned the artless girl, "why should I not go to Sir William Berkeley, and represent to him the harshness of his course, and the propriety of tempering his revenge with mercy?"

"First, my daughter, because I have only expressed my private opinion, which would have but little weight with the Governor, or any one else but you and mother, there. Remember that we are neither the framers nor the administrators of the law. And then you would make but a poor mediator, my darling, if you were to attempt to dissuade the Governor from his policy, by charging him with cruelty and injustice. Think no more of this wild idea, my dear child. It can do no good, and reflects more credit on your warm, generous heart, than on your understanding or experience."

"Hinder me not, my father," said Virginia, earnestly, her blue eyes filling with tears. "I can but fail, and if you would save me from the bitterness of self-reproach hereafter, let me go. Oh, think how it would add bitterness to the cup of grief, if, when closing the eyes of a dead friend, we should think that we had left some remedy untried which might have saved his life! If I fail, it will at least be some consolation, even in despair, that I did all that I could to avert his fate; and if I succeed—oh! how transporting the thought that the life of one I love had been spared through my interposition. Then hinder me not, father, mother—if you would not destroy your daughter's peace forever, oh, let me go!"

The solemn earnestness with which the poor girl thus urged her parents to grant her request, deeply affected them both; and the old lady, forgetting in her love for her daughter the indelicacy and impropriety of her plan, volunteered her very efficient advocacy of Virginia's cause.

"Indeed, Colonel Temple," she said, "you should not oppose Virginia in this matter. You will have enough to reproach yourself for, if by your means you should prevent her from doing what she thinks best. And, indeed, I like to see a young girl show so much spirit and interest in her lover's fate. It is seldom you see such things now-a-days, though it used to be common enough in England. Now, just put it to yourself."

The Colonel accordingly did "put it to himself," and, charmed with his daughter's affection and heroism, concluded himself to accompany her to Accomac, and exert his own influence with the Governor in procuring the pardon of the unhappy Hansford.

"Now that's as it should be," said the old lady, gratified at this renewed assurance of her ascendency over her husband. "And now, Virginia, cheer up. All will be right, my dear, for your father has great influence with the Governor—and, indeed, well he might have, for he has received kindness enough at our hands in times past. I should like to see him refuse your father a favour. And I will write a note to Lady Frances myself, for all the world knows that she is governor and all with her husband."

"Ladies generally are," said the Colonel, with a smile, which however could not disguise the sincerity with which he uttered the sentiment.

"Oh, no, not at all," retorted the old lady, bridling up. "You are always throwing up your obedience to me, and yet, after all said and done, you have your own way pretty much, too. But you are not decent to go anywhere. Do, pray, Colonel Temple, pay more respect to society, and fix yourself up a little. Put on your blue coat and your black stock, and dress your hair, and shave, and look genteel for once in your life." Then, seeing by the patient shrug of her good old husband that she had wounded his feelings, she patted him tenderly on the shoulder, and added, "You know I always love to see you nice and spruce, and when you do attend to your dress, and fix up, I know of none of them that are equal to you. Do you, Virginia?"

Before the good Colonel had fully complied with all the toilet requisitions of his wife, the carriage was ready to take the travellers to Tindal's Point, where there was luckily a small sloop, just under weigh for Accomac. And Virginia, painfully alternating between hope and fear, but sustained by a consciousness of duty, was borne away across the broad Chesapeake, on her pious pilgrimage, to move by her tears and prayers the vindictive heart of the stern old Governor.

CHAPTER XLV

"Why, there's an end then! I have judged deliberately, and
the result is death."

The Gamester.

Situated, as nearly as might be, in the centre of each of the counties of
Virginia, was a small settlement, which, although it aspired to the dignity
of a town, could scarcely deserve the name. For the most part, these little
country towns, as they were called, were composed of about four houses,
to wit: The court house, dedicated to justice, where sat, monthly, the
magistrates of the county, possessed of an unlimited jurisdiction in all cases
cognizable in law or chancery, not touching life or murder, and having the
care of orphans' persons and estates; the jail, wherein prisoners committed
for any felony were confined, until they could be brought before the general
court, which had the sole criminal jurisdiction in the colony; the tavern, a
long, low wooden building, generally thronged with loafers and gossips, and
reeking with the fumes of tobacco smoke, apple-brandy and rye-whiskey;
and, finally, the store, which shared, with the tavern, the patronage of the
loafers, and which could be easily recognized by the roughly painted board
sign, containing a catalogue of the goods within, arranged in alphabetical
order, without reference to any other classification. Thus the substantial
farmer, in search of a pound of *candy* for his little white headed barbarians,
whom he had left at play, must needs pass his finger over "cards, chains,
calico, cowhides, and candy;" or, if he had come to "town" to purchase
a bushel of meal for family use, his eye was greeted with the list of M's,
containing meal, mustard, mousetraps, and molasses.

It was to the little court house town of the county of Accomac, that Sir
William Berkeley had retired after the burning of Jamestown; and here he
remained, since the suppression of the rebellion, like a cruel old spider, in
the centre of his web, awaiting, with grim satisfaction, the capture of such
of the unwary fugitives as might fall into his power.

"Well, gentlemen, the court martial is set," said Sir William Berkeley,
as he gazed upon the gloomy faces of the military men around him, in the
old court house of Accomac. In that little assembly, might be seen the tall
and manly form of Colonel Philip Ludwell, who had been honoured, by

the especial confidence of Berkeley, as he was, afterwards, by the constant and tender love of the widowed Lady Frances. There, too, was the stern, hard countenance of Major Robert Beverley, whose unbending loyalty had shut his eyes to true merit in an opponent. The names of the remaining members of the court, have, unfortunately, not found a place in the history of the rebellion. Alfred Bernard, on whom the governor had showered, with a lavish hand, the favours which it was in his power to bestow, had been promoted to the office of Major, in the room of Thomas Hansford, outlawed, and was, therefore, entitled to a seat at the council which was to try the life of his rival. But as his evidence was of an important character, and as he had been concerned directly in the arrest of the prisoner, he preferred to act in the capacity of a witness, rather than as a judge.

"Let the prisoner be brought before the court," said Berkeley; and in a few moments, Hansford, with his hands manacled, was led, between a file of soldiers, to the seat prepared for him. His short confinement had made but little change in his appearance. His face, indeed, was paler than usual, and his eye was brighter, for the exciting and solemn scene through which he was about to pass. But prejudged, though he was, his firmness never forsook him, and he met with a calm, but respectful gaze, the many eyes which were bent upon him. Conspicuous among the rebels, and popular and beloved in the colony, his trial had attracted a crowd of spectators; some impelled by vulgar curiosity, some by their loyal desire to witness the trial of a rebel to his king, but not a few by sympathy for his early and already well known fate.

As might well be expected, there was but little difficulty in establishing his participation in the late rebellion. There were many of the witnesses, who had seen him in intimate association with Bacon, and several who recognized him as among the most active in the trenches at Jamestown. To crown all, the irresistible evidence was introduced by Bernard, that the prisoner had actually brought a threatening message to the governor, while at Windsor Hall, which had induced the first flight to Accomac. It was useless to resist the force of such accumulated testimony, and Hansford saw that his fate was settled. It were folly to contend before such a tribunal, that his acts did not constitute rebellion, or that the court before whom he was arraigned was unconstitutional. The devoted victim of their vengeance, therefore, awaited in silence the conclusion of this solemn farce, which they had dignified by the name of a trial.

The evidence concluded, Sir William Berkeley, as Lord President of the Court, collected the suffrages of its members. It might easily be anticipated by their gloomy countenances, what was the solemn import of their judgment. Thomas Ludwell, the secretary of the council, acted as the clerk, and in a voice betraying much emotion, read the fatal decision. The sympathizing bystanders, who in awful silence awaited the result, drew a long breath as though relieved from their fearful suspense, even by having heard the worst. And Hansford was to die! He heard with much emotion the sentence which doomed him to a traitor's death the next day at noon; and those who were near, heard him sob, "My poor, poor mother!" But almost instantly, with a violent effort he controlled his feelings, and asked permission to speak.

"Surely," said the Governor, "provided your language be respectful to the Court, and that you say nothing reflecting on his majesty's government at home or in the Colony of Virginia."

"These are hard conditions," said Hansford, rising from his seat, "as with such limitations, I can scarcely hope to justify my conduct. But I accept your courtesy, even with these conditions. A dying man has at last but little to say, and but little disposition to mingle again in the affairs of a world which he must so soon leave. In the short, the strangely short time allotted to me, I have higher and holier concerns to interest me. Ere this hour to-morrow, I will have passed from the scenes of earth to appear before a higher tribunal than yours, and to answer for the forgotten sins of my past life. But I thank my God, that while that awful tribunal is higher, it is also juster and more merciful than yours. Even in this sad moment, however, I cannot forget the country for which I have lived, and for which I must so soon die. I see by your countenances that I am already transcending your narrow limits. But it cannot be treason to pray for her, and as my life has been devoted to her service, so will my prayers for her welfare ascend with my petitions for forgiveness.

"I would say a word as to the offence with which I have been charged, and the evidence on which I have been convicted. That evidence amounts to the fact that I was in arms, by the authority of the Governor, against the common enemies of my country. Is this treason? That I was the bearer of a threatening message to the Governor from General Bacon, which caused the first flight into Accomac. And here I would say," and he fixed his eyes full on Alfred Bernard, as he spoke, who endeavoured to conceal his feelings by a smile of scorn, "that the evidence on this point has been cruelly, shamefully garbled and perverted. It was never stated that, while as the minister of another, I bore the message referred to, I urged the Governor to consider and retract the proclamation which he had made, and offered my own mediation to restore peace and quiet to the Colony. Had my advice been taken the beams of peace would have once more burst upon Virginia, the scenes which are constantly enacted here, and which will continue to be enacted, would never have disgraced the sacred name of justice; and the name of Sir William Berkeley would not be handed down to the execrations of posterity as a dishonoured knight, and a brutal, bloody butcher."

"Silence!" cried the incensed old Governor, in tones of thunder, "or by the wounds of God, I'll shorten the brief space which now interposes between you and eternity. Is this redeeming your promise of respect?"

"I beg pardon," said Hansford, undaunted by the menace. "Excuse me, if I cannot speak patiently of cruelty and oppression. But let this pass. That perfidious wretch who would rise above my ruins, never breathed a word of this, when on the evangelist of Almighty God he was sworn to speak the truth. But if such evidence be sufficient to convict me of treason now, why was it not sufficient then? Why, with the same facts before you, did you, Sir William Berkeley, discharge the traitor in arms, and now seek his death when disarmed and impotent? One other link remains in the chain, this feeble chain of evidence. I aided in the siege of Jamestown, and once more drove the Governor and his fond adherents from their capital, to their refuge in the Accomac. I cannot, I will not deny it. But neither can this be treason, unless, indeed, Sir William Berkeley possesses in his own person the sacred majesty of Virginia. For when he abdicated the government by his first flight from the soil of Virginia, the sovereign people of the Colony, assembled in solemn convention, declared his office vacant. In that convention, you, my judges, well know, for you found it to your cost, were present a majority of the governor's council, the whole army, and almost the entire chivalry and talent of the colony. In their name writs were issued for an assembly, which met under their authority, and the commission of governor was placed in the hands of Nathaniel Bacon."

"By an unauthorized mob," said Berkeley, unable to restrain his impatience.

"By an organized convention of sovereign people," returned Hansford, proudly. "You, Sir William Berkeley, deemed it not an unauthorized mob, when confiding in your justice, and won by your soft promises, a similar convention, composed of cavaliers and rich landholders, confided to your hands, in 1659, the high trust which you now hold. If such a proceeding were unauthorized then, were you not guilty in accepting the commission? If authorized, were not the same people competent to bestow the trust upon another, whom they deemed more worthy to hold it? If this be so, the insurgents, as you have chosen to call them, were not in arms against the government at the siege of Jamestown. And thus the last strand in the coil of evidence, with which you have involved me, is broken, as withs are severed at the touch of fire. But light as is the testimony against me, it is sufficient to turn the beam of justice, when the sword of Brennus is cast into the scale.

"One word more and I am done; for I see you are impatient for the sacrifice. I had thought that I would have been tried by a jury of my peers. Such I deemed my right as a British subject. But condemned by the extraordinary and unwarranted proceedings of this Star Chamber" —

"Silence!" cried Berkeley, again waxing wroth at such an imputation.

"I beg pardon once more," continued Hansford, "I thought the favourite institution of Charles the First would not have met with so little favour from such loyal cavaliers. But I demand in the name of Freedom, in the name of England, in the name of God and Justice, when was Magna Charta or the Petition of Right abolished on the soil of Virginia? Is the Governor of Virginia so little of a lawyer that he remembers not the language of the stout Barons of Runnymede, unadorned in style, but pregnant with freedom. 'No freeman may be taken or imprisoned, or be disseised of his freehold or liberties, or his free-customs, or be outlawed or exiled, or in any manner destroyed, but by the lawful judgment of his peers, or by the law of the land.' Excuse me, gentlemen, for repeating to such sage judges so old and hackneyed a fragment of the law. But until to-day, I had been taught to hold those words as sacred, and as indeed containing the charter of the liberties of an Englishman. Alas! it will no longer be hackneyed nor quoted by the slaves of England, except when they mourn with bitter but hopeless tears, for the higher and purer freedom of their ruder fathers. Why am I thus arraigned before a court-martial in time of peace? Am I found in arms? Am I even an officer or a soldier? The commission which I once held has been torn from me, and given, as his thirty pieces, to you dissembling Judas, for the price of my betrayal. But I am done. Your tyranny and oppression cannot last for ever. The compressed spring will at last recoil with power proportionate to the force by which it has been restrained — and freed posterity will avenge on a future tyrant my cruel and unnatural murder."

Hansford sat down, and Sir William Berkeley, flushed with indignation, replied,

"I had hoped that the near approach of death, if not a higher motive, would have saved us from such treasonable sentiments. But, sir, the insolence of your manner has checked any sympathy which I might have entertained for your early fate. I, therefore, have only to pronounce the judgment of the court; that you be taken to the place whence you came, and there safely kept until to-morrow noon, when you will be taken, with a rope about your neck, to the common gallows, and there hung by the neck until you are dead. And may the Lord Jesus Christ have mercy on your soul!"

"Amen!" was murmured, in sad whispers, by the hundreds of pale spectators who crowded around the unhappy prisoner.

"How is this!" cried Hansford, once more rising to his feet, with strong emotion. "Gentlemen, you are soldiers, as such I may claim you as brethren, as such you should be brave and generous men. On that generosity, in this hour of peril, I throw myself, and ask as a last indulgence, as a dying favour, that I may die the death of a soldier, and not of a felon."

"You have lived a traitor's, not a soldier's life," said Berkeley, in an insulting tone. "A soldier's life is devoted to his king and country; yours to a rebel and to treason. You shall die the death of a traitor."

"Well, then, I have done," said Hansford, with a sigh, "and must look to Him alone for mercy, who can make the felon's gallows as bright a pathway to happiness, as the field of glory."

Many a cheek flushed with indignation at the refusal of the governor to grant this last petition of a brave man. A murmur of dissatisfaction arose from the crowd, and even some sturdy loyalists were heard to mutter, "shame." The other members of the court were seen to confer together, and to remonstrate with the governor.

"'Fore God, no," said Berkeley, in a whisper to his advisers. "Think of the precedent it will establish. Traitor he has lived, and as far as my voice can go, traitor he shall die. I suppose the sheep-killing hound, and the egg-sucking cur, will next whine out their request to be shot instead of hung."

So great was the influence of Berkeley, over the minds of the court, that, after a feeble remonstrance, the petition of the prisoner was rejected. Old Beverley alone, was heard to mutter in the ear of Philip Ludwell, that it was a shame to deny a brave man a soldier's death, and doom him to a dog's fate.

"And for all this," he added, "its a damned hard lot, and blast me, but I think Hansford to be worth in bravery and virtue, fifty of that painted popinjay, Bernard, whose cruelty is as much beyond his years as his childish vanity is beneath them."

"Well, gentlemen, I trust you are now satisfied," said Berkeley. "Sheriff, remove your prisoner, and," looking angrily around at the malecontents, "if necessary, summon an additional force to assist you."

The officer, however, deemed no such precaution necessary, and the hapless Hansford was conducted back to his cell under the same guard that brought him thence; there to await the execution on the morrow of the fearful sentence to which he had been condemned.

CHAPTER XLVI

Isabella.   "Yet show some pity."

Angelo.   I show it most of all when I show justice."

Measure for Measure.

That evening Sir William Berkeley was sitting in the private room at the tavern, which had been fitted up for his reception. He had strictly commanded his servants to deny admittance to any one who might wish to see him. The old man was tired of counsellors, advisers, and petitioners, who harassed him in their attempt to curb his impatient ire, and he was determined to act entirely for himself. He had thus been sitting for more than an hour, looking moodily into the fire, without even the officious Lady Frances to interfere with his reflections, when a servant in livery entered the room.

"If your Honour please," said the obsequious servitor, "there is a lady at the door who says she must see you on urgent business. I told her that you could not be seen, but she at last gave me this note, which she begged me to hand you."

Berkeley impatiently tore open the note and read as follows:—

"By his friendship for my father, and his former kindness to me, I ask for a brief interview with Sir William Berkeley.

"VIRGINIA TEMPLE."

"Fore God!" said the Governor, angrily, "they beset me with an importunity which makes me wretched. What the devil can the girl want! Some favour for Bernard, I suppose. Well, any thing for a moment's respite from these troublesome rebels. Show her up, Dabney."

In another moment the door again opened, and Virginia Temple, pale and trembling, fell upon her knees before the Governor, and raised her soft, blue eyes to his face so imploringly, that the heart of the old man was moved to pity.

"Rise, my daughter," he said, tenderly; "tell me your cause of grief. It surely cannot be so deep as to bring you thus upon your knees to an old friend. Rise then, and tell me."

"Oh, thank you," she said, with a trembling voice, "I knew that you were kind, and would listen to my prayer."

"Well, Virginia," said the Governor, in the same mild tone, "let me hear your request? You know, we old servants of the king have not much time to spare at best, and these are busy times. Is your father well, and your good mother? Can I serve them in any thing?"

"They are both well and happy, nor do they need your aid," said Virginia; "but I, sir, oh! how can I speak. I have come from Windsor Hall to ask that you will be just and merciful. There is, sir, a brave man here in chains, who is doomed to die—to die to-morrow. Oh, Hansford, Hansford!" and unable longer to control her emotion, the poor, broken-hearted girl burst into an agony of tears.

Berkeley's brow clouded in an instant.

"And is it for that unhappy man, my poor girl, that you have come alone to sue?"

"I did not come alone," replied Virginia; "my father is with me, and will himself unite in my request."

"I will be most happy to see my old friend again, but I would that he came on some less hopeless errand. Major Hansford must die. The laws alike of his God and his country, which he has trampled regardless under foot, require the sacrifice of his blood."

"But, for the interposition of mercy," urged the poor girl, "the laws of God require the death of all—and the laws of his country have vested in you the right to arrest their rigour at your will. Oh, how much sweeter to be merciful than sternly just!"

"Nay, my poor girl," said Sir William, "you speak of what you cannot understand, and your own griefs have blinded your mind. Justice, Virginia, is mercy; for by punishing the offender it prevents the repetition of the offence. The vengeance of the law thus becomes the safeguard of society, and the sword of justice becomes the sceptre of righteousness."

"I cannot reason with you," returned Virginia. "You are a statesman, and I am but a poor, weak girl, ignorant of the ways of the world."

"And therefore you have come to advocate this suit instead of your father," said Berkeley, smiling. "I see through your little plot already. Come, tell me now, am I not right in my conjecture? Why have you come to urge the cause of Hansford, instead of your father?"

"Because," said Virginia, with charming simplicity, "we both thought, that as Sir William Berkeley had already decided upon the fate of this unhappy man, it would be easier to reach his heart, than to affect the mature decision of his judgment."

"You argued rightly, my dear girl," said Berkeley, touched by her frankness and simplicity, as well as by her tears. "But it is the hard fate of those in power to deny themselves often the luxury of mercy, while they tread onward in the rough but straight path of justice. It is ours to follow the stern maxim of our old friend Shakspeare:

'Mercy but murders, pardoning those who kill.'"

"But it does seem to me," said the resolute girl, losing all the native diffidence of her character in the interest she felt in her cause—"it does seem to me that even stern policy would sometimes dictate mercy. May not a judicious clemency often secure the love of the misguided citizen, while harsh justice would estrange him still farther from loyalty?"

"There, you are trenching upon your father's part, my child," said the Governor. "You must not go beyond your own cue, you know—for believe me that your plea for mercy would avail far more with me than your reasons, however cogent. This rebellion proceeded too far to justify any clemency toward those who promoted it."

"But it is now suppressed," said Virginia, resolutely; "and is it not the sweetest attribute of power, to help the fallen? Oh, remember," she added, carried away completely by her subject,

"'Less pleasure take brave minds in battles won,
Than in restoring such as are undone;
Tigers have courage, and the rugged bear,
But man alone can, when he conquers, spare.'"

"I did not expect to hear your father's daughter defend her cause by such lines as these. Do you know where they are found?"

"They are Waller's, I believe," said Virginia, blushing at this involuntary display of learning; "but it is their truth, and not their author, which suggested them to me."

"Your memory is correct," said Berkeley, with a smile, "but they are found in his panegyric on the Protector. A eulogy upon a traitor is bad authority with an old cavalier like me."

"If, then, you need authority which you cannot question," the girl replied, earnestly, "do you think that the royal cause lost strength by the mild policy of Charles the Second? That is authority that even you dare not question."

"Well, and what if I should say," replied Berkeley, "that this very leniency was one of the causes that encouraged the recent rebellion? But go, my child; I would rejoice if I could please you, but Hansford's fate is settled. I pity you, but I cannot forgive him." And with a courteous inclination of his head, he signified his desire that their interview should end.

"Nay," shrieked Virginia, in desperation, "I will not let you go, except you bless me," and throwing herself again upon her knees, she implored his mercy. Berkeley, who, with all his sternness, was not an unfeeling man, was deeply moved. What the result might have been can never be known, for at that moment a voice was heard from the street exclaiming, "Drummond is taken!" In an instant the whole appearance of the Governor changed. His cheek flushed and his eye sparkled, as with hasty strides he left the room and descended the stairs. No more the fine specimen of a cavalier gentleman, his manner became at once harsh and irritable.

"Well, Mr. Drummond," he cried, as he saw the proud rebel led manacled to the door. "'Fore God, and I am more delighted to see you than any man in the colony. You shall hang in half an hour."

"And if he do," shrieked the wild voice of a woman from the crowd, "think you that with your puny hand you can arrest the current of liberty in this colony? And when you appear before the dread bar of God, the spirits of these martyred patriots will rise up to condemn you, and fiends shall snatch at your blood-stained soul, perfidious tyrant! And I will be among them, for such a morsel of vengeance would sweeten hell. Ha! ha! ha!"

With that wild, maniac laugh, Sarah Drummond disappeared from the crowd of astounded spectators.

History informs us that the deadly threat of Berkeley was carried into effect immediately. But it was not until two days afterwards that William Drummond met a traitor's doom upon the common gallows.

Virginia Temple, thus abruptly left, and deprived of all hope, fell senseless on the floor of the room. The hope which had all along sustained her brave young heart, had now vanished forever, and kindly nature relieved the agony of her despair by unconsciousness. And there she lay, pale and beautiful, upon that floor, while the noisy clamour without was hailing the capture of another victim, whose fate was to bring sorrow and despair to another broken heart.

CHAPTER XLVII

"His nature is so far from doing harm,
That he suspects none; on whose foolish honesty
My practices ride easy."

King Lear.

When Virginia aroused again to consciousness, her eyes met the features of Alfred Bernard, as he knelt over her form. Not yet realizing her situation, she gazed wildly about her, and in a hoarse, husky whisper, which fell horridly on the ear, she said, "Where is my father?"

"At home, Virginia," replied Bernard, softly, chafing her white temples the while—"And you are here in Accomac. Look up, Virginia, and see that you are not without a friend even here."

"Oh, now, yes, now I know it all," she shrieked, springing up with a wild bound, and rushing like a maniac toward the door. "They have killed him! I have slept here, instead of begging his life. I have murdered him! Ha! you, sir, are you the jailer? I should know your face."

"Nay, do not speak thus, Virginia," said Bernard, holding her gently in his arms, "Hansford is yet alive. Be calm."

"Hansford! I thought he was dead!" said the poor girl, her mind still wandering. "Did not Mamalis—no—she is dead—all are dead—ha? where am I? Sure this is not Windsor Hall. Nay, what am I talking about. Let me see;" and she pressed her hand to her forehead, and smoothed back her fair hair, as she strove to collect her thoughts. "Ah! now I know," she said at length, more calmly, "I beg your pardon, Mr. Bernard, I have acted very foolishly, I fear. But you will forgive a poor distracted girl."

"I promised you my influence with the governor," said Bernard, "and I do not yet despair of effecting my object. And so be calm."

"Despair!" said Virginia, bitterly, "as well might you expect to turn a river from the sea, as to turn the relentless heart of that bigoted old tyrant from blood. And yet, I thank you, Mr. Bernard, and beg that you will leave no means untried to preserve my poor doomed Hansford. You see I am quite calm now, and should you fail in your efforts to procure a pardon, may I ask one last melancholy favour at your hands! I would see him once more before we part, forever." And to prove how little she knew her own heart, the poor girl burst into a renewed agony of grief.

"Calm your feelings, then, dear Virginia," said Bernard, "and you shall see him. But by giving way thus, you would unman him."

"You remind me of my duty, my friend," said Virginia, controlling herself, with a strong effort, "and I will not again forget it in my selfish grief. Shall we go now?"

"Remain here, but a few moments, patiently," he replied, "and I will seek the governor, and urge him to relent. If I fail, I will return to you."

Leaving the young girl once more to her own sad reflections, Alfred Bernard left the room.

"Virtue has its own reward," he muttered, as he walked slowly along. "I wonder how many would be virtuous if it were not so! Self is at last the mainspring of action, and when it produces good, we call it virtue; when it accomplishes evil, we call it vice; wherein, then, am I worse than my fellow man? Here am I, now, giving this poor girl a interview with her rebel lover, and extracting some happiness for them, even from their misery. And yet I am not a whit the worse off. Nay, I am benefited, for gratitude is a sure prompter of love; and when Hansford is out of the way, who so fit to supply the niche, left vacant in her heart, as Alfred Bernard, who soothed their mutual grief. Thus virtue is often a valuable handmaid to success, and may be used for our purposes, when we want her assistance, and afterwards be whistled to the winds as a pestilent jade. Machiavelli in politics, Loyola in religion, Rochefoucault in society, ye are the mighty three, who, seeing the human heart in all its nakedness, have dared to tear the mask from its deformed and hideous features."

"What in the world are you muttering about, Alfred?" said Governor Berkeley, as they met in the porch, as Bernard had finished this diabolical soliloquy.

"Oh nothing," replied the young intriguer. "But I came to seek your excellency."

"And I to seek for you, my sage young counsellor; I have to advise with you upon a subject which lies heavy on my heart, Alfred."

"You need only command my counsel and it is yours," said Bernard, "but I fear that I can be of little assistance in your reflections."

"Yes you can, my boy," returned Berkeley, "I know not whether you will esteem it a compliment or not, Alfred, but yours is an old head on young shoulders, and the heart, which in the season of youth often flits away from the sober path of judgment, seems with you to follow steadily in the wake of reason."

"If you mean that I am ever ready to sacrifice my own selfish impulses to my duty, I do esteem it as a compliment, though I fear not altogether deserved."

"Well, then," said the Governor, "this poor boy, Hansford, who is to suffer death to-morrow, I have had a strange interview concerning him since I last saw you."

"Aye, with Miss Temple," returned Bernard. "She told me she had seen you, and that you were as impregnable to assault as the rock of Gibraltar."

"I thought so too, where treason was concerned," said Berkeley. "But some how, the leaven of the poor girl's tears is working strangely in my heart; and after I had left her, who should I meet but her old father."

"Is Colonel Temple here?" asked Bernard, surprised.

"Aye is he, and urged Hansford's claims to pardon with such force, that I had to fly from temptation. Nay he even put his plea for mercy upon the ground of his own former kindness to me."

"The good old gentleman seems determined to be paid for that hospitality," said Bernard, with a sneer. "Well!"

"Well, altogether I am almost determined to interpose my reprieve, until the wishes of his majesty are known," said Berkeley, with some hesitation.

Bernard was silent, for some moments, and the Governor continued.

"What do you say to this course Alfred?"

"Simply, that if you are determined, I have nothing to say."

"Nay, but I am not determined, my young friend."

"Then I must ask you what are the grounds of your hesitation, before I can express an opinion?" said Bernard.

"Well, first," said the Governor, "because it will be a personal favour to Colonel Temple, and will dry the tears in those blue eyes of his pretty daughter. His kindness to me in this unhappy rebellion would be but poorly requited, if I refused the first and only favour that he has ever asked of me."

"Then hereafter," returned Bernard, quietly, "it would be good policy in a rebellion, for half the rebels to remain at home and entertain the Governor at their houses. They would thus secure the pardon of the rest."

"Well, you young Solomon," said Berkeley, laughing, "I believe you are right there. It would be a dangerous precedent. But then, a reprieve is not a pardon, and while I might thus oblige my friends, the king could hereafter see the cause of justice vindicated."

"And you would shift your own responsibility upon the king," replied Bernard. "Has not Charles Stuart enough to trouble him, with his rebellious subjects at home, without having to supervise every petty felony or treason that occurs in his distant colonies? This provision of our charter, denying to the Governor the power of absolute pardon, but granting him power to reprieve, was only made, that in doubtful cases, the minister might rely upon the wisdom of majesty. It was never intended to shift all the trouble and vexation of a colonial executive upon the overloaded hands of the king. If you have any doubt of Hansford's guilt, I would be the last to turn your heart from clemency, by a word of my mouth. If he be guilty, I only ask whether Sir William Berkeley is the man to shrink from responsibility, and to fasten upon his royal master the odium, if odium there be, attending the execution of the sentence against a rebel."

"Zounds, no, Bernard, you know I am not. But then there are a plenty of rebels to sate the vengeance of the law, besides this poor young fellow. Does justice demand that all should perish?"

"My kind patron," said Bernard, "to whom I owe all that I have and am, do not further urge me to oppose feelings so honorable to your heart. Exercise your clemency towards this unhappy young man, in whose fate I feel as deep an interest as yourself. If harm should flow from your mercy, who can censure you for acting from motives so generous and humane. If by your mildness you should encourage rebellion again, posterity will pardon the weakness of the Governor in the benevolence of the man."

"Stay," said Berkeley, his pride wounded by this imputation, "you know, Alfred, that if I thought that clemency towards this young rebel would encourage rebellion in the future, I would rather lose my life than spare his. But speak out, and tell me candidly why you think the execution of this sentence necessary to satisfy justice."

"You force me to an ungrateful duty," replied the young hypocrite, "for it is far more grateful to the heart of a benevolent man to be the advocate of mercy, than the stern champion of justice. But since you ask my reasons, it is my duty to obey you. First, then, this young man, from his talent, his bravery, and his high-flown notions about liberty, is far more dangerous than any of the insurgents who have survived Nathaniel Bacon. Then, he has shown that so far from repenting of his treason, he is ready to justify it, as witness his speech, wherein he predicted the triumph of revolution in

Virginia, and denounced the vengeance of future generations upon tyranny and oppression. Nay, he even went farther, and characterized as brutal bloody butchers the avengers of the broken laws of their country."

"I remember," said Berkeley, turning pale at the recollection.

"But there is another cogent reason why he should suffer the penalty which he has so richly incurred. If your object be to secure the returning loyalty and affection of the people, you should not incense them by unjust discrimination in favour of a particular rebel. The friends of Drummond, of Lawrence, of Cheeseman, of Wilford, of Bland, of Carver, will all say, and say with justice, that you spared the principal leader in the rebellion, the personal friend and adviser of Bacon, while their own kinsmen were doomed to the scaffold. Nor will those ghosts walk unavenged."

"I see, I see," cried Berkeley, grasping Bernard warmly by the hand. "You have saved me, Alfred, from a weakness which I must ever afterwards have deplored, and at the expense of your own feelings, my boy."

"Yes, my dear patron," replied Bernard, with a sigh, "you may well say at the expense of my own feelings. For I too, have just witnessed a scene which would have moved a heart of stone; and it was at the request of that poor, weeping, broken-hearted girl, to save whom from distress, I would willingly lay down my life—it was at her request that I came to beg at your hands the poor privilege of a last interview with her lover. Even Justice, stern as are her decrees, cannot deny this boon to Mercy."

"You have a generous heart, my dear boy," said the Governor, with the tears starting from his eyes. "There are not many men who would thus take delight in ministering consolation to the heart of a successful rival. You have my full and free permission. Go, my son, and through life may your heart be ever thus awake to such generous impulses, yet sustained and controlled by your unwavering devotion to duty and justice."

CHAPTER XLVIII

"My life, my health, my liberty, my all!
How shall I welcome thee to this sad place—How speak to
thee the words of joy and transport?
How run into thy arms, withheld by fetters,
Or take thee into mine, while I'm thus manacled
And pinioned like a thief or murderer?"

The Mourning Bride.

How different from the soliloquy of the dark and treacherous Bernard, seeking in the sophistry and casuistry of philosophy to justify his selfishness, were the thoughts of his noble victim! Too brave to fear death, yet too truly great not to feel in all its solemnity the grave importance of the hour; with a soul formed for the enjoyment of this world, yet fully prepared to encounter the awful mysteries of another, the heart of Thomas Hansford beat calmly and healthfully, unappalled by the certainty that on the morrow it would beat no more. He was seated on a rude cot, in the room which was prepared for his brief confinement, reading his Bible. The proud man, who relying on his own strength had braved many dangers, and whose cheek had never blanched from fear of an earthly adversary, was not ashamed in this, his hour of great need, to seek consolation and support from Him who alone could conduct him through the dark valley of the shadow of death.

The passage which he read was one of the sublime strains of the rapt Isaiah, and never had the promise seemed sweeter and dearer to his soul than now, when he could so fully appropriate it to himself.

"Fear not for I have redeemed thee, I have called thee by my name; thou art mine.

"When thou passest through the waters I will be with thee; and through the rivers, they shall not overflow thee; when thou walkest through the fire thou shalt not be burnt; neither shall the flame kindle upon thee.

"For I am the Lord thy God, the Holy one of Israel, thy Saviour."

As he read and believed the blessed assurance contained in the sacred promise, he learned to feel that death was indeed but the threshold to a purer world. So absorbed was he in the contemplation of this sublime theme, that he did not hear the door open, and it was some time before he looked up and saw Alfred Bernard and Virginia Temple, who had quietly entered the room.

Virginia's resolution entirely gave way, and violently trembling from head to foot, her hands and brow as white and cold as marble, she well nigh sank under the sickening effect of her agony. For all this she did not weep. There are wounds which never indicate their existence by outward bleeding, and such are esteemed most dangerous. 'Tis thus with the spirit-wounds which despair inflicts upon its victim. Nature yields not to the soul the sad relief of tears, but falling in bitter drops they petrify and crush the sad heart, which they fail to relieve.

Hansford, too, was much moved, but with a greater control of his feelings he said, "And so, you have come to take a last farewell, Virginia. This is very, very kind."

"I regret," said Alfred Bernard, "that the only condition on which I gained admittance for Miss Temple was, that I should remain during the interview. Major Hansford will see the necessity of such a precaution, and will, I am sure, pardon an intrusion as painful to me as to himself."

The reader, who has been permitted to see the secret workings of that black heart, which was always veiled from the world, need not be told that no such precaution was proposed by the Governor. Bernard's object was more selfish; it was to prevent his victim from prejudicing the mind of Virginia towards him, by informing her of the prominent part that he had taken in Hansford's trial and conviction.

"Oh, certainly, sir," replied Hansford, gratefully, "and I thank you, Mr. Bernard, for thus affording me an opportunity of taking a last farewell of the strongest tie which yet binds me to earth. I had thought till now," he added, with emotion, "that I was fully prepared to meet my fate. Well, Virginia, the play is almost over, and the last dread scene, tragic though it be, cannot last long."

"Oh, God!" cried the trembling girl, "help me—help me to bear this heavy blow."

"Nay, speak not thus, my own Virginia," he said. "Remember that my lot is but the common destiny of mankind, only hastened a few hours. The leaves, that the chill autumn breath has strewn upon the earth, will be supplied by others in the spring, which in their turn will sport for a season in the summer wind, and fade and die with another year. Thus one generation passes away, and another comes, like them to live, like them to die and be forgotten. We need not fear death, if we have discharged our duty."

With such words of cold philosophy did Hansford strive to console the sad heart of Virginia.

"'Tis true, the death I die," he added with a shudder, "is what men call disgraceful—but the heart need feel no fear which is sheltered by the Rock of Ages."

"And yours is sheltered there, I know," she said. "The change for you, though sudden and awful, must be happy; but for me! for me!—oh, God, my heart will break!"

"Virginia, Virginia," said Hansford, tenderly, as he tried with his poor manacled hands to support her almost fainting form, "control yourself. Oh, do not add to my sorrows by seeing you suffer thus. You have still many duties to perform—to soothe the declining years of your old parents—to cheer with your warm heart the many friends who love you—and, may I add," he continued, with a faltering voice, "that my poor, poor mother will need your consolation. She will soon be without a protector on earth, and this sad news, I fear, will well nigh break her heart. To you, and to the kind hands of her merciful Father in heaven, I commit the charge of my widowed mother. Oh, will you not grant the last request of your own Hansford?"

And Virginia promised, and well and faithfully did she redeem that promise. That widowed mother gained a daughter in the loss of her noble boy, and died blessing the pure-hearted girl, whose soothing affection had sweetened her bitter sorrows, and smoothed her pathway to the quiet grave.

"And now, Mr. Bernard," said Hansford, "it is useless to prolong this sad interview. We have been enemies. Forgive me if I have ever done you wrong—the prayers of a dying man are for your happiness. Farewell, Virginia, remember me to your kind old father and mother; and look you," he added, with a sigh, "give this lock of my hair to my poor mother, and tell her that her orphan boy, who died blessing her, requested that she would place it in her old Bible, where I know she will often see it, and remember me when I am gone forever. Once more, Virginia, fare well! Remember, dearest, that this brief life is but a segment of the great circle of existence. The larger segment is beyond the grave. Then live on bravely, as I know you will virtuously, and we will meet in Heaven."

Without a word, for she dared not speak, Virginia received his last kiss upon her pale, cold forehead, and cherished it there as a seal of love, sacred as the sign of the Redeemer's cross, traced on the infant brow at the baptismal font.

CHAPTER XLIX

"Forthwith this frame of mine was wrenched
With a woeful agony,
Which forced me to begin my tale,
And then it left me free.
Since then, at an uncertain hour,
That agony returns,
And till this ghastly tale is told
My heart within me burns."

Rime of the Ancient Mariner.

The sun shone brightly the next morning, as it rose above the forest of tall pines which surrounded the little village of Accomac; and as its rays stained the long icicles on the evergreen branches of the trees, they looked like the pendant jewels of amber which hung from the ears of the fierce, untutored chieftains of the forest. The air was clear and frosty, and the broad heaven, that hung like a blue curtain above the busy world, seemed even purer and more beautiful than ever. There, calm and eternal, it spread in its unclouded glory, above waters, woods, wilds, as if unmindful of the sorrows and the cares of earth. So hovers the wide providence of the eternal God over his creation, unmoved in its sublime depths by the joys and woes which agitate the mind of man, yet shining over him still, in its clear beauty, and beckoning him upwards!

But on none did the sun shine with more brightness, or the sky smile with more bitter mockery, on that morning, than on the dark forms of Arthur Hutchinson and his young pupil, Alfred Bernard, as they sat together in the embrasure of the window which lightened the little room of the grave old preacher. A terrible revelation was that morning to be made, involving the fate of the young jesuit, and meting out a dread retribution for the crime that he had committed. Arthur Hutchinson had reserved for this day the narrative of the birth and history of Alfred Bernard. It had been a story which he long had desired to know, but to all his urgent inquiries the old preacher had given an evasive reply. But now there was no longer need for mystery. The design of that long silence had been fully accomplished, and thus the stern misanthrope began his narrative:

"It matters little, Alfred Bernard, to speak of my own origin and parentage. Suffice it to say, that though not noble, by the accepted rules of heraldry, my parents were noble in that higher sense, in which all may aspire to true nobility, a patent not granted for bloody feats in arms, nor by an erring man, but granted to true honesty and virtue from the court of heaven. I was not rich, and yet, by self-denial on the part of my parents, and by strict economy on my own part, I succeeded in entering Baliol College, Oxford, where I pursued my studies with diligence and success. This success was more essential, because I could look only to my own resources in my struggle with the world. But, more than this, I had already learned to think and care for another than myself; for I had yielded my young heart to one, who requited my affection with her own. I have long denied myself the luxury of looking back upon the bright image of that fair creature, so fair, and yet so fatal. But for your sake, and for mine own, I will draw aside the veil, which has fallen upon those early scenes, and look at them again.

"Mary Howard was just eighteen years of age, when she plighted her troth to me; and surely never has Heaven placed a purer spirit in a more lovely form. Trusting and affectionate, her warm heart must needs fasten upon something it might love; and because we had been reared together, and she was ignorant of the larger world around her, her love was fixed on me. I will not go back to those bright, joyous days of innocence and happiness. They are gone forever, Alfred Bernard, and I have lived, and now live for another object, than to indulge in the recollection of joy and love. The saddest day of my whole life, except one, and that has darkened all the rest, was when I first left her side to go to college. But still we looked onward with high hope, and many were the castles in the air, or rather the vine clad cottages, which we reared in fancy, for our future home. Hope, Alfred Bernard, though long deferred, it may sicken the heart, yet hope, however faint, is better than despair.

"Well! I went to college, and my love for Mary spurred me on in my career, and honours came easily, but were only prized because she would be proud of them. But though I was a hard student, I was not without my friends, for I had a trusting heart then. Among these, yes, chief among these, was Edward Hansford."

Bernard started at the mention of that name. He felt that some dark mystery was about to be unravelled, which would establish his connection with the unhappy rebel. Yet he was lost in conjecture as to the character of the revelation.

"I have never in my long experience," continued Hutchinson, smiling sadly, as he observed the effect produced, "known any man who possessed, in so high a degree, the qualities which make men beloved and honoured. Brave, generous, and chivalrous; brilliant in genius, classical in attainment, profound in intellect. His person was a fit palace for such a mind and such a heart. Yes, I can think of him now as he was, when I first knew him, before crime of the deepest dye had darkened his soul. I loved him as I never had loved a man before, as I never can love a man again. I might forgive the past, I could never trust again.

"Edward returned my love, I believe, with his whole heart. Our studies were the same, our feelings and opinions were congenial, and, in short, in the language of our great bard, we grew 'like a double cherry, only seeming parted.' I made him my confidant, and he used to laugh, in his good humoured way, at my enthusiastic description of Mary. He threatened to fall in love with her, himself, and to win her heart from me, and I dared him to do so, if he could; and even, in my joyous triumph, invited him home with me in vacation, that he might see the lovely conquest I had made. Well, home we went together, and his welcome was all that I or he could wish. Mary, my sweet, confiding Mary, was so kind and gentle, that I loved her only the more, because she loved my friend so much. I never dreamed of jealousy, Alfred Bernard, or I might have seen beforehand the wiles of the insidious tempter. How often have I looked with transport on their graceful forms, as they stood to watch the golden sunset, from that sweet old porch, over which the roses clambered so thickly.

"But why do I thus delay. The story is at last a brief one. It wanted but two days of our return to Oxford, and we were all spending the day together at old farmer Howard's. Mary seemed strangely sad that evening, and whenever I spoke to her, her eyes filled with tears, and she trembled violently. Fool that I was, I attributed her tears and her agitation to her regret at parting from her lover. Little did I suspect the terrible storm which awaited me. Well, we parted, as lovers part, with sighs and tears, but with me, and alas! with me alone in hope. Edward himself looked moody and low-spirited, and I recollect that to cheer him up, I rallied him on being in love with Mary. Never will I forget his look, now that the riddle is solved, as he replied, fixing his clear, intense blue eyes upon me, 'Arthur, the wisest philosophy is, not to trust your all in one venture. He who embarks his hopes and happiness in the heart of one woman, may make shipwreck of them all.'

"'And so you, Mr. Philosopher,' I replied, gaily, 'would live and die an old bachelor. Now, for mine own part, with little Mary's love, I promise you that my baccalaureate degree at Oxford will be the only one to which I will aspire.'

"He smiled, but said nothing, and we parted for the night.

"Early the next morning, even before the sun had risen, I went to his room to wake him—for on that day we were to have a last hunt. We had been laying up a stock of health, by such manly exercises for the coming session. Intimate as I was with him, I did not hesitate to enter his room without announcing myself. To my surprise he was not there, and the bed had evidently not been occupied. As I was about to leave the room, in some alarm, my eye rested upon a letter, which was lying on the table, and addressed to me. With a trembling hand I tore it open, and oh, my God! it told me all—the faithlessness of my Mary, the villainy of my friend."

"The perfidious wretch," cried Bernard, with indignation.

"Beware, Alfred Bernard," said the clergyman; "you know not what you say. My tale is not yet done. I remember every word of that brief letter now—although more than thirty years have since passed over me. It ran thus:

"'Forgive me, Arthur; I meant not to have wronged you when I came, but in an unhappy moment temptation met me, and I yielded. My perfidy cannot be long concealed. Heaven has ordained that the fruit of our mutual guilt shall appear as the witness of my baseness and of Mary's shame. Forgive me, but above all, forgive her, Arthur.'

"This was all. No name was even signed to the death warrant of all my hopes. At that moment a cold chill came over my heart, which has never left it since. That letter was the Medusa which turned it into stone. I did not rave—I did not weep. Believe me, Alfred Bernard, I was as calm at that moment as I am now. But the calmness was more terrible than open wrath. It was the sure indication of deep-rooted, deliberate revenge. I wrote a letter to my father, explaining every thing, and then saddling my horse, I turned his head towards old Howard's cottage, and rode like the lightning.

"The old man was sitting in his shirt sleeves, in the porch. He saw me approach, and in his loud, hearty voice, which fell like fiendish mockery upon my ear, he cried out, 'Hallo, Arthur, my boy, come to say good-bye to your sweetheart again, hey! Well, that's right. You couldn't part like loveyers before the stranger and the old folks. Shall I call my little Molly down?"

"'Old man,' I said, in a hollow, sepulchral voice, 'you have no daughter'—and throwing myself from my horse, I rushed into the house.

"I will not attempt to describe the scene which followed. How the old man rushed to her room, and the truth flashed upon his mind that she had fled with her guilty lover. How he threw himself upon the bed of his lost and ruined daughter, and a stranger before to tears, now wept aloud. And how he prayed with the fervor of one who prays for the salvation of a soul, that God would strike with the lightning of his wrath the destroyer of his peace, the betrayer of his daughter's virtue. Had Edward Hansford witnessed that scene, he had been punished enough even for his guilt.

"Well, he deserted the trusting girl, and she returned to her now darkened home; but, alas, how changed! When her child was born, the innocent offspring of her guilt, in the care attending its nurture, the violent grief of the mother gave way to a calm and settled melancholy. All saw that the iron had entered her soul. Her old father died, blessing and forgiving her, and with touching regard for his memory, she refused to desecrate his pure name, by permitting the child of shame to bear it. She called it after a distant relation, who never heard of the dishonour thus attached to his name. A heart so pure as was the heart of Mary Howard, could not long bear up beneath this load of shame. She lingered about five years after the birth of her boy, and on her dying bed confided the child to me. There in that sacred hour, I vowed to rear and protect the little innocent, and by God's permission I have kept that vow."

"Oh, tell me, tell me," said Bernard, wildly, "am I that child of guilt and shame."

"Alas! Alfred, my son, you are," said the preacher, "but oh, you know not all the terrible vengeance which a mysterious heaven will this day visit on the children of your father."

As the awful truth gradually dawned upon him, Bernard cried with deep emotion.

"And Edward Hansford! tell me what became of him?"

"With the most diligent search I could hear nothing of him for years. At length I learned that he had come to Virginia, married a young lady of some fortune and family, and had at last been killed in a skirmish with the Indians, leaving an only son, an infant in arms, the only remaining comfort of his widowed mother."

"And that son," cried Bernard, the perspiration bursting from his brow in the agony of the moment.

"Is Thomas Hansford, who, I fear, this day meets his fate by a brother's and a rival's hand."

"I demand your proof," almost shrieked the agitated fratricide.

"The name first excited my suspicion," returned Hutchinson, "and made me warn you from crossing his path, when I saw you the night of the ball at Jamestown. But confirmation was not wanting, for when this morning I visited his cell to administer the last consolations of religion to him, I saw him gazing upon the features in miniature of that very Edward, who was the author of Mary Howard's wrongs."

With a wild spring, Alfred Bernard bounded through the door, and as he rushed into the street, he heard the melancholy voice of the preacher, as he cried, "Too late, too late."

Regardless of that cry, the miserable fratricide rushed madly along the path which led to the place of execution, where the Governor and his staff in accordance with the custom of the times had assembled to witness the death of a traitor. The slow procession with the rude sledge on which the condemned man was dragged, was still seen in the distance, and the deep hollow sound of the muffled drum, told him too plainly that the brief space of time which remained, was drawing rapidly to a close. On, on, he sped, pushing aside the surprised populace who were themselves hastening to the gallows, to indulge the morbid passion to see the death and sufferings of a fellow man. The road seemed lengthening as he went, but urged forward by desperation, regardless of fatigue, he still ran swiftly toward the spot. He came to an angle of the road, where for a moment he lost sight of the gloomy spectacle, and in that moment he suffered the pangs of unutterable woe. Still the muffled drum, in its solemn tones assured him that there was yet a chance. But as he strained his eyes once more towards the fatal spot, the sound of merry music and the wild shouts of the populace fell like horrid mockery on his ear, for it announced that all was over.

"Too late, too late," he shrieked, in horror, as he fell prostrate and lifeless on the ground.

And above that dense crowd, unheeding the wild shout of gratified vengeance that went up to heaven in that fearful moment, the soul of the generous and patriotic Hansford soared gladly on high with the spirits of the just, in the full enjoyment of perfect freedom.

Reader my tale is done! The spirits I have raised abandon me, and as their shadows pass slowly and silently away, the scenes that we have recounted seem like the fading phantoms of a dream.

Yet has custom made it a duty to give some brief account of those who have played their parts in this our little drama. In the present case, the intelligent reader, familiar with the history of Virginia, will require our services but little.

History has relieved us of the duty of describing how bravely Thomas Hansford met his early fate, and how by his purity of life, and his calmness in death, he illustrated the noble sentiment of Corneile, that the crime and not the gallows constitutes the shame.

History has told how William Berkeley, worn out by care and age, yielded his high functions to a milder sway, and returned to England to receive the reward of his rigour in his master's smile; and how that Charles Stuart, who with all his faults was not a cruel man, repulsed the stern old loyalist with a frown, and made his few remaining days dark and bitter.

History has recorded the tender love of Berkeley for his wife, who long mourned his death, and at length dried her widowed tears on the warm and generous bosom of Philip Ludwell.

And lastly, history has recorded how the masculine nature of Sarah Drummond, broken down with affliction and with poverty, knelt at the throne of her king to receive from his justice the broad lands of her husband, which had been confiscated by the uncompromising vengeance of Sir William Berkeley.

Arthur Hutchinson, the victim of the treachery of his early friends, returned to England, and deprived of the sympathy of all, and of the companionship of Bernard, whose society had become essential to his happiness, pined away in obscurity, and died of a broken heart.

Alfred Bernard, the treacherous friend, the heartless lover, the remorseful fratricide, could no longer raise his eyes to the betrothed mistress of his brother. He returned, with his patron, Sir William Berkeley, to his native land; and in the retirement of the old man's desolate home, he led a few years of deep remorse. Upon the death of his patron, his active spirit became impatient of the seclusion in which he had been buried, and true to his religion, if to naught else, he engaged in one of the popish plots, so common in the reign of Charles the Second, and at last met a rebel's fate.

Colonel and Mrs. Temple, lived long and happily in each other's love; administering to the comfort of their bereaved child, and mutually sustaining each other, as they descended the hill of life, until they "slept peacefully together at its foot." The events of the Rebellion, having been consecrated by being consigned to the glorious *past*, furnished a constant theme to the old lady—and late in life she was heard to say, that you could never meet now-a-days, such loyalty as then prevailed, nor among the rising generation of powdered fops, and flippant damsels, could you find such faithful hearts as Hansford's and Virginia's.

And Virginia Temple, the gentle and trusting Virginia, was not entirely unhappy. The first agony of despair subsided into a gentle melancholy. Content in the performance of the quiet duties allotted to her, she could look back with calmness and even with a melancholy pleasure to the bright dream of her earlier days. She learned to kiss the rod which had smitten her, and which blossomed with blessings—and purified by affliction, her gentle nature became ripened for the sweet reunion with her Hansford, to which she looked forward with patient hope. The human heart, like the waters of Bethesda, needs often to be troubled to yield its true qualities of health and sweetness. Thus was it with Virginia, and in a peaceful resignation to her Father's will, she lived and passed away, moving through the world, like the wind of the sweet South, receiving and bestowing blessings.